THE SEA GARDEN

Also by Sam Llewellyn

The Shadow in the Sands

THE SEA GARDEN

Sam Llewellyn

HEADLINE
FEATURE

First published in 1999
by HEADLINE BOOK PUBLISHING

A HEADLINE FEATURE hardback

10 9 8 7 6 5 4

British Library Cataloguing in Publication Data
Llewellyn, Sam, 1948 –
The sea garden
1. Suspense fiction
I. Title
823.9'14[F]

hardback ISBN 0 7472 2192 8
trade paperback ISBN 0 7472 7373 1

Typeset by Palimpsest Book Production Limited,
Polmont, Stirlingshire
Printed and bound in Great Britain by
Mackays of Chatham plc, Chatham, Kent

HEADLINE BOOK PUBLISHING
A division of the Hodder Headline Group
338 Euston Road
London NW1 3BH
www.headline.co.uk
www.hodderheadline.com

for Miss Innis

Prologue

Revel the weeder was digging where the terrace wall had collapsed by the Sea Garden at Trelise. He was right alongside a pair of old granite steps, six feet down in the black loam, trenching in leaf mould and seaweed and shell, to get the roots groping down and the garden thrusting up, like the new generations what had arrived on the island, and all that crap—

'Fucking Adas,' said Revel, and dropped his spade as if it had gone electric.

There had been twenty more spadefuls till tea time, twenty more turns of muck into the ground, easy as a chef folding egg whites into a soufflé. Bloody years Revel had been a footsoldier at Trelise, doing spuds and bulbs and weeding. Not much Revel did not know about the use of the back.

Then *clonk*, went the spade, and Revel had dropped it.

He was deep down here, on the edge of the red clay underlayer. There were lumps of granite in it, like plums in a cake. But this was no stone. It sounded hollow. It was domed, yellowish white, like an egg. An ostrich egg. An egg the size of your head.

Somebody's head.

Revel scratched carefully at the ground. He exposed the basketwork of a rib cage, the summits of what might have been knuckles folded on the breast. The skull lay rolled to the right, half sunk in clay. The bone was nicotine-yellow when he rubbed the dirt away with a spit-wet finger. No hair, no clothes. Old, old, bloody old.

Revel pulled the roll-up out of his hat and lit it. He trudged up the barrow planks, threaded through the mounds of soil and muck, and stumped through the lacework shadows of the *Dicksonia* tree ferns to the sheds by Davy Jones.

He went to his hook and fortified his nerves with Brooke Bond D from the flask in the gas-mask bag. Halfway through, Darren the driver came in smelling of dinnertime Caffrey's, and Revel told him, and Darren took a fag off him for his nerves, any excuse with Darren. Darren, being a flaparse, told the propagator at her compost mound on the potting bench. Revel sort of wished he had kept his mouth shut. The bones were up now: not buried any more, but out and about, nicotine yellow and clagged with clay, walking. Trelise was full of bones, though. Perhaps another lot would make no difference.

The propagator wandered into the office and found her husband with his nose in a report on *Echium* species, written in Spanish by David Bramwell of the Tenerife Botanical Gardens. A greenish copper plaque on his desk said Head Gardener. As it crossed the desk, the news broke ground and became official.

The Head Gardener went under the tree ferns to the Pharos at the purposeful trot of an animal on passage. He skirted a gaggle of day-trippers, plunged down a small path in the middle of a blocky *Ilex* hedge, and pushed through a screen of *Fuchsia*.

Beyond a small orchard of banana trees just released from their winter chimney pots, a tape barred entry to a series of earth terraces, linked by granite steps, stretching down to the boundary wall. Beyond the wall were marram and dunes and a line of blue Atlantic. A noticeboard by the tape said THE SEA GARDEN – RESTORATION AND EXTENSION UNDER CONSTRUCTION TO MARK THE ARRIVAL ON TRELISE OF MR AND MRS GUY BLAKENEY-JONES. Beyond that was the repaired terrace, finished now, except for the trench by the steps where Revel had been digging, Revel the unstoppable digging machine. At the bottom of the trench the Head Gardener stooped. His fingers worked in the black peat-and-sand soil. Gulls flicked in the blue slot of light overhead.

When he came up out of the ground he headed for the house, still at the trot, following side paths no better than tunnels through thickets of brambles, sheets of bracken mingled with the pale-green blades of *Crocosmia* and belladonna lily. Emerging at last into daylight, he ran up part of a two-hundred-foot flight of granite steps. A laurel-crowned bust of Poseidon peered at him from a thicket at their top. He turned onto a path that became a drive. There was a rockery, overgrown, a thicket of *Agaves* that had flowered and died and shrivelled. Round the top of its cliffs of living granite ran a terrace wall. Above the terrace rose the towers and battlements of Trelise Priory. The Priory stood at the top of Trelise.

And at the bottom, half sunk in red clay like a nasty yellow corm, those bones.

The Head Gardener grasped his nose with his fingers and blew snot over a floral cliff. Then he walked across the courtyard and into the hall.

Chapter One

It had been a thundery June evening. Victoria's youngest sister, Martha, had been visiting London. Victoria had two sisters; sometimes it felt like twenty. Martha worked in PR. In hushed tones, she had revealed to Victoria that she was a close personal friend of a close personal friend of someone Victoria had never heard of, in the movies. There was a movie party. Victoria had not heard of the movie any more than the close personal friend, but Martha said So what? Enjoy. Victoria knew that Martha, who was twenty-three, thought that at twenty-nine she was a weird old frump. So she had taken Martha's efforts to corrupt her as a compliment to her power of keeping up appearances, and agreed to go along.

Martha was picking Victoria up from the Museum of America, where Victoria worked as an assistant curator. In the restrooms by The Shaker Barn she made her mouth big and red. Her hair was dark and her eyes were blue, and there was no point hiding the fact. So she lathered on the kohl and the mascara, and looked at herself out of the mirror like two sapphires in a coal cellar. Then she climbed into a small dark suit with a low silk top and a (for her) dramatically short skirt. Real life was jeans and cowboy boots.

Martha was wearing a halter top and frosted eye-shadow. Two policemen were drooling on the bonnet of her Miata, parked on the double yellow line in Holland Park Avenue.

Victoria got in, rather self-conscious about the knees. The policemen faded into the sticky air. Martha gave her a sisterly kiss, and checked her lips. She said, 'I thought you were going to change at work,' and pulled out into the traffic jam. It started to rain.

The party was at Pinewood, in a cavernous sound-stage paved with damp people. Outside, the evening's fourth thunder storm was rattling away. Victoria found herself nose to nose with a forty-year-old surfer with dyed blond hair and a tan that degenerated into ocelot splotches in the hard-to-see-in-the-bathroom-mirror spots. She could hear very little of what he was saying.

'Bridget n me n Matt,' he seemed to say. 'Totally but like totally. Crowbar.'

Crowbar could not be right. 'Great,' she said, wondering where her next breath was coming from.

She had left East Neck because East Neck was too small and too full of her mother and sisters and other things invisible but worse. She had come to London to enlarge her world. And here she was at an American party after work at the Museum of America, with her American sister. The surfer started to explain something that made it necessary for him to touch her shoulder. Next stop would be her breasts.

She gave a sort of writhe and a stab of the elbows. The crowd parted, cursing over its shoulder. She found herself on the outside. It might never happen again. Head down, she ran through the rain for the parking lot.

She found herself in the middle of acres of wet tarmac, lit violet in a flash. By one of the huge sheds, a panel truck was unloading. Somehow she had expected a cab rank.

There was no cab rank, just a man, frozen in mid-lumber by the flash: a big man, alone in all that acreage, briefcase in each hand, two more under his left arm and one more under his right. The lightning faded to sodium glare, but not before she had seen keys hanging from his mouth, and a banged-up Range Rover on which he was homing.

Victoria watched those keys with lust. Surely a man who worked hard enough to have five briefcases could not constitute a threat?

Don't be stupid, yelled her mother and her sisters inside her head. So *Victoria*, do it now, think later. Don't be *stupid*.

The man said, 'Shit,' and dropped all his cases with a crash. One of them burst open. Files spilled across the wet tarmac.

All of a sudden Victoria was there, scrabbling in the wet. The man gave her a look in which terror and surprise were mixed fifty-fifty. She ignored it. She could not bear to see papers suffer.

After they had finished picking up, he gave her a ride back to London.

She should have been nervous, on guard. Instead she felt oddly relaxed. She leaned back against the headrest and watched him from the side, watching him as a man, not a ride.

He had a thick head of dark brown curly hair, ringlets of which had been stuck to his brow by the rain. His skin was smooth and close-pored, with freckles. He wore round glasses, and had a blobby, unthreatening profile that Victoria actually found sort of cuddly. By the time they reached the North Circular she had discovered that he was tired, he hated the bloody rain, he had been doing post-production on a film about butterflies, that he did not like working at Pinewood but when someone lent you a free edit suite what could you do?, that the Range Rover was clapped out, that he had a great-aunt who used to take her dog for walks in Ealing because she hated Ealing and loved to see it shat on, that he knew a terrific Lebanese restaurant in (amazingly enough) Hammersmith, that her turning up in the car park was an omen, the purport of which he did not specify, and that his name was Guy Farrer. He had not mentioned Trelise.

He had discovered that he had saved her life, that she had failed to finish a doctoral thesis on Research Method on grounds of boredom, that she hated men with fake tans and dyed hair, that she came from East Neck which was painted white and where eighty per cent of the population went to church and only sixty per cent committed adultery, that as far as she was concerned the Museum of America was like some sort of weird space station, and that her name was Victoria Kline. She had not mentioned house fires.

He had said that he had never met an American called Victoria. She had said that her father was weird, and dead. At this point, he had noticed that they were approaching Hammersmith. They had gone to the Lebanese restaurant and got squiffy on Chateau Musar. Then he had dropped her home in Bayswater. And she had discovered that even after three hours together, she missed him.

Next day, Martha had rung. 'Where did you *go?*' she said.

'I met a guy in the parking lot,' said Victoria.

'You're crazy.'

The shock in Martha's voice was deeply satisfactory. 'Not really. How about you?'

'I went home with this stunt man. He tied me up. It was fantastic. Victoria, you can't go round picking up guys in parking lots.'

'It won't happen again,' said Victoria.

'I hope *not*,' said Martha, severely. 'But how can I be sure?'

Perhaps it was this severity that stopped Victoria telling her that Guy had already called, and asked her to dinner that night at 192. Or perhaps it was that she did not want to talk about it, in case it suddenly went away.

In fact, Victoria had left for the Museum that morning in a state of some confusion. There was a Frederick Remington painting to unpack, catalogue and hang: a sun-burnished Apache looking ferocious on a rock, feathers blowing in a primal breeze. She propped it in front of her desk and chewed her ballpoint. The Apache's shoulders were narrower than Guy's. His forehead was lower, the nose longer, fiercer; stupidly fierce, like the blade of an axe. Not like Guy's, which was straight okay, short but resolute. And the shallow eyes on the Apache, black and snapping. She much preferred Guy's, soft and brown, amused and determined at the same time . . .

When she looked at her watch it was one o'clock, and the paper in front of her was blank. She had spent all morning comparing an unfortunate Native American with her dinner date. Was this fair?

Fair or not, she did the same thing to the man in Pret-a-Manger, and afterwards to Dick Blake, her boss, when he came for the Remington copy. Blake was short and gay, with cropped hair and a rosebud mouth. Guy's mouth was bigger, less luxurious, and it certainly would not be capable of assuming the sort of pout Blake was giving her. A much stronger mouth. Without being hard, of course . . .

Nobody was measuring up. Not the people in the elevator at Holland Park tube, certainly not the guy who sold her the irises by Queensway station. She walked home slowly, in case there was a message on the answering machine cancelling dinner; or no message, of course; same thing. She opened the door slowly, keeping her eyes averted while she put the flowers in water. In the end she had to look.

The light was blinking.

His voice. Guy's voice. Diffident, but strong. Oh, Christ, he's thought better of it. I am a casual pickup and so is he, and we will cancel, like adults—

'Listen,' said the voice. 'One nine two at eight o'clock still okay?' Anxious, he sounded. Well, eager, anyway. Of course it was okay. She stopped herself calling him, just. She was in the shower when Martha rang again.

'We're going out to dinner,' said Victoria, dripping.

'You like this guy.'

'I guess.' Victoria gave her full details.

There was a silence, while Martha adjusted her sights. 'Think underwear,' she said.

'*Martha!*'

'For you right now underwear is the bottom line.'

'It's not *like* that.'

'It's always like that, honey,' said Martha. 'Have a great evening.'

Victoria dressed with great care, four separate times. This was pathetic. She had not been sixteen for thirteen years. At the last minute, she decided on a blue muslin shift from Whistles, started from scratch, could not find a taxi, and arrived at the restaurant out of breath.

Guy was leaning on the bar, talking to a woman who seemed far too interested in him, though of course she was the barmaid. He was as solid as she remembered. His hand was big and soft and strong, charged up with about forty thousand volts. They sat at a table in the corner. She felt protected and protecting, both at once. There was a silence. He poured wine. She said, 'Well.'

He nodded, concentrating on the wine.

'Second date,' she said, so callow. 'Weird.'

'Nice,' he said. Behind the freckles, his face reddened. 'I mean, once a day. It feels like about the right dose.'

Sweet. Vulnerable, even. Victoria felt a piercing empathy, mind and body, all at once. Good grief, she thought, what's happening? Must get this back on the straight and narrow. She told him about the Apache.

'Glad you could work,' he said. 'I couldn't. Butterflies everywhere, screen, stomach. The editor keeps asking me do I want two more seconds and will she fade or wipe? and I can hardly even remember where I am.'

Yes, *yes*. 'So what's the problem?'

He shook his head. He was British, after all. From the way his eyes held

9

hers she knew exactly where his mind had been. His fingers brushed hers. The spark blew her back against the wall.

'Okay,' she said. 'So what should I know about you?'

He did not like it (British again) but this time she got some of the stuff behind last night's bald facts. His mother had been tough; seriously tough, messed up, by the sound of it, by some horror in late childhood, or the war, or something. His father had been some sort of academic, a socialist. They had lived in North Oxford, a place she knew little about, but saw as a sort of chilly British version of East Neck. He seemed glad to be away from it, making his movies, living in his house in Chiswick. 'Boring,' he said. 'Going on and on like this.'

'No, it's great.' She meant it. She could have listened to him all night. Preferably at the house in Chiswick. Or her own apartment. It did not matter, as long as there was a bed there, and Guy was in it.

They ate something, she did not notice what. When the coffee arrived she thought he was going to suggest something interesting. Instead he asked her about her. She described the rattletrap machinery of her relationship with her mother and her sisters. He nodded. They understood each other.

Then, shockingly, he called for the bill. She sat there white-faced. It had been about nothing at all. Not a beginning. Just a date, draped in the usual British bullshit. He said, 'I've got to be in Pinewood by eight.'

'Oh.' Could be an excuse. At the very least, could show an unhealthy preference for work over play.

His hand came over the table and held hers. 'I'm sorry.'

Could be gay, of course. Absent father, powerful mother. Lord, please let him not be. Or maybe she had put him off, sitting here like a rabbit in the headlights.

'Er,' he said, pinkish between the freckles again. 'This probably sounds silly. And I'm sure you've got things sort of fixed up already. But . . . are you doing anything special tomorrow night?'

Alleluia.

She said, 'Not if you're not.'

'That's good,' he said. 'Because it's Friday.'

It was all she could do not to climb over the table there and then. 'So it is,' she said.

He drove her home. They did not touch each other, but sparks kept jumping the gap. She asked him up. He said, 'Not tonight.' Still good, she thought, bounding up the stairs. Not as good as him being here, but good.

Twenty minutes later the telephone rang. It was him. 'Just wanted to make sure you got home all right.'

'All twenty-eight stairs. Sure.'

'And of course there was hearing your voice.'

'And yours.'

'See you tomorrow,' he said.

'I'll bring dinner,' she said. Somehow, they hung up. When she looked at her watch it seemed they had been talking for two hours. She did not sleep that night. She did not mind. She had plenty to think about.

Guy's house was in a short, leafy street near the river. Inside it was white, with bare wooden floors and oriental rugs and beat-up sofas; the debris of his parents' household, Victoria guessed, with later additions. The kitchen was practical, as if it was used for cooking as well as defrosting. She made her legendary lobster tagliatelle. He helped. Not bumbling around pouring too much wine and wondering what he should do, but actually being in the right place at the right time.

She watched him as he ate.

'She watched him anxiously while he ate,' he said.

'"This is excellent," he said,' she said.

'He was right,' said Guy, and poured her more Cloudy Bay.

'"You are trying to get me drunk," she said,' she said. He took her hand. No jolt this time. Just a steady current, voltage off the dial. 'Little did he know there was no need.'

And there they were, on the sofa. And after that upstairs in the bed, which was colossal, with a white duvet like a cloud, and sheets that smelled as if they had been aired outdoors. Everything was fresh and bright. Victoria had a suspicion that she would have felt that way even if they had been undressing each other in a mangrove swamp. But here she was, making love to this wonderful man in this wonderful bed, in this wonderful life. And it was just perfect.

Next day they went back to her apartment for clean clothes. Seeing him in the living room, the height of him, the powerful slope of his shoulders, she realised how small the place was, how cramped, how like her life. Her old life. They went walking, ate in again, made love again, a lot. They had Sunday lunch at Kensington Place. Watching him with the waiter, in the noise of the outside world, she felt an awful premonition of loss. This would be over soon. He would go back to his life, and she would go back to the apartment, the museum, the short, unsatisfactory jaunts with passing sisters . . .

He was watching her over the table. He said, 'Do you have to go home?' He was blushing again. She was blushing too. 'I mean, there's lots of room in Chiswick.'

This time she did climb over the table.

Four weeks later, it was apparent that they had moved in together. They got on so well. *So* well. In conversation. In life. In bed. Insanely well.

And all that time, she never mentioned house fires, and he never mentioned gardens.

Though he had given her clues, if she had had eyes to see.

There had been an elderly picture, a good amateur late-Victorian water-colour of a walk, apparently in a garden. In the background was a royal-blue sea. In the foreground, flanked by the spiky plants she used to see on the tequila bottles in Martha's apartment, were a dozen women in navy blue skirts and stout black boots. It looked foreign, but the women in navy blue could not have been anything but English. It went oddly with the other pictures in the room, an Elizabeth Frink horse's head drawing, a couple of Alan Lowndes circus acrylics, and a Patrick Heron. 'Oh,' he said, when she asked. 'That's Trelise. Sort of family headquarters. In Cornwall. An island.' He looked awkward, on the verge of a revelation. Then he shook his head, and focused his glasses on her right foot, and took her hand in his large, dry, soft one. 'Look. Why don't we get married?'

Well, of course.

They did it in Chiswick Registry Office, in the presence of a director friend of Guy's and Helen Torode, a pathologist Victoria had met while dating Native American relics at the Museum. They spent the week afterwards in Paris. They came back by the Tunnel. As the Range Rover trundled across Kent she held Guy's hand. They were Mr and Mrs Farrer, in love. Beginning the straight, smooth road, a little up, a little down: steady as she goes, forever.

Forever lasted as far as the sign to Maidstone, where Guy cleared his throat and said, 'By the way. There's a lecture on Thursday night. Can you come?'

Ahead, the traffic was piling up. 'It's late opening at the Museum,' she said.

'Can't you rearrange things?'

When she looked round she saw his chin was set. The lights of a police car flashed red in his spectacles. 'Lecture?' she said.

'It's a family thing.'

She had never heard of a family lecture, and the expression on his face was new to her. She was going to ask him about it. But the motorway had come down to one lane. There were ambulances. One car's windscreen had been crushed to the size of a letter box. From the letter box protruded a hand. The moment for asking passed.

By fits and starts they continued the road home.

The Merchant Apothecaries' Hall was in London Bridge, a building of sooty stone with a caduceus on the keystone of the door. As Victoria went up the steps in her little black dress, the place exhaled a breath of ancient books, oddly blended with flowers and strong drink. The Merchant Apothecaries (Guy had told her) were famous for their collection of early herbals, and their cellar. Victoria had her hand in Guy's arm – an inordinately tidy Guy, his dark mop of hair actually cut, his jaw shaved and his spectacles overhauled. He was wearing a dark blue suit, a white shirt, and an apprehensive expression.

'You look great,' she said, meaning it.

He smiled at her, or it might have been a stone in his shoe. 'You're beautiful,' he said. 'Too beautiful for this lot.'

Then a butlerine man had opened a pair of double doors, and they were moving forward.

Guy had explained this lecture hardly at all; but then he was never a great explainer. It was, he had muttered, a sort of tradition in his family. They all seemed to be called Blakeney-Jones. She assumed they were like most large families of her acquaintance – a heterogeneous group with maybe a great-grandfather in common, distant, inaudible, non-interruptive, a blur of genetic background radiation with no toxic effects on the soul.

The contents of the Library at the Merchant Apothecaries' Hall therefore came as a shock.

It was a large room, sixty feet on a side, walled with books, the upper shelves being reached by a gallery with a wrought-iron balustrade. At the far end, the gallery broadened until it was a sort of stage, on which was a lectern. By the lectern was a chair. Behind the chair was something that looked like a glass case.

All this Victoria took in during the five seconds between their entry into the room and their burial in a vast throng of people. She found herself being introduced to a stream of elderly faces. She was repeatedly asked if she was Irish. When she said she was American, there was a familiar glazing of eyes. Guy's cousinry did not seem much given to travel outside the islands of Britain.

Somebody pushed a glass of champagne into her hand. She got separated from Guy, made polite conversation, inhaled terrible breath, became desperate with boredom, sidled towards a wall, found herself by an iron spiral staircase, and went up to the gallery, where she discovered to her intense delight a 1633 edition of Gerard's *Herball*. As she reverently turned the pages, a dull beat communicated itself through the iron floor. She looked up.

In the chair next to the lectern there sat a very old man with a crooked face. His nose was huge, hooked and bloated like an elephant seal's in rut. He had a gigantic overbite, so his chin seemed in constant danger of disappearing up his left nostril. His right eye was covered by a black patch, and the right-hand corner of his mouth was turned down, drooling. The vibration in the gallery floor came from the stick in his left hand, with which he was beating the iron. 'You!' he cried in an ancient, reedy voice. He ceased pounding with the stick and aimed it at Victoria. 'Come here!'

On the main floor, Guy stood at the centre of a solar system of his relations. She had never before thought of him being at the centre of anything except her life and his work. She found she was proud of him. She shelved the *Herball* and walked along the gallery to the stage.

'Who are you?' said the hideous old man.

'Victoria Farrer,' said Victoria. 'Married to Guy. Who are you?'

'Harry. You should know who I am. Why doesn't anyone introduce me? Get me a glass of wine. White wine.' He thumped his stick pettishly. 'Flowers,' he said. There was a mighty vase on the table at his elbow.

Victoria had been on the point of scuttling off to get the monster its booze. But it seemed to have forgotten, and was now glaring at the vase. '*Proteas* bloody awful this year,' he said. 'Marvellous. What?'

Victoria was trying to cobble up some sort of reply when her eye strayed over his shoulder to the glass case, and she froze.

A face was gazing from behind the glass: a ghastly orange face, with eyes like glass marbles. A black wig sat askew on the broad orange brow. Below it, a leprous stock hid what was obviously no neck at all, and a black frock coat sagged in rusty folds over what Victoria hoped was a coat-hanger, but was too three-dimensional: a ribcage, for sure. Her eyes travelled down to the knees, the horribly thin knees in black trousers. The hands had been arranged on the knees; dark brown hands, leathery skin shrunk over clawed bones. The hands of a mummy.

The thing smiled at her through the glass, a mad cheeky-chappie smile: the smile of a skeleton with a wax face, dressed as a Victorian gentleman.

'Fucking *gross*,' said Victoria.

'Foul-mouthed woman,' mused the the old man aloud. 'Nothing wrong with that. Married to, ah Guy. Great friend of mine. *Great* friend. Married, are you?'

'Yes.' Victoria thought she might faint.

Phlegm crackled in the old man's throat. 'I like a foreigner, within reason. Who did you say you were?'

She told him again.

'Hybrid vigour,' he said. He waved laboriously at a white daisy in the vase. '*Olearia trelisensis*. Cross between, something or other. Strong plant. Strong plant.' He scowled. 'Why doesn't someone bring me wine? White wine, God damn and blast them. It's not much to ask.'

A man had materialised at his shoulder; a smallish man, not much taller than Victoria, with a lean face, an outdoor complexion and bright blue eyes above a curly chestnut beard. He was carrying a glass of white wine, to which he guided the old man's hand. 'Owen,' said the old man, looking up with a smile of surprising sweetness, and waving a hand at Victoria. 'This seems to be the American.'

The man called Owen stuck out his hand. It was hard, as if he used it for work. He said, 'You're Victoria?'

He was under fifty, and did not smell. She trusted him immediately. 'Everyone else seems to know already. Are you a cousin?'

He smiled, as if it was a silly question. His teeth were white and excellent. He said, 'Come and meet my wife.' There was the suspicion of a wink in his right eye. He was rescuing her from the old monster. Her hero. They came alongside a dark-haired woman. 'Mary?' said Owen. The woman looked across at him, reluctant to be disturbed in her conversation with a tweed suit. 'This is Victoria.' Mary's reluctance disappeared. She wrapped Victoria in a warm, bright smile. 'Victoria's from America. She's been talking to Harry.'

Mary laughed. 'About foreigners?'

'Hybrid vigour, actually.' Victoria found herself talking. She told Mary about East Neck, the oppressions of her sisters, the Museum of America.

'So you're a historian,' said Mary.

'A curator. Who's the mummy?'

'Joshua Jones.'

'He looks terrible.'

'He's been dead since 1865.'

'And son of the mummy's Harry. Who's Harry?'

'Harry Blakeney-Jones. He lives at Trelise. He's the boss.'

Victoria said, 'What is Trelise?'

Owen said, 'Nobody's told you?' He looked genuinely surprised.

'Should they have? Guy said family headquarters.'

16

'House and garden in Cornwall. Built and designed by Joshua Jones up there. He believed in benign despotism, a society organised for the greatest good of the greatest number. Trelise is an island. He used it as a social and horticultural laboratory. Thought funerals were sentimental claptrap.'

'Ah.' The shock of Harry and the mummy was wearing off. Victoria was conscious of a twinge of historical interest. 'Why here?'

'One of the conditions of his will. Annual lecture on a botanical or pharmacological subject, to be delivered from a lectern alongside the head of the family, who is to occupy a chair in front of Joshua.'

Medieval. *Pre*-medieval. 'So the one who lives at Trelise is the head of the family.'

'That's right.'

'Harry.'

'Your husband's grandfather.'

Victoria heard herself say, 'Ah.'

Grandfather. Guy, the grandson of the head of the family.

Guy did not seem to have any uncles or aunts or first cousins.

Her mind floated up to the gallery, to the room as she had seen it from above; planetary cousins, with satellites of connections, each with its atmosphere of halitosis. And in the centre – the solar centre? – Guy.

She began to formulate words to help her find out more. But Guy was forging towards her, and Owen and Mary were drifting away. Guy said, 'We're off to dinner with the Forsyths.'

She said, 'Sure.' She caught Owen's eye above the crowd, waved. He grinned back with those good un-English teeth, too bad.

Then someone banged a gavel, and people found chairs, and someone got up and gave a lecture. Victoria did not hear any of it. She was thinking about grandfathers.

George Forsyth (Guy explained in the taxi) was the great-grandson of one of Harry's aunts, who had married late in life but still had four daughters. His wife, Harriet, was long-jawed, with eyes the colour of blued steel. She was also excessively forthright about Trelise. 'Lovely place,' she said. 'Past ten years, it's gone all to hell. Marvellous gardener there. But Harry won't let him do anything. Jungle now. Such a waste.'

'He was there tonight,' said George. 'Brought the flowers up from Trelise, I hear. I saw Victoria talking to him.'

'I talked to him?' Victoria searched her mind for heavy beards and black-rimmed fingernails.

'Little chap, short beard. Owen Morgan.'

'He was the gardener?' But he had been crisp and neat, with the nails of a professor.

'The garden at Trelise,' said George portentously, 'is a national treasure; a world treasure, even. Plants from all over the world. The biggest *Banksia*, er, can't remember, *in* the world. Bigger than in Australia. So the chap in charge has got be something special. More like a university professor than Mr McGregor, ha, ha, *Peter Rabbit*, you know?'

'Rather yummy, I think,' said Harriet.

George frowned, and changed the conversation to politics.

In the taxi home, Victoria said, 'Why didn't you tell me Harry was your grandfather?'

'You didn't ask. You haven't told me about your grandfather. Morgan told you, I expect?'

'Yes.'

He nodded. His face was bland and stiff. He obviously did not want to talk about it.

Victoria did. All of a sudden, she was part of a brand new world. 'Tell me about Trelise.'

'It's incredibly beautiful.' He sounded as if he was making an admission under torture. 'Everyone gets emotionally involved, one way or another. Harry's lived there like a hermit for forty-odd years, since my grandmother died.'

Victoria wanted to hear him say it. 'How many grandsons does Harry have?'

'Just me. No surviving children.'

'So . . .'

Guy laughed. 'My mother hated him. He hated my father. Dad had a row with him twenty years ago. Told him Trelise was just a farm and a garden, not some kind of kingdom in the sea, so stop behaving like some sort of emperor. So Harry said never darken my doors, and Dad didn't, and I haven't, not since I was what, twelve? He will have left it to George Forsyth, and good luck to the bastard, because nobody's done any planning and the inheritance tax will be a nightmare. Anyway, Trelise kills rightful heirs.'

'Jesus,' she said.

He took her face in his hands and kissed her mouth. 'Gothic, eh?' he said.

She kissed him back.

Gothic sounded right.

Next day Guy went filming for a month, and Victoria did her duty at the Museum, and had dinner with her sister Sarah, the lawyer, who was passing through London on a research-and-Christmas-shopping basis.

They ate in a French restaurant. Sarah was dressed casually, for her (two ropes of pearls, cream silk blouse, navy Chanel suit). She quizzed the waiter about garlic, and looked mildly shocked when Victoria asked for a bottle of wine instead of two glasses. 'Whew,' she said. 'I'm bushed.'

This was by way of a cue. Victoria said, 'Tough day?'

'Tough life. You know, you should really come to East Neck next summer?' Sarah and Martha did go back, most summers. Not Victoria. Not since she had been seventeen.

It still stood in her head: the white house and the picket fence, the family round the table on the lawn. She heard the long-running bicker that passed for conversation, the chink of iced-tea glasses. And Dad's glass, that did not contain iced tea. She saw him shake his head as the argument swelled, walk away from the table and into the house.

In her head was the only place the house stood now.

Sarah was yakking on about a divorce she had fixed up for someone else. Instead of cutting things in half, the parties were buying two of everything, including Bahamas. 'The rich,' she said, 'are different. By the way, this fellow of yours. Is he rich?'

'No.'

'Good.'

*   *   *

Revel – A Day in the Life: Winter*

Alarm clock, eight. Weather forecast easterly, cold. Tea strong, three sugars. Revel kicks his way through limewood shavings in his sitting room. Dawn is coming up; a rainy dawn, icy, smelling of salt. The rotavator is dismembered in the machinery shed. He prods at it, cold fingers, writes out an order for a new crankshaft. It is a day to be indoors. They are cleaning seed in the propagation shed, shake, riddle, dust, chat, drink tea. The propagators are hard at it. Spring is just around the corner.

After dinner, the rain stops. Revel goes out into the damp, empty garden, trudging down to the vegetables. There are winter cabbages to cut for chef at the Castle, potatoes to earth up. A couple of firecrests bob above the wall. Revel leans on the spade, watching. The Head Gardener tells him to do something or other. Revel nods, and carries on leaning. Winter is time to make do and mend, take it easy. It always has been. Nothing anyone says will make any difference. Tea with Daisy. Down to the Castle, three pints of Guinness, game of dominoes. Someone has found a crate of trousers washed up on Plum Orchard beach. Back home; Martin Hayes on the stereo. Continue with carving of bass.

Same every winter, more or less.

Two weeks after Christmas, Guy disentangled himself from sleepy Victoria, and went downstairs. She listened affectionately to the morning noises, sniffed the coffee percolating. He brought up the tray with the mail and the slime-green French cups with the gold rims. He opened the first letter. Then he kicked the tray with the sugar and the milk right off the end of the white bed and onto the floor.

The letter had a discreet letterhead and a nine-line text. It was typed on paper expensive enough to rattle in his hand. When she said his name, he did not answer. Unnerved, she twitched the letter out of his fingers.

Dear Mr Farrer,

Unfortunately prior commitments prevented my attending the Joshua Lecture, but you may remember that we met three years ago at your Cousin

* *Country Times* magazine, feature

Clara Benbow's Ordination. It is now with mixed grief and pleasure that I must inform you that your Grandfather, Major Harry Blakeney-Jones, died last night; and that under the terms of his Will you are his sole heir, on some conditions, the most onerous of which being that you change your name to Blakeney-Jones. Please do come and see me, as there will be much to discuss.

Congratulations, Guy.
Yours ever
Ned Scoresby

The expression on Guy's face was one she had not seen before. It was the expression of a man who has taken an escape route that he suspected all along was a blind alley, and whose suspicions are confirmed by a big, blank brick wall.

'It's great,' she said. 'Isn't it?'

'Yes,' he said. 'Of course.'

'You don't look as if it's great.'

His mouth moved. After a while, words came out. 'Most people have a future,' he said. 'We've just inherited a past.'

'We don't have to live there.'

'If we don't, the lease falls in, and it goes back to the Kernow Estates. It is our . . . sodding . . . *duty*.'

Victoria took his hand. She said, 'As I understand it, someone has just given you an earthly paradise for us to have some babies on. Excuse me, but where is the problem here?'

He grinned at her; not much of a grin, but a reasonable try. 'You wait,' he said. 'More coffee?'

'And come here.'

He came here. She held him close, and he held her. 'It's great,' she said.

'Sure.' He kissed her.

They went to the funeral. And shortly thereafter, Guy and Victoria Blakeney-Jones entered into the enjoyment of the gifts of the dead, and the monstrous inheritance taxes that accompanied them.

Chapter Two

*Lords of the Isles**

A dream came true this February when Guy and Victoria Blakeney-Jones inherited the paradise island of Trelise, off the south coast of Cornwall. It happened on the death, at a grand old ninety, of Guy's grandfather, Major Harry Blakeney-Jones, who had lived on the island as a recluse.

Married just six months, the Blakeney-Joneses previously lived in fashionable Fulham. As a film producer, Guy is used to making dreams come true, and is negotiating an eight-part TV series on the recreation of Trelise's exotic gardens. Victoria, a diplomat, is originally from Massachusetts. 'I had no idea,' she laughs. 'Guy never told me, can you believe it?'

The happy couple drove in one of Guy's ancestral carriages across the causeway that connects their Fairyland with the mainland of England. Under the four hundred year old Witch Tower at the entrance to the village, they were greeted by cheering islanders, and the Trelise Silver Band.

Well, the Witch Tower was the Watch Tower, for a start. It had been bloody cold. East of the causeway, the Hull Bay sand flats had faded into black rain. Ahead, Trelise was a murky stain across the horizon: the causeway felt rickety and insecure.

And to accept Trelise as a fairyland, you had to believe in fairies.

*   *   *

* article from *Hello!* magazine, n.d., framed on downstairs lavatory wall at Trelise

Trelise; First Footprints in the Sand*

Trelise. A glorious place in, as it were, a glorious place. A crescent of granite attached by a causeway to one of the prettiest headlands in the Cornish Riviera, blessedly void of chalets! Six hundred acres of sun-kissed granite and heather-purpled moor – its convex side hunched against the westerly gales that lash this southwesternmost of peninsulae, its concave side sheltering beaches of purest silver. At the end of the causeway closest to the shore stands the quaint village of Old Hull, its whitewashed granite cottages gay with geraniums that in the frostless climes of this Fortunate Isle flower all the livelong year. In the little harbour sheltered by Old Hull quay, bright fishing boats bob at anchor in the crystal water, and ferry boats (weekdays, every hour on the hour; Sats every 20 mins, first boat 8am, last boat 1 hour before sunset – see Quay noticeboard for details. No boats Suns.) serve when the causeway is closed (2 hours either side of high tide. A horn is blown from the Watch Tower [1628] 10 minutes before closing) NB it is not safe to bathe off the quay, owing to the powerful whirlpool at its seaward end, known as the Mixer and specially strong in the middle two hours of both ebb and flood.

South of Old Hull, a road winds behind silver coves, skirting potato and bulb fields and plunging at length into strong shelter belts of the Monterey pine Pinus radiata and Cupressus macrocarpa.

And now between the black-green trees, turrets and spires may be seen to rise. Heart in mouth, scarcely venturing to breathe, the traveller finds herself cast into Faërie.

For here on a frowning rock gay with flowers, overlooking a freshwater pool used as a wintering ground by many fascinating types of duck, stands the battlemented donjon of Trelise Priory. Not, it must be said, the first Priory, founded here by the good monks of Tavistock one thousand one hundred and ten years after the birth of Our Lord. But a new Priory, built in 1847 from local granite by one Joshua Jones, a man of strong and principled motive, in search of a kingdom.

And what a kingdom he found!

From the foot of the donjon walls, the gardens sweep away. They are

---

* Trelise – Cornwall's Lovesome Thing, Jeremy Peebles, Duckworth 1964

*twenty-one acres of Paradise, of flowers and scents gathered from the Cape
of Good Hope and the Canaries, Australia and the Azores, and a thousand
and one other 'faraway places with strange-sounding names'. And beyond
Great Rocks, stretching away forever, rent with black fangs of granite, the
true Kingdom of Trelise – Homer's 'wine-dark sea' itself!*

It had been a February day, and an evil one. A rusting Bentley had met them
in front of the Causeway Hotel on the mainland. They had wallowed across
the causeway and under the Watch Tower. Then there had been the band
droning weirdly in the slate-roof echoes of the village street, faces reflected
cold-red and vein-blue in the bells of the instruments. Then there had been
a reception line of people in best oilskins and Sunday anoraks. The faces
were on the whole wind-whipped and somewhat wary around the eyes.
With the death of Harry Blakeney-Jones, Trelise had emerged from sixty
years of totalitarian rule. Houses went with jobs, justice had been rough,
and nobody knew what came next.

Victoria's excitement had been dampened by the rain. She had not
realised this was going to be a state occasion. The faces crowded in on her.
Then she saw a dark-haired woman forging through the crowd, waving,
smiling. It was Mary Morgan. They had only met once, for five minutes.
But Victoria had the sense of finding a friend. She put her arms around
her and hugged her. 'Welcome home!' said Mary. Owen was there too,
a firm but delicate handshake, introducing her to a chestnut-bearded man
called Revel, and a bright-faced woman called Daisy Parker. There was
also Jeremy Davis, the farm manager, and his nervous-looking wife Irene,
and a black labrador called Patton, and a lot of other people who failed to
register.

In the middle of the road stood a grey tractor decorated with wet flowers.
Guy boosted her onto the seat, squeezed in beside her and let the clutch out
with a jerk. They rolled out of the village street and onto a road that ran
along the landward side of a long silver beach. Guy held her hand, steering
perilously with the other. 'No cars this side of the village,' he said. Victoria
wondered who made the rules. She brushed the wet curls off his forehead
and said it was just marvellous. Bowling along in a luminous blast of sun
on grey-green sea, on this cute little tractor, Guy pleased and proud with

his arm around her waist, marvellous was the exact word. She might be a stranger. But so was Guy. They could learn together. She felt purely, blissfully happy.

The tractor left the beach road, threaded a couple of pine-clad gorges, and rattled under a granite arch and into a courtyard.

Two sides of the courtyard were a granite cliff. Along the other two sides ran the castellated granite facade of an enormous house. In front of a massive oak door a middle-aged man was standing. He was dressed in black slacks and a black polo neck. His eyes were bright and knowing. His face was tanned a coppery orange, his jawline collapsed, and his lips simultaneously compressed and stretched. It appeared he was smiling. 'Guy,' said the man, in a breathy purr. 'And you must be er Victoria. Welcome to the Priory. Come *in*.'

Guy said, 'Victoria, this is Dawkins.'

'Come in come *in*,' said Dawkins.

'Dawkins looks after things,' said Guy, as if describing a headland, or a constellation, or any other unchanging feature of the cosmic order.

Victoria smiled at him, feeling the happiness curdle.

In they went. Into the Priory, their marital home. At the invitation of Dawkins.

There was lunch, laid out in a vast dining room with a window full of sea and served by Dawkins. Victoria found her morale mysteriously low. 'Dawkins'll take us round afterwards,' said Guy.

Victoria felt simultaneously intruded on and intruding. 'Is he really necessary?'

Guy looked taken aback. 'Well. He's . . . Heart of gold. It's a big house, takes some running. So I thought we might as well hang on to him till, you know, things get organised?'

Victoria felt an inner crumbling. She knew nothing about running castles. She was a museum curator, not Mrs goddam Beeton. She nodded, hoping Guy might notice her silence. But he seemed to have other things on his mind.

After lunch, the rain having returned, Dawkins accompanied them on a tour of the house. Victoria found her enthusiasm rising. The ancient oriental carpets were worn, but immaculately groomed. The windows shone, the bed linen, though patched, smelt of lavender. Everything was fresh as a field of daisies. Victoria could not believe it had been the home of the drooling monster she had met at the lecture. 'It's so beautifully *kept*,' she said.

'One has done one's best, Victoria,' said Dawkins stiffly, choosing to interpret her enthusiasm as surprise.

The place was crammed to the roof with ancestral loot, most of it of extreme interest. There was a state room built of timber from the nineteenth-century wreck of the *Society*, lined with panels of hand-painted Chinese wallpaper. There was a state dining room sixty feet on a side with a vast and hideous dresser in the Gothic taste, stacked with K'ang Hsi porcelain, some of which appeared to have been used as a target for small-bore rifle practice. There was a drawing room, with arcaded benches and fantastical Alpine scenes by James McNeill Whistler, and a billiard room perfumed by a badly stuffed tiger and one and a half centuries of tobacco.

'And this,' said Dawkins, pausing in front of a cabinet holding a black and white Grecian urn, 'is the only surviving relic of the *Sophocles*, blown ashore in a gale in Hull Bay in 1806, full of pots from Herculaneum.' Guy looked reverent. Apparently both he and Dawkins saw Dawkins as Permanence. This would have to change.

But not (she realised, as her legs grew weary and her brain clogged with new information) yet. Guy had been right about the scale of the place. There were twelve bedrooms, acres of carpet, catacombs of wine, tons of crockery, miles of corridor. Only Dawkins knew how it fitted together. Presumably it was her job to ask him how.

He obliged, loftily. 'Well there's me, of course, and I do the cooking and the shopping and I organise Sharon and Denise who do the housemaiding, and Jenny who does the ironing and a day's cleaning, and Mrs Jones does four more days and we get round once a week, twice for the studies and the state rooms and the bedrooms if there's anyone staying. Of course I didn't do that for the Major, not at the end, because we never had anyone in the house, but I thought, well, that's all going to change now, so I took the liberty of putting it all together. Temporarily.'

'Excellent,' said Guy.

Victoria nodded, heading for the canvas in the first seconds of Round One.

'Victoria,' said Dawkins. 'One more thing. The flowers?'

Victoria had no idea what he was talking about. Then at the last minute she noticed that there were indeed flowers everywhere, as at the lecture but more so, much more, great explosions and pyramids of flowers, of species that she could not even recognise, let alone name. 'Marvellous,' she said, stretching her face into a gracious Blakeney-Jones sort of smile.

'Someone has to do the flowers,' said Dawkins. 'Generally, I mean until now, it is, has been, I. Perhaps you . . .' His voice trailed away.

'Oh, no,' said Victoria. 'You carry on.' Too abject. 'For the moment.' Christ, the man was fishing for a compliment. 'They're lovely.' Too little, too late. Go away, go away.

Dawkins' eyes were bright with intelligence, and possibly hostility. He looked at his watch. 'Do we drink tea, Victoria?'

'Like a native,' she said.

He glided away to the kitchen.

Guy was watching her. 'He's got eighteen months till he retires,' he said quietly, as if afraid of being overheard. 'Expensive to change anything before then.'

Victoria thought it would be worth the money. But she had no confidence in her opinion, not knowing how you went about living in big houses on islands.

On her way up the stairs that night, she heard from the direction of Dawkins' apartment the yowl of Siamese cats, and the sound of high, pettish swearing. It occurred to her that perhaps this was not an ideal situation for anyone.

Things would settle down.

From the desk of Dave Franklin,
Controller,
Charlesworth TV

Dear Guy
I wanted to tell you about my very great pleasure and excitement that we

have now commissioned TRELISE – A GARDEN REBORN. This will be our major series for next winter, and as you know, we all feel that an eight-parter of rare importance will come out of this. I know that Jules in France, Romka in Holland, Helga in Germany and Benedetta in Italy feel the same way. We were all very glad to hear that ABC in the States has come aboard, and of course that Australia and the Far East have committed themselves. This bids fair to be the TV programme the planet will be talking about, come next winter.

So good luck with it, Guy. One small thing that I have to mention, for the sake of good communications between us. Please be aware of the time clauses. This is a big deal, and it is crucial that everything runs to schedule, which is why the penalties are so hefty and cancellation is an option until such a late stage. All there to concentrate the mind!
All the best
Dave

Next day, Victoria found herself in the State Room with her aching feet for company. The past twenty-four hours were a blur, from which things protruded like headlands from sea-fog. She recalled attics (jammed with boxes three high), the bamboo groves, Coffee the carthorse, the house dog (the labrador Patton), the best bower anchor of HMS *Elephant*, wrecked on Tobaccoman's Ledge in 1784, the collection of figureheads salvaged from the island's wrecks and now attached to the pillars of the loggia known as Davy Jones, greenhouses intact and ruined, the horses in their paddock by the pool, some irises, a silver gilt Chinese junk on the dining-room table, the kennels with fourteen spaniels, the garden lavatories, the slender tower of the Mare lighthouse just this side of the horizon to the south, some noxious emanations from the island's sewage plant, an ostrich egg whose mother had once roamed wild on the garden terraces, the Priory arch blazing (despite the early season) with cunningly potted orange *Quamoclit coccinea*, ruins everywhere, the sea, calm to the east and rough to the west, trees of all shapes and sizes, the undulations of the tide-races off Tobaccoman's Point, the vermin in the Priory's mouldering cellars, weeds, weeds, weeds in bed and terrace, a toy xylophone thick with dust in an abandoned nursery, a highly desirable Dragon class yacht rotting in a huge shed (nearly as beautiful as the Friendship sloops she had sailed in Maine, she told Guy; did they have a sailboat? Hell, said Guy, we've got everything else), and the zeal of gardeners and farmhands and fishermen and everyone else she met; zeal that she strongly suspected of being at best temporary and at worst assumed for her benefit. Because actually the place was a mess. You could tune in to its history and majesty and all that, but only dimly, through a static of bracken and bramble. Someone had let things go to hell, for about fifty years, by the look of it. And she and Guy had to get it back together again. Somehow.

Scary, really.

Dawkins materialised in front of her, face a coppery moon rising over a mesa of books. He said, 'If you've got a moment, Victoria?', put the books on the table, and began. There were lists of indoor housekeeping, outdoor housekeeping, Trelise residents with their connections, and county residents with theirs. There were calendars of village events, county events, garden events, regattas, shows, fetes, charities tradition-ally supported. To each entry was attached a list of people, places, equipment. This was how it was done, then; an order of service detailed as a Mass, to be observed daily, over years, decades; centuries, maybe. Dawkins developed his theme at a steady canter, noting each system as it passed, until Victoria caught the sharp whiff of burning brains. From then on she sat and nodded brightly, and thought, no way. Not ever. I will never understand all this, not if I live to be a billion, and there is no need.

'So there it is,' said Dawkins, shutting the last book with a slap. 'I hope you don't mind my taking the liberty. You'll have time to get used to things, of course. It's quiet just now. Until the Spring Social, in a month. I bought you a diary.' He put it on the table: a fat A4 volume, two pages a day, each day divided into quarter-hour segments.

'You shouldn't have,' said Victoria.

'Not at all,' said Dawkins, and left.

'Exit the Master of Tradition,' said Victoria to the Chinaman on the wallpaper.

Kind of droll, really.

So why wasn't she laughing?

She closed her eyes.

The French windows were open, and a small breeze loaded with the smell of *Pelargoniums* and the cry of herring gulls blew off the terrace. Just for a moment, the world was made new. Her heart soared with the gulls, pure in the blue—

The dining-room door opened and closed. Sighing and tut-tut noises followed. Someone had come in from the flower room, a sort of pantry with a sink just inside the front door. Dawkins was doing the flowers. Any minute now she would be getting more terrific advice about the conduct of his imaginary establishment.

The library door was open. Victoria slid through.

By Trelise standards it was a small room, no more than twenty feet square. Its walls were lined with books. There were French windows over Great Rocks and the sea, the Mare and its outliers in the top right-hand corner. It had a reassuring air of disuse, and above all, no flowers. She walked through the French window and onto the terrace. Below the wall, the rockery fell, a cliff of granite ledges, studded with the dried-up corpses of the succulent plants Guy said were *agaves*. *Agaves* died after flowering, apparently. A lot of them had flowered last year. They would have to clean up the corpses and start again.

It sounded fine to Victoria, in the garden and elsewhere.

She went back into the library and opened the door into the State Room. A vase holding a mighty sheaf of something or other was walking across the Isfahan carpet on black gaberdine slacks. 'Dawkins,' she said.

The arrangement rustled violently. The coppery face appeared among the fronds. 'Oh Dawkins,' said Victoria. 'I'll need a telephone in here.'

'But Victoria there isn't a telephone in there,' said Dawkins. 'There never has been.'

'No time like the present,' said Victoria.

The thin lips opened, as if to speak. Then they pursed instead. By teatime that evening, there was a telephone in the library. After breakfast the next day Guy went off in a restless blur, and Victoria took possession.

It was good. It was very good.

*   *   *

Books as Flora*

One can tell so much about a British country house from its library. Take Trelise, for instance; an island garden, founded in the 1840s, a desert previously. The library is a small, plain room, workmanlike. If one thinks of the books botanically – and Trelise is a place informed by botany – one can see the early years as a rocky desert, populated only with the occasional time-tried oak: a Testament, a herbal. There is a coarse development of seventeenth-century scrub, ill-printed accounts of skirmishes between Royalist and Parliamentarian, small men with bad teeth and rusty armour. The Enlightenment sees some introductions – beeches, perhaps, in the native oak – parsonical attempts to analyse the benevolent microclimate, most of them ending in denunciations of the islanders' fecklessness. By the early nineteenth century, the vegetation has thickened and come under cultivation, with worthy, turnip-like accounts of famine and misery, the impressive sums raised by the conscience-stricken urban bourgeoisie for the relief of the islanders, and the alacrity with which the islanders spent these sums on drink.

Then all of a sudden in the acquisitions of the eighteen-forties, we find ourselves in a dense wood of sturdy but exotic trees: Jeremy Bentham, John Stewart Mill, Adam Smith, primers of muscular Anglicanism and social reform, theology, Naval history, herbalism, organic chemistry, pharmacology, underlain by a litter of boxes containing letters and papers, unsorted, uncatalogued and in some cases unread since the time of writing. It is a growth that shows a predilection for the utile over the decorative, but is none the less glorious for that.

As the century moves on, ornamental plantings start to punctuate the mighty trunks. There are the poems of the Brownings, novels, novels, novels – Dickens by instalments, Disraeli, Ouida, Jane Austen, the Brontes, Flaubert; borders of flowers, annual and perennial. Towards the turn of the century the specimens take on a heavy, orchidaceous air, leaves fleshier, flowers more exotic, habit more drooping. This growth becomes dense and confused in the tens and twenties of the new century. There are the Theosophical writings

* from a lecture given by Humphrey Wheeler to the Women's Horticultural Society of Marblehead, Mass: 'Great Gardens and their Libraries' (n.d)

of Madame Blavatsky, runs of the Yellow Book, early editions of Freud, airship manuals, the Psychopathia Sexualis *of Kraft-Ebing, a volume of the poems of Vita Sackville-West bound in limp beige dogskin, Radclyffe Hall and Wyndham Lewis. These exotic blooms are brought back to earth by a grove of heart-of-oak – G.A. Henty and Angela Brazil, 'Sapper', Edgar Wallace. And under all these books there ramps an undergrowth of serious accessions: botany, botany, botany, in the form of monographs and the memoirs of plant hunters and theoretical volumes on the farming of bulbs and plant genetics.*

But mysteriously, the accessions come to a halt in 1942. After which there is nothing; a broad expanse of emptiness, paved over with bound volumes of Blackwell's Magazine *and the* Garden, *obsolete copies of the Army list and Whitaker's and Crockfords; the dreary wastes of a library in a household that has forgotten how to – or is afraid to? – use its mind . . .*

Rules of Trelise Priory Library
1. Under ABSOLUTELY NO CIRCUMSTANCES are books or papers to be taken out of the library
2. It is VITALLY IMPORTANT that ALL BOOKS AND PAPERS be put back in their RIGHT PLACES
3. Only persons with CLEAN HANDS may handle books and papers
4. SMOKING is a FILTHY HABIT. NONE of it in the library
5. The history of Trelise is in CONSTANT DEMAND. ALL loans to be marked in the book provided
BY ORDER
THIS MEANS YOU

SIGNED
(*illegible squiggle*)

The leather of the loans book was salt-dry, ungreased by handling. When Victoria opened it the cover came away in her hand. The first sixty pages were neatly kept up, with ruled partitions, titles of works consulted and their dates. The last entries were in a looping teenage hand; the writing of Diana, Guy's mother, dated 1944. On the final non-blank page someone had written, in similar writing but apparently with both hands, *go to hell go to hell damn and blast you to hell*. There was a bookmark, a small padded oblong of brown paper. A cigarette end. Judging by the burn mark, someone had laid it in the gutter margin and crushed it out by slamming the book—

'Victoria,' said the voice of Dawkins. 'Violet wants to dust.' He was tapping his foot, the asshole. Victoria said, 'It'll wait till tomorrow. There should be some boxes of letters here. Any idea what happened with them?'

'What do you want them for?'

Victoria said, with enormous patience, 'I'm going to read them.' Go right ahead. Tell me I can't have them.

But Dawkins was watching her with his penetrating eyes. He managed a smile and said, 'You'd better come up.'

The attics seemed to go on for ever. There was no electric light, so Dawkins took a flashlight and showed her endless avenues of cardboard boxes, most of which seemed to be full of paper. 'The tea-chests from the library are here,' he said.

'Have them brought down, would you?'

And by teatime, they were in the library; ten of them, numbered. There had been a system once, but now it was a jumble. Victoria hugely looked forward to putting them in order, then starting on the attic.

She started straight away. There were letters, diaries, some account books; a great tract of virgin past awaiting the mapmaker.

It was going to be wonderful.

All afternoon, the lines of letters on the floor grew longer. At half-past four, Guy's curly head appeared round the door. 'Cup of tea?' he said. With the head came a faint whiff of Lapsang Souchong. Victoria's throat was full of paper-dust. 'Sure,' she said, and went and sat close to him on the sofa in the State Room, in front of the silver teapot and the bone-china cups. There were already stop motion cameras by the clumps of wild freesias, and in the Sea Garden. She could see by the gleam behind his spectacles that he was enjoying it.

The door opened. Dawkins said, 'Owen Morgan to see you.'

'Great,' said Guy, busy, energised.

Morgan came in, short, taut, dressed in Trelise surf 'n' turf, jeans, jersey, seaboots. Victoria offered him tea. He shook his head, teeth ice-white in the light pouring in at the granite-mullioned window. He looked like the better type of Greek god. Not a lumbering powerhouse like Zeus, but Pan or Hermes, bright and agile. He was saying something to Guy. Victoria sat dazed with sun, not listening, happy.

Something had happened. Guy was still leaning back in his chair, teacup small in his large hand. But behind his round glasses his eyes had gone narrow and shocked. He came forward in the chair and he said, '*What?*'

'Body,' said Morgan. 'Skeleton, that is. Revel dug it up in the Sea Garden. By the two steps, there. What d'you want to do?'

*The Pool Garden occupies the site of the burying place of the monks of the Benedictine Priory of Trelise, founded in 1110 and attached to the Abbey of Tavistock. A holy calm pervades this garden; a sense of pious souls sweetly at rest.**

'Better just fill it in,' said Guy. The shock had passed, if it had been anything but imaginary in the first place. He was brisk and practical.

'Surely someone should examine it?' said Victoria. 'As evidence.'

Guy said to Morgan, 'Victoria trained as a museum curator.'

'That right?' said Morgan, interested. 'All round the Arch is where they used to bury the monks.'

'We need that terrace planted up in what, a fortnight?' said Guy. He sounded nervous. His series schedule was punishing. 'Marvellous phosphates, bones.'

'We should tell someone,' said Victoria. 'Archaeologists. At least have a look.'

'You'd get police, Environmental Health, God knows what,' said Guy. 'They'd shut us down for a toenail. So much to do, so little time.'

'So knock down the house, build a ranch home, it's more practical.'

Guy sighed. 'We'll try to work round it while you take a look. Can do?'

'Do our best,' said Morgan. Victoria got the idea that he understood, even if Guy didn't. She hoped Morgan would be a friend.

* *Trelise – Cornwall's Lovesome Thing*, Jeremy Peebles, Duckworth 1964

'I'll ring someone at the County Archeological Survey, see if they can come first thing tomorrow,' said Guy. 'Let's get on, shall we?' He left with Morgan.

After tea Victoria went down the garden. On the margins of the bramble thickets were sprawling mats of geraniums that smelt good, and weird New Zealand trees with roots hanging from their branches. In the Sea Garden a JCB stood yellow and prosaic on the bare black earth. Beside it, the terrace retaining wall had been rebuilt. Where the wall connected with a couple of mighty granite steps, the backfilling was incomplete. A trench remained open. By the trench, a worn spade stood in the ground.

She moved gingerly to the spoil heap and looked into the hole.

It was twenty feet by five, its base rough-dug, except in the extreme right-hand corner next to the steps, where the bottom layer was smooth, still marked with the striations of the digger-bucket. She saw a yellowish dome, half exposed, more bones half buried, yellow stripes in the red ground. She plucked the spade out of the ground and went down the barrow planks. Out of the sun the air was chill. There was a smell of peat, or perhaps mould.

She began to dig, nibbling at the soil with the edge of the spade, trying not to imagine the flesh that had rotted here. She exposed a ribcage, arms folded over it; the top of a pair of legs, stretched straight. She was dry-mouthed and nauseous. What she was doing must be wrong. She was interfering with evidence.

But it was real. Something old, but something new that Dawkins did not know about. Her own personal discovery.

The skull was dirty with soil, turned to one side, half sunk like the rest of the bones in the red clay underlayer. She did not want to expose it, in case she spoiled the scene for the archaeologists. No sign of a coffin. Probably coffins would rot away. She had no idea whether monks used coffins anyway. Why would the head be on one side? The rest of it was neatly, formally laid out. Maybe it had flopped; been buried after rigor mortis had been and gone, or before it had set in. You would need to know the burial customs of the island, however long ago. How long? Well, she could find out. There would be something in the library. It must be possible to carbon-date bones. She would ask the archaeologists when they came. She bent to the ground. Any cloth? None that she could see. Marks? She touched the forearm. The bone was cold and clayey. The feel of it went all the way up her arm and into her stomach. She was in a hole, with a corpse. Panic rose in her like bubbles.

A shadow fell across the trench wall. She looked up so fast she cricked her neck. A pair of shoulders and a bearded head were silhouetted against the sun-bright sky. She went up the planks and into the sun. She found she was trembling.

The man said, 'I'm Revel.' He stood in the flowerbed, framed by the arch.

She remembered him from the crowd by the Watch Tower. She said, 'You gave me a hell of a shock.'

'Tell me about shocks,' said Revel. 'It was me found them bones.' He took a roll-up from his hat and lit it. 'Life, though, innit? Shocks in store.' He crouched, started to rummage in a great mat of foliage.

'What do you mean?'

'New place, always surprising,' said Revel, rooting with a fork, grunting. 'Buggers to weed, *Dimorpotheca*. Must get on.'

Victoria went back to the house.'

Chapter Three

That evening Guy came back pleased about something. He seemed disinclined to talk about skeletons, and opened champagne. They held hands on the terrace. It was unseasonably warm, with a big moon and the Mare sweeping the horizon with its beam. Still, it was February, and the night air finally drove them to bed. Next morning, she woke early. Outside the window the sea gleamed silky green in a peachy dawn. She had her territory now; her library, her skeleton to study. She felt confident and loving. She sidled across an acreage of cold sheet and put her arms around Guy's neck. She found his mouth, and kissed him good morning, soft and deep. One of his arms came across and embraced her. A hard arm, muscular since he had been working in the garden. He had hardened up, mind and body. She liked him this way. Loved him any way, actually.

She lay for a moment in his warmth. The points of her breasts touched him through her Egyptian cotton nightdress. They felt vivid, awake. A heat spread in her body. She rolled away. 'Hey,' he said, groping for her. She pulled the nightdress over her head and crawled back to him. 'Wozzis?' he said.

'Wait and see.'

'It's early.'

She climbed onto him, letting her breasts brush his chest. 'Sleep, then,' she said.

He raised an eyebrow at her, blurred without his glasses. 'Well,' he said.

She lowered herself onto him, very slow.

'In the circumstances . . .'

She started a planetary rocking.

East Neck had been cold. The Museum had been cold. Trelise was cold.

Guy was hot.

Oh, yes.

She felt herself begin to flower like, oh, hell, *oh*, twenty-one acres of Paradise.

Later, Guy got up. 'Tea?' he said.

'Earl Grey,' she said. 'Hint of English Breakfast.'

'I'll get Dawkins to bring it up,' he said.

She rolled her head at him, sleepily. 'Bring it yourself.'

'I've got a film crew to get ready.'

'Hell with them.'

He kissed her, a definite goodbye kiss. She grabbed him by the neck. 'Hey,' he said. 'Leggo.'

'Not yet.'

'Sexual harassment.'

She was up now, hanging onto him tight, nose to nose, sucking his tongue. He disengaged himself. 'I've got to go.'

'No, you don't. I can tell.'

'All right, then.' He picked her up; Christ, he was strong. She locked her legs behind his back. He took her against the wall. They giggled at first. Then the giggling stopped, and the floor shook, and the cupboard doors rattled and slammed. Afterwards, he carried her back to the bed and laid her gently down. 'More?' he said.

'Yes.'

'Too bad. Think film crew.'

'Jerk.'

'Slut.' She lay in a lazy glow. When Dawkins brought the tea, she pretended to be asleep. Give it an hour. Get up, catalogue some letters, walk down the garden with the county bone guy. The walk in her thoughts turned into a dream. In the dream she walked round the west of the island, along the little tracks in the heather above the surge and boom of the sea. Guy was there, at first. Then he was not there. And something bad was happening.

There was a smell in the air, burning, the worst smell in the world. She turned away from the sea and looked down the long slope towards the dark shelter-belts of the garden. It was all there, as usual. Except that as she looked, she saw flames burst out of the roof, crawl around the turrets and pinnacles, just as they had burst and crawled in the house at East Neck. Suddenly she was not on Trelise, but in East Neck, on the grass, running backwards away from the house, watching those fearsome orange flames, feeling the sting of burns on her arms and legs, and the fatal sense that nothing would ever be the same again.

The roof caved in with a roar.

Her eyes flew open. For a second she thought it had been a dream. But the roar was really there; a huge, crackling roar. And a smell of smoke, more than a smell, harsh in the throat, coming in the window, the door.

She was out of bed, up to the window. The world was obscured by huge white billows. She pulled the window open. There were flames down there. A world of flames. She could not get her breath. Her mouth was open and her throat was raw as hamburger, and above the flames she could hear an odd hissing in her ears: a sound she was making. She supposed she was screaming. It would not stop. There were voices from outside: men's voices, bellowing. There had been men's voices last time, in East Neck. It was all just like the last time.

Behind her, the bedroom door swung open with a crash. You had to close bedroom doors. If they were open and windows were open they turned the whole house into a chimney and burned it up real real quick—

Someone was yelling at her. A man. Not screaming, like in East Neck. Just shouting. A pair of arms went round her. She was not wearing any clothes. Her breasts were up against buttons. That was like last time, too. She struggled, hammering away with her hands. The room was vague and blurred.

Then she landed on the bed, and looked up, and the face on the man was Guy's. She heard his voice say, 'It's not the house. It's not the house.'

She rolled away from him and put her hands in her hair. The smell of smoke was strong.

'It was a surprise,' he said. 'It was supposed to be a surprise.'

She began to cry. Someone, presumably him, put a duvet over her. It made it good and dark and safe. She said, 'I was in a house once when it burned.'

'We were only burning the rockery. All the dead stuff. It's part of the clean-up, to get rid of the dead *Agaves*. They've done it for a hundred and fifty years. Usually in autumn, but Morgan said this early in the year wouldn't do any harm.'

She found a voice. 'You could have told me.'

'Sorry.'

She wrapped herself round him. She needed the company of someone alive. 'I've got to go,' he said. 'Will you be okay?'

'Sure,' she said, because that was the answer he wanted.

The door opened and closed. He left. She got back into bed, and lay there, chewing at her thumbnail.

She was a total flake. The whole island would hear. Well, Guy would explain about her house fire. He was good at explaining.

And house fire was true.

As far as it went.

She dressed and drank a cup of coffee and went out into the courtyard. It was half past nine. The county archaeologist would be here already. She trotted down the Poseidon Stairs, past the blaze of the *Camellias*. The air smelt of bitter ash from the rockery, and her head was sloshing with the chemical debris of terror. The garden was empty, quiet. Soon she would hear the fuss and rumour of archaeologists; police, perhaps, coroners.

She turned off the Stairs, past the Priory Arch and into the Sea Garden.

A thrush hopped between two banana trees. An *Enkianthus* shifted in the breeze. Nothing else stirred.

It must be the wrong time. The tide must be in. The causeway must be closed. Someone must be late.

Beyond the tape was the JCB, a yellow monster resting its bucket on the ground. There were the terraces of the Sea Garden, running towards the wall and the low dunes.

There was no trench, and no way of telling where it had been.

When she laid her hand on the JCB's hood, it was still warm.

Someone said, 'Morning.' Revel the weeder got up from the lower of the two steps beside which the grave had been. His smock and jeans were the colour of earth. He had a barrowful of young plants in pots.

Victoria sat down on the steps beside him. He worried a hole with his trowel, tapped a plant loose from its pot, and tamped it into the hole.

'It has been,' said Victoria, as best she could, 'a really weird day.'

'Already?' said Revel. He cleaned his trowel against the granite, *zing*. 'I'm having a cup of tea. Fancy one?'

Anything. Anything normal. He led her down a couple of paths to a stone bungalow. A flight of steps led to a verandah. Behind the verandah were patio doors, and a sitting room that was also a kitchen. There were carvings propped against the railings, half-finished; a gull, a seal in weed. Ravel put the kettle on. 'Daise?' he said.

A woman came out of an inner room. She was blonde, with short hair and a bright gull's-egg face. There was a dustpan in her hand.

'Daise comes and cleans up,' said Revel. 'Out of pity and sympathy.'

'Chips wood in his bedroom, this animal,' said Daisy, with affection. She did not look as if she had been out this morning. Victoria guessed that cleaning was not all she was doing in Revel's bedroom.

'They filled in the trench with the bones,' said Revel.

'Yeah,' said Daisy. 'Saw Darren on the digger at eight.'

'Eight?' said Victoria. Archaeologists? Bullshit, Guy. *Bullshit*. She made conversation. They talked about Trelise as if it was the whole world. She stayed for as long as it took her to swallow the tea. Then she clattered down the steps.

She took a wrong turning, and found herself in Davy Jones, the figure-head cloister. Blank-eyed women gazed down at her over white billows of bosom. They did not care. A wild Turk brandished a scimitar. She said, 'Kill goddam Guy.' Too strong. 'A bit.' She could hear a film crew operating in the Sea Garden. Not Guy's voice, though. She marched back to the house.

Dawkins was crushing the ends of camellia stems in the flower room. 'Where's Guy?' she said.

He consulted his watch elaborately. 'Eleven o'clock, Tuesday. Coffee with Jeremy Davis in the Estate Office. Week's progress review, flowers over, so I expect they'll be talking about bulbs. Victoria, we should discuss—'

But Victoria was on a bicycle, clattering down the road to the Estate Office, at the root of Old Hull quay. There were voices in Guy's room. She marched in. Guy was behind the desk. Jeremy Davis was in the visitor's chair, spidery cavalry twill legs crossed. He took one look, mumbled and bolted. Guy opened his mouth.

'You never rang any archaeologist,' said Victoria. 'You just had the trench filled in.'

'I—'

'This is us living on this desert island,' she said. 'Not your ancestors. So if you want to do something that affects me could you just level with me first?'

His head sank between his big shoulders. 'They're only bones,' he said.

'You made a promise.'

'I am filming a garden show,' he said, thin and tight as a banjo string. 'Today, the weather is perfect. You cannot have open bloody graves in a garden series, that will be watched by several million old ladies and which will pay the tax people if I can get it finished in time, and which will bankrupt us if I do not. Last night the weather forecast said cloud, so I thought, fine, let's get some archaeologists. But this morning I got up and there it was, sun. So we filled in the hole, and did our shots, and now we are planting it up. When the film is done you can dig all the holes you want. All right?'

'All right.' She was oppressed by guilt. He was right. She was acting spoilt. An American, making fuss about things that in this old world were just not important. 'You could have said, though.'

'Yes.' He hung his head. 'It's not being a great morning, is it?'

Which made her feel even sorrier. Bones were only bones. There were other ways of digging.

'I'll come back with you.'

They bicycled back to the Priory. She went into the house. Dawkins was primping daisies in the hall. She was about to walk past him, then hesitated. 'Nice day,' she said.

'Delightful, Victoria.'

'Better than forecast.'

'I beg your pardon?'

'Last night,' said Victoria. 'They were calling for cloud, rain, right?'

'Oh, no,' said Dawkins. 'Not at all. I heard it twice. Pressure high as anything. Sun, sun, sun all the way.'

'Is that right?' said Victoria. 'Well, ain't love grand?'

'I beg your pardon?'

'Nothing.'

Back to the library. Where else did you go?

Notes for a Treatment for a movie, provisionally entitled ISLANDER
© Wallace Diment 1968.

A story based on known historical fact – the life of Joshua Jones, pharmacologist, social reformer, lover, smuggler, explorer; a man of his time. A man of our time. A man for all time.

We meet JONES in a Cambridgeshire workhouse. He is eight years old, an attractive kid with dark hair and blue eyes. Misunderstood by the authorities, he escapes, with his friend AMELIA. It is raining. AMELIA contracts pneumonia. JONES carries her to a farmhouse nearby, and nurses her in a barn, tending the farmer's cattle in exchange for food. AMELIA dies. JONES swears revenge on the workhouse superintendent who has used them so cruelly. He stays on the farm. The cattle fall sick. JONES notes that this is down to them eating ragwort, and makes a draught from herbs that pulls some of them through. The FARMER, BILLINGS (Roy Kinnear?) mentions this to his friend DR PRIVIS, a Cambridge apothecary (Vincent Price?). PRIVIS is impressed. By this time JONES is twelve, a nice-looking lad, with a quiet manner. His gentle ways and good hands have attracted the attention of FARMER BILLINGS' daughter SAMANTHA (Susan George?), as well as her MOTHER (Sylvia Sims?). The MOTHER, jealous, frames JONES for a cheese theft. Just before the Bow Street Runners arrive, SAMANTHA is able to warn him. Placing a sprig of Rosemary on AMELIA'S grave, he flees the farm, arriving in Cambridge.

Here, as he begs on the steps of Trinity College, he is recognised by PRIVIS, who is passing en route to deliver mercury pills to a syphilitic DON (John Gielgud?). PRIVIS recalls his talent as a self-taught herbalist. He takes him on as his apprentice. For the next two years

JONES lives as a virtual prisoner, under threat of exposure for cheese theft.

By now, JONES has become a man (Terence Stamp?). From behind the glass screen in the Apothecary's shop he catches the eye of LADY ANCONA (Julie Christie?). It is love at first sight. She orders some of PRIVIS' patent face powder, and asks for JONES to deliver it. They make far-out love. JONES discovers while at her place that FARMER BILLINGS is dead, and that PRIVIS has been keeping him under false pretences. Thanks to his knowledge of massage oils, his relationship with LADY ANCONA grows daily more sensuous. Then when LORD ANCONA (Jeremy Child?) arrives home unexpectedly, LADY ANCONA explains JONES' presence (he has his oils out, but has not yet uncorked them) by the fact that he is a young botanist, giving her instruction, and that she intends (as an act of charity) to send him to Trinity College. So to Trinity he goes.

Here he gets heavily into drugs. He still visits LADY ANCONA. But her maid, a country woman MISS TIMMS (Barbara Windsor?), knows SAMANTHA is still looking for him. As he awaits the awarding of his degree SAMANTHA comes to visit him in his rooms. While they bounce on the bed LADY ANCONA comes in and catches them in flagrante, *followed by the DEAN OF DEGREES, come to summon JONES to the Viva at which he will be awarded a First by Acclamation. JONES flees over the rooftops, pursued by all, and takes ship for Mexico. He has realised that the world is a place in which* what people say and what people do are not necessarily the same thing. [Underlinings are in red ink. On the T/S in Harry Blakeney-Jones' hand is written 'I should think so too, who on earth is this charlatan? The facts may be right but what has poor Joshua done to deserve this God damn and blast this bloody little man'] *The only reliable thing is the effect of drugs on the organism. He will devote his life to drugs. Mysteriously, as his ship departs, the superintendent of the workhouse is found to have invested his life savings and money embezzled from the workhouse fund in a venture to grow Indian Hemp in the Fens – a venture that crashes. The superintendent hangs himself. The word goes round that JONES is a great lover, a good friend – but a deadly enemy!*

He – [here the page is torn in half. No further material exists].*

Who can venture to say what was passing in the mind of Joshua Jones when at the age of 32, a distinguished medical career already behind him, he first set eyes on the heather-clad hummock that was Trelise? Certainly we know he was a man of parts, respected, in the year before the accession of Queen Victoria, as one of the leading lights of Science in the Empire. Certainly many a Belgravia mamma whispered his name behind her fan, and many a high-born miss lowered demure eyelashes at this bright-eyed savant endowed with a gravity beyond his years. Certainly, he was a follower of Jeremy Bentham, the high priest of Utilitarianism. Certainly, he entertained visions of an ideal society. But as to what it was that clinched his decision to come to this desolate spot, in those days before railways a five days' journey from London, we shall never know – and perhaps it would be presumptuous to enquire.†

Guy said, 'What are you up to today?' They were having breakfast, the day after the rockery and the bones.

Victoria said, 'I'm going to write a book.'

'Ah,' said Guy, writing a note on the script by his plate. 'Anyone to dinner?'

'Nobody knows anything about this place,' said Victoria. 'Or cares. It's all there, letters, papers, the lot.'

Guy's mobile phone chirruped. He stopped writing, switched it on and said, 'Yes?'

'But nobody's ever put it all together. So I'm going to, and if I don't get to look at those bones, I'll work them out for myself.'

'I'll be right down,' said Guy into the telephone.

Victoria finished her coffee. 'I'll take that as a "yes, dear",' she said.

'What?'

'I was just saying that you buried that skeleton, so I'm going to find out who it is.'

He gazed upon her abstractedly. 'If you must.'

She went into the library before he could try to kiss her goodbye.

* fragment of holograph ms, box 5, Trelise library
† from *Great Joshua*, Maria Jones, 1953

In her chair, she relented. Guy was in a hurry, for good reasons. Perhaps it was easier for an Englishman to lie about a weather forecast than to tell his underemployed wife to zipper her American mouth.

She uncapped her pen, and pulled her notebook towards her.

Chapter Four

Falmouth, 1844

Rain. Rain pouring onto the luggers in the harbour. The stink of new fish, and old fish, and coal smoke, and flooded drains streaking slime over the cobbles, pressed down by the weight of water vapour into a thing thick and heavy as a punch in the throat. A short, filthy day, haunted by the masts and yards of the ships in Carrick Roads.

The barber's shop was packed, bear's-greased assistants officiating, scrape, yessir, terrible weather we do be 'aving, scrape, and among and behind the chairs *le tout* Falmouth milling, wet wool and stale drink and a haze of cigars, will there be any other *harticle*?

They were all watching the corner. George Benbow, the notoriously chicken-hearted potboy from the Grapes, was in a chair. Surgeon Penruddock bending over his open mouth. 'The patient is immobilised!' cried a gentleman's voice. 'We have anointed the gum with the Patent Coca Salve. He will feel – well, you will see.' Surgeon Penruddock's shoulders heaved. He stood up, one arm raised. There was a pair of pliers in his hand. In the pliers was something blackish and bloody.

'A molar!' cried the gentleman's voice. 'Well, Mr Benbow. Was it agonising?'

George was up, drooling blood into a brass basin. 'Dint feel nothing at all!' he said. 'Zat my tooth?'

'Painless dentistry!' said the gentleman. 'At last! With the Jones Patent Coca Salve! Thank you, Mr Benbow. With the Coca Salve, all becomes smooth and easy. Even stopping, with the rotary drill and silver amalgam.' The speaker opened his mouth and pointed to a metal-plated left-hand molar. The audience horripilated, imagining the drill. 'Now we pass to the next demonstration.'

Benbow merged with the crowd, grinning bloodily and shaking an incredulous head. No quackery here; everyone knew George, and his cowardice, and his abominable teeth. All eyes turned to another chair; a chair of a different kind. It had straps on its arms and legs, and a cradle for the head, with another strap for the brow. In the straps was a man somewhere between thirty and seventy, emaciated, with a bluish skin. Surgeon Penruddock had taken up position behind the chair in his blood-stiffened frock coat, tall hat crammed down over his butcher's eyes, hands curled like a fighter. Ramrod-straight at his side stood the man who had been doing the talking.

He was an up-country chap, thirtyish, with black curly hair, bright blue eyes, and a forceful jaw thrusting from clean white gills. The posters melting on the doors of the town proclaimed him to be Joshua Jones, the celebrated scientific apothecary, trained in Cambridge, Berlin and Algiers, now according Falmouth the inestimable benison of his presence, bringing that small but striving town to the very scalpel-edge of Science.

The paragon struck an attitude, and spoke.

'Gentlemen,' he said. He had an easy, confident way with him. The audience fell quiet; the finest intellects of Falmouth, and a dozen doctors from parishes as far off as Penzance. 'Gentlemen and learned professionals. I thank you for attending our demonstration here today – a demonstration, I may say, of one of the marvels of the age. You see here beside me a suffering fellow human, ladies and gentlemen.' Here the bluish gentleman in the chair groaned affectingly. 'In his right arm is lodged a fragment of His Majesty's first-rate ship *Bellona*, blasted thither when he was a boy by the Frog at Trafalgar of heroic memory.' The hush was absolute. Falmouth loved to remember a sea battle, even one forty years old. 'It lies grinding against the upper radial nerve, and causes him unspeakable agony. The first surgeons of England have examined our poor friend, and declared that to remove it would leave him lunatic from the pain. But now through the exhibition of Jones' Etheric Draught, this crooked way can be made straight. Gentlemen, you are about to see Surgeon Penruddock remove the foreign body without the slightest pain to this brave Jack Tar.' He held up a black bottle. 'Jones' Etheric Draught. Surgeon! Are the instruments sharp?'

Using the scalpel, Surgeon Penruddock shaved a small tuft of greasy whisker from his jaw. 'Very good,' said Jones. He measured two inches of amber fluid into a graduated medicine glass.

'Laudanum,' said a pig-faced man in the front row.

'Sir, you have the advantage of me,' said Jones.

'Fairey,' said the pig-faced man. 'I'll go bail that's laudanum.'

''Pothecary,' hissed Penruddock. 'Man of large business. Doctor, too.'

'Thank you, Doctor Fairey,' said Jones, dismissively. 'But as we know, the exhibition of sufficient laudanum for the entire dulling of pain can lead to a depression of the vital faculties, with dangerous consequences to the organism.'

The pig-faced Fairey snorted derisively.

'Very well,' said Jones. 'I'll double the dose, and you shall see that there are no adverse consequences.' He poured another two inches into the glass and raised it to the throng, masking the man in the chair with his body.

'Snot enough,' hissed the blue man from the chair. 'I felt the blade in bloody Plymouth and St Ozzle.'

'So!' cried Mr Jones with a circus flourish, presenting the glass to the blue man's teeth.

'I'll shriek, Josha,' hissed the blue man. 'Also kick.'

'Lord bless ye, ye won't feel nothink, not but a tickle,' said Penruddock.

'The patient is nervous,' said Jones. 'We can understand this. Drink, my good man, and your troubles will be at an end.' The blue man's eyes were glassy under the buckle on his forehead, the pupils small. He drank.

'Now,' said Jones, and tipped into the glass another two inches of the liquid, which he fed the blue man. 'This we do without the slightest danger to the patient. Were this laudanum, I need hardly say, the dose would be fatal; double the fatal, even in a constitution accustomed.'

'Aaah,' said the blue man, and smacked his lips.

'Now,' said Jones. 'Unstrap, if you please, Mr Penruddock.'

The surgeon's mouth opened.

'Unstrap, sir, I say. You have my assurance.'

''E'll thrash,' said Penruddock.

'Now, sir!' cried Jones.

Slowly and with reluctance, Penruddock unstrapped.

There was quiet, except for the rain on the windows and the rumble of carts in the street. The surgeon crammed his hat over his eyes, wiped his knife on his coat tail, pulled the white left arm taut on the chair, and raised the blade.

'One moment, Mr Penruddock,' said Jones, addressing himself to the blue man. 'What d'ye feel, sir?'

He saw the glaze in Pancho's eye, the slow pulse in the throat. The Draught was not right: which is to say, the principle was right, but the formulation was not yet correct. Ether was a terrible irritant to the lining of the stomach. Until he found a way to reduce the irritation he must use Pancho, who after a lifetime of opium eating could sustain consciousness under a dose big enough to kill a mule, and feed him a mixture in which the proportion of ether had been reduced to the point where all that remained was the characteristic smell. There were cuts all over Pancho. What had done the damage was the ragged wound torn four days back, by that drunken fool Warbeck on the Barbican in Plymouth . . .

Tonight, Pancho had had too much.

'Mr Mendez,' he said. 'What do you feel?'

The lids lifted, heavy as the shutters on a man-of-war's gun ports. The pupils were the size of Bible full-stops. 'Feel?' he said. He laughed.

'Cut, then,' said Jones.

It was red in Pancho's head, warm, with a deep soothing drone. Someone was poking at his arm, but the Draught soothed that away. There were eyes, too; a flower border of eyes, blue and grey poppies blooming in smoke, fixed upon him. Somewhere in the thicket there would be tigers slinking to and fro, lovely tigers. But now there was only the Place, this lovely red, colour of the velvet curtains of Heaven . . .

Jones allowed the jagged fragment of timber to slide from his sleeve. He said, 'Allow me,' and walked to the chair. Bending over the patient, he paddled the splinter well in the blood on the white arm. Then he turned, and held it up to the crowd. It occurred to him that the blood was flowing very sluggish. 'Behold,' he said. 'Extracted, without pain. Sew him up, Mr Penruddock, if you would be so good.'

Every man in the barber's shop had writhed in sympathy with the man in the chair. But the man in the chair had been still. *Without straps.* If Jones' Coca Salve and Jones' Etheric Draught would stop the agony of the pliers and the knife, they would pay any money for them. The whole of Europe and some of America had drawn the same conclusion, and in drawing it made Jones a rich man.

Someone began to clap. Everyone began to clap.

Pancho slumbered in the chair. A knot of men formed round Jones, placing orders. The Etheric Draught was not yet available: tonight had been a demonstration only. But they scooped up the Jones Coca Salve, the Febrifuge, the Apoplectic Tea, the Stimulant. They scooped it up in dozens, and paid for it in gold. Jones' stocks ran out. He took orders for the rest, cash on delivery. Doctor Fairey scowled at the crowds gathered round Jones' book. Orders placed, the crowd dispersed, except for a couple of men being shaved, and Fairey.

'You'll oblige me by showing me what's in that bottle,' said Doctor Fairey. 'And with your permission, I shall examine your patient.'

Jones smiled, his obliging, hard-as-nails smile. 'I regret, Doctor, that that is impossible.'

Fairey's neck reddened. He put his face close to Jones', so Jones could smell his fearful breath. He said, 'More likely laudanum than not. A hellish big dose of laudanum.'

'Sir,' said Joshua, and his own eye was hard as his jaw. 'I would draw your attention to Jones' Carminative Draught, Jones' Modified Bark Pills, the Jones Febrifuge, the Coca Salve. If you choose to doubt their efficacy you are in a great minority, sir.'

'Senna,' said Fairey. 'Quinine. Willow. Coca. Efficacious, nobody's doubtin' that. No need to pay your silly prices, though.'

'You are paying for quality, reliability, consistency. There are advantageous terms available to the Trade.'

'Squeegin' the local man,' said Fairey. 'Damn quackery.'

From the corner of his eye, Jones could see the carotid pulse under the leaden skin of Pancho's throat. Very slow. And, unless Jones was much deceived, getting slower. But this man had called him a quack. 'I think I cannot have heard you properly,' he said.

Fairey prided himself on being a forthright man, particularly in defence of his personal interest. But he found that under the hard blue eye, he was incapable of repeating the accusation. 'Ether,' he said. 'Gastric irritant.'

'The merit,' said Jones, 'is in the formulation.'

'Pish,' said Fairey.

Surgeon Penruddock emitted the hasty cough of a man with a ten-pound bribe in his waistcoat pocket. 'Shuttin' up shop, sir, doctor, if you please.'

'We can continue at my warehouses in London,' said Jones. 'My card, sir.'

'Damn your card,' said Fairey. 'What's required is the constable, not a card.'

'By your leave, Doctor,' said Penruddock, and swept him towards the door with his large upper body.

'Just because you're a monopolist don't mean you ain't a mountebank poisoner,' shouted Fairey. 'I demand to examine that man.'

'Yessir,' said Penruddock, sweat rolling out of his hat now. 'Out ye go, doctor. Dirty filthy night. Best get off 'ome.' He projected Fairey into the downpour, bolted the door behind him and wheezed nervously back to Jones. 'Chap don't look good, actual,' he said. 'I said to myself, surgeon, e's overdoing that stuff, whatever it is—'

'I am not the one who stuck knives into him,' said Jones.

Penruddock stared at him, open-mouthed.

'I'll take him away,' said Jones. 'With your help.'

'Fairey's in the street.' Penruddock was a nasty phosphorescent green. 'Werry persistent man in defence of his trade, which is what you did threaten here tonight. 'E'll have Mr Walker J.P. on us. By Harry, my boy, what if you've killed him?'

'I am not your boy. He is alive. Where's the back door?'

Penruddock pointed.

'A wheelbarrow. Quick, before he finds a mob.'

Night had long fallen; a grim night, with the rain hardening into sleet. Through this night and onto the quay Jones bowled the barrow, the wet creeping through the broadcloth of his coat, the puddles icy through the pulp of his varnished boots.

The abominable weather had kept the luggers from the grounds. They lay in the harbour like pilchards garbaged in a barrel, huddled out of the wind moaning in the roofs of the town.

Jones dragged Mendez down the steps, hauled him to a boat in the outer rank of luggers, and laid him on the sleety deck.

In the dirty cabin, two men were playing cards under a lantern. One was middle-aged, with a red beard and the fat neck of a seal. The other was a boy, perhaps fifteen, with spots around his mouth. 'Give me a hand down with my friend,' said Jones.

When the boy saw Mendez, his face went slack and frightened. ''E's dead,' he said.

'By no means.' The Mexican's jaw fell open as they laid him on the cabin bunk. Jones was chafing the cold hands, whacking the leaden cheeks. 'Pembarra. What time's high water?'

'Couple of hours yet.'

'We'll sail now.'

'Tent fit,' said Pembarra, keeping his eyes away from Mendez. This chap Jones had chartered him in Plymouth a week ago. Since then, Pembarra had found him a man not over-easy to say no to.

'Mr Mendez is ill. We must get him back to Plymouth.'

'Never Plymouth, not in this,' said Pembarra. It had not taken long to discover that a flat refusal would not do, not with Mr Jones. 'We could pop across to St Mawes, though. Handier for the morning tide.'

'As you wish,' said Jones, fingers on Mendez' pulse. It crossed Pembarra's mind that weather or no weather, it was not like Mr Jones to take up a suggestion. But by then he and the boy were up the companionway, and the apothecary was reaching for his brass-bound chest of medicines.

Canvas roared as they swung the mainsail up into the rain, four reefs in. The sound of retching came from below, the clink of glass, torn away east down the wind; and another noise, fainter, from the quay; hounds' music, perhaps. Or a mob, whipped into full cry after a quack. 'Let go, Denzil,' roared Pembarra, to drown it. He grasped the mainsheet in his hard hand, and gave it the benefit of his back. The *Edward and Rose* wallowed off the raft and into the shrieking coalpit of the night.

In ten minutes Jones was on deck. The rain-smeared lights of the town shone in the silvery pallor of his face. He bellowed into Pembarra's sou'wester, 'We'll go to Plymouth.'

'We bloody will not.'

'Plymouth or hang.'

Pembarra's mind played him a reprise of the shouting on the quay, and his heart turned to lead in his chest. He knew then, in that way this here Jones had of telling you things with his mind and not his voice, that the chap down below was dead as a haddock, and the voices on the quay wanted to know why, and that he would never get back there upwind in the lugger to explain, so he would be seen as a fugitive, an accessory after the fact.

'Better drown than hang,' bellowed Jones.

Which it just showed, thought Pembarra, that he knew bugger all about the sea. But he was not a man you could refuse, this Jones. Not even if you died doing his wish.

Like that chap had down below.

Wedged in the bug-stinking coffin-bunk, Jones dreams.

He dreams of opium the great sovereign. He flows away over yellow fields of goldenrod, *Spiraea filipendula,* master of fever, more effective even than willow – stupid provincial Dr Fairey – in Jones' Febrifuge. He watches the old tramp shit himself drunkenly in Farmer Devis' hayloft, Devis punch the tramp in the nose for fouling his hay, never mind the hay was mouldy. The tramp's nose flooding scarlet, a scarlet that would not stop, ran and ran, never clotted; the formulation of Jones' Apoplectic Tea from mouldy clover hay.

Jones is a man who watches.

What Jones believes in are ventilation, respiration, the circulation of the blood. He believes in bodily cycles, microbial infections, the disposition by Providence of plants as factories for chemicals that affect the human organism, the perfectibility of humanity by hard work, organisation and rational enjoyment. He believes in the absolute obligation of promises, and the ruthless punishment of treachery.

What Jones does not believe in are the beneficial effects of bleeding, the humours, planetary influences, the casting out of demons, untested convention, and the ineluctibility of Destiny.

Jones believes in aloes, balsam of Peru, the Bark, buchu leaves, camphor, castor oil, chamomile, clover, Compound tincture of Benjamin, Cubebs,

Dandelion, Ergot of Rye, Sulphuric Ether but not by mouth, Feverfew, Foxglove, Goldenrod, Helebore, Honey, Henbane, Iodine, Ipecac, Juniper, Kousso, Laudanum, Cod-liver Oil, Opium, Quassia, Rhubarb, Senna, Spider's webs, Strychnia, Sulphate of Quinine extracted from best Bark by his own process, Valerian, Water (rain, spring, river and sea) Willow, Wormwood; tweezers, scalpels, hand-wash bowls, white aprons, clean sheets and comfortable beds in general.

He does not believe in the administration of arsenic, artificial asses' milk, the Blue Pill, Calomel or any other mercurial compound, Blue Vitriol except to excite vomitus when laudanum is used as a poison (the final retchings of Mendez were blue as ink), corrosive sublimate, the lunar caustic, elixir of vitriol, the tartar emetic, liquor potassae, Mindereus' Spirit, nitric acid, prussic acid, sugar of lead, or the instruments of torment: saws, bistouries, hammers, leather aprons and straps in general.

Nor does he believe in magic.

Through his factory he flowed in his dream, past mortars, mills, stills and compounding vats, storehouses of rye and foxglove and umbelliferae in variety, dried and baled, bled into cakes and carboys, tinctured, powdered, rolled, wrapped, bottled—

Jones felt in his sleep that the sea changed. The short lurch and bump ceased. Now there was the long lift of a big swell, the check and weightlessness, the wail of wind in a rag of sail, the long, tearing slide into the trough.

But Joshua did not wake. He flowed on through the dark storehouses. All his life he had travelled, Europe, Mexico, Turkey, the whole patchwork face of the world, restlessly seeking out drugs and money. Always looking for the next place, the improved formula. Here off the coast of Cornwall, remotest corner of the foggy islands of Britain, he was tired. He wanted peace, stillness. Somewhere inside himself, he felt an intimation of brightness: the place Mendez had sought, and perhaps now found.

There had been enough pain.

At the moment of waking, the boards under his shoulder twitched like a thrower's arm and flung him out of the bunk. He brought up with a crash against a bulkhead. There was shouting on deck, the frenzied rattle of canvas. The *Edward and Rose* gave a sort of struggling wallow and fell sideways off a wave. Jones crawled up the companion ladder, hauled the hatch open and clambered out. 'Shut that!' yelled a voice in the dark. A wall of icy water smacked him in the chops. The hatch slammed.

The lugger's deck was a pale leaf writhing in the grip of the black sea. Up she went; up, up, a long hill of water. As she came to the summit, Jones heard a rumble and saw a gleam of white. The crest burst like a bomb against the lugger's windward bow, and another wall of water came down the deck. She shuddered, and shook herself, and started down the long slope into the trough. A body crashed into Jones. The hatch opened, sang a brief bottleneck note in the wind, then slammed. In a moment of quiet he heard the rattle of the bolt. 'Oh Denzil, you bastard!' roared Pembarra. 'Come back, wait'll I tells your mother on you!'

But the hatch stayed mute and closed.

The black shape that must be Pembarra was standing at the tiller. Jones could feel the horrible tautness of the mainsheet, the torrent of the water over the rudder. 'Zay your prayers,' roared Pembarra.

'What do you mean?'

Even over the howl of the tempest, Pembarra could hear the authority in the voice. It made him angry. 'Trelise,' he roared, spitting brine. 'Back of us we've got the mainland. Ahead of us we've got Trelise.'

'Sea room,' said Jones. 'Get sea room.'

'Now that is a thing nobody can do,' roared Pembarra. 'Not even you, damn you, sir, because we are in the bloody bay.'

'What can I do to help?' said Jones.

Pembarra said, 'Well, you could always decide what one you want to hit, Gwineas Cliff or Trelise?'

Jones fixed him with his cold grey eye. 'What,' he said, 'is Trelise?'

'Trelise, damn your higorance, sir, is a bloody great rock of an island what is dead ahead of us the way we are going, sir. Like a pile on the arse of Cornwall, sir. Which you cannot pass it to the north because of shoals and a causeway, and you cannot round it to the south by Tobaccoman's Point because of where this wind do blow, and even if we was to make Tobaccoman's, sir, there is rivers of tide and a jawful of rocks off of it called, should you be interested, the Mare, sir. Which I hope you are now contented, Mr Bloody Jones.' Another explosion of icy water. Another shriek and heel and wallow. Pembarra said, 'Being as this year whole bloody mess is up to you.'

'I am aware of that,' says Jones, clear and stony.

'Then be sorry, bugger you.'

Jones said, 'Do whatever you think gives you and the boy the best chance.'

'Trelise,' said Pembarra. He leaned on the tiller. The lugger's heel steepened. Icy water flew aboard in sheets. After ten minutes there was a bang and a long rattle. Where the black shadow of the sail had been there was charcoal-grey cloud, with something whipping against it like a long fringe. The sail itself had gone.

Pembarra ran forward and flicked turns of rope off the halyard pin. Jones was beside him. The yard started down. Halfway to the deck, a puff of wind came round the wrong side of what was left of the sail. Pembarra roared as the blast tore the rope from his hands. The yard came down with a run. There was a heavy *clonk* as it caught him at the base of the skull. He fell on his face and slid. Jones grabbed the skirt of his oilskin smock, feeling his fingernails go. Pembarra was limp as a sack of potatoes. The yard bounded across the deck and leaped over the side, where it lay pounding like a maul. He pulled the knife from Pembarra's belt, groped for what ropes he could find, and sawed at the wet hemp. After a while the thudding stopped.

Jones lay in the lee of the low bulwark and let his heartbeat slow. He pressed his palms together against the sting of the salt on the rope-flayed flesh, and turned the cold machine of his mind to the subject at hand.

Pembarra was senseless, the boy useless. Even if he found a new sail and the strength to hoist it, Jones did not have the knowledge to bend it onto the yard. The wind had not abated. It had veered west in the night; an area of low atmospheric pressure, Jones deduced, was moving eastwards across England. Sooner or later, the wind would turn northwest, more favourable. The tide would turn. Once turned, it might wash them south along the western shore of this Trelise.

So Joshua Jones sat with the wind whipping his hair across his eyes, and waited for his fate at the hands of the shore or the dawn, whichever would come first.

He was not a man to give himself over to unprofitable anxieties. Instead, he rehearsed his life. He smelt the air of freedom outside the workhouse door. He rolled pills with Dr Privis, slept with Lady Audubon, sat in the lecture theatre at Cambridge. He walked laughing with Pancho in the blazing heat of the Sierras. He sat in the evening with the women while the mariachis played, trying the efficacy of the herbs they had collected. Pancho had been a strong man then, but loyal. His loyalty had lasted better than his body. In the end, it was loyalty that had undone him.

And now they were all undone by Jones, his arrogance and folly and greed, in the cold February sea off Cornwall. If they lived, there would be reparations to be made.

If they lived.

All of a sudden he became aware that the night was no longer black. There was a grey heave out there, like the chest of a vast animal, breathing. The sea, in the dawn.

With the sight of the sea came a noise: a rumble so deep and dull that at first he thought it was the cold-thickened blood in his ears. Then to the east he saw what might have been a range of black mountains crested with snowfields that came and went. The spittle left his mouth.

The mountains were the cliffs of Trelise. The rumble and the snow were waves, breaking.

The light grew. Jones studied the cliffs with great attention. The wind had not shifted into the northwest. Tide or no tide, there was no way of weathering Pembarra's Tobaccoman's Point. Away to the south, the sea was a white swamp of tide in the ledges girdling the rock Pembarra had called the Mare.

So Joshua Jones, having as usual carefully considered the options, reached his decision.

He knocked on the cabin hatch, and called gently to the boy Denzil. Denzil scrambled into the cockpit, eyes rolling at the cliffs thundering a mile to the eastward. 'We must anchor,' said Jones.

'Too deep,' said Denzil, chattering his teeth. He began to cry, poor child.

'Then we shall prepare, and wait,' said Jones, soothingly. He went below, and measured eighty drops of laudanum into a glass, and gave the draught to Denzil. The boy drank it, mixing it with tears. Jones watched his eyes glaze, his movements steady. 'Now,' he said. 'Hang out your anchors. They may catch.'

Denzil fumbled the anchor off the bow. Then, assisted by Jones, he opened the hatch of the fish hold, pulled out net corks, threaded them in garlands on tarred lines and wrapped them round his chest, and Pembarra's, and Jones's, and even Mendez, by now stiff as a tunny in the bunk.

The next part was at least quick.

The shore was a mere cable's length away, the air thick with spray blasted back against the wind. The waves slid and crumbled with volcanic boomings. The lugger was floating nose to sea, held head-to-wind by her mizzen. She pitched up on a wave so the deck was a wet wooden hill rising at forty-five degrees. The wave went under, roaring as it broke. The nose went down. Stayed down . . .

The anchor had caught.

The blood flowed warm in Jones's face. All the anchor had to do now was keep holding, while the tide turned and the wind abated, until such time as they could raise a sail, or people from the land would come in rowing boats—

The nose rose to the next wave. Hull and anchor rope moaned together like the string of a bass-viol. Water poured down the deck. In that white wave Jones saw something rise; something huge and square, that bowled past him on a shoulder-high torrent. The lid . . . *cover* of the hatch. Left unsecured by Denzil when he had gone for the corks. Left out of Jones' calculations.

The lugger was suddenly soggy underfoot. The hatch was a gaping hole in the deck, the mouth of a tank into which gushed roiling grey water.

'She'll sink on us!' shrieked Denzil, his terror suddenly more powerful even than opium.

'What, then?' said Jones, linen-pale.

'I'll 'ave the mizzen down,' said Denzil, wild-eyed. 'Do you cut 'er off 'er anchors. Put us all ashore afore she goes down.'

So Jones went up the deck, waist-deep now, awkward in his caddis of net-corks, and cut the anchor rope.

The mizzen had gone. The lugger wallowed towards the black granite shore.

The wave ahead curled over and broke. To left and right it smote pillars of rock and leaped at the sky. Another wave, another. Now they could see water roaring white up a black tongue of granite that licked from the cliff-base.

The last wave began to pile up beneath them. The lugger hung at the crest of a long grey slope of water, high above the white shallows two hundred feet ahead and thirty feet below.

The boy began to scream.

The crest reared and thinned, becoming hollow. The boat yawed ahead and across, bow down. The wave broke with a collapsing roar.

Jones felt the world roll under his feet. He was far, far underwater, the corpse of the lugger huge above him. He rose, was smashed about in a mixture of air and water too tenuous for floating, too thick for breathing. His hand brushed another body, found rope. He twisted it tight round his wrist and held on. He spun. Things slammed into him. Once he surfaced, saw nothing, breathed, tumbled again, found a great horse-kick of pain blooming in his ribs and shoulder. Again he surfaced, caught a glimpse of a steeple of rock dizzy against the overcast. Bitter salt was in his mouth and nose and lungs. He longed passionately for the smell of his warehouse, musk of opium, dust of dry clover, sweetness of umbelliferae—

Another ringing blow to the head. The wave receded. He was on the granite incline at the head of the bay. Out in the white water, something dark was rolling. He did not waste any time wondering what it might be. He scrambled for the shore, boots slithering on slimy rock. Two waves flattened him. Then he was behind a boulder, a boulder shaggy with ochre *Xanthoria parietina*, his lips moving as he said the words, tolerates spray but not heavy water, a dyeplant when matured in urine, lichen of the upper part of the upper shore.

The upper shore.

Only then did he look at what was attached to his right hand.

It was the body of Pancho Mendez, half naked, webbed with the cuts of his demonstrations.

Joshua dragged himself and the corpse laboriously up a slope of rock and onto something that might have been a meadow. With enormous effort, he laid out the body of Mendez. Then he crawled further inland to look for help.

But he was tired. He had been wandering all his life. That he was still alive was a sign that the time for wandering was over. This place, wherever it was, was journey's end.

He ceased crawling and lay down. He felt warmth, and the spring of sea-pink under his face. He went to sleep.

In his sleep he could hear the shriek of the wind. But in the lee of the wall where he lay, it was quiet and warm. He dreamed that he woke. A group of narcissi nodded, a species he did not recognise, spreading perfume across the air. A woman looked at him: a beautiful woman. Then the quietness and the scent and the woman's face wrapped him soft as down, and in his dream he closed his eyes.

But it was not a dream. It was Trelise.

Chapter Five

When Joshua Jones opened his eyes, he was looking up at a thatch of bracken on rafters in which woodworm were at work, and a plank shelf carrying a Bible. His nostrils were full of peat smoke. Someone had taken his trousers. The smell was turning his stomach. He lurched into the air and stood shivering in the spinning brightness of the world, and vomited into a pile of shells.

'Food?' said a woman, some time later.

He was back in the bed, looking up at her. She had a wide, pointed face, bright, greenish eyes. It was the face that had been beautiful. It was dirty, and younger than he remembered. 'If you please,' he said. 'What's your name?'

'Alice Jenkins.' She stared at him with the intense curiosity of someone to whom not much happens. 'What's yours?'

He told her. She brought him his trousers, rough-dried, salt-stiff, reeking of turf smoke. When he had dressed, she steered him to a three-legged stool and gave him a bowl. There were rubbery lumps in the bowl, with a faint taste of the sea. 'What is this?' he said.

'Sea beef,' she said. 'Limpets, you call 'em. Break your teeth, then your heart.' He smiled at her knowingness. Under the matted shawls she was a scrawny fifteen. When she smiled back, he could see why he had thought her beautiful. Her teeth were good, her eyes grey washed tropical lime-green in her windburned face.

Jones swallowed potatoes and limpets. The potatoes were good. The limpets were not. He said, 'There were two—' he remembered Mendez, dead, covered in the cobbled-up scars of surgery, and in a burst of self-preservation Doctor Fairey '—three men on the boat. Where are they?'

'Two dead,' said the girl, eyes lowered. 'Old chap's in the Castle.'

A boot clashed in the limpet shells outside the door. A voice said, 'What the buggery you burning fuel for?' There was the sound of struggle. 'Bugger me, someone's puked up on my legs. *Girl!*' roared the voice.

'My father. That is to say my stepfather,' said Alice in a new, thin voice. It was not a change that pleased Joshua. 'Father,' she said, with an attempt at brightness. 'We have a guest, you will remember.'

A man darkened the door. He was rubbing with a handful of bracken at Joshua's vomit on his seaboot. 'So he woke up,' he said. He had a matted grey-and-yellow beard and vicious eyes. 'A waking man eats. A waking man must pay for his sleep and his grub, my dear.' He smiled, a cozening smile that exposed to Joshua simultaneously the blackness of his teeth and his heart. 'Have you fucked her yet, cully? Because that's more again.'

The girl turned red, then white. She said in that same thin voice, 'Stow your nonsense, father.'

Jones chewed steadily at a limpet, counting the contractions of his jaw. To these people he presented an opportunity. This man had been celebrating in advance. Now he sought to continue the celebration by doing someone violence. As for the limpet, two hundred and eighteen mastications had produced a negligible result. A chicle substitute, if only one could get rid of the noxious flavour, thought Jones, waiting. But he would not let this be just another phase of his wandering life, seeking improved plants. He had promised himself as he lay in the sea-thrift that this was journey's end—

The man's hand rose in a lazy swing, and whacked the girl on the side of the head. She lurched sideways. The cooking pot spilled on the earth floor. 'Pick it up, bitch,' he said. 'Now then, you. Let's see your money.'

Jones heaved himself up and helped the girl to her feet. She would not look at him or take his hand. 'I am but recently shipwrecked, sir,' he said, in his calm, reasonable, infuriating voice. 'I have no money. When I am reunited with my friends, I shall make it my business to see that your daughter is rewarded.'

The man loomed over him like a cloud. 'Bugger your friends,' he said. His arm came round. In his haze, Joshua was slow. The man's hand knocked him backwards, through the door and out of the hut. 'So I'll 'ave your buggering coat,' said the man. 'And your buggering boots, and everything else you bloody got.'

Jones put himself upright again. His eye was cold, his face still. 'You may have my ring,' he said. 'It will give you something to remember me by.'

The man stopped. His swollen fingers closed on the signet. 'Not by the time I've drunk this 'ere.'

Jones gave him a smile that had an oddly spine-chilling effect. 'I shall remember you, at any rate. Miss Jenkins, I am very much obliged to you.' He turned his back and began to walk away. Behind him there was a crash. The man had fallen into the shell-midden. Now he was clawing through the filth, having apparently dropped the ring.

It was a ring Jones valued, having come from Lady Ancona on her deathbed. Just now, however, he saw it not as lost, but as invested.

The girl caught him as he walked away. She said. 'He's a devil when he's drunk. Most times he don't have the money, though, so he's quiet.'

'Did he hurt you?'

She smiled at him and shook her head. A blue bruise was rising on her temple. They walked a few yards in silence, Alice hanging back, looking at her feet.

'Is there something wrong?' said Jones.

'It was what he said. About—'

'My dear Miss Jenkins,' said Jones, with firmness. 'I heard the slabberings of a drunkard. I do not recall him *saying* anything.'

She nodded, and sniffed, and raised her chin. 'Well, then,' she said. 'I shall show you the island.'

'I should like that of all things,' he said. 'But first, my fellow survivor.'

He seemed a firm and solemn man. She hoped he could laugh. She should like to see him laugh. But of course he was only now shipwrecked, and had lost his friends. He was not to be blamed. It would be hard to blame a gentleman as handsome as he was.

The wind had dropped. A fine drizzle was falling. 'The town,' she said.

The town was a huddle of houses crumbling at the seaward end of a causeway that wound towards a rain-dim smudge of mainland. Weedy nets hung drying in the rain. The Castle was a tavern sited in the damp ground floor of what might once have been a watch-tower at the side of the causeway arch. Pembarra was on the floor above, in a dirty bed. Rain blew into the glassless window from the pale sands beyond. He looked old and shrunk, and when his eyes swivelled at Jones, Jones saw he had been crying. 'What am I going to tell her?' he said. 'The mother of poor bloody Denzil that is dead?'

'I am sorry for the boy,' said Jones.

'We should never have sailed,' said Pembarra. There was drink on his breath. 'Why did you make me sail?'

'I asked,' said Jones, looking out of the window. 'You agreed.'

'So it's my fault, is it?' said Pembarra, knuckles twisting in his red beard. 'Cold bloody fish you are. Clammy drat-you-deaduns-I'm-alive bastard. But I'll tell the world on you. I'll tell 'em, and you'll be proper famous, my dear.'

'The reason you sailed,' said Jones, 'was that you had an objection to hanging for murder.'

'Me?' said Pembarra. '*Me?*'

Jones paid no attention. 'I suggest that you console yourself with the thought that poor Denzil was not the only corpse that came ashore yesterday morning.'

'What?'

'The law will draw its conclusions from the evidence it finds,' said Jones, calm and clear. 'Two bodies after a shipwreck is no more than nature. I shall speak to the landlord. Your reckoning will be paid until you are quite recovered. And you will not be the poorer by the loss of your boat.'

'How's that?' said Pembarra, frowning, as if thinking caused him pain.

But Jones was already on the stairs, with the girl. 'Where will I find the parson, Miss Jenkins?' he said.

'Isn't one.'

'Who is then charged with the welfare of your souls?'

'Can't afford souls.'

Joshua looked at her as if he had only just noticed her. She looked straight back, a look that made him aware of his imperfect manners. He said, 'Miss Jenkins, I fear I have been taking you for granted. I thank you for your great generosity to me, and the hardship you have undergone on my behalf.' She blushed. 'Now tell me, where do you bury your dead?'

She shrugged. 'Anywhere. There's the Arch, though.'

'The Arch.'

'Old church place. Other end of the island.'

She watched as he went back into the Castle taproom. She watched him talk to Dunster Hicks, dirty Dunster, who would rather fight than drink and drink than breathe. She watched with close attention as Jones allowed Dunster a peep into his soul, and Dunster's face turned dirty yellow, and Dunster touched his forelock and said, yessir, and went about his errand like a man asleep. Five minutes later she and Jones were walking south along the track to landward of the beach, and she was explaining the world to him with a new and thrilling lightness in her tone.

Jones had a sore throat that might become a cold, and his body ached like a tooth. But there were other things to occupy his mind.

This leeward side of the island was packed with cabins jammed midden to midden. Behind them, little fields ran up to heather moors studded with rock quoits, and the cliffs of the windward shore. Clouds of spray rolled down the slope, torn by the rocks from the ground swell left over from the gale. There were no trees. Thin pigs rooted listlessly in mounds of limpet shells. It was still raining, a soft rain squalid with turf smoke, that diluted the salt on Jones' lips and fought the brisk iodine smell of the shore. The heathery ground where the fields ran up to the western cliffs bore the scars of peat-cutting. The inhabitants were burning the soil by which they lived.

But in the angles of the buildings the daffodils were nearly over, and in the potato lazy beds, the haulm was up and green. Jones stopped at a little field that came down to the road. The green potato leaf was faintly shrivelled.

Up, and green, and blighted. *Phytophthora infestans*, Ireland's bane.

'Bordeaux mixture,' he said.

'What's that?'

'Against the potato disease.'

'No money for no mixtures,' she said.

Jones nodded, in the way he had, storing it away, what for she could not tell.

The Arch must once have been part of a Norman chancel. It was granite, coped with red sandstone. It stood in the middle of a lawn-like meadow. The air was full of a thick, ferny scent that beat even the stench of the cabins on the margins of the green area. From one of the cabins, Jones borrowed a spade. It was like him to have gone without thinking to Revel's house, home of the only spade in the Priory, and to take what he found there for granted. He went to the place beside the Arch where there was a little group of rotting wooden crosses, and began to dig.

He dug until the sweat poured out of his hair and his shirt turned from dirt-grey to black: burying Denzil, and Mendez. Burying the wandering past. A pale and ragged crowd gathered, men and women from the hovels. A man with a heavy chestnut beard said, 'I'll take a turn, mate.'

Jones looked at him. 'What's your name?' he said.

'Revel.'

'I thank you, but no.' They had been his friends, his wanderings.

The crowd thickened. The only sound was the rasp of his breathing, and the clang of the spade on pebbles. The soil here by the arch was dark and deep, and he seemed to swim down into it like a mole.

When he had finished the first grave, he took the hands offered, and allowed them to lift him up. He swallowed a draught of water, cleaned the blood off the spade handle, and started to dig again. Three feet into the second grave, he was seen to fall forwards. Revel lifted him out, and Alice wrapped him in her outermost shawl. He was feverish hot. She mopped his forehead with a rag. Revel finished the grave.

The cart creaked up, Dunster at the ass's head, two shrouded corpses in its bed. Jones roused himself, blue-white and swaying. But the voice in which he recited the burial service (from memory, all observed, not a syllable wrong) was firm. The islanders stood silent in the rain, storing his every movement and gesture for later discussion, as was the Trelise way.

After the words were spoken, Jones directed his face at the ground and stood awhile. He was brought back to himself by someone tugging at his sleeve. It was the girl Alice, with a handkerchief. He took it, and dried his eyes. She squeezed his hand and smiled, those good teeth again, but hardly shown now, timid. He disengaged himself, shrugged into the rags of his good black coat, and walked up onto the low hill that gave a view over the Pool and the sea and the ledges round the Mare. Alice moved behind him, quietly, like a mother behind a child she fears may fall.

On the summit of the hill he sat on a flat rock, and watched a skein of teal skid onto the Pool. Suddenly he was looking at Alice with eyes that seemed lit from behind. 'What do they do for water here?' he said.

'There's a well. A good 'un.'

He bounced to his feet. The eyes were positively blazing. 'Good,' he said. 'Good, good, good.' He took a last look down on the cottages huddled against the rain. Then he was off, scissoring long-legged down the road behind the beach.

Alice, trotting beside him, found herself battered with more questions than she had answers to. She had a tenancy inherited from her dead father, used till she was of age by John Eavis her stepdad, that Mr Jones had . . . met, who sublet her farm to four other families from the mainland and spent his life in the Castle on the proceeds. It was terrible crowded and limpets was bad food, but there was not a lot else to eat with the quay just about ruined and the weather so horrible and last year's potatoes running out, so thank Heaven this year's were up now . . .

Before she properly noticed where she was, they were back among the houses of Old Hull. She knew that now Jones would go. She found herself praying that he would not.

The tide was coming in. Beyond the Arch of the Castle, the causeway was a ruinous black ribbon across the grey wavelets. 'Well,' he said. 'Thank you, Alice.' And he smiled.

The smile jolted her like a fist; or rather, the prospect of losing the smile. She felt her face stiffen with tears. She quickly said, 'Well, then,' and turned away.

'If I might trespass one minute more,' he said.

'Yes?' She kept her voice cold. She was cross at herself for being so weak as to cry, and redirecting the crossness at him.

'I was meaning to ask,' he said. 'The name of your landlord.'

Odd question. But then all his questions were odd. 'Earldom of Kernow,' she said. 'Agent's a Mr Dawson of Looe.'

'I thank you kindly,' he said, and his hand strayed to where his hat should have been, but his hat was somewhere off Ushant.

'You won't forget us then,' she said. She passionately wanted not to be forgotten.

'Never in life,' he said. 'That part of it is over.'

71

She had no idea what he was talking about. But all of a sudden she found she had kissed him on the cheek. He kissed her back. She jumped away from him. He would be believing Eavis's filthy lies. What had possessed her?

But he had turned, and was limping purposefully across the causeway and into the grey curtain of the rain.

From the *West Briton*, March 1847:

> *Intelligence reaches us that the lease of suffering Trelise has been taken up by Joshua Jones, Esquire, of Grosvenor-Place, London, W. Those of our readers who have lately visited this Isle will have observed the sad state of the Lands, Buildings, Tenantry &c &c since the late Potato disease. Mr Jones has made a vast amount of money in the Apothecary line, particularly in the formulation of effective nostrums against pain and illness. Many readers will have derived personal benefit and surcease from such marvels as Jones' Carminative Tincture, and the recently perfected Jones' Etheric Inhalation, which has all but removed from the surgeon's art the agonies once its inescapable concomitant.*
>
> *We hear that Mr Jones purposes to apply his great fortune to relieving the misery of Trelise, and restoring it to prosperity, and offer him our congratulations. In which we hope our readers will concur, and give a hearty 'Three times three' to this noble enterprise.*

Letter from Joshua Jones, esq, Grosvenor-Place, London, W, to his agent at Trelise, Hubert Vyvyan.

Dear Vyvyan

I am sure that you will by now have done those things I mentioned in the matter of the grant of money to Alice Jenkins and the mother of the late Denzil Treberthy, and opened discussions with Captain Pembarra.

I have now placed my main business in the hands of trusted agents, appointed managers in my warehouses in Calcutta, Lisbon, Valparaiso and London, and realised a great sum from the licensing of my various patents and pharmacological processes. With those funds, we can now proceed in the manner I foreshadowed to you at our meeting in March, the object being for me to make a Home at the end of my wanderings, for myself and for all who live on Trelise. To restate:

First – I must reform the Leases and abolish the evil of sub-letting. All sub-lessees will be evicted. I charge you with this task.

Second – riot, debauchery, lawlessness. Any found habitually Drunk will be removed from the Island, as will loose women. Any Illegality particularly in the matter of the smuggling of Spirits Tobacco & c, to be punished by removal of the culprit's House Roof.

Third – cutting of turf for burning – any apprehended will be evicted – the turf is the seed-corn of the Island.

Fourth – there will be grants-in-aid for the Fishing and the construction of Boats, Fishing being an occupation both healthful and profitable, hitherto much neglected at Trelise.

Fifth – the School. Fees, 1d a week for children who attend, 2d a week for those who do not. A Schoolmistress is to be found, not under 35 yrs.

Sixth – you have received my plans for foundation works as to the House, Church and Gardens. Please undertake as per drawings. Also, Masons and Carpenters will be needed, and I charge you with the finding of 'em.

I am resolved, as you know, to establish my Island according to the best principles, viz. to ensure in its constitution a happy, rational life for all, my Rules being aimed at securing the greatest good of the greatest number. I sh'd therefore like you to call a meeting of Tenants – principals only, of course – for Saturday fortnight, 4th April. Meanwhile to avert trouble I require you will continue the Relief of any whose health seems in danger of Blight and to pursue the Sowing of a Corn Crop.

Yours &c

Joshua Jones

Revel – A Day in the Life: Spring*

Alarm six a.m. Weather, southwest two to three, not bad at all. Tea, three sugars. The sun is laying gold bars down the paths. The growth

---

* *Country Times* magazine, feature

spurt is on. Mow the bloody orchard, set the blades down, mow two lawns, do bloody edges with hand shears, no strimmers because of the noise mucking up the filming. Back to the greenhouse for the big barrow. A hundred *Pelargonium* in variety for the bedding out on the Stairs, thirty *Geranium maderense* for the urns in Africa on the Middle Terrace. Then into the pram and row across the pool to the Island, plant three *Metrosideros excelsa*, New Zealand flame trees, replacement for frost-burnt corpses. Bite of dinner. Then bloody run for it back into the Sea Garden and the Pool Garden for an afternoon of hack and slash. Every bloody thing is coming out of the ground at once. The boss and the film crew want you to pose here, pull out a bramble there. Tea time. Then some idiot wants to interview you about what it is like, living in an island, working on a garden. Very silly question. They watch you do the last of the tail lines for the pots and slap on antifouling. The boat shed is handy for the Castle. Six pints of Guinness. Home, carry on with mermaid carving.

Same every spring, more or less.

In March, a stream of people began to flow through the house: cameramen, soundmen, pundits, producers, cousins, cousins, cousins. Victoria could shut herself off in the library. But Guy was in the thick of it, day after day, in meetings, directing Owen Morgan's campaign against bracken and brambles, filming when flowering times and architectural discovery permitted. By disposition, he was a solitary. But every time he came back from his dayful of people, there was a houseful of people to pour drinks for and make conversation to.

No wonder he was edgy.

It was seven a.m., and the sun was shining in at the bedroom window, and there had been only a couple of cousins to dinner the night before. Victoria could feel him awake, staring at the ceiling, chewing stuff in his mind.

He said, 'Letters again today?'

'Letters and ledgers and diaries.'

Guy yawned. 'So whose bones are they?'

'Give me a chance.'

'But you're getting somewhere.'

'Sort of. Joshua seems to have poisoned his assistant.' The papers were laid out on the library floor, ready to start writing up as a story, a long, infinitely expandable word-processor document, one column for narrative, one for references. Soon she would have a chapter ready, and she would show it to Guy.

At eight-fifteen she headed for her desk in the library, full of cheery anticipation of her notes of Joshua Jones' early diaries, and his advertisements, and his newspaper cuttings, and his letters and bank books and rent rolls: his whole life before and during the arrival at Trelise. This was not going to be a sensational film treatment or a wad of reverential garbage written by someone who wanted to be asked to stay in the house. This was the truth.

She opened the library door. The morning sun lit strappy green *Agapanthus* leaves on the terrace. Everything was as usual.

But the papers had gone.

She looked under the desk, in case a rogue breeze had crept in, even though she had shut the room hermetically, and the night had been still as a pond.

She knew.

She ran across the hall, down the passage into the kitchen, her lips numb with rage and shock. Mantovani was drivelling away on the radio. Calm, calm. She opened the door.

Dawkins' eyes rose from behind the *Daily Mail*. 'Good morning, er Vic—'

'Who has been in my room?'

'Your room?'

'The library.' She could feel the pressure rising.

'Oh, the *library*. Yes, I knew you are in there all day every day so I thought I'd get in there early and give it a super clean.'

Victoria said, 'What did you do with the papers?'

'All that scribbly paper? I put it out for Hodges.'

'Hodges?' Hodges was the odd-job man.

'He'll pop it in the incinerator later. Perhaps he has already.'

Droning in the ears. 'Where is he now?'

'Somewhere in the yard, I should think. Is there some kind of problem, Victoria?'

But Victoria was gone.

Hodges was standing by the pierced fifty-five-gallon drum at the back end of the yard by the stables, rummaging for a match in the pocket of his old blue boiler suit.

Victoria shouted, 'Stop!'

But Hodges was deaf as a post and twice as stupid. He found the matches, struck one, lit his cigarette, tossed the match onto the paper in the oil drum.

Victoria knocked him flying, pulled out the two sheets that had caught, crushed the flames against her jersey.

'Oi!' said Hodges.

'You're burning the wrong paper.'

'Only what Mr Dawkins give me.'

They pulled it out, smoothed it, stacked it; Hodges was quite a stacker, once he got the hang of things. There was no harm done, as Hodges pointed out. Victoria took the sheaf back to the library, keeping her breathing slow and regular. Then she went to see Dawkins.

She said, 'That was three weeks' work.'

'But it was paper. On the floor. I thought it was rubbish. I mean it was on the *floor*.'

'I told you. I'm doing research. Maybe for a book.'

'A book?' Dawkins looked entirely mystified. 'Goodness.'

'So I would appreciate it if you did not touch anything in the library? Ever? At all? Even if it's on the floor?'

'But somebody's got to clean, Victoria.' The face was puzzled, but the eyes watched her like twin gimlets.

'I'll clean it myself,' said Victoria. 'Is there a key?'

'Key?'

'To the library.'

The lips pursed. 'I don't know—'

'Could I have it please? All of them, if there's more than one.'

'But honestly, Victoria—'

'In case of accidents.'

Dawkins went and fetched the key. Victoria locked up, smiled, and went out. Writing books was evidently an unworthy pursuit, leading to neglect of lists and schedules.

She stamped out of the yard and walked onto the heathery West Downs and watched the waves smashing themselves to bits on the rocks, and imagined Dawkins out there, treading water. When she felt better she walked back through the pine woods and the garden.

Guy was in the dining room, frowning at a script. He acknowledged her with an unfocused, hostile look. 'What have you been doing to Dawkins?' he said.

She was taken aback. 'What are you talking about?'

'He thinks you're angry with him. He's very upset.'

'What a bizarre thought.'

He said, stuffily, 'Sarcasm doesn't help.'

She said, 'He tried to burn my papers. He's a lunatic. We live here, not him.'

He said, in a new, sharper voice, 'What the hell are you talking about?'

And suddenly they were having a real row, and there was no way out but forwards. 'Even if he is afraid I'll make Joneses stink, it's none of his damn business. Isn't it time—?'

'Shut up. He looked after Harry for years. Every year he sent me a birthday card and a Christmas card with a fiver in it. He's loyal and devoted to Joneses and Trelise.'

'And it's never occurred to you that if he looked after Harry all that time he probably knew what was in his will.'

His eyes turned hard and furious. 'That's a truly shitty suggestion.'

'I hate his guts,' said Victoria. 'He hates mine. Listen, Guy, he works for us, and he's making these disapproving noises, and I'm supposed to roll over? What the hell is this?'

'You're just going to bloody well have to put up with him for the moment.'

She knew that was it. Guy was plugged into his million volts of obstinate passivity. It was time for the final compromise. 'Okay, then. But I told him. I don't want him in the library. Ever.'

He spread his hands. 'Okay. Fine.'

So there it was.

There were cousins in the drawing room. She did not know them well enough to be able to face talking to them. She went out onto the terrace. In the far corner was a figure with a rake. Revel's friend, Daisy.

She hardly knew Daisy, but next to the cousins, she looked like company. She said, 'I didn't know you worked in the garden.'

'Revel asked me to come up.' Daisy's shoulders moved easily, raking a series of perfect overlapping clam-shells onto the path. 'Darren's Jill left last night so he got pissed and he's too hungover to work, so it's muggins.' She raised her freckled face. 'You all right?'

Oh, the relief. 'Since you ask, no,' said Victoria. 'I am writing a book, and Dawkins thinks it's not ladylike or something, and my husband takes his side.'

Daisy nodded. 'Do you think you ought to be telling me this?'

Ah, yes. The great British class system. 'I'm American,' said Victoria.

'Course you are,' said Daisy, and giggled, in a nice way, Victoria thought.

'Well, thank you for this,' said Victoria.

'Must be hard, up here on your own.'

'Not if I get to work.' Pause. 'Thanks.'

'Any time.' Scrape, scrape, went Daisy, away down the terrace. Victoria sailed through the cousins and into the library.

Later, when she went into the kitchen for coffee, she heard voices in the house. Guy's voice. 'I can look after myself!' it said. Then Dawkins' voice, whiny.

Then a door banging, and silence.

Chapter Six

From the *West Briton*, October 1847.

> Reports reach us of great changes on Trelise, for so long the abode
> of poverty and the home of misery.
>
> Monies distributed at the late failure of the Potato crop will for
> Tenants be commuted to a 1d surcharge of rent. For squatters, sublessees
> and lodgers, the Debt will be forgiven in full on the event of their remov-
> ing from the Island within one month of notice being issued. In the event
> of their remaining on the island, however, the Debtors to be prosecuted
> with the full rigour of the Act, leading to certain imprisonment.
>
> Furthermore the energetic Proprietor has caused to be built in the
> town of Old Hull a Church. He has appointed a Parson thereunto, a
> want greatly felt, and instituted a Penny School. He has offered to
> the Elder Brethren of Trinity House to collaborate in the building
> of a Lighthouse to replace the ancient beacon on the Mare Rock.
> And last of all, he has undertaken the construction of a Gentleman's
> Residence at the South end of the island, together with a Pleasure
> Garden laid out according to the latest principles.
>
> It is to be hoped that the outcome of all these projects will give
> satisfaction to the Proprietor and his tenants. There are those who say
> that Pasha Jones is building not a gentleman's estate, but a Kingdom:
> others, that in a place as deep sunk in misery as Trelise, any change
> must be for the better. The West Briton takes no side in the matter,
> reminding Pasha Jones only that Cornishmen are a free people, who own
> kings but when they are Constitutional, Benignant and Unoppressive. So far
> as he respects the liberty of his Tenants and the property of his Neighbours,
> we know we speak for all when we beg to wish him strength to his Elbow
> and good success to all his efforts.

*   *   *

After the wreck of the *Edward and Rose*, Captain Pembarra had left Trelise in a state of despair – without boat, without employment, and faced with the melancholy task of consoling the mother of Denzil Treberthy. But within a week of his arrival back at Helford, he found himself in a sort of whirlwind; as a consequence of which he left the fishing, and found himself supervising the building of the brig *Deliverance*, sixty tons, destined to serve as the Trelise packet, in which he had been allotted free gratis shares to the tune of forty-eight sixty-fourths, Jones owning the balance. Poor Denzil's mother, whom nothing could ever console for the loss of a son, had been allotted a munificent pension. All in all, given the amount of misery he had been at the root of, Jones had come out of it very handsome.

To his friends, that is. Not to Doctor Fairey the Falmouth apothecary, who had precipitated the flight of the *Edward and Rose* into the gale.

Pembarra had watched first with puzzlement and then with fascination as the Pasha had opened, next to Mr Fairey's shop in Falmouth, an apothecary's of his own, under the management of Eli Prideaux, a bright young chap of modern views. The beauties of the new shop, together with (to quote Eli's many advertisements) the extraordinary cheapness, purity and efficacity of the medicines therein purveyed, had gained him a large following in the town. His Comprehensive Chests found a market among the captains of the swarms of emigrant ships provisioning for the run to Queenstown, and thence west to America. The shop was, in fact, a splendid success.

And every bottle of medicine sold over Prideaux' gleaming counter was a bottle uncompounded in Fairey's dispensary.

Last time Pembarra had been alongside in Falmouth, Fairey had button-holed him. 'So, ye dog, ye dog!' he spluttered. 'Murder, hey?'

'Watch your lip,' growled Pembarra, confident of his innocence but nonetheless out of countenance.

'Murderin' cheat Jones. Killed a man with laudanum. He knows I'll have him. Knows. I'm gettin' a warrant from the Lord Chancellor for exhumation and assay of his Dago's bones. A warrant, sir!'

'Which you can stick up your arse,' said Pembarra loyally.

'Suit yourself, sir, suit yourself!' cried Fairey. 'An information has been laid, sir!'

'Meaning by John Eavis,' said Pembarra, very scornful. 'Silly drunken man that he do be.'

'Mr Eavis has been cruelly used, sir. Overweeningly, sir. Thrown from what was rightfully—'

'Mr Eavis tried to steal young Alice Jenkins' farm, and Pasha Jones put him off the island,' said Pembarra. 'Which if you goes on like, this an action in slander will like as not be brought and will unless I am a Dutchman lie.'

'Alice Jenkins is nothing but Jones's who—' Here Fairey stopped abruptly, because Pembarra had grabbed his shirt front.

'She has showed him the island, and he showing a proper spirit of enquiry,' said Pembarra.

'Never showed a proper spirit of anything,' growled Fairey. 'Wouldn't know how.'

'Away, misery,' said Pembarra, releasing the apothecary and turning back to his beloved *Deliverance*. Fairey was not a man to forget an insult, nor forgive a competitor.

Which made him and the Pasha a pair, of a sort. Outcome uncertain, thought Pembarra. Except for one sure thing.

No good would come of it.

The Pasha took out his old knife and pulled back the heather. There was black peat below, mixed with sand, the acid surface slimed with green algae. In the surface of the peat he cut a little slit, and popped in a couple of gorse seeds. Since his arrival on the island last June, he had planted two and a half tons. Here in the heather of the Downs, gorse would make shelter for trees, and trees would shelter his home against the Atlantic gales. He had it in his mind to plant sycamore and sea buckthorn, for a beginning. For the rest, he had since before his arrival been in correspondence with William Hooker, Director of Kew, and William Lobb, hunter-in-ordinary for Veitch of Exeter, nurserymen, apprising them of the extraordinary climatic advantages of this place. Narcissi bloomed from October to March in variety. It seemed a greenhouse without glass.

Kew had sent him (among many other things) seed of something called a Chile Pine, an *Araucaria*, a timber tree with leaves sharp enough to vex an ape. A specimen of this he had planted close to the new house now building on the hill where he had sat after the burials of Mendez and Denzil. Of more immediate interest were a gross of seedling *Pinus radiata*, the Monterey Pine, reputed to make excellent shelter against strong and continuous salt winds.

It was now three o'clock, and Joshua had been planting since breakfast. It was a pleasant activity, here in the sun and the mild breeze off the sea. It freed his brain to think about the governance of Trelise for the greatest good of the greatest number.

He stood up, hands on his back, stiff from much bending to plant. Even in a year the landscape had changed. A gang of men was working on the road behind the beach. It was becoming a real road, not the crazy track that had serpentined among swamps and boulders this time last year. Where once tumbledown hovels and ill-patched walls had stood, there were now neat hedges of stone at the margins of tidy fields. There was corn, and potatoes grown from clean seed in new ground, sprayed with copper sulphate against the blight. In the most sheltered fields, there were acres of goldenrod for the Jones Febrifuge, Aloe for the Cooling Balm, and glaucous sheets of poppies for the Soothing Draught; *Papaver somniferum*, a variety Pancho Mendez had shown him in the Sierra Madre, poor Pancho, that produced plants of high potency even when grown in a temperate climate. There were no frosts at Trelise. Still in his mind there was the aromatic warmth of the wall to which he had crept after the wave had washed him ashore, the sense that his wanderings were at an end. And Alice Jenkins' face, aged and solemnised by his delirium, now the face of a friend.

He climbed to the top of a cairn of rocks.

Ah.

From his point of vantage, he could see the whole east coast of Trelise. The tide was in. Hull Bay was a sheet of blue, lined at its edges with the dustier blue of the mainland. On the near fringe of that blue, a brig was crawling under a pile of tan sails.

'*Deliverance!*' piped Jimmy the groom. The Pasha was already striding downhill on spidery blue legs, telescope slung over his back like a carbine.

He vaulted a couple of walls, took a moment to check the gang tipping shingle into a soft patch of the new road, then strode off northwards, stout boots crunching in the new white grit. A hundred yards behind him came Jimmy, dragging the balky Isaiah.

'Owd cunt,' said one of the gangers, giving two fingers to the Pasha's retreating back.

'Sh,' said another, so Jimmy could hear. 'There's his bumboy.'

Never seen with a woman, the Pasha, except the girl Alice. Never no pity nor sympathy in his cold grey eye. Never no generosity except in exchange for something. Jimmy flushed scarlet, and would have thrown a rock, except that it was more than his life was worth not to keep up with the Pasha.

By the time Jones reached the quay, the *Deliverance* was alongside. People were climbing from her deck up the granite steps, skirting the men mixing cement on spot-boards and manoeuvring new coping stones into position. There were a couple of pedlars, and a foursome of tourists, the women in green veils and crinoline, the men in loud-checked tweeds and wide-awake hats. Jones ignored them. ('Bear!' said the younger and prettier of the women to her companion) What interested him was the contents of the *Deliverance*'s hold. 'Cap'n Pembarra!' he yelled. 'What we got?'

Pembarra looked up at him across his prophet's beard. 'Mornin', Pasha,' he said. 'Lot of seed. Some of they glass cases. Left Kew day afore yesterday forenoon, the Railway chaps did say.' He came onto the quay. 'And that man Fairey's making a nuisance of hisself.'

'What about Mr Fairey?' Pasha Jones' eye, always cool, had taken on a January chill. Pembarra told him.

At dawn today, as his boys were casting off ready to take the last of the ebb down the Roads, and so on the flood to Trelise, Fairey had appeared, muffled in shawls, with two men. 'We will come with you to Trelise,' he had said.

Pembarra had given him a pebbly stare. 'Your shoes soled and heeled?' he said.

'What?'

'Then you can use 'em to walk.'

'I demand . . . I insist . . .'

'Cast off forward!' roared Pembarra. 'Aft!' He sprang up the tarry side.

And Fairey watched blood-boltered as the *Deliverance*'s topsail rattled down and filled, and her bow peeled off the quay and nosed for the blue horizon.

'So he's a-coming,' said Pembarra to Jones. 'And he means to make trouble.'

'Sticks and stones,' said Jones cheerfully. 'Let's have those boxes up, shall we? Gently, now.'

A couple of deckhands began to sway up Wardian cases – little greenhouses, hermetically sealed – from the hold. There were luggage labels on the lifting rings. The tourists gawped: so this was the notorious Jones. He was rich as Croesus, of course, a patent-medicine czar among czars. His past was a collection of shuddersome rumours; drugs, quackery, conversations with plants, wanderings in strange lands, shipwreck and (whisper it) murder. And his appearance: the sailorly frock coat and drainpipes, the yachting cap, the clean-shaven jaw, burnt now with sun and wind; the eye bleak and faded, yet commanding. Savage. *Romantic* . . .

The women tourists exchanged glances and shivered deliciously.

Early the following afternoon, Alice was with the Pasha on the terrace of his half-built house, at a table made from a door on two trestles, the real terrace table being still under construction in the farm workshops, taking tea. Beyond the stubby iron tower of the Mare beacon, the sails of the *Deliverance* were sliding towards Plymouth. The air was full of the *Pelargoniums* in the terrace tubs and the raw whiff of new mortar from the walls of the cabin-like bedrooms rising above the state rooms.

Alice was now seventeen, upright in her shawls and her wine-red skirt. She had become in truth the beauty of Jones' delirium, with cheekbones and a firm but delicate jaw that just now showed signs of being clenched. It was a month since the eviction of her stepfather, Eavis. The Pasha was quizzing her.

'Shall you be lonely?' he said.

'I think not.' She looked at him with her amazing eyes, grey washed lime-green.

'No,' he said. 'It is our good fortune to have found one another.'

A pause. She blushed. Then she said, 'Shall I see you later?'

'If you can find the time.' Their fingers touched. A silence fell.

In the door that led to the terrace, a throat was cleared discreetly. Neither Joshua nor Alice had moved, but their eyes unclasped, and shifted to Drage, the butler, standing by the door in his swallowtail coat and striped vest that smelt of the Castle taproom, above which he was lodging pending the completion of his quarters. 'Doctor Fairey,' said Drage, in a voice oddly breathless, and proceeded suddenly backwards into the house; the reason, it became apparent, being that the man behind him had caught the tails of his coat and jerked him in.

Doctor Fairey stood on the terrace, feet planted, with the presence of a pantomime Demon King. The boots squelched slightly; evidently he had been in a great hurry to cross the causeway. 'To what,' said Jones, 'do I owe the honour?'

Doctor Fairey's eyes followed Alice off the terrace. Then he blew out his cheeks and slapped the paper in his right hand on the palm of his left. 'To this, sir,' he said. 'To this warrant from . . . the . . . Lord . . . Chamberlain. For the exhumation and assay of the man Mendez. On the orders of the Truro coroner. The inquest being re-opened. For opium in his damned bones, sir.'

Jones, sat, and poured himself some tea. 'You would like me to show you where my poor friend lies, then.'

'That will not be necessary,' said Fairey. 'An information has been laid. I have two labourers and a constable. Having been refused passage by your creature Pembarra, I may say.'

'Wet feet are dangerous,' said Jones. 'May I offer you a prophylactic dose of the Febrifuge?'

'Damn your Febrifuge,' said Fairey. 'My men have already commenced their excavations.'

Jones raised an eyebrow. He said, 'Civil in you to call.' He picked up the *Morning Post* that had arrived yesterday with the *Deliverance*. 'Drage, Doctor Fairey is leaving.'

When he had read and digested the paper, he walked down to the Priory Arch.

There was an oblong hole by the arch's foot. Beside it was a pile of earth, onto which more earth was flying out of the ground. Drage, who had been marching duck-footed behind Joshua, opened up the camp chair he had been carrying. Joshua seated himself.

Fairey was standing in the mud, by a cart. A small crowd of islanders watched, silent. 'You should be nearly there,' said Joshua.

The green meadow by the Arch was taking on the appearance of a garden. The ground had been dug, and trodden, and hoed, and raked. A terrace was in the course of construction, and tapes and pegs marked out more.

A voice came from the hole in the ground. 'Got it!' it said. There was a murmur from the crowd. 'Shroud's still good,' said the voice. 'Cuagh! Dunnee stink.'

'The coffin,' said Fairey, grim as Justice.

One of the men pulled a yellow deal box off the cart, and dumped it on the ground by the grave. Joshua took a handkerchief from his pocket and held it lightly to his nose. A solitary thrush sang in the silence.

A bundle came from the ground; a long bundle wrapped in an earth-blackened cloth. The crowd shrank back. It landed in the coffin with a sound somewhere between a thump and a clatter. The navvies dusted their hands on their moleskins and spat. Fairey came over to Joshua. There was another paper in his hand, a pen and a portable inkwell. 'Receipt,' he said. 'One corpse, suspected poisoned.'

Jones yawned and signed.

The yawn disconcerted Fairey horribly. 'We'll see,' he said. 'Yessir, we'll see.'

'I would remind you that opium is a common specific, and not necessarily fatal.'

'Damn you, sir, I know that.'

'Giddap!' said the carter. The corpse rattled off towards Truro. When it had vanished onto the Priory road, the crowd dispersed. Oddly, for people who had attended an exhumation, many of them seemed amused about something.

As for Jones, strolling down his new terraces, he did not seem worried at all.

A little way from the Arch, he had caused to be built a glasshouse and a couple of potting sheds, arranged round a granite-cobbled yard. The Wardian cases that had arrived on the *Deliverance* lay in the shade. When Jones' footfall sounded on the cobbles, a sandy-haired man stuck his head out of the potting shed door.

'Murdoch,' said Jones. 'What do you think of the young entry?'

'Load o' rubbish,' said the gardener. 'Stove plants, conservatory subjects. Waste of my time and your money.' Murdoch gave an ironic tug to his sandy forelock. 'But anything you say, Mr Jones.'

Jones had opened a case. '*Agave americana ferox*,' he said. 'Native of Mexico. Two.'

'I telt you. Conservatory subject.'

But Jones was thinking of Mendez, cut apart for gain, dead in a place that in life he had never even heard of. He took out the agaves – little things like yuccas, but succulent, their pygmy leaves edged with thorny sawblades. He carried them to the lowermost terrace. A pair of great granite steps had been laid. The mortar of the coping was new, the soil on either side fresh-dug into beds six feet by six. With the knife he used to plant his gorse seeds, Jones hoed the ground into a fine tilth. Then he planted the agaves, one either side of the top step, and tamped them well home with his knuckles.

When he had finished planting, he remained a while on one knee, almost as if he was praying. A shadow fell across him. When he raised his eyes, Murdoch was standing over him. 'Look after these plants,' said Jones.

'They'll die,' said Murdoch.

The eyes were the colour of cold water. 'If they die, you lose your place.'

'Mphm,' said Murdoch, and would perhaps have said more, but by then Jones was gone, striding past the raw slot of the open grave, past the Priory Arch, zigzagging up the stark new ramps of his terraces.

At the house, Drage brought him the sherry decanter. Jones ate his turbot and mutton chops on the terrace. The turbot was excellent. Doubtless due to the building works, there was a certain amount of plasterer's horsehair with the mutton. Below, the quacking of mallard on the Pool mingled with the quacking of the four tourists, who would be taking a constitutional before embarking on another flea-gnawed night at the Castle. After dinner he sent the servants to bed, and sat on the terrace under a sky heavy with stars. A meteor sputtered from Great Rocks to Tobaccoman's. He was lonely and tired; a man weary with defending his home.

A footfall in the grit behind his chair.

So Alice saw him: a powerful darkness hunched against the stars. She was frightened at what would happen. He had become her friend. Tonight, he would become more, or less; she could not tell. She clutched the ring that hung on a thong round her neck; the ring the Pasha had given Eavis that first time, and Eavis had dropped it in the midden. Slovenly Eavis had given up the search. Alice had searched diligently, and found it, and kept it as a reminder of the best thing that had ever happened to her.

So tonight she clutched it, and hoped.

Even when her mother had been alive, Eavis' hands had wandered up the smoothness of her neck, and round her bodice, and once, when mother was away, between her thighs. Of course it was not something you could tell about, for shame. But after Mother had died, Alice had made quite sure that she slept bolted in the bedroom, while Eavis slept as best he could in a chair by the fire. One night he had kicked the door in, and whipped off the bedclothes, and crushed her with his stinking weight. She had struggled hard, but he had been the stronger; twelve, she had been. She had cried for the best part of a week. But she had made a big bar for her door and showed it to him, and told him that if anything like that ever happened again, she would kill him. He had believed her. She had a way of making herself believed.

But always she could feel his eyes on her. In the autumn of the year before Jones arrived, he had made his move. She had been washing her clothes in the half-barrel tub. She had felt somebody behind her as she bent. Then her skirts were lifted and her head was in the filthy water, and there was a cool breeze on her suddenly naked thighs.

Her hand found the broken crock with the washing soda in it. She flung it backwards. Behind her, something roared like an animal, and the pressure went. She rolled out of the tub, towards the tripod cauldron and jars of fat that did duty as kitchen gear. Eavis was splashing his eyes with water from the bucket, swearing. Her hand found the iron rod that did duty as a poker. She grasped it, came to her feet, felt the shock as it took him behind the ear and knocked him into the washtub. She went over and hit him again. He was on his knees. She put the iron into the back of his neck and pushed his face into the tub. Bubbles rose in the scum, thinned, ceased. Her mind was settling. It would be foolish to hang for his sake. She grabbed him by the hair and pulled him from the tub. He lay and sucked air.

'Never,' she said. 'Never. Ever. Not ever again. Touch. Me.' Then she took the bucket of hot water from the fire, and poured it on the unbuttoned crutch of his trousers.

After he had healed up, he had left her alone.

She had to live with him, because her mother had asked her. When Mr Jones had sent him away that had been good, the Pasha's being a commandment stronger than her mother's. He had set her free. Then earlier today their eyes had caught, and . . . well, she hardly knew what. But first, there was a terrible admission.

'Mr Jones,' she said.

The black shape moved against the stars. 'Miss Jenkins.'

'Doctor Fairey,' she said. 'He came asking. It was Eavis told him where the grave was. I'm sorry.'

She saw the white of his teeth against the stars. 'Eavis is Eavis,' he said. 'You and he are not connected.'

'But will you not get into trouble?'

He leaned back in his chair. 'I have been expecting his visit for some time,' he said. 'Ever since Revel told me about Eavis. And Pender, and Odger, and Mumford. They saw no reason why the good order of the island should be disturbed by the arrest of the landlord.' A hand came out of the darkness, warm, with perhaps the faintest hint of nervous dampness. 'You will forgive me, Miss Jenkins,' he said. 'Mine has been a wandering life, and I am not used to dealing with ladies. But will you sit with me, and take a glass of wine?'

She thought he was only play-acting, but nonetheless she felt a warmth; more than that. An excitement. 'With the greatest of pleasure,' she said.

They sat very close together. After a while, she said, 'If you will permit,

I shall take off my stockings. My feet are wet. It's the dew on the plants between the rocks.'

Jones said, 'Permit me to assist.' His dark shape moved towards her. And Alice Jenkins was filled with the knowledge that things had indeed changed, as she had hardly dared to hope.

Next morning, after she had gone, Jones instructed the masons to make a secret staircase through the rockery and up to the French windows of his bedroom. He could not, he explained, tolerate stockings wet with dew. And o, said the masons, you should have seen the bugger grin while he said it.

A small room, underground. Below an Argand lamp, a slab with a gutter round its edge. On the slab, a thing once a man: limbs, a ragged skull, a ribcage. Below the ribcage, a long incision, from which a man in a black frock coat is drawing a putrid slab that might once have been a liver. Six men round the table, Jones among them. In the corner Mr Bolitho the coroner, retching over the sink. The stench is dreadful.

'The peatiness of the soil,' says one man, Mr Waldegrave, a surgeon, retained by Jones from London as a witness to the operations of the Court's own surgeon, 'has preserved the tissue in some measure. We find the same in the bogs of Denmark, the Fens of—'

'This is Truro,' snaps Fairey. 'Not Baden Baden with the ladies. Carve a big sample, a very big sample, surgeon, and enough chat.'

The liver flops onto a dish. 'Halve it, if you please,' says Jones to the surgeon. 'Then let us dine.'

The Coroner said, 'Urgent appointment,' and bolted into the catacombs.

The surgeon cut the liver into small pieces, which he macerated in water. From this putrid soup he prepared an aqueous extract, which he evaporated and scrutinised for tell-tale yellow crystals of meconic acid. None appeared. Conscientious in pursuit, he added to a solution of the evaporate perchloride of iron, looking for the liquid to turn cherry-red. It remained obstinately pale. He dipped his finger, and tasted, seeking the typical bitterness. It was no more than disgusting. He therefore reported to the coroner that he had found no more opium than you would expect if the drug had been used as a palliative at the point of death.

The coroner was furious. He had never had a nastier day, and its only cause, the way he saw it, was the pig-headed jealousy of that drunken little Turk Fairey. Both Jones and Captain Pembarra were adamant that the man Mendez had been alive until the fishing boat was wrecked. And when all was said and done, Mendez was only a foreigner. *Stupid* man, Fairey.

The inquest was reconvened. The verdict was not in doubt. The coroner made remarks of unusual potency about Mr Fairey; remarks that were heeded in the whole of the west of England. And Jones went home.

On the grave by the Sea Garden steps, the *Agave* shoved out roots and began to grow.

Chapter Seven

Message found in a bottle, September 28th 1849, on the Farm Beach at Trelise.

I, Jeffery Bowyer, Keeper of the Mare Beacon, rite this my Last Account and Farewell. Last evenin the breeze was a warm light so'westerly under a heavy overcast of cloud, the sea swelly but calm. I proceeded to the Beacon, climbed the ladder trimmed the wick and filled the Reservoir, and at sunset did light same and retire to the cabin, where I did work upon my Bark in the medicine bottle give me by mr Jones and then turn in without a-sayin my prayers, for which God forgive me, thinking that the calm would continue with perhaps a storm of Thunder and Lightnings.

In the night I heard the sea rise, a thing I am used to after long habitation on this rock. It rose and rose, the wind also, from the south, shrieking most unearthly in the legs of the Beacon and rattling at the Cabin roof. At five-and-twenty past Two, I did hear a great sudden Noise like an explosion of Gunpowder, and another, and Jos that was with me said, There's the beacon gone! With which same words there was a fearful smash and a wave blew in the windows, and took with it poor Jos, that was by the lee window. Then I heard the cables that anchor the cabin go, and felt her shift, God help me. There has been other noises, perhaps a ship, but it is high water, and we are swept by seas, and I cannot go out. Now another great sea and another. She is wedged, for that instant. But as I write this she moves again. I takes the bottle and the cork. My poor, poor wife and sweet infants! May God have mercy on my soul.

SHOCKING TRAGEDY AT TRELISE*
This day our cruel Cornish rocks claimed another victim – this time

* *West Briton*, October 8, 1849

the schooner Poseidon, *Capt James, for Saltash with Boscastle slates. She struck early in the morning of April 12, a dark night with a great gale sprung up sudden from the south, and held fast on the Mare, off Tobaccoman's Point, until with the falling of the tide she worked a great hole in her side and, filling, sank. The violence of the tempest and the remarkable Height of the Tide were such that the Mare beacon was itself overcome and utterly destroyed, together with its unfortunate Keepers. By this same frightful tempest much devastation was wrought in our Coasts and Islands.*

Jones woke in the black night to a ragged shouting. Alice was not in the bed. He crammed his nightshirt into his trousers and stumbled onto the terrace. The wind took him full in the face; southerly, a huge booming southerly, hot and violent as a tiger. Where there should have been the white glimmer of the Mare's beacon, there was only black. Then, far away, a sharp streak of red; a signal rocket. There was a ship on the Mare.

So he ran down to Davies Porth by Plum Orchard Point, where a little crowd had already collected, drawn by ancient Trelise instincts, bearing lanterns, and long poles with hooks.

The boxes and barrels came first, bobbing round the white surge of the point and into the bay. Then came other, slower-floating things.

The first of these things was a grating. To the grating were lashed two small bodies. The Captain's children, perhaps, launched tenderly overboard, to drift to salvation among the little yellow lights on the black land. And to salvation they may have drifted; but not among the lights of Trelise, or anywhere else in this world.

The light grew. The wind had veered southwest, and increased. The islanders had left the beach, except Joshua, and one other, a hulking figure with a chestnut beard hoary with salt-crystals. Revel.

A slab of dune face slid down to the beach. There were two hours' tide to go, and it was already a foot over high water springs. Another dune-face slid, taking with it a little pile of boxes and barrels someone had stacked above high-water mark.

Inside the rampart of dunes, next to the Pool, a flat meadow of rabbit-grazed turf ran up to the garden wall. Joshua was halfway across the turf when the sea came through the dunes. The first wave merely sent a skim of water under his feet. The next wave was a little ridge, and suddenly he was ankle-deep. The third wave splashed against the garden wall. Revel went through the gate. Joshua followed. As he shut the gate, sea water flooded into the bottom-most beds.

The waves took the dunes down, and roared across the meadow, and burst on the garden wall, where the wind took their spray and blew it in sheets up the terraces. At high water, Joshua sat on the steps where he had planted his first *agaves* with his feet in the sea. Ahead of him was a sheet of water, from which Great Rocks and the other cairns stood out like islands.

Revel said, 'Sorry 'tis spoilt, Pasha.'

Joshua. His eyes ran over the ruins of his garden. 'Never let go,' he said. 'Never let go.'

The tide ebbed. The Sea Garden had gone, agaves, steps and all. The waves no longer found their way through the dunes. The sand dried, and began to blow.

On the morning after the wind dropped, Joshua prowled devastation: rank upon rank of wind-blown, salt-burned, water-logged plants; sheds and glasshouses without tiles or panes, mats of weed and jetsam.

Then someone shouted from the bottom of the garden. Joshua strode down the steps, kicking aside the litter. The crowd by the gate parted. He found he was looking at the wooden head of a sea god, curled hair, beard, pupils blank and imperious. The figurehead of the *Poseidon*, come to rest at the foot of the stairs.

Jones stood and looked at the vast, hoary head. He had founded his island according to rational principles. But a garden was more than rational, or less. It satisfied needs he had not even recognised, during the years of his wandering. Needs that disturbed him, because they demanded to be fulfilled without being understood.

Later that day, he arranged a great fetching and carrying. The mortals he had buried in his new churchyard. The god he had carried through Arcadia and set up at the top of the granite stairs. Then he set about the repair of the shelter belts and the replanting of the garden.

★   ★   ★

Some saw it as a rich man's caprice; others, as a map of Joshua's inner life. Joshua himself revealed nothing about its meaning.

The Top Terrace ran under the ridge of a long hill clothed with new Monterey pines. At its eastern end Poseidon's head, clad now in a lead paint reinforced with sand from Hull Bay, glared out across the sea.

From Poseidon, a great flight of granite stairs descended from the imperial Top Terrace across the hierarchies; the senses in the spicy whiffs of the Middle Terrace, the intellect in the Endless Walk, an allee in the form of a figure-eight infinity symbol; past Love of Country in the Union Jack garden and Peace of Spirit in the Priory Arch and the Sea Garden; and thence to the Pharos, at the end of which, miles away, the seas boomed sullenly in the black rocks of the Mare, lightless since the horrors of the Great Storm.

To the west of the Pharos, round a lawn fringed with borders of blue *Agapanthus*, was Davy Jones. Here Joshua caused to be built a loggia. On the pillars of the loggia, he mounted the gifts of death: the rock-ground nymph once the figurehead of the brig *Circe*, blown ashore in Hull Bay in a black easterly; a battered cannon from the frigate *Camperdown*, wrecked on Tearing Ledges, trawled up by a Brixham boat that put in at Old Hull. There was the nameboard of the *Twee Gebruder*, type unknown, lost nobody knew where, washed ashore by the Glory Hole. Each pillar of the loggia had its figurehead. Under the roof lay haphazard a mass of curious stones, and turtle shells, and conch and cannonball and coral, washed in a green gloom of ferns; the debris of a sea bed, paving the kingdom of Davy Jones.

All this Joshua planned and caused to be executed inside shelter belts doubled in thickness since the Storm, behind ramparts of dune now hand-planted with bracken and marram. The vast *Ilex* hedges, the oaks and elms and eucalyptus, he would never see himself. But that did not matter. This was not a place for single lifetimes. He had started out to found a home. Now he was founding a world.

People whispered about his habits of life. They credited him with a harem, an opium mania, sodomitical leanings. But Joshua listened only to his inner voices.

One morning from his study window he saw the *Pasha* heading out to sea. The *Pasha* was an eight-oar gig, painted blood red and named in his honour, pulled by eight stalwart ex-loafers from Old Hull. There were three masts on the horizon; a big ship. Standing in the *Pasha's* sternsheets was Alice Jenkins.

Alice had left Joshua's bed at six that morning, moving dryshod down the new stairs through the rockery. Now she was pursuing her life; specifically, she was heading out to sell eggs and vegetables from her holding to sailors who for three months had seen no green thing but the mould on their hardtack . . .

No green thing.

Joshua folded his telescope.

Next brig on the horizon, he was out in the *Mab*, his own launch.

On a Bordeaux wine snow he was given cuttings of a blood-red geranium he called Chateau Petrus.

From a returning convict ship he acquired seeds of two kinds of wattle.

From a ship bringing general cargo from the Cape he secured by bribery a collection of *Mesembryanthemums* destined for Kew Gardens, together with an improved aloe of great value in the preparation of medical astringents.

From the half-frantic captain of a becalmed tea clipper he acquired a *Euonymus* new to cultivation, a large bronze temple urn he cemented into the West Rockery, and threats of personal violence.

And these were only the first few. As the years passed they came thick and fast, and the terraces were populated with glasshouse exotics, and in the drug fields there grew new varieties that made stronger medicines. The house began to fill with trophies, and Davy Jones' with the dark proceeds of storm and wreck.

Then on the deck of the New York packet *Albion*, Alice Jenkins met Josia Macleod, and at his earnest request conveyed him to Trelise in the *Pasha*.

'I've worked out what happened to Mendez,' said Victoria.

'Sorry?' Guy was crouched over the breakfast table. Another goddamn script.

'Joshua buried him by the Arch. But they moved him. Later, before the exhumation. Put another guy there instead. And I think they put him by the bottom steps, left hand side, in the Sea Garden.'

Guy made a note, looked up over his glasses, distracted. 'What?'

'Eavis told Fairey where Mendez was buried. So Fairey got his exhumation order. But look.' She put a couple of sheets in front of him: a page from Joshua's diary, and another from the estate ledgers.

Wm Odger, died in a fever, 9 May 1847. Dosed him pre mortem, for his comfort etc etc with some drops Laudanum. Buried by Arch. The ledger bore an entry for 10th May. *Revel 1 gn. for digging by Arch this night.*

'The dates would fit. William Odger's not in the churchyard. A guinea's an incredible amount of money for digging. So I think Joshua paid Revel to dig up Mendez, rebury him further from the Arch, and put Odger in Mendez' hole. One of the first agaves was planted on Mendez, one of a pair, on either side of a pair of steps. Those must be the steps you found for the Sea Garden. If I could just have a little bit of that skeleton, send it off for analysis, I could find out—'

Guy said, 'Revel dug the hole?'

'Yes.'

'Typical Revel behaviour. Always on the fiddle somehow. Bound to be his idea.'

'Joshua's.'

'Don't you believe it. No whimsy about Joshua. Anyway, if it's Mendez, you'll be happy now.' He went back to his script.

Dimly somewhere she heard the echo of Dawkins' voice, whining after he had thrown out her papers; Guy, shouting: *I can look after myself.* She had the vague, irreverent suspicion that somewhere in Guy's insistence on the primacy of present over past was the desire to protect his lilywhite ancestors. What did it matter which laws they had broken all that time ago?

'Don't you think it's interesting?' she said.

'Within reason.'

She felt a twinge of claustrophobia. 'Yes, dear,' she said.

'Don't be like that.'

'No, dear.'

He made a hissing sound between his teeth, and dropped his eyes. 'Where are the Foxes?'

The Foxes were the current house-guests, cousins of his, a grim, tweedy duo unused to the company of people with American accents. 'I do not know,' she said. 'Nor do I care.'

He nodded. He was trying to make up. She was not going to let him. 'And,' he said. 'Did you remember the Social?'

'How could I forget?'

The Spring Social was – *always has been*, was the phrase Dawkins used – held on the last Friday of March in the Mission Hut in New Hull. At twenty past six, Victoria found herself in a roaring press of people, holding onto a glass containing gin, which had just been filled for the fourth time. She still felt claustrophobic and off-balance, but the gin was helping. The Mission Hall was a grey stone building with a slate roof and a clogged tea urn. Tea had once been the drink of the Social. It had been Guy's idea to introduce alcohol: a popular idea, but (Victoria speculated, eardrums spasming in the roar) possibly an unwise one. She could see Revel, descendant of Revels, already slumped on a folding chair, apparently asleep; Darren, demonstrating how to smoke a cigarette the wrong way round. And Morgan, calm and sober, smiling, working the room.

She found herself next to him. 'How are you getting on?' he said. *Great* teeth.

'Fine,' she said. 'Great. Doing history.'

'What history?'

'Jones. I'm trying to work out who that skeleton is.'

'Best of luck,' he said. 'Skeleton there, it's a needle in a needlestack.'

'But the skulduggery.' She told him about Joshua and Revel, and the autopsy.

Someone else came up. He said, 'If I can help . . . ?'

'Sure.'

Victoria remembered him at the lecture; quiet, in control, even amused by it all. Victoria had a weakness for people who knew stuff, instead of just reporting what other people knew. Interesting. Interested. Actually, really attractive—

Hey. Victoria, you are a married woman, half full of gin. Stop that right now.

'Bit horrifying when you see them all together, isn't it?' said the voice of

Mary Morgan, behind her. Her hair was like black snakes, her eyes faintly glazed. She had been drinking too. 'Let's go to the pub.'

Across the room, Guy jerked his chin, summoning her. She could not imagine Morgan acting that way. 'Sure,' she said.

The Castle was only forty yards down the road. Victoria brought large gins to the table in the bow window overlooking the sea. The gin went, and the next lot. Mary had no children. Nor did Victoria. It was all right for Victoria, she was still young and all that. Mary was just bloody past it. She had been a singer once. Folk. Then she had married Owen when he had been at Kew. Now she was doing the same job living in the same bloody place for bloody years and she sometimes thought she was going crazy. She loved Trelise of course and it would be better now Victoria was here, things happening again. Owen and Harry got on like a house on fire. Except Harry wouldn't let him touch the garden, really. But all that was changing, with Guy, these films. It was all great. She loved Owen, of course, if love was a word you could still use, well, the usual amount of the time, maybe a bit less. But something had got into him, the bastard. It did, sometimes.

It was at about this point that Victoria realised they were both very drunk. 'Perhaps it's Guy,' she said.

'Guy what?'

'Guy arriving. That's changed Owen. I mean Owen's been running things. Like Dawkins has been running things in the house. And Dawkins doesn't like me, well, maybe it's not me, but the fact I'm new, and there. So maybe in the same sort of way Owen's resentful of Guy.'

'Dawkins is a prick,' said Mary, with surprising venom. 'Stupid plotting gossiping arsehole. I hate him.'

'I'm not saying Owen—'

Mary said, 'I know, I know, I know, I know, we know. We know Owen and I know it wasn't Guy's idea to inherit this place, you know? Give him credit. Give him credit.' Victoria was somewhat lost, but their heads were close over the table. 'It's just Owen's gone cold,' said Mary, settling back into monologue. 'Mind on other things. I expect Guy does it too.'

'No,' said Victoria. 'He doesn't.'

Mary laughed, short and ironic. Victoria felt her smile turn hollow. There was a new distance between her and Guy, certainly. Well, he was so busy. But she had had no idea it was visible. She felt like crying. Then she told herself, no, it was only a manner of speaking, and got some more gin, and pretty soon there was nothing left but a vague memory of upsetness, no specific cause.

At some point she must have gone home, because next morning there she was, at breakfast with Guy and the Foxes. Their long grey British faces smiled perfidiously, ticking off (Victoria was sure) the inventory of recent gin, nicotine, disorientation. Dawkins brought in more coffee, and smiled with cloying sweetness. The Foxes were making unnecessarily elaborate plans to watch birds on the Pool. Guy put his head round the door and said, 'Have you got a minute for a word?'

She smiled ravishingly, gave Dawkins the order of the day and went to the library.

Guy was waiting for her, reading a page of her notes. He looked up, said, 'Have a good time?'

'Most jolly.'

'We wondered where you were.'

This did not seem to call for a reply.

'I never thought you'd land up in the pub,' he said.

That did not seem to call for a reply either.

'Thing is . . . well.' He was looking hot and bothered. 'The pub's where the Island goes to get away from the Priory. I wouldn't want anyone in the village to think they're being spied on.'

She smiled at him, to hide a surprising upwelling of anger. 'Talking about spying, how did you know I was there?'

'You told me last night.' Well, that was possible. 'Who did you meet?'

If this was an olive branch, Victoria was not impressed. 'Mary Morgan,' she said. 'She's not too happy.'

'She never is,' said Guy. 'You don't want to pay any attention to her.'

'I like her,' said Victoria. 'Is that all?'

Guy sighed and departed. She sat and tried not to feel guilty, staring numb-headed at the paper on her desk.

The telephone rang.

A voice said, 'Victoria?'

101

'Yes.'

'Owen Morgan. Nice morning.'

Victoria checked out of the window. 'Yes.'

'Look,' said Morgan. 'I was thinking about what you were saying last night. About bones, and so on.' Pause. 'I've got something you might like to see.'

'What?'

He laughed, tantalising her. 'Come down and I'll show you. I'll be in the propagating shed.' The telephone went down.

Victoria put back her own receiver. She was intrigued. Teased, even. Perhaps indignant at being treated like this, on her own island—

Pompous cow.

The propagating shed was a small, dark building on the site of the furnace room for the greenhouse erected during the latter years of Jones' reign. Plastic bags of twigs and shoots lay piled on a bench mounded with compost.

Victoria sat on the stool at the bench and shoved her hands into the cool compost. It would have been nice to stick her head in too.

A shadow fell into the bright rectangle from the doorway.

'Morning,' said the voice of Morgan. He took her into the sunlight. Tame thrushes hopped in front of him. He spoke, in the manner of a tour guide. 'We are now at the back of Davy Jones,' he said. 'The undersea kingdom. Originally it was a grotto, as in grotesque. But the Major wanted it cleaned up. Loved painting things white. By the time I got here all the original stuff was on the rubbish dump.'

'What original stuff?' said Victoria.

They climbed an awkward twist of steps and arrived at a glasshouse, a small structure Victoria had not seen before, lurking in a hollow of the rock. It was a complicated thing, with ironwork curled and twisted and fragments of stained glass. Fern fronds pressed against the panes. Victoria had the feeling that she had been shown through a curtain into another Trelise, deeper, odder. 'The Doll's Greenhouse,' said Morgan. 'Harry could never get down here, so I could do what I wanted.' There was a bracing sense of conspiracy between them. He opened the door, and stood aside.

The air was warm and humid, with the musty smell of things rotting to grow. As Victoria's eyes became used to the dim green light, she saw tree ferns, blacker, shinier, more exotic-looking than the *Dicksonias* outside, things climbing on trellises.

'This is what Davy Jones is meant to be like,' said Morgan. 'Was, when Joshua built it. The kingdom of the drowned.'

Victoria felt at last that she was behind Joshua's eyes, in a Victorian mind, barbarous by modern standards, suspended between logic and magic. Under the ferns, the ground was carpeted with a litter of fossils, conch shells, cannonballs, anchors. On the carpet were strewn turtle carapaces, a thing like an ivory Henry Moore that she realised was a whale's vertebra, and the skull of a . . . not a dinosaur, even among these cycads . . . of a rhinoceros. 'Over there,' said Morgan. In the background, gleaming in a ray of light filtered by half-a-dozen layers of fern, was a small stone platform, scrolled, that might have been (she realised, with a quickening of excitement) a Roman altar. There was something on the altar. An egg; a big one. She stooped to touch it.

It was not an egg. It was a skull: an ancient yellow skull, its left-hand side cracked and starred, perforated. The skull of a person who had died by violence.

Morgan was watching her, quite still. He said, 'That's the one Revel dug up.'

She stared at him. 'But Guy said they reburied it.'

'That's Revel all over,' said Morgan. 'Bit of a scavenger, world of his own, really.'

'Why didn't you mention this before?'

'I didn't want Revel to get into trouble.'

Victoria liked Revel, what she knew of him, and Daisy. Guy would have seen the whole thing in black and white. Morgan was right, there would have been trouble.

'So there it is, anyway,' said Morgan. 'I must get on.'

'Do you mind if I stay?' The hairs were sharp on the nape of her neck.

'My dear Mrs Blakeney-Jones,' he said, with the hint of an ironic bow. 'This is your garden, and you can do what you want in it.' The door closed behind him. He left her there, in this little greenhouse, with the skull. In the unofficial world.

She picked the skull up.

It was surprisingly light in her hands. The lower jaw was missing, the orbits blank and empty. Were you Mendez, or a monk? Were you one of the ones who brought the sandstone arch from Normandy as ballast in a ship's bilges, assembled within the sound of the sea a red arch to hold up the blue roof of Heaven? She turned the skull in her hands.

She stopped.

The teeth of the upper jaw were regular and unworn. The right second upper molar had once been decayed, though. Until someone had drilled and filled it with silvery-black metal.

Victoria was just about sure that dentists did not do the rounds of Medieval monasteries.

She pushed the tooth. It gave a little, loose in its socket. She took it between finger and thumb and moved it from side to side.

It came out in her hand.

No big deal. It was old, dead, cold, no more than a stone, really.

But already she could feel warmth from her hand spreading into the tooth; the warmth of life, brought back by contact with the present. She should return it to the past, where it belonged . . .

Her fingers closed around it. She put it in her pocket.

The woman at the Dental Museum was an enthusiast. 'People have been having fillings for much longer than you probably think,' she said. 'I mean *centuries*. All the way back to, well, in its modern form certainly the middle ages, gold-leaf fillings, lead, what have you. If you were posh, of course. And you didn't mind someone grinding away at your teeth with a brace and bit and cramming lead or gold leaf into the hole. It didn't do much good because it never fitted properly. You got new decay down the walls of the cavity. Then in the 1830s the Cracou brothers introduced the Royal Succedaneum, made of filed five-franc pieces and mercury. Exactly the same as our amalgam, give or take an ingredient and not counting plastics, of course, but they're very recent, very recent indeed. Filled the cavity completely, no access for air or food fragments or bacteria. Marvellous stuff.'

'So there's no way of telling whether a filled tooth is a year old or two hundred years old.'

'Not if it was an amalgam filling.'

Victoria hung up. The tooth was a big, four-horned thing, yellow bone inlaid with metal. The filling looked like part of the tooth. Amalgam, for sure.

The monks had left five hundred years ago. The meadow round the Arch had been the burying ground for Trelise. Dirt-poor islanders filled cavities with rum, not silver. Had Joshua used Mendez in his demonstrations of the Jones coca salve?

Guy's head came round the library door. He said, 'Aren't you dressed?'

'Dressed?'

'The Jansons. Dinner. Remember?'

She looked at her watch. 'Oh my Lord.' She ran upstairs and climbed into dark red silk St Laurent, shortish, lapis lazuli beads strung up with gold spirals. In the pier glass she looked bright, chic and happy.

She got down to the drawing room at the same time as the Foxes, and kept out of their way by dodging around with drinks. The Jansons arrived. The Foxes spoke reverently of the splendour of Trelise in the Old Days, while the Jansons nodded politely. Camilla Janson was Scottish and satirical. Her husband Denis was a farmer, pillar of the county, Justice of the Peace, with a sharp piratical edge ground onto him by generations of Cornishness. Victoria liked them. At last it was time for dinner. Victoria had found oysters in Truro. 'Goodness!' said Mrs Fox. 'We never would have had oysters in the Old Days!'

'Harry thought they were foreign muck,' said Denis, slurping. 'Silly old fool.'

There was a short, pregnant silence, broken only by the clatter of shell on plate. Victoria realised it was perfect-hostess time. She said to Denis, who was sitting on her right, 'Did you hear about our bones?'

'Bones?' Denis had been punishing the whisky, and was now storming in on some excellent Chablis.

'In the Sea Garden. We were digging a terrace.'

'For God's sake,' said Guy, with the weariness of an Old Worlder faced with American callowness. 'You start digging around in a monks' graveyard, you find monks' bones.'

'So what did you *do*?' shrieked Mrs Fox.

Victoria said, 'It wasn't a—'

'Buried 'em again,' said Guy, ignoring her. 'Good phosphates. It's going to be a jolly interesting garden. We're making a film about it. A series, actually. Just as well. Inheritance tax is a crippler. Vic, for God's sake give Denis some wine.'

'Delicious,' said Denis. 'Series, eh?' And away they went, on gardens – Camilla and Denis had a famous one of their own, though not in the same league as Trelise.

The guests left at ten-thirty; they had come by car, and the tide would be over the causeway by eleven. Victoria sat weary at her dressing-table, taking off the lapis beads. Life felt flat and boring this side of the curtain. She saw Guy in the mirror, coming towards her, mountainous at her back. His big hands fell soft and heavy on her shoulders. He said, 'Will you keep quiet about those bones?'

'Just keeping the folks amused,' she said. 'Did I cause trouble?'

'No,' he said. 'Well, in a way.'

'Tell me. I'm American.'

'Denis is a magistrate, goes to meetings with the Chief Constable, you name it. If he knows about it officially he'd have to tell someone. We'd have Heritage, planners, coroners everywhere for weeks. He knows that as well as I do. So he let us off the hook. Now for God's sake, darling, do your research but please I beg you let's keep the bloody law out of it, because it's meant for murderers in council houses, not people trying to run estates on holy ground.'

'And you don't care whose bones they are.'

'No.'

'Well, I do. That's the difference between us.' She caught an ugly glimpse of herself, dabbling in history and sulking because her husband refused to live like a tourist in his own country. She put her arms around his neck and kissed him softly on the mouth. His hands locked in the nape of her neck, held her to him, captive. As if he needed to chain her up, to make sure she did not go away. He seemed so unsure of himself, since they had come to Trelise.

She found herself thinking of someone else: confident, living in a real world. Morgan. Claustrophobic again, she pulled away.

'Sorry,' said Guy, flushed.

She was shocked at herself. But it was too late now. They went to bed without speaking. She lay and stared at the ceiling, the night cool on her eyes. In stealing the tooth, she had left the body unburied. Never mind all this bullshit about moving between worlds. She was being disloyal.

She found herself out of bed. The tooth was in her hand.

The moon was high over the rockeries. As she padded down the Poseidon stairs, the sea sounded like the breathing of a huge creature; a garden, perhaps. In Davy Jones the figureheads would be staring haughtily with their blank eyeballs, and she could not face them. The stripes of moon-shadow under the bamboos were bad enough. Even the homely litter of boxes and pots outside the greenhouses was a threatening pile of darkness. She wished she had brought Patton the labrador.

But Patton was in his kennel. She was Victoria Blakeney-Jones. She dealt in facts, not ghosts.

She opened the door of the Dolls' Greenhouse and brushed quickly through the Cycad fronds. She would put the tooth back in the skull, and tell Morgan to bury it again. She and Guy, speaking with a single voice. She owed him that much.

The flashlight beam flicked over coral, whalebone, cannon barrel and on to the Roman altar where the skull had been.

The skull was gone.

Victoria ran.

She sat panting in the library, her homely library. She should throw the tooth over the terrace. Or perhaps since the skull was gone she could just send it to Helen Torode, her friend, who was a pathologist at Charing Cross. And bury it afterwards. Facts, not ghosts. Why not?

She put it in a ring-box, scribbled a note to Helen the pathologist, and put the box in an envelope. She left the envelope on her desk and padded upstairs, under the eyes of the ancestors, and into the Big Bedroom.

She slid in as quietly as she could, put her arms around Guy and pressed her body against his.

'Cold,' said Guy.

'Sorry.'

''Sfine,' said Guy, and went back to sleep.

It was all fine; except that if you did not confide in the man you had married, was that not the same as betraying him?

Well, there was more than teeth she had not told him about. Much more.

It would have been 1975. The sun was out, and the breeze was ruffling the leaves of the big maple outside the white clapboard house. Everyone was on the porch: Daddy in his black suit, Mommy in her print dress with a straw hat, and the girls, Victoria, eight, Sarah, five, and Martha, two, in identical blue dresses, white socks, black patent-leather shoes. Everyone had just been to church. Now it was time for Daddy time.

Daddy pulled the Bible out of the drawer in the dresser where it lived. He said, 'Martha first.'

Martha held the book the wrong way up. 'La ba dee da,' she said. Mommy smiled. Her eyes went across to Daddy, who was frowning. Martha started to bounce and giggle, carried away.

'That's enough,' said Daddy. 'Sarah now.'

Sarah could read. She did it right. Trust Sarah to do it right. She read from the Epistle to the Galatians, in a flat monotone, slow, syllable-perfect. Victoria waited her turn, stomach knotted with hatred.

'More expression,' said Daddy. Mommy was looking anxious. Nothing new in that.

'What's expression?' said Sarah.

Daddy reached across the table and swatted her on the ear. 'That is,' he said.

'David—' said Mommy.

But Daddy had taken the Bible and given it to Victoria, and Victoria had opened it at the place she had selected. 'Blessed above all women shall be Jael the wife of Heber the Kenite,' she said. She was not reading. She had learned it by heart, and as she said the words she was looking right at Daddy. 'He asked for water, and she gave him milk. She brought forth butter in a lordly dish. She put her hand to the nail, and her right hand to the workman's hammer; and with the hammer she smote Sisera, she smote off his head, when she had pierced him through and through the temples.'

Victoria put into it all the feeling she had about Daddy, how terrible it was to be scorned, and made to do things, and for poor Sarah to be hit. She knew Daddy knew, because she could see it in his face.

'Well,' said Daddy, when she had finished. He was smiling, like glass breaking. 'Very . . . good.'

Victoria heard Mommy start to laugh. It was a high, hooting laugh, really awful. It turned all of a sudden to crying. Mommy ran into the house.

'Wait here,' said Daddy, and went in after her. There was a lot of shouting.

They waited till three o'clock. Then Victoria took Martha and Sarah to their room, and the three of them played till it was five o'clock, TV time.

It was nothing unusual.

Next day, she walked down the garden in the light. It was hot and aromatic. Morgan was in his office. 'Lovely morning,' he said.

'The skull's gone.'

He swung his boots gracefully to the floor. 'Come up the garden,' he said.

He led her to the Abbey Arch. The beds hereabouts were looking better already, unidentifiable bushes shooting unhampered by bramble, patches of black soil shrinking between spreading mats of *Pelargonium*.

'I've been doing a bit of work on the Arch,' said Morgan.

There it was, the peaked swoop of it, lined with red sandstone, the granite ashlar dotted with *Crassulas* and *Convolvulus mauretanicus*. And there beside a rosemary bush growing from the wall was a new-looking stone, mortared in. Victoria had a curator's eye for buildings and their condition. Last time she had looked, this stone had been an alcove, and there had been no rosemary.

'Rosemary's for remembrance,' said Morgan. 'Nice and warm, and on holy ground.'

So there was only the tooth unburied.

Nothing wrong with a tooth.

Chapter Eight

Josia Macleod was a thickset man of small height and plethoric countenance, dressed in black, with a flat-topped straw hat and trousers strapped tight under stout boots. Leaving his traps by the *Pasha*, he perspired his solitary way inland from the South Quay, arriving soon at the tablet of slate marking the garden's seaward entrance. WELCOME, STRANGER, it said. A pained expression flitted over his thick face.

A gardener, once, Josia Macleod. Brought up in Dundee, apprenticed to the Duke of Lothian's Henry Montagu, sent by His Grace to look for novelties in Patagonia. But Macleod was a drinker and a whoremonger, a man without loyalties. He had deserted the Duke long ago. At forty-eight, he was a hunter of plants, a seller of plants, a trader in futures, a speculator in orchids, a bagman, a runner in all things about to grow, growing, or having grown. He had stepped off the packet at Falmouth to see if there was any business to be drummed up in the way of new potatoes, hybrid *Camellias*, improved daffodils. Things were bad, and Macleod needed money.

In the course of his enquiries, he had landed up opposite a bottle of brandy, and a pig-faced apothecary by the name of Fairey. Fairey had lost little time in expounding to him the beauties and iniquities of the region. After a list of respectable garden owners, his puffy brow darkened. 'Trelise,' he said. 'Man name of Jones. Begun a garden, they say. Dreadful things he grows. Against Nature. Amazing instance of a cruel man. Satan of a man. Patent medicines. Saw him kill a man once. Built himself a palace. A bordello. Disorderly house. Shares his women with all comers. Debauched man. Licentious man. Sodomitical man, thankee Mr Macleod, just a drop.'

So it was that Macleod had taken the arrival of Alice in the gig as a sign that Trelise should be visited and carefully investigated.

Had his face been given to expression, what it would have betrayed during the thirty minutes following his arrival in the garden would have been astonishment, changing gradually to cupidity.

It was ten years since the Storm. The shelter belts were now between fifteen and thirty feet high, and Lady Amherst's pheasants skulked picturesquely among the dark firs. There were three large greenhouses, in which Macleod's trained eye detected the apparatus of plant hybridisation. Away from the steps and walks and terraces were trial plots, in which grew poppies and herbs and what looked very like aloes. The beds of the main garden were full of plants that filled Macleod with lust and covetousness. There were succulents of inordinate choiceness, mimosas to make a florist salivate, *Strelitzias* of a perfection seen hitherto only in the West Indies. A well-planted garden, indifferently kept.

It was being a remarkable day. First, the tip from Fairey. Then, the meeting with the remarkable pretty woman on the packet's deck, one of Jones' harem, he dared swear. And now this perfumed and coloured place where before there had been only the flat stink of the sea. Josia Macleod farted luxuriously.

Ahead, the path turned sharply round a projection of rock. On the rock grew clods of *Mesembryanthemum*, while to the left the beds rolled down a couple of terraces towards a ruin of some kind. He slowed his pace, planning to round the bend after due pause, to give himself the pleasure of the next vista.

But from the blind side of the bend there came a curious sound. The sound of many feet, running, with a thump and a click and a weird rattle. Macleod hesitated, walked up to the corner and looked round.

Galloping down on him with huge, stately strides was a herd of ostriches.

The lead ostrich clattered its beak irritably, and tried to swerve, but was prevented by the narrowness of the path and the press of its fellow birds. Macleod found himself barged flat, face down in the grit as a score of clawed feet trampled him and sped off into the distance.

As the sound of the feet died, Macleod pushed himself to his hands and knees. His head rang. Blood from a rip in his cheek pattered into the grit, ruby-red in the sun. 'Damn me,' he said. 'I'm killed.'

It was only a long time afterwards that it occurred to him that it might have been better all round if this had been the literal truth.

Meanwhile rescue came quickly, in the shape of a tall figure, keen of eye and long of jaw, who bore down on him from a distant bed, where it had been scrutinising with a hand lens the sex organs of a promising tulip. It introduced itself as Joshua Jones, and told the unprotesting Macleod that it insisted on his accepting the hospitality of his house until he found himself quite cured.

Macleod was borne up, as if on wings of angels. He received a draught that stripped him of pain but not consciousness. His wound was bathed and stitched, his person cleaned, and he found himself in a small but beautifully appointed bedroom, with a view of blue sea. A charming dinner of soles and lobster sauce was brought him, with a bottle of Chablis. And before closing his eyes for a night of sweet repose, Macleod blessed the good fortune (though not the ostriches) which had brought him to the very heart of this place, without the need for assault by guile.

Next morning he woke at nine, to find his clothes brushed and darned, his linen clean and ironed on the bedroom chair, and his traps brought up from the South Quay. He dressed and followed his nose to breakfast.

It had been an ordinary morning for Joshua Jones. He had risen at five. He had, as was his custom, ridden a circuit of the island on the cob Isaiah. When he returned to the house at half past eight, Hawtrey his secretary was waiting at the table. Joshua dictated as he ate. The first letter was to the Curator of Kew, dangling a couple of tempting *Crassula* hybrids in return for a *Myrtus luma* his spies had noticed. Then he wrote to his friend Ethanie Burrows, a cousin of poor Lady Ancona. Miss Burrow was a maiden lady of some fifty years, whose habit it was to act as his hostess at Trelise when he absolutely could not avoid having people to stay. Just now, he was writing to her about certain other matters. He was forty-five, and to all intents and purposes alone in the world. His mind was turning to the succession.

Hawtrey finished that letter. Joshua started ordering a new plough from Parsons of Exeter. 'I beg you will dispatch these per railway,' said Jones. 'I remain, Sir, and so forth. My dear Mr Macleod, I hope I find you quite recovered?'

Macleod, placed at table and presented with kidneys, bacon, pullet's eggs, beefsteaks, kippered herrings, bloaters, bread fresh and toasted, farm butter, Majorca oranges, early peaches from the glasshouses, tea and coffee, found himself recovered most amazingly. The process was accelerated by a tour of the estate, including the model farm and a repaired causeway leading to the mainland from a largely rebuilt village. Along this causeway Macleod had the satisfaction of watching the garden ostriches transported off Trelise, downcast in a menagerie man's cart. Then Mr Jones took him fishing in a most elegant gentleman's cutter, from which his men hauled a net in which were discovered two red mullets of great size, which they ate later, with the livers in. McLeod found this all quite in keeping with general rumour about the mysterious past and eccentric present of Pasha Jones. It did not for a moment occur to him that to Jones, these were no more than the pursuits and comforts attention to detail could bring to a well-run home.

One morning about dawn, as Macleod returned from a bout of diarrhoea brought on by a queasy overindulgence in lobsters and port, he saw something that clinched his notions of Jones' libertinism. On the terrace he saw Jones and the remarkable pretty girl from the *Pasha*. Jones was in his night-clothes. The girl had her skirts up to her waist. She was on a patch of grass, dancing; laughing. Damn fine ankle. Also knee and thigh. A whore, if ever he had seen one. A deuced pretty one.

Macleod was partial to a pretty whore.

On the fifth evening of his convalescence, he was sitting over the white tablecloth in the dining room, swilling his third bottle of port and figuring with a bloated hand in his book of accounts. Mr Jones had drunk hock and seltzer and retired, pleading early engagements on the morrow. Macleod was extremely drunk, had been for three days. He rose, and took himself to the terrace to smoke.

Wedging himself against an urn, he lit a cigar on the third attempt. The night was clear, with a moon. Below him the rockery stretched away, mats of membryanthemum and agave and yucca, uncanny in the dim silver light. Through that weird landscape, a woman's figure was moving.

The woman. Jones' whore.

Macleod licked his lips.

Shares his women, Fairey had said. Well, Macleod was certainly ready for a bit tonight. Squaring his shoulders, he started along the terrace to intercept.

He saw the woman's pale face, the gleam of the moon in her eyes, on her . . . legs, damme! those legs, all the way up to the thighs, her skirt in her hands. She was a beauty, light and airy. Macleod longed to hear her squeak. He leaned his arms on the wall and said, 'Hey!'

'Sir?' said Alice Jenkins, letting fall the hem of her skirt.

'Come up here,' he said.

She dropped a small curtsey, and came up the steps towards the terrace. Demure and willing, the minx. 'Good evening, sir,' she said.

Macleod's prick was a rod in his breeches. He mumbled something about his pretty maid, and made a grab. His hands made contact with a waist, unlaced, firm and willowy. This was a ripe one. And she was not pulling away.

It did not occur to Macleod that there was a woman in the world who under such an assault would remain still not through compliance, but because after eleven years of Joshua's unswerving courtesy, the fact this was happening was of itself unbelievable.

She stood for perhaps five seconds frozen on the moonlit steps, her narrow waist caught in Macleod's port-thickened fingers. 'You're a long way from your bed,' he said. His lips came at her out of the dark, a puffy-walled crater fruity with drink. At last she turned to run.

He felt her waist twitch out of his fingers, saw her stumble down the steps, and lunged after her. He was savagely disappointed, so the lunge was halfway between a grab and a swipe. The side of his hand caught her on the hip, a mere nudge, but enough to divert her foot a couple of inches, so that instead of finding the path it bent on a granite kerb-pebble. She fell sideways and outwards.

He saw her go over a low cliff-face. She seemed to go slowly, face downwards, so that her cloak billowed round her and made her for a split second a great grey moth under the moon. Macleod stood with his mouth hanging open, rooted to the spot by drink and shock and the fading remnants of his lust. She landed with a crash, face down in the vegetation.

Suddenly sober, Macleod prayed she was dead. Dead, she would not be able to tell anyone about an attempted rape. He could report it as an accident, a missed footing, a shocking tragedy—

The grey figure stirred. It whimpered. Its hands moved towards its face. It rolled onto its back, and lay still.

Macleod faded off the terrace and into the dining room. He gulped a glass of port and took himself to his bed. There were times to call for help, and times to beat a strategic retreat. This was definitely one of the latter. Teach Jones to loose his damned ostriches hither and yon. He slept.

Jones sat in his nightshirt under the lamp in his bedroom, writing in his diary while he waited for Alice. She did not arrive. His mind was unsettled. Perhaps it was merely the presence of Macleod. The man was a vulgar sot. The obligations of hospitality were fulfilled. It was time to be rid of him, and for happiness to continue.

He looked at his watch. Where was Alice?

He rose from his chair and padded onto the terrace.

And saw the grey figure sitting on the stone halfway down the rockery, apparently composed. The hands were white, pressed to the eyes. She did not move, but she was making a small, strange noise. As he drew nearer he saw that between the fingers of her hands there oozed something that shone black as tar in the moon, and dripped into the spiny bed of new-planted agaves that had broken her fall.

Doctor Bellars was a steady man, a craftsman in his way. Joshua received his report sitting upright behind his desk, in high white gills and a new black coat, as if on his way to a funeral, or a wedding.

'The wounds to the face are insignificant,' said Bellars. 'I am afraid that the spines of the vegetable objects have penetrated the eyeball, torn the iris, scarred the cornea, mangled the retina and may indeed have destroyed the optic nerve. I much regret to say that I cannot in all fairness and goodwill see any prognosis but a complete and permanent blindness.'

'Yes,' said Joshua.

He conveyed Bellars to the quay in his trap, bade him a civil farewell, and watched unsmiling as he was rowed to invisibility on the charming blue face of Hull Bay, that poor Alice would never again see.

He drove from the quay to the house he had built Alice, a neat, square edifice of slate and granite just outside the garden wall. An old woman met him at the door. 'She's been asking for you,' she said.

The bedroom curtains were half open, admitting a white-hot bar of Cornish sun. Alice's head was on the pillow, the eyes heavily bandaged. When she heard his step, she said, 'Joshua.'

He nodded. Then, remembering, 'Yes.'

'Here.' He sat on the bed. Her hands found his face. 'What's this?' There was wetness on her fingers.

'It's raining.'

She held tight to his hand. She could feel the sun on her cheek. She said, 'Will you stay with a blind woman?'

'Alice,' he said. 'It will be my duty and my pleasure to be your eyes.' A silence. 'Can you tell me what happened?'

Her cheeks were bruised and cut. Even so, he saw the blood rise to darken them. 'I fell,' she said.

'It is not like you to fall. Was Macleod there?'

'What would he have wanted with me?' She turned away from him. Joshua's whore, the man had called her. He had been right.

'There is something I wanted to ask you,' said Joshua. 'We have been tolerable good friends these ten years, you and I. Now you must become my wife.'

She made a scornful noise. 'What would people say?'

'That Joshua Jones has married his love.'

'They would say he has married his whore. Out of pity. They would say it was too late; once a whore, always a whore.'

'These are their assumptions. Not the truth.'

'There is no difference. I am known to be your whore.' The chin went up. 'I am proud to be your whore. Why should I become your wife? To make you respectable?'

Jones took her hand. 'We are already respectable.'

'So why change?'

'I thought you would like it.'

'Thank you.'

He rose to go, opened the door. Instead of walking away, he paused.

She turned her head towards him. On the white gauze of the bandages there appeared two red stains.

Alice was weeping.

Macleod had left that morning – out of consideration, his note put it, for this dreadful accident. He was surprised to receive from Joshua shortly afterwards an order for Canary palms, which he found and dispatched. For a year, he heard nothing from Trelise. This suited him admirably; he himself preferred to forget, and besides, he had other things on his mind. Competition was growing in the nursery line. His damned wife was whining about the butcher and the baker, and the dratted child screamed all the time, more like a girl than a boy.

It was at this moment that his clerk brought him a letter, on heavy cream paper sealed with a rich red wax bearing the impress of a ragged staff. The letter, he was delighted to note, was from Joshua Jones, and bade him in the most cordial terms to Trelise, to see the progress of the new palms he had sent, and to discuss a matter close to Mr Jones' heart, with consequences (the letter said) beneficial to all concerned.

So Macleod packed a portmanteau, and set off in search of fortune.

Chapter Nine

The summer had dealt kindly with Trelise. The sea was green satin under a sky of Himalayan poppy. Over all there lay an entrancing clarity, in which ships hull-down on the horizon revealed every spider's thread of their rigging, and bees in the heather of the Downs were visible at a hundred yards to the naked eye.

Macleod was brought to the house in the carriage this time, the tides being favourable. In the State Room he found to his satisfaction Mr Jones. He was much less pleased to find, dispensing tea from her position on the sofa, Alice Jenkins. An Alice Jenkins still beautiful, but with her features pocked with the scars of small punctures, and with her eye sockets concealed behind a black silk bandage.

'I do not believe you know Miss Jenkins,' said Jones, smiling affably.

'Indeed not,' said Macleod.

Miss Jenkins bowed in his direction. He sweated. But as far as he remembered he had said nothing that night, and of course she could not see him now. He decided on a frontal attack. 'I see you are injured, madam.'

'A fall,' she said. 'It cost me my eyes.' He saw a tear steal from the bandage, and thanked God he was safe.

After tea, they walked the garden. Collectors were taking seed on the beds. In one of the stoves, lines of dark-green plants were growing: like camellias, but not. 'What?' said Macleod.

'Rubber,' said Jones. 'A seed of short viability, never as yet grown outside Brazil. I have an idea it will do in the Eastern colonies. I found some seed on an American steamer, and exchanged it for some bags of coal.'

'Remarkable,' said Macleod, in a voice thickened by cupidity. Nobody had yet succeeded in the transport of rubber seed to the Eastern colonies.

There was a fortune there. A vast fortune. Damme, this cove knew how to make money. Catch a ride on his cart, that was the ticket.

'I say . . .' said Joshua. 'No. Never mind.' And he would say no more.

With the passing hours, the thing Macleod was never to mind grew in his head. As Joshua took him for the third time to contemplate the Canary palms in their wide-spaced ranks down the Poseidon stairs, his curiosity burst like a boil. 'Mr Jones,' he blurted, as they walked between the shrub-sized trees that would one day make a tunnel of the Endless Walk. 'You mentioned a scheme.'

At the eastern extremity of the walk was a granite bench, a massive thing like a dolmen, facing west. On this they sat, Macleod gingerly, for he dreaded to think what the mossy dampness of the stone would do to his piles. 'Now then,' said Jones, when they were settled. 'What do you think of my gardener?'

'Choice subjects,' said Macleod, not knowing what was the right answer. 'Kept tidy.'

'Quite.' Macleod had forgotten his piles. He was being taken into the confidence of the great Joshua Jones. 'But he is less of a hand in the greenhouse, I fear. Now, I need a man to help me bring on these rubber plants. As a partner.'

'A partner?'

'Someone to assist practically. Who will share the profits, in lieu of pay. And the risks, of course; it is a risky business, growing such plants.'

'Of course.' The spittle had gone from Macleod's mouth.

'So this is what I propose. You are a man who knows tropical plants. You will come here and look after our rubber in the stove, and participate in the proceeds of the venture. You will require time to think about this. Till dinner, perhaps?'

'Yes,' croaked Macleod.

He spent the afternoon pacing the garden. If this Jones had rubber, he had a goldmine. And the silly fool wanted to share it.

Well, if he was handing out money, Macleod was not the man to stand in his way.

After dinner, the blind woman (she disgusted Macleod) had dispensed tea in the State Room. Jones led her away. Macleod was bold and red with port. Jones sipped a green-stemmed glass of hock and seltzer.

'Now then,' said Macleod. 'The rubber enterprise, hey.'

'You have considered it?'

'I should rather think I had. Up, down and sideways. And I can tell you that I like it.'

Jones smiled, his sudden, dazzling smile. 'Splendid,' he said. '*Splendid.*'

'But.'

'But what?'

'The usual,' said Macleod. 'The ballast. The ducats. The mint sauce, the rivets, the rowdy.'

'Ah,' said Jones. 'There will be no salary. You can draw a bill against the profits from selling on the plants. And of course there is the consequential effect on your reputation. Macleod, the man who brought rubber to the East!'

'Yes.' Macleod was without funds, dogged by bailiffs. To live on an island would have been enough. The rest was handsome. More than handsome.

There was one thing, though.

'Tell me,' said Macleod. 'Why are you asking me to come in on this with you?'

'As I told you,' said Jones. 'Risk is best shared between friends.'

'Quite so,' said Macleod, flattered.

Macleod used the money raised on the bill to stave off his most pressing creditors. A week later, he, his wife and eight-year-old son took up residence at a house on Trelise. There, benignant in his family circle, he felt that yet again he had put one over on Pasha Jones.

Jones and Alice went away to Carlsbad for six months. It was rumoured on the island that the Pasha was having her eyes looked at by the finest physicians of Europe. Macleod did not care what they were doing. He saw to the plants in the greenhouse with loving care, every new leaf a sovereign in his pocket.

In the month of November, a letter arrived from Joshua. In it, he said how much he was looking forward to seeing his rubber plants.

It was a cool November; very cool. On St Andrew's Day, the dusk sky was high and clear, the air razor-edged with coming frost. Macleod banked up the stoves, shut the house tight, and went to his bed.

When he awoke next day, the fuchsias outside his window sparkled with hoarfrost. He stuffed his shirt into his breeches, waddled past his small son, who was drawing a fern leaf by the kitchen range, and went out to the greenhouses.

The cool house was steamed up on the inside. The stove, where the rubber grew, sparkled clear as a great diamond in the early morning sun.

Macleod frowned. The panes should have been running with condensation. Unless—

His heart leaped into his mouth. He began to run.

The furnace was out, the ashes wet, as if someone had poured on water. The doors and lights stood open.

Every single plant was dead.

A week later, Joshua and Alice returned. Macleod met Joshua and told him the news.

'Who opened the house?' said Joshua.

'Devil in human form.' said Macleod.

'Or an avenging angel.'

'I beg your pardon?'

'Well, no good crying over spilt milk,' said Jones, and Macleod's hopes rose. Could have happened to anybody. Try again, he would say. 'We have no further use for you here,' said Jones. Macleod felt the words as a blow to the heart. 'You will be off the island by tonight.'

'Tonight?'

'And the bill falls due at Christmas, I think.'

'But—'

'Pray excuse me,' said Jones, and went back to his ledger, in which he was entering the sum of one guinea, paid to Revel for services in the stove on the night of the 30th November. The rubber plants were no loss. They had been *Hevea guianensis*, an ornamental stove plant, similar to *hevea brasilensis*, the commercial rubber plant, but of no practical value.

Money could blind as efficiently as the spines of *Agave*.

When Macleod returned to his cottage he found his furniture on a cart, with his wife and son. The cart took them to the mainland, and dropped them by the Causeway Inn. He was forced to sell his furniture, and take lodgings in Truro. All his attempts to get work failed; he had no capital, and nobody wanted a gardener who left a stove wide open on the coldest night of the year.

When Jones' bill was presented for payment, the customary pleas for renewal were made, and refused. Macleod's remaining effects were sold up lock, stock and barrel, and he was taken with his family to the workhouse.

Just before Christmas, the door of the visiting room opened and Jones walked in, the ice-white of his linen contrasting disagreeably with the mould-stained drab of the walls. 'Deliver me!' cried Macleod. 'Have you no heart?'

His wife appeared, pinched blue. Clinging to her hand was a boy, eight years old, with a wide forehead and pale hair. 'Have mercy!' cried the woman. The child said nothing, but contemplated Jones steadily from eyes bright with hatred.

Jones walked across to the window, and looked through a barred tunnel of wet stone at a view of slimy brickwork. 'You took Alice Jenkins' eyes,' he said. 'So I have taken it upon myself to effect a curtailment of your own horizons.'

Macleod stared at him from a face the colour of lead. 'Fairey was right,' he said.

'Doctor Fairey is dead, I believe,' said Jones. 'Now I will leave you.'

'Here?'

'Where else?'

'You're mad.'

'So people say. What do you think? Really?'

There was a silence, in which Macleod's breath came harsh and papery. 'My wife,' he said at last. 'My boy—'

'You should have thought of them earlier.' Jones left. The doors slammed, one by one, fading.

Macleod began to weep, tears as hot as blood. Though of course in his case they were only salt water.

Alice loved the spring air in the window. She loved the salt of the sea, and the murmur of the breeze in the pines and palms, and the feel of Joshua's face, ridged with hard lines now at the corners of mouth and eyes, a deep cleft vertical between the brows. An unswerving face.

Alice took the head and held it to her breast, so he could hear the life in her, and perhaps so she could catch a distant echo of whatever was in his head.

But what was in the head was silence, as always. You did not hear his thoughts by listening. You heard them by being in his garden.

He stirred under her hand. She heard the crackle of paper; the mail had arrived earlier. 'Macleod has died,' he said.

Silence.

Paper crumpled and was thrown. More letters were opened.

'James and Emily Blakeney are coming to visit,' he said. 'This week.'

'That will be lovely for you.'

'Yes.' James Blakeney was a cousin of Lady Ancona, known to Ethanie Burrows. James was a splendid fellow. Emily was . . . well, Joshua would have to decide about Emily.

'And Professor Rowntree, and Lord Mackay.'

'Summer again.'

'Yes.'

In winter, Alice spent much time at the Priory. As the days lengthened and visitors began to arrive, her presence became an outrage to good taste.

She rose from the bed, and dressed herself in her sky-blue skirt and rose-pink shawl. She adjusted the black bandage over her eyes. She kissed Joshua on the cheek, grasped her wand of bamboo from the Pool thicket, and tapped her way to the door.

Joshua watched her pick her way down the path through the rockery. Regret tugged at his breast. Not for her blindness; the blindness was an avenged fact. It was the visitors. Unmarried, she could not be in the house. But she had been right when she had refused him. Marriage would not diminish the scandal; would increase it, if anything. He and she were of a different station. What he could change he had changed. But it was as she said. Some things were ordained.

He sat and gazed from the window at the sea. There was a pricking in his eyes, a mist, painful in its way as spines of agave. Society was made up of men and women in their station. Upon that depended the smooth running of the civilised world.

But Trelise was not the civilised world, said a small voice in his head. Trelise was his. Changeable at his whim.

But Alice was part of Trelise, and nothing could change her.

He shut his mouth, and let her go.

Chapter Ten

The coach had rolled onto the marshes out of the purple tors and the dark-green valleys of small oak. Now it stood gleaming at the root of the still-drowned causeway. There was a coat-of-arms on the door, a juvenile groom in livery picking his nose on the rumble; the carriage and four (no less) of Mr and Mrs James Blakeney of Taplow, Buckinghamshire, containing James, Emily, a French maid, and Fate. James and Emily and the coach and their servants and horses had come by train, at frightful expense. This (said Emily) was the moment to make an Impression.

So far, it was not going well.

They had arrived at the causeway half an hour earlier to find Hull Bay full to the brim, and a dirty-looking pair of men in the most disgusting rowing-boat at a jetty above which a board announced FERY – 1d. LUGAGE EXTRA. The sky was blue, the light strong and unflattering to Emily, a pale young woman with a long nose and hay-coloured hair, dressed in mourning. James, lanky in travelling tweeds, lurked under a sort of pith helmet, the brim lined with green baize, specified by his wife against the dangerous Cornish sun. He inspected the ferry boat, and saw from the corner of his eye Emily's nose, wrinkled. 'We shall wait,' he said, before she could.

Emily nodded sharply. She was here not from family feeling or even curiosity, however James might feel. She was here because Ethanie Burrows had suggested it, pointing out that Jones was exceedingly rich, and without relations of any kind.

There was a low building by the jetty, a public house from the gorse bush hanging over its door. 'Some refreshment, my dear?' said James.

'Tea,' said Emily, tight-lipped.

The spotty groom was dispatched to the interior. The tea proved night-black and undrinkable. Emily sent it back. Tray and cups then flew from the public house window, followed by a woman's voice, swearing horribly. The green baize lining of his hat gave James a drowned appearance. He was a kind but irascible man, continuously at the mercy of his wife's sense of the fitness of things. 'Pay 'er no mind,' said the dirtier of the two ferrymen confidingly to Emily. 'Which tis only her monthlies, my dear.'

James burst into a cold sweat. Action was required. There was a sort of measuring-stick by the root of the causeway, sunk in water to the number 2. Hastily, he said, 'Drive on!'

'But it's all water,' said the coachman.

'I said drive!' roared James, in one of his passions.

Tucking his head between his shoulders, the coachman jobbed his horses forward. The causeway root was no more than a slipway, across which the tide streamed with silky vigour. The ferrymen began making satirical bets about how far they would get before they drowned. As the land in the windows was replaced by smooth water, Emily sat up straight, compressing her lips to vanishing point. James glowered greenly under his hat brim. The wheels sloshed and rumbled, then stopped.

'What is it?' roared James.

'Osses don't take to it,' said the coachman.

James was good with horses and cattle and vegetables. He was about to say they would wait, when Emily leaned forward and said in a high, irritable voice, 'Whip them, man! Whip them!' Five years of marriage had taught James that it would be suicide to gainsay her.

The coachman sucked his teeth, and chucked the reins, and applied the whip. The horses started forward, rolling their eyes. The carriage rumbled hub-deep, two hundred yards from the mainland, half a mile from Trelise, the ebb-tide leaving a long wake to the westward.

Down in the stones of the causeway, a conger eel was messily devouring a crab, and a shoal of grey mullet were cruising half-heartedly among the debris.

It was the mullet that caused the problem.

The rumble of the coach caused the conger to slide back into his crack between two of the causeway's boulders. The crab debris tumbled away down the tide. The mullet shoal rose towards the silver mirror of the surface.

In that mirror they saw a terrifying shape, boxy, sixteen-legged, glinting aggressively in the sun. A hundred and ninety-eight fish turned as one fish, and fled across the broad green wall of the causeway.

Ten yards ahead of the lead horses, the mirror of the water was suddenly, shockingly churned to foam. It lasted perhaps a second; but a second was long enough.

The nearside horse reared in the traces, and came down sideways. Where its front hoofs landed it found not causeway, but deep water. It plunged in, thrashing, dragging its harness-mate along, twisting the coach's front wheels so the whole equipage lurched sideways. The nearside wheels came off the causeway. The body of the coach grounded with a crash and a surge of white water. The coachman fell in.

Inside the coach, there was pandemonium. James had been flung onto a tangle composed of Emily and her maid. Their screams mingled with the crash of breaking plate-glass and the roar of green water flowing over the window's sill. Outside, horses were neighing, and a sledgehammer concussion hinted broadly at kicking. 'The other door!' roared James.

'Don't *shout* at me!' shouted Emily. The maid, pretty enough to be used to rapid self-defence, was already scrambling for the uphill door. Between them, she and James shoved it open, and hauled Emily towards the patch of sky. Emily's crinoline held a terrible weight of water, and she kept screaming; her boxes, her trunk, his hand was hurting her wrist, the maid was too wet, the water too cold—

They got her up to the door. The world was a dazzling place, all blue sky and kicking horses. The coachman was nowhere to be seen. The tiger was sitting on the causeway, water up to his chin, moaning with agony from a kick on the knee by an offside leader. The horses plunged and struggled. The coach ground on the stones, slipping sideways in the tide.

'Get out!' roared James, hauling at his wife's bony wrists.

'My hoops!' she screamed. She stood waist-deep in the carriage window. Her crinoline held her in.

'Take 'em off,' said James.

'Never!'

With a grinding noise, the carriage shifted again. James said, 'Dearest, when the carriage falls off the edge it falls into deep water, and it will take you with it.' The world had the slow, treacly feeling of a nightmare. 'I implore you.'

'Monster!' cried Emily. The horses plunged again. The carriage lurched.

'Release her!' said James to the maid. 'I'll take care of the horses.' He pulled out a clasp knife. He always had found horses easier than women.

'Madame,' said the maid, soothingly. 'It is important. Very important. For if you are not alive, you cannot be *chic*.'

She knew the vanity of this poor bony thing, her wish to shine at this meeting with her important connection. She talked to her soothingly, and the hysterics soon gave way to sobs; and under cover of the sobs, the maid's fingers untied the tapes of the crinoline hoops. 'Now, madame!' she cried. 'One last, a great effort!'

At that moment, James detached the last of the horses. The carriage must have been delicately balanced, for as Emily braced herself for the effort, the whole equipage lurched backwards. For a terrible moment, the carriage was a vast black shape under the green water, the wheels rolling uppermost.

Now, finally, the maid screamed.

Emily's head appeared above water, gasped and sank. At that moment, with a huge knock of oars, the ferryboat arrived from the quay. They threw a plank to the coachman, who had surfaced and was floundering among the capes of his greatcoat, and turned their attention to the carriage. While one of them held water, his mate plunged his unclean right hand armpit-deep, groped around, and straightened up with a grunt. And there at the end of his arm, his dreadful blood-pudding fingers gripped in her hair, was Emily, drenched and gasping.

James was on the causeway, struggling with four horses, up to his knees in the rush of the tide. The boatmen placed Emily, speechless, beside him. The French maid stood at her side, her soaking dress clinging to her body like a second skin. 'Wor, Kenny,' said the ferryman. 'Looka the bum on that.'

But the maid was not looking at lecherous ferrymen, or shocked mistresses, or speechless masters. She was gazing south.

Ahead lay a broad sheet of satiny sea. And in the middle of that blue sheet was a creature: a creature like a centaur, with four endless legs that started thin and black, but ended broad and wavering—

A voice came over the water, four hundred yards if it was an inch. 'Kenny!' it roared. 'What in hell's name do you mean by letting my guests start on the causeway at this time of tide?'

Kenny went red and started to stutter.

'Now pick them up, God damn and blast you, and bring them ashore and get their bags and send the groom on with the horses and I will talk to you later, damn your eyes.'

Kenny had turned white. He touched his forelock. 'Yessir,' he mumbled. 'Yessir, certainly sir, Mr Jones.'

The horseman turned and rode back towards the island.

Things began to happen with magical smoothness. James and Emily and the maid found themselves in the ferryboat, wrapped in blankets. The men began to row with Naval precision.

The maid, now she was over her shock, was in ecstasies. '*Mais c'est inouï!*' she said, pink and beautiful with delight. '*Comme le Mont-St-Michel.*'

Emily sniffed into her handkerchief. James was acutely aware that she had nearly drowned, and that this was no time for admiring the view. But this was indeed a truly remarkable thing that they were seeing, and he was not a man who found it easy to hide his delight.

There was the Watch Tower, with behind it the neat houses of Old Hull, and the chessboard pattern of field and wall, and the stubby tower of Joshua Jones' new church pale against the dark blanket of the woods, and beyond it, the spires and turrets of the new Priory, copper gleaming. There it all was, reflected in the glassy sea, perfect, double. On its reflection, James' ludicrous hat floated away down the tide. Gliding on water so clear that it might have been floating on air, the ferry bore sulking Emily and her consort alongside the quay, where Joshua was waiting for them.

The luggage had been rinsed with fresh water, and the coach was undergoing a scheme of restoration. But it was foolish to pretend (as Emily did not tire of pointing out) that either wardrobe or conveyance would ever be the same again. James, though naturally enthusiastic about a place conducted on such perfect principles, was humiliated by the business of trying to make a good impression. He made solitary explorations of the farm, while Emily stalked the policies, thrusting her nose before her like a heron. She found much to approve of on the ground floor of the house, with its two great state rooms and its cosy drawing room. The spare bedrooms, designed as ship's cabins, she found pokey. The garden was absurd and barbaric. And as for the greenhouses and the plant breeding and the drug fields ... well! Her husband was related by blood to Lady Ancona. Her parents had lived in the utmost respectability at Clifford Lodge near Guildford. Trelise's greenhouses and drug fields were a constant reminder that Joshua was not only in trade, but as a merchant apothecary little better than a quack.

The dignity that had suffered so horribly in her near-drowning returned with double strength. It was not to be expected that a respectable person such as herself, with a position to maintain, should be anything but shocked by the ... *eccentricity*; a harsh term, but there was no other word for it ... of Trelise. Yet Jones gave himself such airs about the place, in his quiet way. Well, thought Emily, sniffing; Mr Jones' fortune was a great chance. She must show herself a person worthy of its charge, by improving him.

She therefore put herself out to explain to him the application of Taste where gardens were concerned. The natural granite cliffs of Trelise would be much enhanced by additions of fancy stonework, even possibly by the creation of artificial mountain ranges. The higgledy-piggledy harum-scarum beds, with plants perhaps rare but horribly undisciplined, would with a little blasting and edging lend themselves to carpet bedding of the most distinguished type – had Mr Jones seen the divinely elaborate work at Drummond Castle, resembling nothing so much as Seville terra-cotta tiling, so rich and grand? And on the rockeries, instead of the staring mesembryanthemum and Gothic succulents, she proposed cascades of roses and verbenas, sweetly pretty and so much calmer. This was such a *wild* place. As a matter of taste it was vital to shut out the wild, and create an oasis of what was nice. Dear Lady Brierton had said to her only the other day ...

Joshua nodded abstractedly, which she took as an earnest acknowledge-ment of the deep thought he was giving her wise words.

'He is coming round,' she said to James, in their bedroom on the morning of the sixth day of their visit.

James was struggling with a shoe-horn. 'How the deuce can you be sure?'

'All of life,' pronounced Emily, 'is a striving from the Lower to the Higher.'

'Strikes me this is all pretty high already,' said James. 'You should see the farm. Wonder of the world. And the works! Splendid quay. Best of housing for the tenantry—'

'I am not interested in farms,' said Emily. At Clifford Lodge, the factor had dealt with the tenantry. 'If we show him the benefits of cultivation, he will be grateful. You'll see.'

James finished with his boot and stood up. He looked out of the window, at the dazzle of sea and beach. 'Yes,' he said, gloomily. 'I'm sure I shall.'

'Well, then,' said Emily, whose grasp of irony was weakened by her inability to understand any point of view except her own. 'Shall we go down?'

On the eighth day of their visit, she delivered the summing-up of her informal programme of lectures. She spoke of the odiousness of Trade and the pleasures of Society. Farming was best left to rustics. As to commerce, the right place for money (if she might speak as a mere woman) was not in Trade, but in the Funds.

The lecture had started at the breakfast table. Jones had recollected an urgent errand at the quay, and had risen swiftly while she had been in mid-sentence. She had insisted on accompanying him. As they passed out of the garden gates, she continued to give him the benefit of her thirty years' experience of Life. Jones turned up a path following the garden wall and accelerated his pace, impelled, she presumed, by intellectual excitement. She had to trot to keep up, but breathlessness did not check her flow of speech. They were passing in front of a hedge of *Pittosporum* growing over a low granite wall beyond which was a square grey house roofed with slate. The garden of the house was peculiar. The colours were higgledy-piggledy and random. The paths had six-inch kerbs, over which trailed not only geraniums but jasmine tangled with tobacco and bushes of lemon verbena, so that the scents rolled off it like a fog. 'Good *heavens*,' said Emily. 'What a freakish place. Are they *blind*?'

There appeared at this exact moment from behind the cottage a woman in her thirties, with reddish-gold hair flowing unbound to her shoulders. She was dressed in bright, sun-washed blue and pink. Her cheekbones were high, her lips soft and voluptuously shaped, though her cheeks were oddly cratered. Over her eyes was bound a broad black ribbon.

'Oh!' cried Emily, in whose mind blindness and deafness mingled indistinguishable. 'She *is*!' She stopped, grabbing Joshua's sleeve. 'Now there you have it,' she said. 'Wildness unchecked. The terrible garden. And—' she lowered her voice significantly, but not far '—disease.'

Jones was watching her from his great height. He said, 'I do not think I understand you.'

'The blindness,' she said.

Marble, his face. 'What of it?'

She felt a heat in her face. 'The diseases of evil living.'

'What diseases?'

She was blushing now. 'I do not have to spell it out, I think.'

'Madam, I insist.'

She was as if mesmerised. 'The . . . vices of the lower orders,' she muttered. 'The diseases concomitant.'

'Ah,' said Jones. He raised his head. 'Alice,' he called. 'Have you got syphilis?'

'Hard to say, Pasha.' The voice was warm, with laughter in it. 'If I have, you have.'

'Well, a trouble shared is a trouble halved,' said Joshua. He walked on, quickly. Emily trotted after him, her sharp face on fire. 'Now then,' he said. 'Mrs Blakeney. You have been entirely wrong about my friend Miss Jenkins, as in so much else. I think it would be best if you were to leave the island.'

'Leave?' she said. 'I . . . it was a speculation . . . a foolish one, perhaps.' She drew a handkerchief from her reticule, preparing tears. 'One is merely trying to—'

'You object to my bedrooms, my garden, my means of livelihood, and the hygiene of my friends,' said Jones. 'I conclude that you do not like it here, so you would be better elsewhere.'

'It was a natural assumption,' said Emily, white-lipped.

'I have known you for a week,' said Jones. 'I have known Alice Jenkins for twenty years, at the beginning of which period she saved my life, and during which period she has been my intimate companion. And yet you presume to think that there is some bond between you and me that disposes me to share your judgements at Alice's expense. Your coach will be in the yard at six. I bid you farewell.'

The Blakeneys went over the causeway on the tide. Jones, according to his normal habit, went to take tea with Alice. Alice heard him drink and set the cup (gold Spode, that he had bought her) with a clash in the saucer. She had a sense of a kettle on the boil. As she had learned, she said nothing.

'Damn and blast it,' he said. 'I won't have it. I damned well won't have it.'

Soothingly, she poured him more tea.

His joints creaked faintly as he rose. His footsteps crossed and recrossed the room. 'Look here,' he said. 'That woman will tell everyone. You'll have to marry me.'

She smiled. 'I told you, I'm quite happy as we are. So are you, I think. She's put you out, that's all.'

The chair by the fire groaned as he sat down. 'Quite,' he said, with a return of honesty. 'But she has made things plain that were not plain before. I have exploded. No, flowered. Oh, blast. I must be married to you, Alice.'

'No.'

'But until we are married, I can put you off, turn you out into the world. Aren't you worried?'

She said, 'I'm a freeborn woman with a cast-iron lease. You can't put me out. And I cannot believe that this sentimental idiot I hear talking is my Benthamitical Mr Jones.'

She heard him sigh. He said, 'You are indeed a designing woman, and I see we are bound with hoops of steel. What are you grinning at?'

She threw the slops from his cup into the bowl. 'Grinning?' she said. It was nice to be wooed, and that was a fact.

They sat for a time in silence. She could hear his mind working. Finally, he rose. 'I find I must go to London,' he said.

'When?'

'In the morning.'

'In that case, shall I come later?'

'By all means.'

So at nine o'clock that night she tapped her way surefooted up the stairway through the East Rockery to his room. And at nine o'clock next morning his carriage rolled across the gleaming causeway and onto the white dust road to Truro.

Behind him, Trelise lay across the sea like a blessing, neat-walled, dark with woods and shelter-belts, the steep gables of the Priory stabbing the blue at its seaward end. He felt the discreet prick of a tear; a sentimental man, Joshua Jones, in the end.

He turned his head forwards. London lay ahead, with much business. It was time that the question of succession was settled, once and for all.

Mr Williams of the Temple was tall, fair, pink and highly polished, with nothing of the bumbling family solicitor about him. He remarked to Mr Jones on the inclemency of the weather. Mr Jones replied that it was said at Trelise that the Gulf Stream was moving out to sea, though small credence attached to such notions, the contortions of the Gulf Stream being used in his experience to justify phenomena ranging from waterspouts to outbreaks of Cabbage White butterfly. He then fell into the silence of a man with much on his mind.

'Well, sir,' said Mr Williams, briskly. 'What can we do?'

'My will,' said Jones. 'When did I make it?'

Williams had already had the will brought up. Jones was fifty-five, an age at which wills tended to come to the forefront of minds. 'Fifteen years since,' he said.

'I must change it.'

Mr Williams was not surprised. It was a young man's will; the estate – not inconsiderable then, much greater now – left in its entirety to Lady Ancona's unsuitable cousins the Blakeneys. A couple of loyal retainers provided for, and a Bentham provision, that the corpse be stuffed and mounted.

'Change,' he said. 'By all means. What will be your instructions?'

'I intend to marry,' said Jones.

'Pray accept my congratulations,' said Mr Williams.

Jones nodded perfunctorily. 'The estate is to be my wife's, for the remainder of her life. Failing issue, it is then to pass elsewhere.'

'Where in particular?'

'I neither know nor care. In this Mrs Burrows will be my trustee, and she is to choose. I shall be dead. You may carry over from the old will the provisos that the garden is to be kept up, particularly by the Arch and the Pool, and that the inheritor reside on the island for nine months of the year at least. Under no circumstances is the estate to pass to James and Emily Blakeney.'

'Very good,' said Williams, writing.

'And there is a bequest.' Jones' face was marmoreal as ever. 'To the child of the late Josia Macleod the sum of one hundred guineas, to be expended in the acquisition of a fitting profession, at the discretion of yourself as trustee.'

'One hundred guineas.'

'I have been over-hard,' said Joshua. 'Against the child I have no grudge.'

Mr Williams made another neat note. 'Now, sir. The name of the lady who is to become your wife?'

'Alice Jenkins, of Higher Ground Farm, Trelise.'

Mr Williams turned his face down to the paper to hide an involuntary pursing of the lips. This Alice Jenkins was named in the old will, as a faithful servant, a small tenant of the Trelise estate. She was by its terms given an irrevocable life-time lease and a pension, and other benefits in kind. It was generous provision for an upper servant: for servant she seemed to be.

'I love her,' said Jones, suddenly.

Mr Williams smiled and bowed. Jones seemed put out by his confession. He rose, abruptly. 'How soon can you have this ready?'

'This afternoon.' Williams cleared his throat, and raised a smooth eyebrow. 'As a friend ... I may venture to describe myself as a friend, after all these years?'

'Indeed.'

'You have reflected and considered?'

'I have,' said Joshua, in a voice that left Williams in no doubt as to his view of the limits of friendship.

The solicitor made a small gesture, flattening the air with his hands. 'Shall we say three o'clock?'

Jones walked into the City, a brisk, smartly dressed man in late middle age. He felt perhaps less brisk than he looked. London smelt of stale gas and unwashed people. He missed the strong air of Trelise. He missed Alice. He wanted to write to her, to summon her to London, to tell her of the future he was building for her.

But that would keep. So he sublimated his enthusiasms in a chop-house, where he took on board *The Times* newspaper, a rump steak, apple pudding, and a pint of claret. He left at two o'clock, and went to visit an acquaintance in the Bank of England.

Here he spent a drowsy half-hour, lulled by the drone of bluebottles and the lucubrations of his acquaintance upon the National Debt of Peru. At half-past two by the bells of St Mary Woolnoth he was standing at the top of the steps by the pillars, looking at the throngs below: the black-coated river of male humanity, fat, thin, bearded, sidelocked, Christian, Jewish, Hindoo: and beyond it cabs and carts and horse-omnibuses, seething and stinking. He stood hands in pockets, ruminating. At Trelise, only nature seethed. For a second he was transported. At his feet, the Bank steps extended and narrowed until they became the Poseidon Stairs. The pavements became dark walks, Threadneedle Street a bed agitated by the wind from the sea: and the sparkle of a tiny slot of Thames was the noon road the sun made from Great Rocks to the Mare—

'Mr Jones?' said a voice.

Jones came out of his reverie. A woman was standing next to him; a thin woman, with deeply pouched eyes under a rusty black bonnet, and a mouth loosened by discontent. At her side was a child, a boy of perhaps ten years. The child held her hand protectively. 'Mrs Macleod,' said Jones.

'As requested,' said Mrs Macleod.

In the hurrying crowds on the steps, they made a little island of awkward silence. 'This is the boy, then,' said Joshua.

'It is.'

The boy had a wide forehead, yellowish hair cut ragged, and blue eyes stony with dislike.

'Well?' said Mrs Macleod.

'My intentions were towards your husband,' said Jones. 'Not yourself nor your family.'

'Never mind your intentions,' said Mrs Macleod, with bitterness, 'it's the consequences we has to live with.'

'You ruined us,' said the boy. His mother hushed him half-heartedly.

Joshua said, 'I would like the boy to be bound prentice to some respectable trade.'

'Oh?' said Mrs Macleod, fury and incredulity kindling in her sour eye.

'Therefore,' said Joshua, drawing from his pocket an envelope, 'I bring an advance of funds the balance of which will be provided by my lawyer, whose particulars you will find herein.'

The woman's mouth opened, then closed. Her hand came out for the letter. The child said, 'Don't take it, mother,' and tried to knock it out of her hand. The mother snatched it away from him and tucked it in her breast. The child was scarlet with humiliation.

Joshua said, 'It is for his good.'

'He killed papa.'

Joshua paid no attention to children, ever, on principle.

'I hate you,' said the child, the eyes implacable under the broad brow. He stepped forward and kicked Jones in the shin.

The boot was small, but it was thick-soled, built to last until outgrown, when it would fetch its price against the next pair. It was a painful kick. It made Joshua step back smartly, into the path of a fat man trotting down the step behind him.

Joshua felt a hard shoulder in his back. It jolted him down a step. He landed on the outside of his left foot. The ankle buckled. Next thing he knew he was falling like a tree, trying to save himself. But his hands were in his pockets.

The pediment of the Bank whirled sharp against the sky. His shoulder slammed into a step. His head, carried on by its momentum, smote the angle of another.

A great red explosion blasted Joshua back to Trelise, not standing now

139

but flying, down the Poseidon Stairs, the Pharos Walk, and deep into Davy Jones.

He felt the eyeballs of the figureheads upon him. They were not blank now, but full of a watchful sort of vigour. *Man proposes, God disposes*, they whispered, as he flew between the pillars and into the cool green grotto at the heart of the loggia. The light faded. The surface became a dim radiance wobbling high above, with the rumour of voices and wheels, or perhaps it was the sea. Then even that faded. Everything turned a cool, soft black and became still. After all his wanderings, Joshua was finally home.

There was a crowd round him now. Somewhere, a woman was screaming. 'Christ,' said someone. 'It's Pasha Jones.'

They gaped at the huge dint at the side of his brow. The trickle of blood from his forehead stilled, and the pulse in his throat and wrists faded to immobility.

In time, they took him away.

The funeral was held at Trelise, without a body. Joshua himself they sent to Venus of Clerkenwell for setting up, then installed in the Apothecaries' Hall with a face of wax. The words *Man proposes – God disposes* were carved on the base of Poseidon. And six weeks later, in accordance with the terms of Joshua's original and only will, the Blakeneys – who had now changed their names to Blakeney-Jones – arrived at Trelise and took possession.

Chapter Eleven

The night before Victoria's birthday, it rained. Guy did not turn up, and there was no one staying, so Victoria worked late in the library.

She thought of the cheeky-chappie smile on the wax face in the library, the decayed and leathery hands. The repulsive display was in keeping with early Joshua, the vengeful, eccentric nabob-mountebank. Late Joshua had put that behind him. Look at the garden. Look at his proposals of marriage to Alice, the attempted legacy to the son of Josia Macleod. Behind the implacable Benthamite had lurked the sentimentalist who had wept on leaving Trelise. It had been sentimentality that had been his undoing.

The house felt big and lonely. At the foot of the stairs, a voice was cooing, 'Sheba? Sheebies?' It was Dawkins, in a Noel Coward dressing gown with a saucer of cat milk. 'Have you seen Guy?' she said. Dawkins always seemed to know where everyone was.

'Not lately.'

'Any idea where he is?'

He gave her a smile implying deep knowledge of ancestral timetables. 'Back soon,' he said, and shuffled up the stairs.

Guy appeared three quarters of an hour later, at half past nine, when she was most of the way down a bottle of premier cru Chablis. His shoes left a wet trail across the Belouch rug in the State Room. He hooked her bottle by the neck and drained it, loose and cheerful. Victoria found herself laughing in the kitchen as she fried eggs and bacon and opened more wine. Next morning, he woke her with a cup of tea.

'What time is it?'

'Eight o'clock,' he said. 'Happy birthday.'

'Aspirin,' she said. 'Coffee.'

'Up,' he said.

'Why?'

'Get dressed.'

She hauled on a pair of jeans and a T-shirt. There were croissants for breakfast, a great rarity on Trelise. After breakfast, he said, 'Time to go.'

Willie Davis the estate fitter was waiting in the courtyard, at the helm of the cart, Coffee in the traces. 'Casting off,' said Willie, nautically. They clattered down the island to Old Hull.

A woman was standing on the quay, wearing white shorts and a blue-and-white striped sleeveless top, talking to Morgan. She had dark hair that stirred in the breeze under a flat-crowned straw hat. She laughed at something Morgan said. She looked like her sister Sarah. God, but it would be good to see Sarah. But Sarah was far away in Virginia—

The woman turned round, and took off the dark glasses.

She was Sarah.

'Happy birthday,' said Guy. 'Part one.'

Victoria's brain was feathers. She was afraid she would faint.

'Thought you might be lonely,' said Guy. 'Flew her over.'

'Oh, wow,' said Victoria. '*Wow!*' Then she was off the cart and running over the quay, and hugging Sarah. Some senator Sarah was attached to was laid up after bypass surgery, so she had got on a plane and flown to London and here she damn well was. There was an avalanche of stuff about how beautiful it was here, and she was looking so well, and isn't Guy *great*, and how it was not surprising Victoria would not come to East Neck. Then there was a pause, in which Guy said, 'Climb in the punt.'

'What's this?' said Victoria.

'Go *on*,' said Sarah, impatient, same old Sarah.

They climbed into the green punt at the quay steps. Guy rowed out into the harbour, towards the boats on the moorings. What with the Chablis and Sarah, Victoria's head was spinning. They came alongside a yacht; long and slender, varnished mahogany that gleamed in the sun, a golden pine mast scraping the heavens. Beautiful.

'This is *Fly*,' said Guy. 'Happy birthday, part two.'

Victoria was confused. 'What?'

'You said you wanted a boat,' he said. 'We did her up. She's yours.'

Then she remembered: the tour, that first frantic tour, the ancient boat, her talking about Friendship sloops. 'The boat in the shed?' she said.

Guy grinned at her. 'Your life is now complete,' he said.

Victoria went and put her arms around his neck and kissed him on the lips, very soft. It was all back again, that wonderful time before Trelise; Guy, her, the pleasure of the moment. Christ, she loved him.

He said, 'I've got to go to the office. Take Sarah.'

She said in his ear, 'I want to fuck you.'

'You'll have to wait,' said Guy, pleased, though. 'Hop on.'

For a second she was oppressed by the return of her sense of distance from him. But the boat was properly beautiful, a jewel in varnish and teak and narrow-panel cream Dacron. Victoria loved her to pieces, her and Guy.

Sarah said, 'Who's that I was talking to on the dock?'

Victoria glanced up. There he was, square-shouldered, narrow-hipped, leaning on the crane, elegant in dirty jeans and leather seaboots. 'Owen Morgan,' said Victoria.

'Attractive guy.'

They pulled up some sails and dropped the mooring. The golden hull slid through the glassy water. The land fell away.

'Who's Owen Morgan?' said Sarah.

'Head gardener. He's married.'

'I'm not.'

Victoria said, 'Local custom. Fornicators we peg out to drown.' But she could see Sarah's point. To anyone not happily married, Morgan would look good. Well, to anyone at all, really. 'How *are* you?'

They caught up, a year in a long, noisy burst. Victoria was happy, and Sarah guessed she was too, but was Victoria sure, she was looking kind of tired, it was hard to tell, she was getting so like English? And Victoria was sure, it was just that she was doing all this work, but then so was Sarah, and Sarah said tell me about it, all work no play till now; and it was *so great* to see her.

The boat slid smooth and easy to seaward, the silver beaches drifting by, then the house, the mica in its granite winking in the sun. A porpoise rolled and blew. The sun was hot, and the sea was ruffled jade, and on the northern horizon Trelise was a toy island furred with dark trees, tiny, manageable.

Fly heeled, accelerating like a chestnut sea-horse. They had raced in the summers, at East Neck; catboats when they were really young, then sharpies, and eventually in Friendship sloops. She had been a much-valued Friendship crew, until . . .

She lived at Trelise, now. She did not want to think about that any more.

But there was Sarah, smiling at her, as if she knew what she was thinking.

'What I said about East Neck. Going back. You don't have to.'

'Thank God.'

'You could, though. It's all over.'

Victoria waved a hand at Trelise. 'Would you, with all this?'

'I guess.'

Victoria turned for home, let the mainsheet out with a long, sweet jingle of ball-bearing blocks. In the heat and stillness of before-the-wind, Sarah took off her top and lay on the foredeck. 'That gardener,' she said. 'Organ.'

'Morgan. I told you. Hands off.'

'Not my problem,' said Sarah.

'What do you mean?'

'Yours.'

'*Sarah!*'

'He fancies you.'

'No way.' Not Morgan. Never. Not on her *birthday*. Not just because Sarah said so. This was prurient spinster talk.

Happy birthday, she told herself. From your husband, your sister, yourself.

The future was secure.

On the stairs, the creaking wooden stairs, a blanket of snow on roof and yard. Victoria, ten years old, aching nicely from tobogganing on Signal Hill, hungry. Smell of pot roast from downstairs. Sound of bottleneck against Daddy's glass. Daddy's voice. 'Victoria, where are you?'

'Stair twelve.'

'Good. First question. What's the capital city of Albania?'

'Tirana.'

'One step.'

Victoria took one step down, towards dinner. She was *starving*.

'Capital of Morocco?'

'Tangiers.'

'Rabat is the correct answer. Up one.'

Victoria wanted to cry. She stepped up a stair, away from dinner. Mommy said, 'My turn.' Before Daddy could object, she had done the capital of the USA, a state beginning with U, the name of the first man on the moon, the date of George Washington's birthday, and Victoria's favourite dessert. Victoria was far enough down to see the table, now. Her sisters were sitting quiet, waiting to start. The pot roast looked great.

'Capital of Outer Mongolia,' said Daddy.

Blank. Then, 'Ulan Bator.'

'Very good.' A little fuzzy, his voice; sarcastic. 'New island in the sea off Iceland.'

'I know it.' She didn't. Her stomach really hurt. 'Newfoundland.'

'Is wrong. Up one'

'No,' said her mother. 'Let her eat.'

'She's got to learn,' said Daddy.

'Not this way,' said Mommy. 'Why—'

'Shut up,' said Daddy.

The voices rose. Victoria stood there for a couple of breaths. She would not hear the next question anyway, not like this, with her hands over her ears. So she went upstairs.

Mommy brought her some food later. 'He means well,' she said.

Then why doesn't he do well? thought Victoria.

Letter from Dismas Stott, Head Gardener, Trelise, Summer 1868, to his brother Arthur, Gardener to His Grace the Duke of Shropshire, Borley Court, Salop.

Dear Brother,

Well well well, we have got a mess up here I am sorry to tell you Brother.

What we got is a Devil of a climate where you cannot get nothing to stop growing. In this I includes not just weeds — weeds is always with us and we know how to deal with them I think — but also the commoner subjects for bedding-out &c. viz pelargonium, rocket, begonia, musk &c. &c.

I arrived here with family all complete six weeks ago today. A shock as I think I told you at the time. This is a place which is three terraces joined by steps and the biggest rockeries you ever did see, plus some glass what was once used commercial but has now fallen into more gentlemanlike employments viz orchids, &c. Sounds very nice pleasant ornamental and manageable. But there are features that mitigate again such a happy state of affairs. Number one and foremost is the master and mistress. Master is I must say too interested in his plants by half, always poking his nose in where you and I know dear brother it has no right to be. The Mistress is a body of good instincts spoiled according to me by loneliness and distance from the centres of Fashin. She has many interesting schemes in the proper taste and has read widely in the correct authorities. But we are cursed as I said with a climate in which things will grow, and without a little dormance of course there are deaths. Just now she is all over me to create a grand bedding scheme representing the triumph of Moses at the Red Sea, Moses to be in blue Lobelia, the Israelites in yellow Antirrhinums and the Red Sea in Salvia, but the master expects me to grow on the plants in the open air not the Glass. Well a gardener is not a gardener unless he be left alone to plan and manage his garden as he sees fit, so as you will see this is a ground for discontent, and when I tell you that Miss Harriet who is five year old is permitted the run of the peach houses and plays merry hell with my other top fruit you will see that matters are far from ideal.

As if this were not enough the staff we have here is very moderate indeed. There is twelve under-gardeners and six boys, an ampoule sufficiency I hear you say, except that at the first suspicion of a wreck or a holiday — the same thing, in this barbarous quarter — they are away drinking, and do not come back for a week. One of them got hisself to France for ten days the other day, and laughed heartily when I give him a piece of my mind when he came back. And when I clipped his ear for his impertinence he laid me out on the ground. Which is not to be tolerated by a tradesman.

So it is no wonder as I see it that there have been twelve head gardeners here these past six years. No man of proper pride can be expected to put up with this sort of nonsense, no indeed. In the light of the above I expect it will come as no surprise to you dear brother that one of the purposes of this letter is to ask if you will keep your ear open for another situation with good pay, decent house, respectful staff, obliging master and coals found. I can wait, but not too long. An early reply will oblige.

    Your brother

    Dismas Stott

From an interview with Horace Pender, 89, conducted by Harriet Blakeney-Jones in 1910.

The estate was the only place there was to work, in them days. When Mr Joshua had been alive there had been the big improvements at first, the house to build, the walls, that damn garden to hack out of the Downs. Then later on there had been the greenhouses and those plants he used to grow, very active that was, and the crushing and milling of the drugs, whatever; though Trelise people did not much take to regular hours, so in the end the milling was not gone on with and the stuff used to go away raw on the train. But there had still been a sort of an atmosphere of hard labour, as you might say, and Johnny Dawson and Kenny and a couple of other chaps, they started up a bit of a boatyard and built some luggers and cutters and Kenny was a most artistic man with a gig, too, finest things you ever did see. Then steam changed all that, steam ships and steam tugs, straight into Falmouth so there was no pilots required and the railway had took the coasting trade. And there came the day when the yard shut and Mr Joshua was dead and nobody could think of anything much to do. We thought the bad old days was back, my dear. But we was reckoning without the Captain. It was the Captain saved our bacon, and no error. Bless him.

Sweet Success*

The arrival of James and Emily Blakeney-Jones at Trelise was marked by a sudden shattering decline in the island's fortunes. Buoyed up hitherto by

* *Trelise – Cornwall's Lovesome Thing p191*

147

the floods of money that gushed from the drug-mills of Joshua Jones, it was now as if – as in the mill at the bottom of the sea! – all that had been gold became salt. Among the Gothic towers of far-off Germany, organic chemists – wizards, once would we have called them – slaved over test-tube and retort to produce synthetic quinine and morphine, aspirin and digitalis. Joshua Jones must have sniffed this in the wind before his fatal trip to London. But the hand of God had snatched him away before his farsightedness could become action; and his successors, estimable folk though they were, had not his deep knowledge and restless imagination. The storm, when it came – first the disintegration of the Jones drug empire, then the stock-market collapse of the 1870s – swept all away. And the lords of Trelise became lords of Trelise alone. Something must be done.

When poverty once again smote the isle, some, ancient reprobates, took refuge in crime. A Horace Pender was apprehended landing a cargo of French brandy on Gimble Point, and evicted forthwith. Blood will tell; and in the case of James Blakeney-Jones it was the blood of the Joneses, rich, red, British. It will be remembered by the alert reader that Joshua Jones' attention had first been drawn to the possibilities of Trelise by the Narcissi *blowing sweetly in the interstices of the rocks. Now, the sweetness of the* Narcissi *was to spread itself beyond the silver beaches of our Fortunate Isle, to perfume the great, smoky world beyond.*

On the day after their arrival, Emily took herself on a solitary journey of exploration. It was only at the end, when her mind was fortified by a sense of her possessions, that she was able to bring herself to walk by the granite house abutting the garden wall, where . . . *that woman* . . . lived.

But when she peered through the iron gate, the garden was overgrown, the windows blank-eyed with shutters. Warm blood surged in Emily. 'She is gone!' she cried.

'Who's gone?'

'Alice. That woman. Jenkins.'

'Only for a time. She's on her travels.'

Emily's blood cooled. 'Can a tenant do that?'

'Long as she pays her rent. Brave woman, if you ask me. Blind as a bat, off goodness knows where—'

'James, you understand *nothing*,' said Emily, and cast herself into her programme of improvements with an all-excluding energy.

This programme she maintained until a November morning, at breakfast. She suddenly exclaimed, 'Lawk, how charming!' Gathering up the Army and Navy Stores catalogue she tripped round the table to her husband, who was gazing at his letters with the set expression that had lately accompanied most Trelise breakfasts. 'Here. The Spode jardinieres. Are they not sweetly pretty, dearest? I shall have a dozen, and you may build me a conservatory, and—'

'You will not, and I cannot,' said James, dully.

Emily stopped. 'But dearest,' she said, something steely entering her voice. 'I *must*—'

'Then you shall pay for them yourself.'

Emily burst into a sudden shower of tears. 'Mr Blakeney-Jones, you are pleased to be cruel.'

'No money,' said James, waving a handful of letters under her nose. 'This is not a paying sort of place, my dear. I'm not the man to make a garden pay. Farming's about the size of it, for me. Look.' He bashed the paper with the back of his fingers. 'New roof for the Penders. Dry rot in the Watch. Twenty yard of causeway with a hole underneath, conger the size of your leg living there—'

'Mr Blakeney-Jones, you are pleased to be indelicate,' said Emily. 'I demand you do your duty as a man and a husband, that your family may not starve.'

'Then I recommend we eat fish,' said James, with something of the volcano in his voice. 'Also potatoes and vegetables. Sack your damn parson. And cease ordering rubbish from the Army and Navy God-damned bloodsucking Stores.'

James walked into the air, waiting for the beating of his heart to slow. He did not like being short with Emily, silly though she could be. But he loved Trelise, and was horrified by the idea of losing it. He walked quickly to the farm. The farm he understood.

The buildings murmured with the cluck of chickens and the stamp and low of milking. 'Pig,' said a small voice from the back of a low line of roofs. 'Pig, pig, pig, pig, pig, pig.' James rounded the corner, and saw his daughter, Harriet. She was dressed in a miniature fisherman's jersey and a blue serge skirt, no hat. That was because she had just fed her hat to Graham, the black boar who was her particular friend.

'Christ!' roared James, erupting. 'You feed your *clothes* to the pigs? Damn and blast you, girl, will you go naked into the spunging-house because the pigs have ate your raiment?'

Harriet had leaped to attention. She was pale and long-faced, not a pretty child, but her eyes were a brilliant sea-blue, and now sparkled halfway between tears and defiance. James' heart, which was a kind one, began to fail him. 'Only . . . we must mind our money, Hattie.'

'Yes, papa. Only he does like it so.'

'All very well for a pig.'

'Yes, papa.' Pause. 'Sometimes I feel he is very much a person.'

'People don't eat hats.'

'I have heard you promise to do so.' Her face was solemn, as always.

'Ah.' As so often with Harriet, James found himself stumped. He dimly perceived that she was a strange little thing; a contented inhabitant of the small but complicated universe that was her Trelise, but awkward beyond it. 'We shan't tell Mama,' he said.

'Thank you,' she said. '*Dear* papa.' But she still did not smile.

Emily found out, of course. 'Her hat,' she said. 'A perfectly good sixpenny straw.'

'The pig stole it,' said James. He was about to add a shrewd riposte about jardinieres; but happily at this point Mr Bishop came in.

Mr Bishop was a lawyer, from St Austell, but with metropolitan airs, based on a few visits paid to London by means of the railway. These extended to a taste for Aesthetic scarves, and a potent fog of patchouli round his locks, which he wore flowing. The reason he was dining at Trelise was to negotiate the extension of certain bills that would cause great embarrassment when they fell due: and as far as Mr Bishop could see, would continue to do so, until a great but inevitable smash. In the most supreme taste house and garden might be. But the farm was no better than Cornish, and small at that. Miss Harriet would be ten years before she could marry money, and even then (Bishop fancied himself a judge of women) showed signs of deficiency in both looks and parts.

With these melancholy thoughts, he sat down and began a stilted conversation. The State Room door opened, and a nurserymaid appeared. 'Miss Harriet,' she said.

'Goodness,' cried Emily, feigning surprise. Not understanding Mr Bishop's purely executive role in the matter of the bills, Emily imagined that a display of sweetness might soften him. Harriet came in, starched to the last degree, eyes firmly on the bouquet of flowers in her red-scrubbed hand. 'Curtsey to Mr Bishop,' snapped Emily.

'What charming flowers,' said Mr Bishop.

Disliking the smell of Bishop, Harriet improvised a change of plan. 'They're for Papa,' she said. She marched on her short legs to her father, stood on tiptoe, and thrust the flowers into his hand.

They were narcissi, many-headed, orange-cupped, yellow-petalled, radiating an intense perfume. 'From the garden?' said Mr Bishop.

'Wild, silly,' said Harriet, gazing fixedly at his knees.

'Goodness,' said Mr Bishop, spotting a chance for metropolitan reminiscence. 'In London, such flowers at this time of year would cost a mort of money.' He took the bunch from James. 'A mort,' he said. *'Charming.'*

Mr Bishop passed the day on the estate, seeing many places in need of outlay, and few promising profit. Dinner, at which important negotiations were supposed to be undertaken, passed in brittle pleasantries between Emily and Bishop, while they both waited for James to speak. But James remained mute, eating steadily, frowning at his thoughts. Next morning, when Bishop took his leave, James was not to be found.

He was in fact with Gowrie, his head gardener of the moment. 'I want you to find every daffodil and narcissus on the island,' he said. 'Pick 'em. Mark the plants, label 'em. When they die back I want you to dig up the bulbs, and line them out in the poppy fields on Middle Downs.'

'I am a gardener, not a farmer,' said Gowrie, sniffing.

'Do as you're bloody well told,' said James.

That day, James sent a single box of the flowers Gowrie had picked to Alfred Biggs at Covent Garden, overnight on the Truro train. He received an envelope by return from Biggs. Inside was a pound note, and Biggs' visiting card, with 'Send more' scrawled on the back. A pound. For one box. Unheard of.

The bulbs were lifted and replanted by variety, and left to multiply. The pound notes multiplied, too. The bills were paid, and Mr Bishop came no more.

One Sunday in the third year of her occupancy, Emily had sent Harriet to pick buttonholes for the gentlemen to wear to church. Harriet was dawdling. It was ten o'clock, five minutes short of the time appointed to start the mile walk to the church above Old Hull. Mr Davies the parson would be hurt if they were late. The governess was nowhere to be seen. So Emily herself had run out of the house, sweating in black Barathea.

By Poseidon, she heard female voices. She opened her mouth to emit her broken-glass-edged call.

Then she closed it again.

There were two voices. One of them was Harriet's. The other was older, with a common sort of burr to it. As she recognised it, her stomach clenched like a fist in its tight vase of whalebone. The voice belonged to Alice, the blind woman who lived over the garden wall; who had been Joshua's . . . she could not bring herself to use the word. That filthy woman, with her black ribbon. She was back.

She forgot about church. She set herself to listen.

'So tell me what you see,' said Alice.

'It's time for church,' whined Harriet. 'Mama will be so vexed.'

'Nothing new about that,' said Alice. 'What have we got here, my love?'

'There is a bed of red flowers,' said Harriet. 'Beyond it is the Alpine Rockery, which is a pile of limestone that Mama says is very delightful, in an approximation to the shape of Mont Blanc. It is planted with saxifrages, gentians, other Alpine things. Most of them are dead, by the look of it.'

'Poor things,' said Alice. 'They're a long way from the Alps.'

'Beyond the mountain, a sweet Gothic pavilion with green paint and the dearest stained-glass windows after Mr Burne-Jones.'

'Sweet,' said Alice, in a voice in which Emily seemed to hear sarcasm.

Emily found herself marching forward, with a roaring in her ears that she assumed was her blood boiling. 'Harriet!' she screamed. 'What do you think you are doing, pray?' Harriet's face was plain and white and frightened. 'Take that, madam!' She dealt the little girl a box on the ear that set her wailing like a vixen. 'And as for you,' she said, turning on Alice, 'I suggest you keep your odious ideas to yourself.'

Alice curtseyed. She was more than forty now, but her face was fresh as a daisy below the black ribbon. It made Emily acutely conscious of her own waxy pallor, and the white-headed spot at the corner of her mouth. 'I beg your pardon, ma'm,' she said. 'I meant no offence.'

'Then watch your tongue,' snapped Emily. 'You know nothing of the fashion, so . . . just hold your tongue.'

'All right,' said Alice. 'But it's not Miss Harriet's fault.'

Emily grasped the sobbing Harriet by the wrist and dragged her out of the garden.

At dinner, she snapped at the parson. That night, after the maid had brushed her thin brown hair one hundred strokes, she lay rigid next to James and broached her plan.

'The woman Alice is back,' she said.

James was reading *Principal Attributes of the Genus Narcissus*. His pale, biddable face had hardened and darkened. An earring would have turned him into a very convincing pirate – not that he would have dreamed of an earring; appearances to the contrary, James was the soul of convention. 'What?' he said, testily. Straight on, was James' motto. He hated diversions.

'Alice Jenkins. Mr Davies and I are of one mind. She must be got rid of.'

'Can't be done,' said James, turning the page. He liked and respected Alice. Furthermore he loathed the parson, who resembled a sanctified weasel.

'Put the lawyers onto it. Bishop. He'd do it.'

'Hell and damnation.' James shut the *Genus Narcissus* with a slam. 'May I remind you that lawyers cost a fortune, and that when Joshua did something he made quite sure it was done so it could never be undone, and that poor Alice Jenkins is blind and does no one any harm—'

'Your own daughter, sir,' said Emily.

'Wha?'

'Alice Jenkins has been poisoning Harriet's mind.'

153

'Alice Jenkins?'

'Are you not listening to a single word? I heard her force the poor child to describe the garden to her. And when she did so, Miss Jenkins construed Harriet's poor innocent lispings in the most uncomplimentary terms. All our good nature to her, and the first thing she does when she comes back from her gallivantings is to bite the hand that feeds her. James, that woman is a viper in our bosom.'

James had found only one feature of interest in this speech. 'Doesn't like the garden, hey?' he said. 'In particular what?'

Emily sniffed. 'If you must know, she was dismissive of the New Pavilion, and ignorantly scornful of the Alps. And the bedding. She said the plants on the Alps were—'

'Dead,' said James. 'Got a point, what? Can't keep alpines alive here, not limestone ones, and you don't get the frost, which they get in nature, of course. The carpet bedding, well, pretty ghastly, what? Tell you once told you a thousand times. But do you listen?'

'James,' said Emily, icy. 'I should like a husband who takes my side, not the side of a prostitute who seeks to corrupt my child.'

James stared at her with eyes suddenly horrified. 'Good Lord,' he said. 'I thought you were talking about *gardens*.' He put out his arms and gathered her to him. Under the voluminous folds of her night-dress, her body was stick-like and unyielding. 'Let me *go*,' she said, struggling.

'Tell you something,' said James. 'Something I've found out. Case you haven't noticed. If you live here, you do things the way things work here. What?'

Emily pulled away. 'Are you defying me?'

'Not me,' said James. Like walking into a chaff cutter, Emily in one of her moods. 'Rather not. Perish the thought.' Agree with everything she said. She'd come round.

Soon he began to snore.

Emily eyed her husband with scorn. It was as Mr Davies so often said. James had been seduced, the weak-minded fool.

Well, that was no reason for her to be seduced too.

*   *   *

Next day, Davies the parson caught Emily on the Truro Road, the track behind the beach. 'My dear Mrs Blakeney-Jones,' he said. She gave him the wan smile of a patient sufferer. 'You are troubled.'

She stared out to sea, her eyes misty with rage.

'In marriage, a Christian resignation,' said Davies, eying her beadily. 'In life, true friends. Among whom one has the honour to . . .' He let his voice trail away.

She looked at him. She saw a thin man, with a questing nose and a pursed mouth in which she mistook conniving for sympathy. 'He is a brute,' she said. 'He takes the part of . . . oh, my poor, poor daughter!'

Davies had no idea what she was talking about, but he had his own plans for Harriet. Delicately, expertly, he probed the wound. 'Poor, dear lady,' he said. 'And more important, oh! such influences on a tender girl. Do you never think – pray pardon the impertinence of my suggestion – that a broader appreciation of life might be indicated?'

Emily tried to look deep. So exquisite was Davies' tact that it was sometimes difficult to work out what he was actually saying.

'Dear lady,' said Davies. 'Living here, even with the best of governesses, the mind of an impressionable girl cannot be alerted to the full range of possibilities offered by Learning. My cousin Amy runs at a most convenient remove from London an establishment for young ladies that without exposing its pupils to the dangers of the world introduces them to its riches – in short, she runs a boarding school in Cheam.'

'Really?' said Emily, jerking her nose at the sky. 'Well, Mr Davies, I am grateful for your concern, and bid you good day.' Davies, who knew her well, went about his business imbued with the holy expectation of a Galilean fisherman who has cast his bait into a stewpond.

It was ten days later. Lessons were over. James was in from the farm. There was an hour to go before nursery tea. Emily was jabbing away at her work.

Harriet was missing. From far away, there floated the sound of children's voices raised in song. The sound grew louder. It was not a familiar song: more a chant, really, partaking of the barbarous. James and Emily moved to the edge of the terrace.

Below, winding up from the South Quay, was a small procession. There were perhaps a dozen children in a loose swarm, heading through the gate and starting on the serpentining of the drive. They seemed to be dancing, in time to what they were singing. In the middle was Harriet.

'What *can* she be wearing?' said Emily.

The small figure was dressed in dark blue jersey and skirt, with a knitted red beret on its head and small sea-boots on its feet. Round its neck was something that looked like a grey scarf; a heavy grey scarf, by the way she was stumping up the drive.

The song floated through the yuccas on the rockery.

Is it a teal?

NO!

Is it a wheel?

NO!

How does it feel?

SLIMY!

It's a longer, stronger, wronger, Conger

EEL!

'Well I'll be blowed,' said James, and ran down to meet the procession. The scarf was not a scarf, but a conger, a big one, comatose, wrapped round his daughter's neck.

The procession arrived on the terrace. James was laughing heartily, the children jumping around him. The conger had been in the rocks at Plum Orchard. Harriet and Jimmy Hicks had got it with a hook and dragged it ashore, tall as them it was, look, it was still a bit alive.

In the grit of the terrace, the conger writhed weakly and snapped its razor teeth at a chairleg. 'Splendid,' said James. Then, remembering, he said, 'But get it off the terrace before your mother sees it, what?'

Too late.

There was a sound by his ear, like (as he put it later, talking to Danes the farm manager) a rushing mighty wind. Emily cleared the terrace in eight seconds flat. An ominous silence fell, and remained.

Harriet was scrubbed, and allowed downstairs. She sat with her father on the long bench that ran under the drawing-room window, playing chess. It was not a very advanced game; it was merely that James and Harriet took pleasure in each other's company.

'Oh, papa,' said Harriet, gazing out of the window at the terrace and Great Rocks fading into the rain. 'This is so lovely, and that was such a sweet eel. I wish we could be like this for ever.'

'We will be,' said James. 'Why ever not?'

She smiled – such a trusting smile, a smug, happy-in-its-lot, *provincial* smile that Emily thought she would be sick. Eels, forsooth. Vulgar children. Happy fathers. Fathers who were undutiful to mothers.

So next week, there Harriet was on the quay, standing beside her trunk with her father – Emily had not come from the house, being busy with her catalogues. Harriet was crying. James was very red, not far from crying himself. 'Well, old girl,' he said.

She held very tight to his hand. 'Must I go?' she said.

'Your mama . . . that is to say, yes,' said James firmly.

'But you must hurry back,' said another voice. They both looked round, and saw Alice, with her black ribbon and her bamboo. 'Real life here,' she said. 'Not anywhere else.'

'Witch!' said Harriet, delighted to have found something on which she could vent her despair. 'Go away!'

Alice smiled. Harriet climbed into the launch with Mr Davies, who was accompanying her to Cheam. James watched her to invisibility. Then he turned heavily back towards the house.

'I'm sorry she's gone,' said Alice.

He made an affirmative sound. He could not speak.

'She'll be back,' she said. 'Pop and have a cup of tea, why not?'

James looked at her, thinking. Then he said, 'That would be very pleasant. Very pleasant indeed.' He plodded back to the empty house.

Chapter Twelve

The arrival of *Fly* gave Victoria wings. She began to neglect the library. The early May weather was beautiful, and every tide she was down at the quay. She would row out to the mooring, haul up some sails, slide into Hull Bay or out beyond the Mare, to fish, or sing, or just be, feeling the lovely cut of the sails in the breeze, weightless.

Sometimes she found a crew; a house guest, or someone from the holiday cottages. But then she had to make conversation, which spoiled the weightlessness. She asked Mary Morgan if she sailed. 'Can't stand it,' she said. 'Try Daisy.'

Victoria thought that Guy would probably freak about sailing with the staff, so she decided not to tell him, and to plead Americanness if he found out. It turned out that Daisy had come to Trelise in the first place on her way back from a Fastnet, and got stuck. So they started making plans about Falmouth Week, and practising when they felt like it.

But mostly Victoria sailed alone.

At low water Old Hull was dry, except for the pool where the moorings were laid. An hour into the tide, the sand was covered. Two hours in, the main stream was moving clockwise round the bay, except for an eddy that came off Bob Rock south of the quay, hit the rock spine that made the quay's foundation, and shot out to sea. The Bob Rock stream met the main stream fifty yards off the end of the quay, heading in the opposite direction. Where they brushed, the water writhed and spun, and made the Mixer.

The ferries and tripper boats used the whirlpool to take them on and off the quay. Victoria watched them for a while, then tried it herself in a punt. One oarstroke from the quay, and you were into it; the world spun half a revolution, and you were almost among the moorings. It was a strange and wonderful sensation, as if you were the still point, and the world was moving to oblige you.

One day, she met Revel on the quay as she was untying the punt. The Mixer was running, making a long, snoring gurgle. He said, 'Getting the hang of it, then?'

'Just about.'

'Ever been right in?'

'How do you mean?'

He looked at his watch. 'Got half an hour?' he said.

Actually, she had been planning to go sailing. But she liked Revel. He seemed to run on his own time, immune to clocks. He knew more about Trelise than anyone else she had met, and communicated very little of it. 'Sure,' she said.

'Get in the punt. I'll row.'

They pushed off. Revel took the one stroke that put you into the Mixer's orbit. The world began to turn. Revel took another stroke. 'Watch,' he said.

The sound of the Mixer grew suddenly louder. Victoria found herself gripping the punt's sides. The boat lurched violently. The nose was pointing downhill, into a funnel of water. 'Jesus!' she said. They spun dizzily, accelerating. Then suddenly the world went flat.

'Here we go,' said Revel.

The sea was calm. The beach was going by. They were moving briskly, not north with the main flow of the tide, but south, smooth, on some sort of counter-current. Revel pulled in his oars and began to roll a cigarette. 'What's happening?' said Victoria.

''Ang on,' he said.

The beaches had gone now. The land was rising towards Tobaccoman's Point, low cliffs planted with the trees that sheltered the fields inland. The point stuck out ahead, barring the road to the open sea.

Suddenly the world moved again. Victoria was looking at a rocky bay with a shingle beach, backed by steep but not unclimbable cliffs, thirty feet high. The current swept the punt towards the beach. There were the shadows of rocks in the pale green bay.

'They call it the Glory Hole,' said Revel. 'Anything that falls into the Mixer, you can look for it here. Weird, innit?' He gave a casual tug of the oars. The punt came out of the cove, into the main flow of the tide. Ten minutes' rowing brought them back to the quay.

'So there you are,' said Revel, and winked. It was a significant wink. Victoria had no idea what it meant. She smiled, at something of a loss. Revel left. It was too late to go sailing. She tied up the punt. As she wheeled her bicycle past the estate office, Guy came running out of the door. 'Hi,' she said. 'I've—'

'What the *fuck* did you think you were doing?'

She was taken aback. 'Rowing. With Revel. Is that a problem?'

His face was the colour of ivory, and the whites showed all the way round his eyes. 'Never do it again,' he said. 'Never.'

'What did I do?'

'Oh, Victoria,' he said, and took her hands.

'Are you okay?'

'Of course.' The colour was coming back into his cheeks. 'Sorry. I was thinking . . . never mind. Someone got drowned. Long time ago. That's all.'

'Who?'

'Doesn't matter. I'm sorry. See you later.'

'Sure.' She started to walk back towards the Priory. Someone fell into step. Morgan. Sensible Morgan. She said, 'What happened in the Mixer and the Glory Hole?'

'What sort of what?'

'A disaster. A drowning.'

Morgan shrugged. 'Search me,' he said. 'But I wouldn't go swimming there myself. How far have you got with the project?' They walked on. He suggested some books, and promised her a planting list for Araby.

It was nice to have someone like Morgan to talk to; a bright guy, doing his job.

Morgan was a comfort.

Revel – A Day in the Life: Summer*
Alarm, five o'clock. Winds light and variable, bloody hot. Tea, strong, three sugars. Breakfast on balcony, in sun. Distant sound

---

* *Country Times* magazine, feature

of head gardener's tractor. Hurry down to rake paths. By ten-thirty, three miles of paths are shining patterns of linked clam shells. Pick up coach party from garden entrance. Has he ever worked in the Lost Gardens of Heligan? Revel has never been to Heligan. He has been off Trelise three times in the past five years. He tramps on at the head of the crocodile, mucking up his paths, but raking paths is like that. These are magazine readers, not gardeners. He shows them Before (brambles, bracken) and After (South African daisies, *Geranium maderense* luminous purple). Next tour at twelve. Dinner in the shade. Barrow to the kitchen garden. Cut rocket and radiccio for the Priory and iceberg lettuce for chef at the Castle. Another sowing of rocket and coriander. Hoe between rows, slowly, in case someone wants something done. Four sharp, knock off. Haul pots. Nice-looking girl topless on Pumphouse beach. Three lobsters from the Foals. Sell them at back door of Castle. Round to front door of Castle. Lot of visitors. Gig crew showing off. Two pints of Guinness. Back home to finish mermaid carving.

Same every summer, more or less.

Harriet's career at Cheam did not fulfil her mother's hopes. She learned nothing except how to make dear female friends, and returned to Trelise in the holidays with an eagerness that delighted her father but was the despair of her mother.

She secured her ticket-of-leave (as dear Papa put it) from Cheam in the year she was seventeen, and was dragged reluctantly to Eaton Square, where her mamma had set up a headquarters from which to wage a campaign among the balls and teas of the Season. She had grown tall, with her mother's long, pale face and wispy blondeness, and her father's lankiness of frame. She was an expert clam-digger, a good helmswoman, and an authority on the garden. At balls, it was only through the most devious conspiracies that her mother could induce any young man to dance with her. Harriet despised balls. She liked to *do things* with female friends. Even Emily had to admit that as a début, it was a non-starter.

One night in a house off Belgrave Square, Emily looked over her fan at the group of future spinsters that included her daughter, and came to a decision. It was useless to try to bring Harriet to Society. Henceforth, Society must be brought to Harriet.

To Harriet's delight, the Blakeney-Joneses therefore left London in early June, to spend the summer at Trelise.

Thanks to James, prosperity had been re-established. He spent much of his time on the farm, scheming innovations in cut flowers, bulbs and early potatoes. Further, a new gardener had arrived, Arthur Robbins by name, a well-set-up fellow of twenty-odd, who had served an apprenticeship at Tresco Abbey, and came with excellent references from Mr Dorrien Smith, Lord Proprietor of Scilly. He had intelligent blue eyes under an intellectual brow. Other gardeners had refused to accept James' advice. Robbins had the tact to appear to consider the opinions of all; and as a result, earned the trust of all, and was left to his own devices more entirely than the most obstreperous of his predecessors.

Though a personable young man on an island with a shortage of personable young men, he seemed perfectly happy to keep himself to himself, devoting his leisure moments to study in the lodgings he had taken in Castle Row. He came to prominence only after the events of Miss Harriet's birthday.

This fell on the 12th September. Traditionally, the weather was benign – indeed, there had come into being an island saying to the effect that as long as a regatta, cricket match or picnic took place 'before Miss Harriet's nameday', it would be untroubled by rain or gale. But her seventeenth birthday dawned grey and wet, with dirty squall-lines driving in from the southwest. James let it be known that the scheduled picnics were to be postponed, and retired to his office.

Among the house party were Harriet's dear cousins Georgina and Barbara Mentmore – women a couple of years older than her, sisters, dark of hair and firm of jaw. Their Naval father George had died before he had put up his Admiral's flag, and they were home; 'home' in their parlance meaning Trelise, and in particular the house behind Old Hull previously occupied by the Earl of Kernow's steward, which James had made over to their penniless mother, Tabitha. George (she hated to be called Georgina) was a passionate rigger and builder of sailing boats, both full-sized and miniature, and Babs was an expert water-colourist and naturalist. Their mother, now a gimlet-eyed seventy, presided over a drawing room whose curtains were of cheapest sailcloth, painted with garden scenes by Babs, and whose mats were of rope, dyed and knotted in plat sinnet by George. And so it continued throughout the house, and their lives.

For Harriet, the lovely thing about George and Babs was that with them you did not have to consider what was thought of you; you simply got on with it. With the people Mamma was always throwing at her, she felt so *conscious*. George and Babs were easy, everyday girls, awfully interested in Trelise. Like her.

Actually, though, Algernon Phipps was interesting too. Algy was tall and languid, with a most wonderful moustache, an incessant smoker of the new 'cigarettes'.

So on the afternoon of Harriet's birthday, she and the Mentmore girls were sitting on the bench that ran along the drawing-room windows of the Priory, watching the raindrops trickle down the plate-glass windows, and the restless heave of the seas towards the Mare. Tarquin, Harriet's hunt-terrier, lay curled up on a cushion. Harriet was pining faintly for Algy, who was in the billiard room with the other boys. Suddenly Georgina said, 'What's that?'

Into the grey square of the window had drifted something new; something dark and low, round which white water roiled with a sullen churning. George was up, training the heavy brass telescope that stood on a tripod by the terrace door. She hauled the door open. It let in a blast of wind and a burst of rain. She crouched over the eyepiece. 'A ship,' she said. 'By the powers, it's a ship!'

'*Hoorah!*' cried Harriet, beating her hands together. A ship was an event, a *something*, a birthday present—

She rushed to the telescope in a flurry of skirts, put her eye to the eyepiece.

It was an exceedingly powerful telescope. The ship was too big for the disc of the objective. She saw only half of it, the after half.

She saw a black iron hull, listing towards her. The deck was a pale slope of planking, festooned with a web of masts and yards and rigging, a tight-looking web, cranked taut, apparently, by the paddles in their great boxes to port and starboard. The paddles were not turning.

Horror.

In that taut web that covered the deck she saw little creatures caught like flies. But they were not flies. They were women, shawls flapping in the screaming wind, clutching children to them. There were men, too, working at a boat chocked in the middle of the web. The boat was not moving.

The objective of the telescope filled suddenly with a hill of grey water, toothed with foam. When it passed, the ship's stern was moving out of the picture, and when Harriet tried to follow it she moved the tube too far, so it focused not on the ship but on black teeth in grey gums of water, and a smooth black column that rose to a tip that winked a brief chip of light, then darkened. The Mare.

The circle blurred with her tears. She moved away from the eyepiece.

'I say,' said a man's voice. 'Beastly draught, what?' Algy strode forward and slammed the door. Tarquin the terrier started to bark.

'There's a ship,' said Harriet. 'What are we going to *do*?'

Algy bent to the telescope, shrugged. 'Not much we can,' he said. He took her arm.

'You're so *silly!*' she screamed, tearing her arm away. Then she was outside, running, and she knew that George and Babs were with her, and that Tarquin was galloping along behind.

A tree was down across the Abbey road – a big tree, one of Joshua's earliest eucalyptuses. They dragged their skirts over it, and went on between the wind-thrashed pines onto the Truro Road. The bays east of the rain-grey beach were full of sheltering gulls. There was nobody on the harbour. Slate-grey squalls raced across the bay. The tide was halfway in, the Mixer churning.

'Those poor, *poor* people,' cried Harriet, not because it was new information, but as a rallying call for herself and George and Babs.

'We'll take the *Fan*,' said George, assuming control.

The *Fan* was a heavy black cutter, much used for picnics – she should indeed have been being used today. Tarquin jumped into the dinghy after them. They rowed out to the mooring, hauled up the mainsail. ('Two reefs,' said Harriet. 'Three,' said George, and three it was.)

In five minutes the sails were up and roaring, Tarquin barking on the bottom boards. George took the tiller. 'Cast off,' she said.

Babs, a navy-blue tempest of skirts on the little foredeck, let go the loop of the mooring pennant from the samson post. Harriet hauled in the staysail sheet. The deck tilted underfoot, and Babs scrambled aft, and the quay was slipping by. George caught the outer spin of the Mixer, and let it hurl them out of the harbour. 'Not long in this breeze,' she said.

Harriet always felt so safe with the Mentmores. Tarquin stood with his back paws on the thwart, his front paws on the foredeck, wrinkling his nose at the wind. Those poor women and children. Well, help was at hand.

They were past the silver beach. The Priory woods loomed above the Glory Hole. There was a lift to the sea now, an echo of the swell beyond the point. The uneasiness of the water found an echo in Harriet. When she looked at Babs and George she saw them propped against the coamings, eyes narrowed, tanned jaws outthrust, not minding.

Tobaccoman's Point was abeam. Beyond it, a wave hit a rock, blew up into a vast white elm that darkened as it came down the wind at them, and arrived cold enough to take their breath.

Then they were out of the shelter of the land.

The wind hit them like a runaway waggon. *Fan's* sails were reefed down as far as they would go, but still the blast laid her over until green water poured in over her downhill side. At the same time a wave arrived, a long grey roller that toppled and broke and came thundering down on them. Harriet heard a voice screaming with terror, and knew it was hers.

The crest smote *Fan* like an avalanche. The air was full of water, and the deck had gone away again, and there was water above and below, cold and solid, and a feeling that something had gone terribly wrong.

Harriet knew she should have been thinking about the poor people on the liner, but all she could think about was here, and now, and *Fan* lying on her side, filling, sinking. My goodness, what fools we are. What *absolute* fools.

Fan came upright. The water inside her was waist deep. Harriet and Babs bailed furiously. Then Harriet said, 'Where's Tarquin?'

There was no sign of the dog.

'Tarquin!' she shrieked, over the roar of the sea and the wail of the wind.

'There,' said Babs, in a strange, quiet voice.

And there was poor Tarquin, downwind, downtide, to the east, on the upslope of a monstrous wave. He had his chin up and his ears pricked, and he was swimming, eagerly, loyally.

'Good dog!' cried Harriet. 'Good *dog*!' And for a moment everything was all right again.

Then the next wave was upon them, breaking, and Harriet was sobbing over her bucket, trying to call Tarquin at the same time, knowing that somewhere out there was a liner with people on it, drowning, but that she was here, in a little boat that might be sinking and that her dog was overboard and that the world was too big for her, too awful, too, *too* awful.

The wave passed. She looked for Tarquin's plucky little head. But Tarquin's head had gone.

'Where is he?' she said.

'Who?' George was shoving the tiller, getting *Fan* head-to-sea, chewing her lips, narrow-eyed.

'Tarquin.'

'Goner,' said George. 'Bad luck, Hatty.'

The next wave went under. Through a stinging veil of spray and tears, Harriet looked for the little head on the grey upslope.

There was no head. Like water poured out, sand between the fingers. Gone.

'Bail,' said George.

And Harriet noticed that they were back in the shelter of Tobaccoman's.

Everything that had happened had happened in the first fringes of the tide. *Fan* had stuck her nose the merest cable beyond the shelter of Tobaccoman's. The merest fraction. Outside the protection of Trelise, they were useless.

As they wallowed into the full shelter of the island, the two gigs pulled past them, heading out, the old red *Pasha* and the new black *Falcon*, the men grim-faced, bent-backed. One man raised a hand in greeting: Robbins, the gardener.

Worse than useless.

Algy was on the quay in a silly small-peaked cap. 'Where's Tarquin?' he said.

Harriet felt George's arm go round her shoulders. It was a kind, strong arm. A Trelise arm. The women walked away, stiff-backed, the blue serge of their skirts clinging wetly to their legs. The islanders would not meet their eyes. They had risked life when enough life was being lost already.

Oh, Tarquin.

Algy made it his business to go round the island finding out exactly what had happened. At the end of eighteen hours, among the silver domes of the breakfast dishes in the dining room, he told his story. He told it in a slack-jawed, Algified sort of way. But Harriet filtered it with her own mind, until she had a version that sounded like the truth.

As the *Fan* had been driven back, the *Falcon* and the *Pasha* had pulled steadily on across the wind, four oars on the windward side, five to leeward, the coxswains putting the boats' noses up to meet the seas. They had moved out through the race off Tobaccoman's, and into the long trail of flatter water behind the Mare. Here the coxswains had found the eddy made by the obstruction of the tide.

Up the seam they slipped, until their noses were in the white backwash of the Mare, the lighthouse a dizzy black column against the sky. 'Give her ten!' roared the coxswain of the *Pasha*. The oars bit, and the hulls drove, and the gigs were out, neck and neck in the full fetch of wind and sea and tide.

Then began the hard scrabble. Yard by yard they clawed upwind. Bow on the *Pasha* caught a crab, and the oar-loom smashed one of his ribs. Robbins scrambled forward from three, and took the oar, and rowed on. Dogged and steady, Robbins, not a seaman bred to the sea, but once he knew what needed doing you could not stop him doing it.

The gigs inched up on the great ship jammed slantwise in the Foals. There were people huddled in the lee of the deck-houses, soaked, freezing, too cold even to wail. Ridges of water sluiced down her deck with a lolloping grace. Where they smacked a paddle-box or a stanchion, they showed a white-toothed snarl of energy that bent iron and tore away plating. On a seventh wave the hull shifted uneasily, with a grinding of rock spikes in metal bowels.

The coxswain of the *Pasha* pointed and roared. Robbins and John Pender scrambled into the gig's bow. The crew gave a long pull and a strong pull. On the next wave, the bow rode up over the packet-boat's deck. The crew backed water, hard. The gig dropped astern. And as the trough came by, there was the gig in deep water, and Robbins and John Pender standing on the deck.

'She's ready to go,' said Pender.

The passengers behind the deck-house set up a muted wail. The crew were there too, exhausted. A bigger wave. Robbins clamped his hands on to one of the cables stretched across the deck. An icy flood covered him. The wave receded. He felt a downward shifting of the hull, an unwinding of the spring of life. 'Officers!' he yelled.

A man lurched down the deck. 'Third mate.'

'What's the matter with you? Why didn't you launch the boats?'

'Jammed,' said the mate.

'Give me an axe,' said Robbins.

The man led him down a hatch into a carpenter's shop half full of water. Robbins found two axes. They went back on deck.

The launch was lashed on chocks between the two paddle-cases, mired in a web of fallen rigging. Robbins gave John Pender an axe, and yelled in his ear.

Pender moved round the tangle, hacking. Lengths of cordage began to come free. Robbins went over to the passengers. He said, 'You must get in that boat.'

They looked at him as if he was talking Chinese. The mate said, 'You'll never shift it.'

'Never you fret,' said Robbins. 'Now, then, my dears.' And one by one, between waves, he led the twenty-three survivors in the lee of the deck-house the sixty sodden feet to the launch.

A wave licked down the deck and burst against the launch's bow. The boat did not move. 'She's going!' cried the mate, in a high, panicky voice.

'Never,' said Robbins soothingly, and put his cupped hands to his mouth, and roared something at the *Pasha*, a scarlet peascod of men on a black

169

upslope. Another wave thundered in. This time the ship's hull settled perceptibly, bringing the launch's bottom below the level of the sea.

Then things moved with bewildering speed. The *Pasha* glided in on the next trough, hove a line, which Pender made fast in the launch's bow. Robbins was racing round the gunwales with the axe, hacking at the last lashings. A wave was coming, a big one, its crest hanging over the launch. And in the trough preceding the wave, the ship's hull, deprived of support, gave up the ghost. With a dreadful metallic creaking, bow and stern broke one from the other, and began to slide their separate ways.

The people in the boat raised a wail of terror. The crest hung over them, teetered and fell. The steel hull was dragging them down.

A last flash of the axe. The last lashing parted. The ship slid away into the deep. The launch floated free, rose cork-like, bobbed on the slope of the wave. The line from the gig tightened. The *Pasha*'s oarsmen held her against the sea while she yawed out of the surge and the backwash, and into the swing of the swell.

So (said Algy, lighting another of his cigarettes) Robbins came home.

In the afternoon, the black overcast split into lakes of blue. The gigs went to and fro, towing wreckage and corpses. All along the south and west coasts of Trelise bodies came ashore, broken things, floating, jammed in rock crevices, the clothes shredded off them. They were laid out in boxes knocked up by Kenny: sixty-seven in all, varnished wood for the grownups, white paint for the children, in the Mission Hall. The relatives of the dead came, from Belgium, many of them; the ship had been bound for Blankenberge. The Castle and the village and the spare rooms at the Priory were full of slab-faced people, weeping.

Harriet knew she should have done more. Much, much more.

Testimony of Abraham Gropius, third Mate*.

Gropius: So we were at sea with a good position 5°57'W 49°56'N by the St Martin's Daymark and the Wolf Rock when the wind pipes

---

* Proceedings of the Enquiry into the loss of the *Voltaire*, Falmouth, n.d.

up to quite a gale, quite a gale indeed. It had been a clear day but he came thicking up that night from the west until it was dimmy, dimmy, with a great sea running. There was a young man, a John Smith, I do not know what has happened to him, but he was always with the Captain where he had no business to be, and the Captain send him away—'

Mr Serjeant Morpurgo, for the Inquiry: With all due respect, Mr Gropius, in what way is this of relevance to the purpose for which we are here gathered, namely to determine the circumstances of the wreck of the *Voltaire?*

Gropius: You will see, you must wait. Well, the Captain send him away, I do not know why. So he go to see the second mate, who has the job to navigate the ship. And I know that he pay the second mate to take us not out in the Channel, safe, but too close to the island. But he make a bad calculation. There is much tide, much, and a very great sea, with the wind over the ebb. So we go first under topsails, and then the foretopmast comes down. Now it is night, you understand, so nobody see. All we know is that the fore topmast is down. We get up steam, and starting paddles. But the cord from the topsails is round the paddles. The paddles wind down the foremast, then the mainmast. All jam. All jam tight. The tide now turns. It is not good seeing. Ahead ... we see this light tower, much water ... breaking ...

Mr Serjeant Morpurgo: Pray compose yourself, Mr Gropius. Usher, a glass of water. Good. Now, then. Are we to understand that you contend that this young man, this John Smith, induced the navigating officer by bribery to make a course dangerously close to this inordinately dangerous shore?

Gropius: That's right, mister.

Mr Serjeant Morpurgo: Is it not simply that, in a case such as this, it is easier to blame the dead – the Captain, the Second Mate, and this ... John Smith ... rather than take responsibility yourself, as the senior surviving officer?

Gropius: This is bad suggestion. Very very awful suggestion. A God damned lie. This John Smith say he was born on Trelise, was near as

171

dammit the owner of Trelise, but could not go back there, not ever. But he wanted to take a look. He had money, he could pay. He had been in America, of course. Now he was going to Belgium, he said, before off to Africa. But he wanted to have a look at his home, so he bribe the Second, and that is why—

Mr Serjeant Morpurgo: I thank you, Mr Gropius, I think we have heard enough of Mr Smith for the moment. If he was indeed the owner of Trelise, perhaps someone on the island will have recognised this fact. Though to the best of my knowledge, the island is in safe enough hands with Mr James Blakeney-Jones.

Revel remembered a time when the Farm Net got you all you ate, except spuds and limpets. That was why he still helped haul, to remind himself where he lived, him and them before him, and that the high times could pass away, and they would be back eating limpets.

So he clamped his leathery hands on the sand-rough rope, and put his back into it, John Pender in front of him, Albert Jenkins behind. No younger men. Nobody took the farm net serious these days, as if these times would last for ever.

Normally, the Farm Net produced a few horse mackerel, a bucketful of atherines, maybe a conger or a skate, and a hundred-odd Hector crabs. The corks came in in a steady curve. Then suddenly, the outermost half-dozen sank.

Normally, this would have sparked up some excitement. But today, the teams just hauled on. The thing in the net was not kicking like a ray, or hopping like a shoal of mullet. It was just dead weight: dead, as in death.

They pulled it ashore, and picked the meshes away. It had been a man, before the crabs had got at it. A young man, by the clothes. Now it was a mass of corruption, snipped ragged by crabs.

Revel was not fussy. He went to the thing, stooped, and searched the pockets. There was a wad of pulp that had been papers. There was a purse, with five golden sovereigns. In the waistcoat pocket was a watch and chain, with seals.

Revel examined the seals on the watch chain. Then he threw the purse into the fish basket and walked away up the beach.

They watched him stump inland at his steady plod, grey beard blowing in the small breeze from the sea. Revel never explained. Nobody ever asked him to. Revel would do right. Revels were known for it.

When Revel knocked at the door, Alice Jenkins opened up immediately. She had heard him coming; her hearing had become as acute as her sense of touch. Revel handed her the watch and chain. When her fingers reached the second seal, they worked, then became immobile. 'Where?' she said.

'In the net.'

She was pale as a candle. Her fingers moved on the agate surface, tracing the crest of the ragged staff. Revel left her.

Later that night, she finished crying. She took from her neck the chain on which she wore the signet that Eavis had dropped in the limpet-midden all that time ago. She put the seal next to it. The two ragged-staff seals clicked faintly between her breasts; the breasts of the lover of one, the mother of the other: a family, of which only she survived.

Later, Revel read her the account of the enquiry, and her face became hard with anger. 'That Robbins,' she said. 'He should have left that devil Gropius on board.'

'Come on, there, Alice,' said Revel. Something in her had turned, like milk going sour. 'He did a brave thing, him and all the gig's crew.'

'He should have left him,' said Alice. 'Some things is better not known.'

And from under the black velvet ribbon, the tears fell like a final curtain for Joshua and his son.

Chapter Thirteen

The night before the funeral, Harriet was sitting on a wall above the church, looking west into the blue Atlantic, rubbing with her thumb at the rough lichen on a boulder.

'Evening,' said a man's voice behind her.

She looked up, displeased at being disturbed. Her displeasure lessened when she saw the speaker was Robbins. He was carrying a shovel. Sweat had carved runnels in the dirt on his face.

'You've been digging,' she said.

'Graves,' he said.

Normally, she would have frozen him out; it was no part of a gardener's place to have conversations with young ladies. But Algy's story of the rescue had entered her heart, and grown into a warm upwelling of admiration. It did not signify who was a gardener and who was a lady. This was a matter touching the very soul of Trelise, and all it touched were equal.

'Sorry to hear about your little dog,' he said.

'My fault,' she said.

'Were you thinking about him, up here?'

'He was only a dog,' said Harriet. She must make light of her loss, much as she felt it. Robbins had been really brave. 'If you must know, I'm here because the house is full of Belgians and I can't bear the smell in the village.'

'Oh.' He fell silent.

Not wanting to appear utterly callous, Harriet felt the need to explain. 'I have a very sensitive nose.' What a silly thing to say to a hero. She felt herself blushing. But there across the heathery down came George and Babs, striding along, waving. She waved back.

'Well,' said Robbins. 'I'm sorry about the little dog, anyway.'

175

She slid down from the wall. 'Thank you,' she said. He was quite nice-looking; handsome, even. His skin was golden brown, his eyes clear and bright and direct, his forehead clever, almost intellectual. And so brave. He had succeeded where she had been a miserable failure. Harriet had a sudden extraordinary urge to put her fingers in his crisp golden curls, smell the warm, working scent of his body—

Goodness.

She turned. Without looking back, she began running at her ungainly lope towards her chums.

Memorandum of a meeting between James Blakeney-Jones and Arthur Robbins, in the form of a letter to Harriet, his daughter, at the Pensione Gibbs, Florence.*

Robbins appeared this morning absolutely festooned with pieces of paper, nursery catalogues, letters from Australia &c &c. He projects some sort of development in scent, a walk, to improve & gain mastery of the ragged piece behind the Arcadias, leading up to a sort of Summer House at the top. He says – and I know he is right – that the sun shines very hot there, and that there is a never-failing drip of water from a spring at the top of the Priory Ridge; and that it is a mere waste just now, all moss fern and bramble and could be made much more of by the plantings he proposes.

Being a gardener of course he has little idea of the conveniences of life, so I was able to suggest to him a backbone to his design, which will take the form of a serpentine walk. And that the apex of the walk shall be a summer house made from the great cabin of the poor Voltaire, *wrecked with such fearful loss on the Mare these three months past.*

Mem – it will be important to guide this scheme past your Mamma with the greatest of care. It is not the sort of thing that delights her heart, and I know she thinks I listen too much to Robbins. I must say he is an excellent gardener, and whatever she may say I think of him not as a servant but as an ally and even friend. With him I can speak my mind as with few others. So the men are coming from the farm Tuesday to start construction of the

* Trelise garden archive, RHS, Vincent Square, London

walk, our steadfast Revel in command of the excavations as usual, at a rate of 1s 2d per diem. I shall occupy myself with the architecturals, and Robbins will look after the plants, and I flatter myself we shall have a very stylish addition, pleasant to all. I know you will be very pleased by it by the time you come back from Florence – still in May, I hope? The new part we shall call Araby – 'the perfumes of Araby', you know. I mentioned the project to old Alice – she loves a scented garden of course – and she declares herself highly delighted. Again, no word to Mamma!

Robbins asked after you, and sent his regards, as he put it. I hope you are thinking of us, and not becoming too sophisticated in your tastes & habits. My love to George and Babs.

Your father.

The girls found much of interest in Florence. George was greatly delighted by the sculptures of Michelangelo, whose women she found splendidly sturdy. Babs painted several reams of watercolours of the Arno, making the water look marvellously wet. As for Harriet, she quite liked the drowsy golden light that flowed thick through the colonnades; but she always felt it was not quite real. (Nothing was, except Trelise.)

Besides, the drains were ghastly and the men were impudent, and a Marchese who showed Harriet his Palazzo tried first to sell her a disgusting Cupid and Psyche, and then pinched her bottom. But on the whole it was a perfectly decent place to spend a winter and spring, on condition that the light at the end of the tunnel was the light off the Atlantic at Trelise.

With the arrival of May, the city began to be hot, and the Arno to stink. Sitting on a terrazza, the girls drank tea made with water really no more than lukewarm, and complained.

'Man does not live by drains alone,' said Babs, who being artistic was probably the keenest.

'One is not a man, thank goodness,' said George stoutly.

'The smell is really unbearable,' said Harriet. Each knew the other was thinking of the light scents of Trelise, bracingly mingled with Cornish ozone, and suddenly Italy was just not bearable another *minute*. They went to the *pensione*, gave a week's notice to Lady Gibbs, and boarded the train with a relief verging on delirium. In only three days, they were rumbling over the causeway, and Trelise was lying like a multicoloured quilt across the brilliant face of the waters.

Bliss!

'*Really!*' Emily had said, crumpling the telegram into a ball.

'What is it?' said James, through a mouthful of devilled kidney. He was suspicious of telegrams at the best of times, let alone at breakfast. From the expression on Emily's face, it looked as if this one was going to spoil a perfectly nice day.

'The girls are coming home,' said Emily, in a voice like an escape of steam. 'Already. They will be in Truro on the half past two train.'

'Marvellous.' said James, his ruddy face brightening. 'I'll—'

'It is *not* marvellous,' said Emily. 'It means she has decided to end her education and will now fritter her life away in this wilderness. How pray am I to find a husband for a daughter who is no better than a savage? How—'

'I'll just order the trap,' said James, secreting a couple of slices of toast in his waistcoat pocket. 'And . . . Good Lord, is that the time? I should be at Castle Down.'

'You have spoiled her utterly,' said Emily, white-lipped. 'I shall not meet her.'

But James had gone.

At six that evening, he was in the courtyard, talking to Robbins. 'Tell you what,' he said, in a state of high excitement. 'I'll show her what we've done on the farm, the new milking parlour and so on. You show her Araby.'

'I'm sure she'd rather be shown by her father.'

'Not a bit,' said James. 'Your idea. Your execution. You show her. Ah!' The clop and jingle of the trap sounded on the Abbey Road. 'Here she comes!'

The trap's wheels crunched under the Arch. Harriet had dropped George and Babs at the Steward's House. She looked well, in a white muslin dress with leg-of-mutton sleeves. Her skin was not its usual dead winter white, but creamy from the Florentine sun. Her eyes were bright with excitement, and as they settled on Robbins they picked up the blue of a clump of *Meconopsis* at her back.

James stalked forward to embrace this tall, elegant, and (in his eyes) incomparably beautiful girl who was his only child.

Only later, when he and she were sitting in the State Room waiting for Emily, did the subject of Araby rise again. 'By the way,' said James, unable to restrain himself. 'Have you been in the garden? No. Of course not. Only Robbins has made a new part, known as Araby, from the perfumes you know, and something he calls the Paradiso, can't think why. I flatter myself it is rather good.'

Harriet said, 'I should so much like to see it!'

'Then Robbins shall take you.'

She smiled at him. How like Papa; credit where credit was due.

'Don't tell your mother,' he said. 'She's . . . well, you know.'

Harriet nodded. There had been a scene, nothing out of the ordinary. Mama had gone to bed with one of her headaches. It was so pleasant to be left with dear Papa. The evening passed with white peaches from the greenhouse, and a few sips of her favourite Gewurztraminer. It was *lovely* to see dear Papa. But, occasionally, her thoughts did stray to Robbins. He had smiled at her in the courtyard. A most charming smile. Good shoulders. Brave, too. And what was this Paradiso? She was conscious of a small itch of curiosity.

Or was it something else?

Next morning she found Robbins in the myrtle grove, piratical in boots and canvas trousers and a leather waistcoat, cleaning the burnt-orange trunks. She found herself awkward. She said without preamble, 'I hear you are to show me the Paradiso.'

He looked round at her over his shoulder. His face had a heavy, brooding look. 'Not yet,' he said.

'But I should very much like to see it.'

'The time is not right.'

'What on earth do you mean?'

'It's better in the evening,' he said. 'You'll see.'

Harriet swallowed the set-down hovering on the tip of her tongue. Now she saw him, things were coming back to her. That time above the church, after the shipwreck. She had been so feeble, and he had been so brave. They had talked about him in Florence. All the girls had agreed that he was a proper chap. But Harriet had not liked them agreeing. She had wanted to keep him to herself . . .

'It'll be warm,' he said. 'Eight o'clock?'

'Very well,' she said. Mamma would hate it, if she knew. Well, she would not know. She trusted Robbins.

More than trusted him.

'Be at the Pharos,' he said. No please.

She wanted to tell him she would not be bossed about. But she discovered that she did not mind. It made her feel safe. Somehow, their hands touched. 'At the Pharos,' she said.

The fingers he had touched were radiating a warmth that spread up her arm and into her breasts and belly, places before only to be hidden and fed . . .

Whatever was happening to her was wrong.

But whatever it was, she wanted more of it.

Her friends put her quietness that day down to fatigue consequent on travel. George was on splendid form, and all afternoon they sailed and caught pollack, it being one of those high, innocent spring days, with a sea like green silk.

But as she walked down the Poseidon Stairs after dinner, Harriet knew something had changed. The sky was darkening, with a rose-pink flush at its western edge. The song of a storm thrush rolled heavy among the trees. They had grown, the trees; everything had grown and swollen and branched, until the crisp outlines of Joshua's terraces were blurred. He must have planned it thus, she realised. For posterity. But she could not keep her mind on solemn thoughts. The paths radiated the heat of the day, amplifying the scents of geranium and verbena; and behind them, more scents, less well-defined. Deeper scents, darker, muskier; the scents of things forbidden.

A giddiness was in Harriet's head. She clasped her hands tightly in front of her, and marched on to the Pharos.

The Pharos Walk was in shadow, a ravine of black against the brightness of the sky, Joshua's ilexes already fifteen feet tall, the Mare a strong column, glowing white, darkening, at their focal point. She clicked her tongue, ready to be vexed, but actually disappointed. There was nobody here. A wild-goose chase. It was too bad.

'Evening,' said a voice from the deep shadows.

Her eyes accustomed themselves. She saw the compact set of his shoulders, the crisp gleam of his hair in the dusk.

'This way,' he said.

He led her between ranks of pale *Abutilons*, up and away along the northwestern loop of the Endless Walk. He did not speak. She could hear her breathing, absurdly loud in her ears. He walked well, light and easy. The familiar northern extension of the Endless Walk had changed. In place of a group of *rheum* someone had erected a sort of dolmen of boulders.

'Through here,' he said, and stood aside.

She knew that something was going to happen; something irrevocable. She knew she should go back to the house. But she was so excited she could hardly breathe. As she passed through the granite arch, her skirt brushed fronds of geranium and a scent rose to her nostrils, heavy and exciting, like incense. It was too late.

'Araby,' he said.

There were pale ranks of lilies now, marching upwards, white and gold below the deepening flush of the sky.

'*Auratum*,' he said.

She tried to reply, but a thickening in her throat prevented her. The scent of the lilies lay in the path like water in a canal. In the tree tops a breeze rustled. Down here, the air did not move. She was suffocating. She wanted someone to lean on. No. Not someone. Robbins. Specifically Robbins.

'I can't see,' she said. Silence, except for breathing. She knew what she was going to say, but she could not believe it. 'Give me your hand.'

His hand came out of the dark and clasped hers. They were in a tunnel that turned sharply left, up a couple of great steps made of granite slabs.

'Honeysuckle,' he said. His hand was firm and dry. 'The woodbine, and one of my own breeding.'

After the heaviness of the lilies, the honeysuckle was intoxicating. Her knees were weakening. The air barely moved, but the leaves on the plants lining the path were shivering, interspersed with pale flowers that smelt like honey.

'The *Acacias*,' he said.

She was floating up the steps not knowing how she could walk, her mind wrapped in veils of scent. She knew that these things did not flower at the same time, but the fact was insignificant. He has planned it all, she thought. How clever he is, how beautiful; how he understands what I need. She knew perfectly well that her mind and body were separate; the mind controlling the body. But the person who had thought that separation real was distant in the past, no relation to whoever she was now, this symphony of nerve-endings moving through the twilight, towards—

'*Daphne*,' said the voice behind her, male and strong, buoying her up, drawing her back. '*Mezereum, Odora, Cneorum*, some others. We are nearly there.'

She walked on, in a trance. They were moving slowly; the light had faded. Above, she saw a square shape with the faint gleam of gilt. It seemed to be the stern of a ship, buried in the hillside; great windows, a door. Her hand went to his waist. She was leaning on him. They were walking up the last steps together, hurrying. For a shocking moment, she saw what she was doing; tramping the garden with a servant, longing to do . . . something she had no word for.

Then the last of the scents came upon her; ancient, wicked, sweet as the corruptions of Satan; jasmine, and heavier, looser, the dark whiff of *Stephanotis*, twined together over the gates of heaven, the gates of hell . . .

The door opened, then closed behind them. They were in a warm room of odd angles, the after-cabin of a ship. Floating in the scents that filled it, she beheld a thing that was long and wide and low; a day bed, with flowers strewn upon it, she could not see what kind in the darkness. He planned this, she thought. It is a seduction. He has planned it perfectly.

'The *Paradiso*,' he said.

She saw his white skin gleaming in the half-light. Then she was holding him close, and he her, and she was opening herself to the urgent thrust of that hardness into her own universal softness. The moment of agony; then the pleasure spread, and the universe was full of it.

Robbins looked down at her, the pale hair spread on the green velvet cushion, the hard-tipped breasts, the lips thickened with passion. He smiled.

He had had no idea it would be so easy.

There was a new dog since Tarquin, another terrier, Raphael. On her immediate return from Italy, Harriet had loved it deeply, and taken it to her bed. All of a sudden, it became lonely, unloved. It took to hanging around the Steward's House, mingling uneasily with the menagerie attendant on George and Babs. 'Poor Raphael,' said George, absent-mindedly caressing its ears with a tarry hand. 'Poor Raphy Waphy. Issa mama not interested?'

'Where is she?' said Babs, who was painting the flower of an *Aloe succotrina*, a many-barbed harpoon of coral tubes.

'Goodness knows,' said George, frowning at a coal brig unloading at the quay. 'She's awfully hoity-toity.'

'Looks awfully well,' said Babs, dabbing.

'Awfully . . . womany,' said George. 'Something's up.'

'What?' said Babs. 'Don't be silly.'

'I suppose so,' said George, with resignation. 'I mean, how would *we* know?'

The new Mare lighthouse had been built by Robert Stevenson, father of Robert Louis, soon after the Great Storm. Girt about in cork lifejackets, his navvies laid the lowest course of shaped granite on the Mare, anchoring it with bolts of bronze to the matrix at lowest astronomical tide. Steadily, the tower rose.

Stevenson was a wrathful man. Joshua delighted in teasing him.

After the replanting of the ilex hedges on either side of the Poseidon Stairs and the Pharos Walk, he had ordered the servants to set up, under the head of Poseidon on the top terrace, a table with a white cloth, and two chairs, and a bottle of champagne. Having received Stevenson at the Priory, he walked him through the garden and up the stairs to the table, beside which Drage waited, tail-coated, white-gloved.

Drage had filled the glasses. Then Joshua had turned, and directed his eye outwards and downwards. Stevenson had glanced with curled lip at the frivolities: little steps, stone urns, agaves two by two, the new-planted hedge fronted by its twin borders, rocket behind, lupin before.

Then he became still and his face darkened.

He was having a Vision.

The Stairs and the Pharos Walk were like the backsight of a rifle. The foresight was out there on the sunlit sea, halfway to the horizon; the tower of the Mare. The tower over which he and his men had toiled waist-deep in icy water, to which they had clung in hurricanes and frozen in blizzards. Transformed into a mere gewgaw in a vista. A frippery in this man's garden, like some disjaskit sundial.

'You've stolen my light,' said Stevenson.

Joshua smiled. 'My dear Mr Stevenson,' he said. 'May I offer you some Passion-flower drops? Apoplexy is a constant danger.'

The glasses had gone left, the table right. Stevenson had knocked him down the top flight of the Stairs. But (as Joshua had pointed out, in his polite acknowledgement of the damages extracted by Mr Williams from Stevenson after the assault) not even the fists of the Game Cock himself could beat away the fact that the Mare was Joshua's, by right of horticulture.

So now Robbins knelt behind Harriet, as Harriet leaned forward over the day bed in the Paradiso, and in the hot, dark perfumes of Araby he fucked her from behind. Far away, over the terraces and the half-grown trees, the eye of the Mare opened and swept the sea. It lit the silver swell of Harriet's buttocks, the narrows of her waist as she moved, the pale gold of her hair as she bent her head, groaning, and said please, more, again. But Robbins waited until the Mare was staring full upon him. He bared his teeth, glared straight back into Joshua's eye, and thrust, thrusting not just into Harriet, but at Joshua, the blighter of lives. Harriet moaned like a dove, trusting him.

Thirty minutes later they parted. He did not say goodbye. He dressed quickly, ran a rough hand over her breasts, and left her on the day bed, naked, her arms behind her head.

He walked through Araby quickly. There were pots in there, a lot of pots, to get the effect. By the smell, some of the lilies needed renewing.

His way home led down the Pharos Walk. Every ten seconds, Joshua's eye flicked out at him from the Mare. 'You be buggered,' he said. 'What you going to do about me, you murdering bastard?'

'Language,' said a voice in the dark.

The hair on Robbins' arms and back stood straight up. By the next sweep of the light he saw a figure sitting on a stone bench. It seemed to be a woman. A black band was round the eyes. 'Alice,' he said, the wind going out of him.

'What have you been up to, then, Mr Robbins?' said Alice.

'Walking,' he said.

'In the dark. Swearing and cursing.'

'That's right.'

'You get the smells, in the dark.' She was sniffing like a spaniel bitch. 'Very loverlike, the smells.'

His heart lurched. 'I beg your pardon?'

'You planted a new place,' she said. 'Very powerful, the smells.'

'Araby,' he said. 'The Paradiso.'

'Is that what they call it, nowadays?'

What did she mean? Silly old woman, full of riddles. 'You're a long way from your bed,' he said.

That phrase. That voice. Alice felt her breathing stop. Time collapsed. It was twenty years ago. She was on a rockery. She had eyes. She was seeing the last things she had ever seen: a fleshy crater of mouth, the lights of the house, spinning as her head spun. Those words. In that voice.

This one had lived, while hers had died. Her man, her boy. Her eyes.

She made herself smile, and said, in a brisk, cheerful voice, 'It's a long time since I heard anyone say that.'

He had no idea what she was on about. 'Well, goodnight, then,' he said. 'Do you want seeing home?'

'It being dark, you mean.' She laughed, and trotted away, tapping at the path-sides with her cane.

After a while she stopped. Her ears were very good. She heard him go. She heard the glide of a tawny owl over Davy Jones, and the faint crunch of other feet, lighter, going slowly along the Top Terrace towards the abbey. She hurried herself.

Harriet felt slow and drowsy, full of a loose, delicious ache. Arthur, Arthur, she was thinking. I will marry you, and we will do this here, for ever, in this place. We will do anything you want, for ever. Arthur—

'Out walking?' said a cheerful voice in the dark.

Harriet jumped. Her clothes were unhooked, her hair anywhere, her face thick and flushed, numb from his mouth. She began tucking herself in, pulling herself together. Then she saw that it was only the blind woman. She said. 'Oh, Alice. It's such a lovely evening.'

'Lovely place, the Paradiso.'

Harriet said, sharply, 'What do you mean?'

'Just that. No offence.'

'Oh.' Harriet's heart was galloping under her ribs. She sensed something new in Alice. Something knowing.

'You should be careful, dear,' said Alice.

'What do you mean? Why?' There was a new, sharper note in Harriet's voice. Terror.

'You get snakes in gardens,' said Alice.

'There aren't any snakes on the island,' said Harriet, babbling now. 'Everyone knows that.'

'I wasn't talking about the island,' said Alice. 'I was talking about Eve, and that old Adam.'

'Oh. Goodness,' said Harriet, in a voice like glass breaking. 'Well, goodnight, Alice.' Alice went away.

When she was gone, Harriet shook her head, smiling a smile proceeding from pure insanity. Of course nobody could know. This was between her and dearest Arthur, a great secret they would reveal in due season. She was a woman who had found her man. Nobody would be able to resist the awesome power of her love. Nobody. Not her father, when he understood. Mama would be difficult. But Papa loved Arthur. He would understand.

Nothing would stand in their way. Her life belonged to Arthur, and his to her.

It was as simple as that.

Next day, James was riding his cob in the bulb fields. The flowers were long picked, and the leaves were dying back. In some of the fields the lifting had begun, cartloads of bulbs heading to the farm sheds for the steam-riddle and the bagging girls, and the mainland disciples of William Robinson, apostle of the Wild Garden.

'Morning, Mr James,' said a voice.

He looked down. It was old Alice. Though why they called her old Alice he couldn't think. Not a day over fifty-five. He was fifty himself, dammit. Perhaps it was her hair. Used to be a nice fairish colour. Grey now, of course. Handsome woman still. Had brains, too, dear old Alice, knew the island like a book. As for the eyes, she didn't seem to miss 'em. 'Mornin',' he said.

'Tell you what,' said Alice, sudden and blunt, as was increasingly her way. 'Did you ever hear tell of Mr Macleod?'

'Macleod,' said James. 'No. Should I have?'

'I think perhaps,' said Alice, in a sort of a purr. 'Though he's dead, of course. Mr Joshua made sure of that, bless him.'

James was watching a hen pheasant by the hedge. She had some chicks in there somewhere. His head jerked round. 'What are you talking about?' he said.

'He had a son. Get off your horse, I'm getting a stiff neck.'

James slid off. He stood holding the cob's head while Alice talked.

After a while, he sat down on a granite boulder and put his head in his hands. The cob wandered back to the stable on its own. James went back to the Priory later, and shut himself in his room. At half past eight, he came out, and took a stick and a lantern from the hall table, and strode out of the front door.

The night was hot and drizzly. If the Mare had been visible, it would have been a mere glow intermittent to the south. But there was no chance of a glow being visible on the Top Terrace tonight. The grit was splashed with crazy yellow patches of lantern light, loud with the crunch of boots on ram and shingle, the roar of angry breath.

The boots crashed up to the Paradiso, pulping tendrils of sweet-smelling flowers. The door walloped open.

The lantern light gleamed on gilt deck-beams, the scales of the serpent carved above the lintel. The air was heavy with the smell of sex. On the day bed, Harriet lay.

The woman sprawled on the bed seemed rounder, more voluptuous than James's daughter. There were rose-petals stuck to her breasts, a shawl veiling her loins. She looked like a Roman whore painted by that filthy foreign sewer, what was his name, Alma-Tadema. She was alone. By the look and stink of the place, she had not been alone long. The blood thundered in James's ears. He thought he might be going mad. 'Where is he?' he said.

She sat up. She covered her breasts with her arms. 'Papa!' she said, and suddenly she was Harriet, lanky and awkward on a rainy night.

She said in a high, frantic voice, 'Arthur has asked me to be his wife.'

Silence fell. The rain made the air thick and unbreathable.

'And I have told him—'

'Never mind what you have told this damned gardener. My poor girl.' He was suddenly on the edge of tears. His darling daughter. Violated. And he had as good as encouraged the whole thing. It was partly his fault. *Mostly* his fault.

Harriet said, 'He is my husband before God.'

'Don't you God me.'

She put her hands over her ears. 'I shan't listen.'

He did not know what to do, so he followed his instincts. He took two steps forward, shoved her back on the day bed and rolled her clumsily in the shawl. She twisted away. He hit her, hard, open-palmed across the face, hauled her up and draped her across his shoulder, grunting with the effort. Then he marched back through the drizzle, over the bridge to the upper-floor door of the house, along the dark passage under the eyes of the portraits and into her room. He threw her at the bed, and missed. She landed on the floor with a thump. He heard her sob. He slammed the door and turned the key on the outside. He went to the gun-room, and took a double-barrelled shotgun from the case, and filled his pockets with swan-shot cartridges, and went out of the front door, locking it behind him. The night swallowed him up.

*　　*　　*

Victoria, fourteen. Pedal pushers, sequined tube top, sitting on the porch playing gin rummy with Sarah and Martha. She was going to the disco with George Latsis. She had never been to a disco before, but Mommy said she could go because Daddy was away at a conference or something and if nobody said anything he would never know. Victoria was so excited that she kept smiling, and Sarah had to keep reminding her about her braces.

A taxi drew up in front of the house. Victoria got up. It would be George. Her insides were dancing already.

But it was not George who got out of the taxi. It was Daddy.

A heavy weight came and sat on her head.

'Got flu,' he said. He was grey in the face. 'Came home. Going to bed.' He saw Victoria, frowned. 'What are you dressed up as?'

'She's going out to a disco with George Latsis,' said Martha proudly, before Victoria could shut her up.

Daddy stayed still, swaying. He smelt of drink. 'She is doing no such thing,' he said.

'But—'

'At your age, looking like that? No way. To your room,' said Daddy. 'I'll find you someone to go out with. Real dancing.'

'But—'

'No buts.'

Victoria rang George. Later that night, she climbed out of the window and went dancing anyway. But it was not the same, because all evening she was looking over her shoulder, and when she came back she could not tell anyone. So Daddy had spoilt it. Again.

Next morning, the sun came pouring into Harriet's room; nobody had thought to draw the curtains. She lay with her hands on the covers, watching the shapes her eyes made on the new paint of the ceiling. She had cried most of the night. Now she felt empty and powerless. Dear God, let it be that Papa had not injured Arthur . . .

Voices were talking outside her door. There was the clink of china, the turning of a key. Papa was in the doorway, taking a tray from the footman. There was tea on the tray, toast; she could smell it, inordinately strong. Her mouth filled with water. Her gorge rose.

'Where is he?' she said.

Her father locked the door and pocketed the key. 'Where is who?' he said. His face was grey and pouchy. He had not shaved, and he seemed to be wearing last night's clothes.

'Arthur.'

He put the tray on the bedside table and sat down heavily on a spindly chair. 'You can stop all that blasted Arthur nonsense,' he said. 'You won't see him again.'

'What do you mean?'

'We will speak of him no more. Nothing has happened.'

'Something has happened,' she said. The tears were pouring down her face. 'It happened. It *happened*!' She was howling, scarcely comprehensible.

He smiled at her, a tender smile, mad. He stood up. 'I must shave. Your mother is in bed. She must not be allowed to think the world is out of order. Eh?'

Harriet said, in a cold, dry voice, 'She will know in the end.'

James shook his head. 'I think not. There is no need.'

Harriet said, 'I am going to be sick.' And sick she was, into her chamber-pot.

'You're ill,' said her father, full of solicitude.

Harriet turned on him a face that was grey and obdurate. 'No,' she said. 'It is what is called morning sickness. And if the child is a boy, I shall call him Arthur. A pretty name, do you not think?'

Ten days later, they unlocked Harriet's room and she went outdoors. Everywhere she went, she asked after Robbins. She asked the coachman, and the under-gardeners, and Revel, leaning on his shovel by the fresh-turned earth of the terrace below the Arch. Everyone shook their heads. Their eyes would not meet hers. Her father had been there first, she guessed. White-lipped and shaking, she harnessed up the trap and rattled across the causeway to the mainland. She asked as far afield as Truro. But it was like looking for a button on a shingle beach. He had vanished.

Back on the island, she got George and Babs to help. They wrote letters, hunted high and low. There was no trace.

Then in August she sat on the bench below Poseidon, looking as always for his square shoulders down by the Pharos. She sat with her hands on her belly. He would not come.

Under her hands, something turned. Something alive.

Her baby, moving.

She stood up. She turned her back on the figure who would not be arriving at the Pharos. She went back to the house and turned her mind away from emptiness.

There was plenty to do.

Chapter Fourteen

*Shocking Tragedy at Trelise**

Recent events in our Eden, Britain's Fortunate Isle, have once again proved the mournful adage that in the midst of Life we are in Death.

  It seems that Eliza Hicks, a nursemaid, took an infant staying at the Priory at Trelise for an airing in the garden. At the summit of the long flight of steps known as the Poseidon Stairs, the girl left her charge, hoping that the child – troubled with its teeth, she said later, and fractious – would benefit from the freshness of the air from the sea. Hicks, it was said, went along the Top Terrace 'to pick flowers'. As she returned after an absence of some twenty minutes, she was appalled to see from a distance of some hundred yards the perambulator in motion. By the time she had arrived at the top of the steps, the perambulator had tumbled from their apex to their base at frightful speed. The unfortunate infant within had been flung clear, dreadfully injured, and is now despaired of.

'The Lord moves in a mysterious way,' said James, lowering the paper. 'Where is Harriet?'

  'Good morning, papa,' said a voice from the door. Harriet came and sat down. Her face was pale and wooden, with dark circles under the eyes. Her eyes were upon her hands, clasped tightly in the lap of her black dress.

  'Some tea?' said Emily.

  'No, thank you. I shall see whether Babs and George would care to do the flowers in the church.' Harriet stumped from the room like a lanky black ghost.

* *West Briton*, January 1890

'She is taking it so well,' said Emily. 'Mr Davies was saying only yesterday. What Christian resignation!'

What nonsense you talk, thought James. He said, 'I must go up to the West Wood.'

'Mr Davies is coming to luncheon.'

Mr Davies was always coming to luncheon. James cared neither for him nor his works. It was largely thanks to Mr Davies that his feelings for Emily had changed, over the years, from a sort of grateful loyalty – he had indeed been a gawky youth, sadly lacking in accomplishments, and she had turned a blind eye to this – to something no more and no less than dislike. Particularly, he found it hard to bear her scorn for all things Trelise. And as for the affair of Harriet's child, well, it had indeed been shameful, but a child was a child, and to harden your heart as Emily had was deuced un-Christian, whatever Davies might say.

It would have been hard to live on an island with no friend. Things had improved since Harriet's return; the two of them got on remarkably well. She was good, and dutiful, and loving, and intelligent enough to know that he would not hold past lapses against her. But all along, there had been one person he could not have done without, and that was Alice Jenkins. He visited her often, ostensibly to talk about island matters far beneath Emily, but actually for tea and companionship.

Circumspectly, of course.

So instead of going to the West Wood, James turned up the little path that led to Alice's gate.

This morning, they talked about the planting of *Pittosporum* hedges, which Joshua had done to such effect, and which James had it in mind to continue. Alice recalled what Joshua had done, width of trench, quantity of muck. 'And how,' she said, after they had dealt with that subject, 'is the girl?'

'Quiet,' he said. 'Sad, I think.'

'It is not to be wondered at.'

'No.' On the list of things James did not talk about, Harriet's child was right at the top. 'Awful ground elder in your pinks. I'll dig it out for you.'

'I'll get a boy to do it.'

But James was already hunting up tools. He spent an enjoyable twenty minutes rummaging round clumps of Mrs Simkins with a hand fork, while Alice sat in a chair and talked about her own child.

And it was in this position, James kneeling, Alice sitting, that Mr Davies saw the pair of them as he made a slight detour to pass the gate en route for luncheon at the Priory.

James found Emily at the dining-room table. Davies was there too, eyes rolled piously to the ceiling. 'Why haven't you started?' he said. 'Go on. Get the beauty of it hot.'

Emily said, 'How dare you speak of luncheon?'

'Hungry,' said James, who was used to her displays of spleen.

'Did *she* not give you luncheon?'

'I beg your pardon?'

'That woman.'

Ah. 'No. Where's Harriet?'

'With Georgina and Barbara. I thought it best.'

'Why?'

'Because against my wish you visit that woman. Do not attempt to deny it. Mr Davies saw you. You were laughing, he says. About what, may I ask?'

'No, you may not,' said James. His face had turned a deep crimson. 'And how did you see me, pray? It is not a place you pass by accident. Snooping, were you, Davies?'

'How *dare* you!' cried Emily.

James said, 'Alice Jenkins is my good friend. She had a child out of wedlock, with unsatisfactory consequences. I was seeking advice from her about managing the happiness of our daughter Harriet. I seek her advice often, because the advice I get from my own wife is either silly or comes second-hand from a weasel in a cassock. Eh, madam?'

'Villain!' hissed Emily.

'Fie, Mr Blakeney-Jones!' cried Davies. 'To seek advice from one sinner about another is doubly to kindle hellfire under your poor daughter!'

James could not bear to look at him. 'When I want advice about my daughter, I'll ask you for it.' He champed at a bit of bread. 'Now get off my island.' He went to the sideboard and picked up the carving knife. 'Now, sir!'

Davies cast a desperate glance at Emily. Emily said, 'Never, sir!'

'Off,' said James. 'Before I call the police.'

'If Mr Davies goes, I go with him!' shrieked Emily.

James made her an old-fashioned bow. 'In that case,' he said, with a calm infinitely more frightening than his usual explosion, 'farewell. Your maid can pack.'

Emily saw that she had walked into a trap. She started to cry. 'Taking advice from a whore about her bastard!' she snivelled. 'Monster!'

'If she is a whore, how else can you see your daughter?' said James. 'I prefer to look at both of them otherwise.'

'You will burn in Hell.'

'So you will be happier elsewhere, for the remainder of my sinful life,' said James. 'Godalming, perhaps. You speak of it so often. I will buy you a house.'

Davies said, 'In the name of God—'

'In God's name, go,' said James.

They went.

'Dawkins,' said Victoria. 'There are two years missing.'

'Two years of what?'

It was raining. It had been raining for ten days. There was a nauseating fug in the kitchen, aggravated by Radio 2.

'Diaries,' said Victoria. 'They're in the catalogue, but not the boxes.'

'Haven't the *foggiest*,' said Dawkins.

'In the attic?'

'You have been through the attic.'

Brick wall.

At lunch, she asked Guy. 'Diaries?' he said. 'What would I want with diaries?'

'I don't know. I thought you might have them for one of your scripts. It's an interesting moment. She's going to have a child, then the diaries go missing, and there seems to be a dead baby that doesn't show up in the registers. I checked.'

Guy said, 'I'm making a series of garden films, not a historical romance.'
'Oh,' she said, chilled.

'Though naturally I am fascinated. Except that you don't seem to be getting far with your bones. And I am sitting here waiting for this bloody weather, so I can do something about filming the merry month of frigging May, while you are amusing yourself—'

She stood up. She said, 'This is a conversation we have had before and it wasn't a conversation in the first place.' She heard his voice shouting after her as she left the dining room. She tried to make excuses for him; rain, pressure. They sounded pretty feeble. Or was it her?

That night, she and Guy did not speak. Next morning she woke full of good resolutions. The sky was blue, and the air was full of thrush-song and myrtle. Guy had a party of people arriving at eleven: big shots from Carshalton TV, a couple of feature writers arriving to do interviews that would come out around the launch, some PR flacks to plan an offensive. Thank God for the weather. And thank God for no filming; two hours free. So she cooked him a sinful breakfast of fried eggs and bacon and kidneys, and he scarfed it down with the innocent delight of a future weight-watcher. After breakfast they fetched Patton from the kennels, and went for a walk. Guy looked happy again, made her laugh, the way he had all that time ago in Chiswick. Things felt normal. Times were good.

The sun illuminated the flecks of gilt that still clung to the Paradiso, the fleshy green radio-telescopes of the *Aeonium* species on the cliffs of Africa. The tangle of Harry's garden was gone. Trees stood uncluttered by brambles. Bright vegetation was spreading across bracken-free soil to clothe raw black beds. There were pheasant pens in the musty pine woods. The bulb fields beyond were dying back neatly in ridges, and the tractor was plying the Priory road, towing a jaunting car crammed with people clutching entry tickets, obtainable from the booth outside the Castle. 'Seven pound fifty a go,' said Guy. 'Roll up, roll up.'

She was proud of what he had done. She took his hand. They walked across the springy turf mounded over the ruined walls of hovels pulled down by Joshua, into the churchyard.

They passed the little group of stones with the foreign names, the dead from the *Voltaire*. After them came Drage, a parcel of Revels, and Alice

Jenkins among others of her clan, alive in the library, rotted in the flesh. There were gaps in the stones: two gaps, in particular. She said, 'I really don't understand why the child's not here.'

'What?' said Guy, looking at his watch. He hated churchyards. 'Five to eleven.'

'The child that went down the steps.'

He said, 'I honestly don't care one way or the other. Does it ever occur to you that it is a bit obsessive, all this digging around?'

'It's real.'

His face darkened. She felt the air between them curdle and sour. What had happened to them? 'It is not real. Victoria, let me tell you you have changed. You are not the woman I married. We just do not communicate any more. Or perhaps you haven't noticed?'

There was no blood in her face. She said, 'I have noticed.'

Down there on Hull Bay, a launch was sliding towards the quay. 'That's my people,' said Guy.

She was thinking of Harriet, frozen, while her father carried on as if nothing had happened. No man. No baby, apparently. Only George and Babs to talk to, and they did not understand. What would that do to you?

It looked as if she was about to find out. Except that she had no George and Babs.

Guy went down to the quay. Victoria went back to the library. She desperately needed to hear friendly voices. Her sisters' voices. Who else?

She knew it was a mistake as soon as Martha answered.

'What is it?' said Martha.

'Oh, you know. How's tricks?'

'Great.' Martha launched into a disquisition on boyfriends (treacherous) work (successful, if it had not been for treachery) their mother (interfering, ill-tempered, and in the final analysis treacherous). Victoria's sadness solidified into depression. 'How about you?' said Martha.

'Yeah. Great.'

'You don't sound great. You need to get off that rock.'

Her defenses were down. 'I guess. I have to go,' said Victoria.

Sarah was better, but not much. She sounded calm, in control. Victoria envied her. 'So how's Guy?' she said, telepathic as always.

'Difficult.'

'Terminal?' At least Sarah had the grace to sound worried. No. Not terminal. It was all a failure of calm, not an irrevocable rift. As she heard herself explaining it to Sarah, she was not sure she believed it. There were phones ringing in the background, the sounds of a busy office, people who would have lunch soon, meetings, work in teams. Trelise was a huge, thick silence.

'Bye.'

'Bye.'

Silence, with gulls. The sea, blue, glittering. Victoria went straight out of the house, grabbed her bicycle, and aimed it at the Arch. Twenty minutes later she was on the sea.

The mackerel sky had thickened, fading in the southwest to a long, dark smear of cloud. But *Fly*'s bow cut a crisp shaving of water, and her tall sails slanted against the sky, and she moved into the bay, and Trelise began to drop. She passed Tobaccoman's, zipping into the tide. She felt the knots in her coming undone. The Mare was growing out of the sea ahead. Right in among the Foals was a brown triangle over a slim red blade in the water: the steadying-sail of a pot-boat, hauling. Revel's boat. The man in the boat looked too compact for Revel. She put the glasses on him. It was Owen Morgan.

She shoved the nose round until the Mare was on the forestay. There were black fans of wind on the water. The horizon was brushed with rain. The luff of the mainsail shivered, then tautened as the puff laid the boat far over. A swell blew a white fountain up the Mare.

She watched the potting boat rising and falling against the jagged background of rocks. Morgan was a minute figure in yellow oilskins. He should have been up in the nose by the wheelhouse, at the winch. But he was down the back end, peering over the stern. The boat was tail-to-sea, wallowing.

Something was wrong.

Revel had made a lot of fuss about Morgan taking the boat out; too early in the year, he had said. But Morgan had fancied dropping a few pots. He had borrowed the boat; all right, pulled rank. He had shot last night. Now he was out hauling, and he had decided it was going to blow, so he had better bring them in. Revel had been right, it was too early. You had to give it to him, he knew about things like that; symbiotic with Trelise, uncanny really.

So there was Morgan in the swell where it creamed ice-white in the black spines of the Foals, hooking the buoys, looping them onto the winch, hauling, with the thunder of the rocks in his ears. If he looked up, he would get dizzy on the suck and slide of the water-slopes. His eye travelled down the buoy-line into the water. Last two pots coming up, and about bloody time.

Then something on the horizon caught his eye. A sail; a white fin of sail. He saw a blast of wind whirl down on it, the sail lie far, far over, come up again. Morgan watched, teeth clamped together.

For a moment too long.

The pot-boat lurched sideways on a wave. The bottom blade of the slow-ticking propeller plucked up the buoy-rope, ran it down to its base, rolled it delicately round the shaft, and kept on rolling. In five seconds, the propeller had become a ball of polypropylene hard as a brick, cranked tight against the pots now jammed against the rudder.

The engine stopped. The roar of the swell in the black rocks was fit to beat the eardrums together in his head. The nose of the boat lifted, caught the wind, slewed sideways. She rolled horribly, was pulled straight by her mizzen.

Fifty yards downwind, a crater appeared in the sea. From the crater there rose slow and violent and streaming with water a jagged molar of rock. Then the next swell rolled on, and the waters rose over the rock and clapped together, and an explosion of spray jumped twenty feet in the air.

Morgan struggled for the oars under half a ton of lobster pots. By the time he got them, the rock was ten feet off. He slapped them in the crutches and gave one great heave. But Revel's was a heavy boat, and it would take a dozen strokes to get it going.

He managed three.

The boat went up. The crater opened. The boat came down with a huge crash. The starboard side went suddenly floppy, and the pots tumbled out of their stacks. Morgan knew that if he let the tail lines get round his boots he was dead, drowned He was probably dead anyway. Which was bloody silly. Anyway, he jumped backwards at the same time as the boat rolled to port. Over the side he went. And as the icy Atlantic closed over his head, his mouth was open, because he was swearing.

Victoria saw it all from the top of a wave: the smash of the pot-boat on the rock, the cloud of spray as the waters clapped together; then the red hull in the water rolling down-tide, the half-seen pile of bubbles in a wave. Then there were only the ink-blue swells, the Mare blinking against the sooty sky, gulls.

She stood at the tiller, her knees buckled under the crushing weight of Trelise, squinting at that cauldron of rock and sea. A wisp of yellow rose and fell against the black. Her heart was suddenly pounding, sending warm, relieved blood through her body.

The yellow again. A body, in oilskins.

She found him. She brought the boat alongside him, sails rattling. He had kicked his boots off, and lay back in the water, eyes closed.

'Grab!' yelled Victoria, both hands on a boathook. The eyes opened, blue-grey, fixed her. He gripped the boathook. She hauled him in. His hands took the coaming, precise, gentle, even at a time like this.

'Hold tight,' she said. She hauled in the mainsheet till the sail was full of wind, the lee rail under, water pouring in. She heaved at his oilskins. He rolled in with a green surge of water.

'Pump!' screamed Victoria.

He crawled to the pump. Victoria turned for Hull Bay. White water roared from bow and counter. His teeth were chattering. She gave him her coat.

It took half an hour to get back to the quay. Morgan crawled up the steps and sat down in a heap, elbows on knees, head in hands, bluish with cold and shock. 'Go home,' she said. He smiled, rueful, perhaps; annoyed with himself. Then his eyes went past her, and hardened.

Revel was standing at the root of the quay. 'Having trouble?' he said.

'I lost your boat.'

Revel nodded. It was impossible to tell what he was thinking.

'We'll sort it out.'

'Bloody right we will,' said Revel into his beard. 'You want to be careful, Victoria.'

'She saved my bacon,' said Morgan.

'She should have bloody left you to drown. I told you, it's not fit.'

Then Guy was there, hands in the pockets of his jeans, deck shoes planted, drops of rain on his round spectacles. His film people were at the quay root, watching. 'What the hell's going on?' he said.

'Boat sank in the Foals,' said Morgan. 'Victoria pulled me out of the water.'

Guy should have grinned all over his face. Instead, he said, 'The Foals is a damn silly place to be on a day like this.' He walked back to the estate office.

Unfair, unfair, thought Victoria, hating him. 'Let's go,' she said to Morgan. 'Can you walk?'

Mary was in the kitchen at the Garden house. 'Get in the tub,' Victoria told Morgan. Then she told Mary what had happened.

Mary got a bottle of Australian shiraz off a shelf, pulled out the cork. She drank her glass quickly, refilled it. She seemed close to tears. 'He does dangerous things,' she said. '*So* dangerous.' Not looking at Victoria.

Victoria was hurt. She had saved this man. She felt a sort of warmth, a closeness to everyone. But nobody seemed to feel close to her. Except Morgan, of course.

She pushed her bike up the drive to the Priory. She hung up her clothes in the drying-room and put on the dressing gown she kept behind the door. She went into the library and dialled Morgan's number. Mary answered. 'Is Owen all right?' said Victoria.

'Yes.' Mary sounded cold.

She wanted to talk to him, to hear his voice, to feel that closeness. 'He's in bed,' said Mary. 'Any message?'

'No. I . . .'

She never found out what she would have said next, because Mary said, crisply, 'Goodbye,' and put the telephone down. People hated being under obligations. Perhaps that was it.

The front door slammed. When she went into the hall Guy was there, hulking and angry in the dim light coming through the glass cases of ship-models in the windows. He started talking, on and on, sense, danger, film. She tuned him out. Harriet walked in the garden, hearing James's good-natured bellow behind a hedge; alone. With the memory of her lost lover, and her lost child. Poor Harriet.

Poor Victoria.

And there went Guy, on and on.

'I'm sorry you see it that way,' she said, and went upstairs.

She showered, threw some clothes into a case, and her make-up bag after them. Then she went quietly down the back stairs, opened the garage door, and started the Bentley. The tide was still six inches deep over the causeway, the Bentley too old for salt water. Victoria did not give a shit. She drove through the sea at forty miles an hour, raising huge fans of water. By six o'clock that evening, she was in Chiswick.

After Trelise, the house felt small and stuffy. The rooms that had once seemed bright and airy now looked poky. And she had to admit that the worst thing about it was that Guy was not there.

She found a bottle of gin, and some tonic with the remains of fizz in it, and poured herself a stiff one. She picked up the telephone, and dialled.

And there was Helen Torode. The pathologist. Her friend. Well, acquaintance. Except for her sisters, the last person from her old life that she had talked to on the telephone.

'Victoria,' said Victoria.

'Did you get it?' said Helen.

'Get what?'

'The report.'

'What report?'

'Isn't that what you're ringing about?' said Helen. 'You sent me a tooth. I sent you a report.'

'You did?'

'Where are you?' said Helen.

'The house. It's just the same.' Why did she say that?

'Are you all right?' said Helen.

'Yes. No. Not really.'

'What's happened?'

It all seemed very hard to explain. 'I don't know,' she said.

'Listen,' said Helen, the doctor, prescribing. 'What are you doing this evening?'

'Don't know.' This evening, or ever.

'Kevin and I are having dinner at the Brackenbury. Come too.'

'Oh, no.' She did not want to bust up anyone's date. She wanted peace, and quiet, and time to think, though she did not feel as if she would ever think again.

'We'll pick you up in an hour.' The telephone went down. Victoria fell asleep in the chair. The doorbell woke her. Helen kissed her. 'I was Victoria's bridesmaid,' she said to Kevin, by way of explanation. Kevin looked like another doctor. If he minded having a gooseberry on his date, he was keeping quiet about it.

After a glass or so of wine, Victoria's courage returned. She found herself explaining Trelise. No doubt about it, it sounded weird, described in London. By the time she had disposed of her salad of goat's cheese, roast tomato and chorizo, she was thinking straight. She said, 'What was that about a report?'

'On your tooth. Didn't you get it?'

'Probably in the mail.'

'I sent it a month ago.' Helen cut her calf's liver. 'Registered. Well, hell, there's not a lot you can say about a tooth. Amalgam filling, as I remember. Drilled, not brilliantly well; with a low-or medium-speed drill. Obsolete here, but state of the art in the Third World.'

'Opium residues?'

Kevin's eyebrows went up. They were thick and dark, quite nice eyebrows. Helen said, 'Not according to my tests. But it would have been hard to tell.'

Victoria looked down at her plate. There was a bass there, on samphire, with saffron potatoes alongside. She was not hungry. Not Mendez, then. Robbins, possibly. 'What age of person?'

'Adult,' said Helen. 'Depends on diet. Middle-aged, by the wear.' Not Robbins, then.

'Is there a problem with this?' said Kevin, looking worried.

There was a problem.

Victoria was not in the restaurant any more. She was in the hall at

Trelise, in the dim light that crept through the ship-models onto the big salver on the hall table, where Dawkins brought the mail every morning.

The package had been registered, so Dawkins would have had to sign for it. And it would be traceable. Victoria made herself smile. 'Mix-up,' she said. 'Happens all the time in Cornwall.' She heard herself talk about politics, Wimbledon prospects, shoes: a normal sort of dinner, but an illusion. Reality was Trelise, and someone stealing her mail. She left Helen and Kevin to their coffee, threw her clothes into the Bentley, and headed home.

Violet said Dawkins was sunbathing on Tobaccoman's.

Larks were singing as Victoria tramped along the narrow path in the heather. The air was full of the scent of honey and a murmur made of bees, and the swell in the Mare, and the hum of anger in her ears.

She came to the edge of the beach. Somewhere on the rocky promontory to the east, tinny music was playing. She climbed the rocks fast, brushing shaggy grey lichen. The music was Mantovani.

The summit was a sort of plateau. Most such plateaux at Trelise bore vile green pools that stank of old men's trousers. Not this one.

On a short pole in its centre sat a large plastic owl, to keep the gulls at bay. Below the owl was a carpet, Belouch by the look of it. On the carpet stood a ghetto blaster and a small but highly polished silver salver bearing the Jones crest and bottles of suntan oil. Beside the salver lay four Siamese cats, and Dawkins.

The cats heard her first. Eight Oriental eyes locked on. Eight shoulders tensed. Dawkins was an oily copper-coloured starfish, stark naked except for a pair of white eye-protectors, a Mills and Boon face down at his side. She advanced. The cats fled. She turned off the tape.

Dawkins' hands moved suddenly and violently. One of them covered his nakedness. The other palmed away the eye protectors. His mouth was a round O for outrage. When he saw Victoria he composed himself and drew breath to speak.

Victoria spoke first. 'I want a word,' she said.

'This is my afternoon off,' said Dawkins. 'What do you think you're doing?' He draped a Trelise silver cloth over his lap, picked up the salver and used it to direct the sun under his chin.

Victoria said, 'From now on, the silver stays in the house. Someone has been stealing things. I want everything in order before I go to the police.'

'The police?' said Dawkins. The cats peered sourly from behind boulders. 'Stealing what?'

'My mail.'

'Oh, *well*,' he said. 'The Post Office nowadays, what d'you expect?'

'A registered letter.' said Victoria. 'Signed for. By you, as it happens. And somewhere between the door and the hall table, it just vanishes. I see you've been at the carpets, the silver. So why not the mail?'

'I don't like your tone.'

She said, 'The police will be much worse.'

There was a silence. 'Sometimes things can slide down the back of the hall table,' he said.

'Take a look, would you?'

'If you insist. But there's no need to be rude.'

She held his eye. 'I know you're interested in whether you're doing your job right. And I just think there are some little adjustments you could make.'

He stared at her out of a face suddenly reptilian. 'I have been here forty years,' he said. 'Since a boy. What it might be hard for you to understand, being American and everything, is that for those of us who have spent our lives here – as for the Family – the place is not a place where we live, or a job. It is a *vocation*. My vocation has been to look after the house, and the Major, and now Mr Guy.'

Victoria smiled, brightly. 'I'm family, too,' she said. 'Well, this has been a good meeting. Perhaps you could have a hunt for that letter?'

'Yes, Victoria.'

'Oh, dear, look, the sun's gone in.' She walked back to the house feeling much better.

That evening, she found the letter on her desk. As she opened it, she noticed that the gum on the flap was not quite right: not sticky enough. As if someone had steamed it open, to read it. And having read it, had decided that it should not be delivered, so had not bothered to close it up while it was fresh, but had filed it away somewhere, for some reason.

This was a forensic report on a tooth from a skeleton in the island burying-ground. So what was there about it that in the eyes of the housekeeper of Trelise made it unfit for the eyes of Trelise's new owner?

She had her confidence up, now. She went up the scrubbed back stairs, and knocked on the door of Dawkins' flat. There was a scuffle of cats. Dawkins opened up, releasing a waft of litter-trays and Ma Griffe. 'I found the letter,' she said.

'I put it on your desk.'

'And why exactly did you open it?'

'Me?'

'It was you, wasn't it?'

'Certainly not!'

'Then who the hell did?'

'Mrs Blakeney-Jones I feel I honestly must say that I am deeply shocked that I need to inform you that it is not my custom to open the Priory mail, and never has been, not in the forty years I have been on Trelise—'

'Where did you find it?'

'Under the blotter,' said Dawkins.

'Which blotter?'

'The one on Mr Guy's desk.' Silence. Complete silence, broken only by the shriek of the gulls over the Pool. Dawkins' eyes were narrow with triumph. 'I feel an apology is in order, Victoria.'

'When you bring back all the carpets and the silver. If you're lucky.' But she was shaken, okay.

What the hell was going on?

A Meeting in the Hills*

The Monsoon came early to the Min-shan in the year 1892. Our little party made camp at the base of one of the great rock-fans that lie at the mouths of the tributary valleys of the Haishui. I had returned from a foray in the nearby jungle, accompanied of course by my loyal

* From *The Pamirs My Pergola*, Col. Ephraim 'Lhasa' Hartford, John Murray, 1903

Fong. We had during the afternoon collected seed of what I believe to have been a new Rosa, and a Meconopsis of great interest from the meadows above the woods, and some bamboos. As we descended the sky darkened, and the nearby peaks were blotted out as if by a wash of China ink. I remember as we descended through the forest I was singing a song – bamboos are the jolliest of grasses – and I here crave the reader's indulgence as I relay it:

'Listen to the breezes in the Sinarundinaria
Listen to the zephyrs in the new bamboo
there will be rejoicing in a minor London area
when our specimens arrive at Kew'

Fong, who loves a tune, joined in with his usual gusto, and the refrain made our marching music as we threaded our way in a drenching rain down the last three or four miles to the valley floor. I was sure the bamboos would do pretty well at Trelise, and happy pictures formed in my mind of their reception by dear old James Blakeney-Jones and his lovely Viking daughter at that hallowed oasis. What with this and our singing, we kept discomfort pretty well at bay, until the rain became so fierce as to render song inaudible with its beating on the skull. The ground underfoot had become a moving sheet of water. As we reached camp, a little rotten temple to one side collapsed with a piteous groan and a frightful lamentation from the porters, who voted it the worst kind of omen.

So I dished out sugar pills to the silly fellows, ate a paltry dinner of stony rice, and turned in.

I awoke to perfect blackness and thunderous noise. The rain was still falling, and my first idea was that we were in a thunderstorm – but a thunderstorm without lightning. Having lit the lamp, I observed that the water in my night-carafe was trembling to a hard, subtle movement of the ground. I turned out pretty sharp and roused the camp; not before time. It seemed that the rains, accumulating behind a boulder dam at the summit of the fan, had created a reservoir so vast that its waters had thrust themselves deep into the slope of debris

208

at whose base we had pitched camp; and that the rumbling that had roused me from sleep was the sound of the whole, six hundred feet high and a quarter of a mile across, entering a state of dissolution.

I shall not here attempt to describe the panic that ensued. Suffice it to say that we lost a score of porters, the mules, a two months' collection of the choicest subjects, all the tents, furniture and equipment – everything in short, but what we stood up in. This in my case amounted to my speculum, a pair of striped pyjamas, one bedroom slipper, the tin of shortbread I keep at my bedside in case of night-starvation, and the water carafe, this last being otiose, as it was still raining in torrents.

The surviving porters chose this moment to desert en masse. Fong and I, having waited for daylight, walked down the valley until we arrived at the river, and made the best of our way to Wu-tu, three days' walk downstream. We made tolerably good progress, allowing ourselves half a biscuit per diem. I was able to collect an interesting lily on the way, together with some seed of a rhododendron for which I have high hopes. Thanks to sidetracks of this kind, it was in fact five days before we reached Haw-sen, upon which Fong found that the time was auspicious for the burial of his father's bones. He therefore departed in some haste for Sian, appropriating as he went the sum of money I had been able to borrow at extortionate interest from the Provincial Governor, a strabismic opium fiend of a character simultaneously luxurious and serpentine.

So I found myself alone, delirious with fever, on a lousy kang, in an inn of surpassing filthiness whose bill I had no means of paying.

It was at this debatable moment in my fortunes that I had the luck to make the acquaintance of George Bird.

Bird was a sturdy chap of some thirty years, entirely bald, with a great chestnut beard. The bearers called him Water Face, on account of the blue spectacles he habitually wore. He was something of a collector in his own right, having worked his way up from the Burmese border, and so far sent home five tons of material, a creditable effort in one so young, though perhaps reflecting some inexperience. He seemed most impressed by my own twenty-three tons, and particularly so by my connection with Kew and Trelise, in the latter of which he professed great interest. He lent me a suit of clothes, paid my reckoning at the inn, and generally showed that fellow-feeling so gratifying between one European and another, even as we hung like swallows under the eaves of Empire. Since we found each other jolly companions, we decided to join forces, and proceed into the mountains of the Min Shan.

Letter to James Blakeney-Jones, Esquire

Hangchow
27 January 1893
Dear Mr Blakeney-Jones,

I write to introduce myself. I recently had the good fortune to be of assistance to your colleague Colonel Hartford, after an accident in the eastern foothills of the Himalayas. I have been collecting for only two years, and am best classified as an enthusiastic amateur. But I think you will find Sir Joseph Hooker of Kew will vouch for my modest skill, and I can provide other references should the occasion arise.

I had occasion to visit your garden as a tourist some five years ago, and think that perhaps I have a small notion of what might suit.

Having fulfilled my commissions here, I propose to continue to the coast, and there take ship for Australia, where I think I may find much that will be of interest in the Gum and Banksia line. I am taking the liberty of enclosing with this letter a small package of material that I hope will be of some interest, and hope it will serve as a consolation for the inability of poor Hartford to remit – he is I fear still very weak with fever.

Please excuse the writing in this letter. I have lost the use of some fingers of my right hand after an accident, and must therefore learn to write with my left.

I beg that if you find yourself in agreement with any of the proposals I outline above, or have any commissions you would wish executed, you will send a letter care of our Consul in Canton; and that otherwise you will forgive the impertinence of your obedient servant

Geo. Bird

Reply sent to George Bird, care of the British Consul at Canton.

Trelise

3 April 1893

Dear Mr Bird,

Thank you for your interesting letter, and your news of Hartford. And thank you for your kindness in remembering us in your parcel, much of which looks to be of immense interest. My gardeners particularly like the sound of the Rosa xanthina, and the Actinidia kolomikta, climbers of decent scent being something for which I have a great weakness. We shall see what we can do about bringing them to the attention of some of our nurserymen friends, in particular Mr Veitch, who is always pestering us for new things. If we arrive at an understanding with him you may be sure that you will not be the loser by it.

Now, then. I must tell you that we have been making some changes here at Trelise. As you may perhaps have guessed, my own interests lie more with the farm than with the garden. We have therefore decided that management of the garden will pass to my daughter, Harriet, who has been working with me here for seven years now. Naturally it will give me the greatest of pleasure to hear all your news. But as far as garden matters are concerned, it will be best if you correspond with Miss Harriet in future.

Yours sincerely

J. Blakeney-Jones

To George Bird, care of the Black Tree Hotel, Melbourne, Australia.

4 May 1895

Dear Mr Bird,

Another marvellous parcel of Gums and Banksias comes back. The big Gums will do well down the Priory Road, and the Banksias can go on the Endless Walk. [Here much technical detail has been omitted.] I am glad that you found it restful in Canton, after your great travels. It was diverting to read about the habits of the Chinee. We lead quite a provincial life here, and your letter is a great breath of fresh air. I shall look forward to your next.

With all my best wishes,

H. Blakeney-Jones

From George Bird to Miss Harriet Blakeney-Jones

Sydney
18 April 1896

Dear Miss Blakeney-Jones,

    I am enclosing some specimens from a voyage I have made to New Zealand, including one or two shrubby Veronicas *that I venture to hope you will find both curious and beautiful. They are of a large and spreading habit, with bottlebrush flowers in shades as marked. The smaller the leaf, the hardier the subject, as so often. It seems to me that they may be crossed to very good advantage. I hope you will not think I am taking a liberty in making this suggestion. I am also shipping to you some trunks of* Dicksonia antarctica, *which I think will grow in the open ground at Trelise in a well-sheltered spot.*

    I have heard from Colonel Hartford, now living in retirement in Hong Kong. He tells me he is still active – remarkable, in a man now seventy-odd, whom I found three years ago at death's door, deserted by his people. His cunning in the matter of collection is unabated. He tells me that one of his neighbours cultivated a very beautiful golden-stemmed bamboo, as yet unclassified. This neighbour is an ill-tempered Mandarin, and for three months steadfastly resisted all requests from the Colonel for a stool-cutting of the plant, however trivial. So the Colonel sought to achieve by guile what he had failed to achieve face to face. Next to the wall dividing his garden from that of the Son of Heaven he buried a dead donkey. Now you know as a grower of bamboos what gross feeders they are, and how briskly they will travel to filth. Well, a year later, there was his bamboo, sprouting happily in half-a-dozen places on the donkey's grave, lured under the wall by the Colonel.

    The sun is properly up now, and the crickets are shrieking beyond the stoop, and the heat is making the gum-woods smell like a patent cold cure. My guides tell me of a low gum not far from here with a flower like red-hot wire. Sometimes I think about Trelise, and I remember what a cool place it was, with a quiet, steady feeling. Down here it is as if the world is raw, just created, not yet finished—

But there can be no interest for you in my ramblings. The truth of it is, I have had nobody but plants to talk to these five years, as it seems. I expect I shall cross out the above; no, I shall not. Excuse me for trespassing on your time, madam. I remain

Your obedient servant

George Bird

Trelise

27 June 1897

Dear Mr Bird—

Thank you for another wonderful parcel. Last week we had our first Dicksonia frond, black and exquisite, coiled like the head of a violin. I am so glad you did not cross out those parts of your letter you say you thought you might – how Papa and I laughed at your news of Hartford, and how we felt for you! When you return to England, as I hope you soon will, you must at the very least come and visit us here at Trelise, and see how romantically your discoveries scramble in the walks and terraces!

Here I should like to broach a matter I have been discussing with my Father. I wish extremely to begin to fulfil the original designs of Joshua Jones, the founder of this garden, and at the same time to bring them into tune with my own feelings and those of my dear cousins, the Mentmores, with whom we share our lives here. There is much that can be done and developed, or could be, by the right person – for profit, we think, as well as for beauty and the public benefit. But it needs a more experienced hand than I or my dear cousins or my Father can provide. I hope therefore that you will not be insulted, in the light of the protestations of affection for Trelise in your last letter, if I tell you that the individual to whom we have it in mind to offer this task is you. Please do give this matter your earnest consideration. There is much we owe you, and much we can do together.

Your friend

Harriet Blakeney-Jones

Chapter Fifteen

There were stairs; funny stairs, coiling up, up. Keeper showed him a snail and said it was like the stairs, winding round and round. Up they went. Stairs, stairs, stairs. There was a bottom room that smelt as if it would make you sick. Then a room where you got food. Then a room where your bed was with a window that was blue. Then a room with shelves in it and books and some sitting-down places, but the only things in the books were black writing, very little and stupid, no pictures. He wanted to make noise about that. But Keeper said, up you go, less of your nonsense, and nobody wanted back-of-the-hand. So he went up, tired legs, wet chin, bit of a sniffle.

Into the Heaven Room.

It was all white, and light, and the light itself was in great curves of silver and rainbow, and outside it was glass, and beyond the glass air, great singing miles of nothing, rolling away to the edge of the world. It was warm in there, most beautifully warm, with a smell of oil and metal.

He found himself looking at a great piece of green and brown, white-edged, that lay across the world in the opposite direction from the sun. There were little things like houses, and a ship, and tiny creatures like ants that were people. He crowed and shouted and waved. He had never seen anybody that small, and he longed to get to know them, have them in his box, perhaps.

Keeper growled at him and told him he would get used to it, and he knew he never would, but he did not say so, because of back-of-the-hand.

He did, though. Suspended between sea and sky, it became just the usual thing. Day after day, year after year.

His life.

From the *West Briton*, April 1899.

> *That jewel in fair Kernow's crown, the Trelise Garden, has welcomed one*
> *of its principal begetters. Mr George Bird, who has for many years sent back*
> *from faraway places to the fortunate isle Nature's choicest bounty, is now*
> *to make his home at Trelise, and take on the running of the gardens his*
> *intrepidity has done so much to people with the Lovely and the Rare.*
>
> *He was met by a Committee of welcome on the quay. The Trelise*
> *Prize Band gave a spirited rendering of 'Poet and Peasant' and Mr*
> *James Blakeney-Jones made a short speech, to which Mr Bird replied*
> *in the kindest terms. The only sombre note came when Miss Harriet*
> *Blakeney-Jones was overcome by the unseasonable heat, and had to be*
> *assisted from the quay by her cousins, the Misses Georgina and Barbara*
> *Mentmore, who also reside on the Fortunate Isle . . .*

Victoria found Guy in the drawing room, standing in front of the fire. There was a smell of jasmine and champagne. He was holding court to half a dozen people. There was the man from Carshalton TV, whatever his name was, his assistant, a couple of a city-pretty PR girls, and a matched pair of magazine writers, one English, one American. Victoria stood clutching the registered envelope with the tooth report. She could see that the women would like to screw Guy. The men were laughing too much or making strenuous efforts to amuse. No doubt about who was the dominant male here.

He introduced her. The American feature writer crinkled his eyes at her and said, 'Where are you *from?*' She ignored him. She said, 'Guy, come here.'

A little chill swept the room. He patently did not want to come, but he could not refuse without a scene. She led him into the study. She held the registered envelope in front of his nose and said, 'How did this get under your blotter?'

His face slackened. A red glow brightened the freckles. 'Accident,' he said.

'Bullshit.'

'It was—'

'It's addressed to me. Not you.'

'Do you want to know what happened, or do you want to shout?'

'Tell me.'

'It was on my pile. I thought it was for me.' He would not look at her. He was lying. 'I opened it. Then I saw it was some sort of rubbish for you and I put it under the blotter to put on the hall table and forgot it. I'm sorry.'

Under the blotter, to put on the hall table? Bullshit. And if his conscience had been bad enough to glue it up, would he have forgotten it? And why glue it up? Why not just say, whoops, and hand it over? It was not as if they had secrets from each other.

Not till now.

She said, 'No.'

'What do you mean, no?'

'I don't believe you.'

He drew breath. He would not meet her eye. 'Okay,' he said. 'If you really want to know. It had some hospital name on the front. Mrs Price at the post office said you posted off a little box, a specimen, maybe, and was there any news yet, you know what she's like.'

'Mrs *Price* told you.'

He shook his head. 'So I thought you were pregnant and I wanted to know. So I opened the envelope, and there was all this nonsense about a tooth or whatever, and I thought, oh shit, and tried to stick it up again, but it was a bad job and I thought I'd get to it later, so I stuck it under the blotter, and all this PR stuff started to happen, and I forgot about it.'

She said, 'And are you still interested?'

'In what?'

'Whether I'm pregnant.'

'Of course.'

'Well, I'm not. And if I want a test, I'll get one from Boots in Truro.' She was furious now. 'To save you checking with Mrs Price.'

He said, 'Not now, Victoria. Please.'

He was still lying. About babies, now. So she would be touched. *Creep.*

She said, 'I'm out to lunch. Goodbye.'

She found herself on the terrace, walking into the garden.

Liar. Liar. Liar.

But why?

She did not understand.

She did not care.

She must have sat down. A man's voice said, 'Hello, Victoria.' She looked up.

Morgan was at her elbow, eyes sharp and kind above his faun's beard. He said, 'Come and have a cup of tea.'

Morgan. Thank God. Someone who trusted her. So she could trust him.

She let him steer her round to the little hut behind the bamboos. Outside, it was just a potting shed. Inside, it was a little room with an old leather armchair, a table and a couple of chairs, a wall of books, and an electric kettle in the corner for the tea. 'So this is where you keep your books,' she said.

'Lot of plants to look up.' Pause. 'How's it going in your library?'

'Not bad.' She did not want to talk about it now. She wanted company. He made tea. She sat at the table with her head in her hands. Showing weakness in front of the staff.

Go to hell, Guy.

She trusted Morgan.

He poured the tea. They chatted. The problems began to look stupid, floated away. 'By the way,' said Morgan. 'I don't know if you're interested. But I found this.' He pushed a book towards her. It was an album of garden pictures: watercolours, drawings, prints, photographs of the Poseidon Stairs, Davy Jones, the Endless Walk, the Antipodes. Plants, not people. She could see the garden grow in front of her eyes, from the starkness of the early Joshua, agaves and figureheads and bedding in bare earth, through the burgeoning and blooming, the growing of hedges, the creation of vistas; the paths writhing as they changed, a kaleidoscopic flicker of planting and replanting: a history moving, alive. 'Where did you find it?' she said.

'In a stack of garden stuff, in a box. It was mixed up with a lot of plant lists, magazines. Nothing else interesting.' She leafed through the thick, rust-spotted pages. It was such a relief to be helped forward instead of constantly held back. 'Have a sandwich?' He shoved a tin at her. 'Not very elegant, I'm afraid. Mary's on a course at Wisley.'

She took one. It was delicious: home-made chutney, decent cheese, bread full of grains. The tea was good, too, Lapsang Souchong, fragrant and powerful. It was solid stuff, in this solid little room, with the solid books and solid armchair, and this solid man, in the middle of all that . . . bullshit.

She found that her head was very close to his. He smelled good, faintly of honey, perhaps. Comfort came off him in waves. The house was far away, hostile as a wasp's nest, and as papery. She felt as if she was watching herself on TV: but not herself. A little creature blown by the winds that powered history at Trelise.

Blown towards Morgan.

In tiny voices her sisters shouted insults, parking lots, craziness. She ignored them.

She saw herself lean further into Morgan. She saw herself look for his mouth with hers. She saw his hands, meticulous and careful, unbutton her blouse, caress her breasts. She saw her own hands, clumsier than his, unbuckle his jeans and push them down and away. She saw the two brown and white bodies, on the chair; Morgan below, herself astride him, lowering herself onto him. Then she was not remote any more. She was in the shed, with her husband's head gardener and the husband of her friend broad and strong inside her, and she was fucking him slow and powerful, right there and right then, and as the burning sweetness welled outwards from her thighs and breasts she knew for absolute goddam sure that this was wrong, and crazy, and that nothing but disaster would come of it. Then suddenly everything crashed bright and beautiful around her, and she knew that the world had changed for ever in that explosion of heat and joy, but she did not care.

That came later.

Afterwards, she could not quite look at him. The shed was suddenly only a shed, the air not fit to breathe, smelling of sex. She picked up the book. 'I'd like to take this,' she said. 'Do you mind?'

'It does belong to you,' said Morgan, buckling his belt. He sat down in the armchair and put his boots up on the table. He looked feline and graceful. She was really not surprised that she had fucked him. 'Will you come back?'

'It is not,' she said, through a throat that did not want to let the words out, 'a good idea.'

He said, 'But do you want to?'

She held the book over her breasts. She opened the door.

'Because if you do,' he said, 'I'll be here tomorrow, half five.'

She took a deep breath. Her lips felt swollen. She could feel his book touching her breasts through her shirt. 'No,' she said.

'I'll be here anyway,' he said.

She went back to the house and took a bath and tried to scrub herself guiltless. She sat at the dressing-table and looked at herself in the three-leafed glass. The face was the one she was used to, the short dark hair, the blue eyes. She saw her lips thickened, the skin under the eyes a little slaty, the set of the eyelids drowsy and passionate. This was not her. This was an adulterer. The woman at the big house, who fixed her itch with the gardener's dick.

It had to stop, right now.

It had already stopped.

She pulled on a new pair of jeans and her Nudie boots, and went down to the terrace, and dived in.

At dinner, the crinkly eyed feature writer thought he had made big progress, and the PR knew she sympathised about the difficulties of her office politics. She could see Guy watching her, saw his nervousness subside into confidence as he kidded himself that lunchtime had been a spat, a disagreement, past now.

She went to bed early. Guy followed soon after. 'Darling,' he said. 'You were fantastic.'

She did feel pleased. She really did. If she was nice to Guy, it felt better about Morgan. She heard Guy brush his teeth, felt the weight of him in the bed. She felt his hand at the nape of her neck. The place Morgan's hand had been that afternoon.

But Guy's hand was not soft and strong, any more. It just felt big and awkward.

She pushed it away. 'Tired,' she said.

'Oh.'

Oh, Christ.

When she went out next morning, Victoria could hear Guy and his people on the Top Terrace. She took the labrador, Patton, for a walk on the Downs. But the previous day refused to blow out of her head. She saw the long swells licking white tongues into the rock crevices, heard the sullen explosions of the waves mingle with the drowsy thrum of the blood in her ears. She told herself to stop being so goddam silly, it was only salt water slopping around stones. She could not make herself listen.

After lunch she sat at her desk and opened the Morgan album. She flicked through the botany. There was only one picture with people in it, a gouache-and-watercolour from the same series as the one in Guy's London house. The usual figures, sturdy, blue-clad, stood round an agave in flower. It was not as good as Guy's. It was out of balance; lousy composition, heavy on the left, blank on the right—

She frowned. She switched on her desk light and took a magnifying glass out of the drawer. (At half past five, Morgan would be in his shed, waiting for her) There was Harriet, long-faced, feet apart, fists clenched. Standing on either side of her, yachting caps over their eyes, black boots planted, were George and Babs. There was no James: only a man standing apart, square, heavily bearded, wearing blue glasses and an extraordinary flat-topped, curly-brimmed straw hat: Bird, presumably. There were two small children, wearing frocks, and a scattering of dogs. In those days all children had worn frocks until the age of continence. There was no way of telling if they were male or female. To the right of the man in the straw hat was an upright oblong of paint, differently textured from the rest. It was the oblong that spoilt the composition. It was just the wrong colour. The wrong sort of paint. A later obliteration. One of the party who had fallen into disfavour, perhaps. But why had she not read about this person?

Victoria went into the flower room and found the scalpel Dawkins used for trimming the flowers for the specimen vases along the drawing-room window-sill. Very gently, she began to scrape the paint from the top of the oblong. It was watercolour, in a thick impasto. It crumbled easily under the blade.

She found herself looking into a face.

It was a boy's face, pale, the eyes underslung with black. The mouth hung open. The painter had conveyed with remorseless skill the shine of the loose lower lip, the slabber of drool at its corner. Yet the face wore a smile of pleasure and delight.

Victoria took a couple of deep breaths to stop her hand shaking. Then she scraped again.

Perched on the matted hair was some sort of cap, blue, with a peak. The lanky body was clothed in a suit of the same colour, creased, too small. A uniform.

Why? What was this figure doing in a family group?

She felt a thought surfacing. A wild, speculative thought. Testable, though. Given time.

She looked at her watch.

It was twelve minutes past five.

Well, Morgan could wait in the hut as long as he liked. She would not be there. She would start the next tranche of research, and ignore this thing that had come out of nowhere . . .

She found she was standing up, spraying Chanel on her throat. When she got to the shed, she was seven minutes early.

Morgan was already there.

Bird was an unassuming man, upright and square-shouldered. It may have been out of modesty that he sported an ink-black beard that covered him to his cheekbones; or it may have been that the beard's purpose was to compensate him for the fact that upon his broad and intellectual cranium, he permitted no hair to grow.

This, and the flat-topped straw tile and blue glasses he wore winter and summer, gave him a somewhat freakish aspect.

What his letters had not betrayed was the energy of the man. The first time he had walked into James's office, he had made no concessions to the fact that he was a stranger in a new garden. Harriet had looked out of the window while he had expounded his views. The treasure of Trelise must be laid out in the gardens of the nations. Mass propagation was vital. Under glass, naturally—

'Hold hard!' cried James, tomato-faced – the years had thickened him, and his enthusiasm seemed to have generated too much blood for his veins, which laced his face and body in thick purple ropes.

'—and it is vital to embark on a programme of hybridisation,' said Bird, ploughing on. 'The purpose of this will be to promote perfect form and abundance of bloom without losing perfume, to determine vigour, and to increase hardiness where possible. I have drawings here.' He laid a large roll of blueprints on the desk.

James opened them up, weighting them with a conch shell, a glass sphere, a calabash pipe and the loaded revolver from his desk drawer. 'Glasshouses,' he said, peering.

'Indeed.'

'Glass means money.'

'Glass makes money. I will guarantee it.'

'Harriet?' said James. 'What do you think?'

The years had treated Harriet kindly. She had the smooth, ruddy skin of a woman who ate good food, worked hard but not exhaustingly in the open air, and thought positive thoughts. Her hair was scraped into a bun, and she wore the blue serge skirt, guernsey and thick black boots that had become a sort of uniform with her and George and Babs. She stood at her father's desk and looked at the plans, not Bird. She said, 'We haven't decided how much we will pay you.'

'Five hundred a year.'

'No. A house. A quarter of the profits.'

'A third.'

'A quarter. Take it or leave it.'

'Steady on,' said James, appalled at the thought of losing this gold mine.

'Mr Bird?' said Harriet.

Bird looked at her through his blue glasses for a long time. 'I accept,' he said.

My word, thought James, isn't Harriet a lovely girl when she smiles?

So Bird moved into the granite cottage on the far side of the Pool, onto which James had built a new wing. Miss Harriet herself took a great interest in its appointments, or so the maids said, sparing no effort to make the gentleman feel at home. She arranged the many curious and interesting objects he had brought back from his travels, and lent him things from the Priory. Who would have thought (said the maid) that Miss Harriet, who never cared much for the company of men, would be capable of acting so motherly?

So the Garden House, as it was known, became a charming villa now, with a lawn – a great rarity on the island – running down to the shores of the Pool, masked from everywhere except the Pool itself by a dense growth of bamboo species and giant *Gunnera*, planted in the days when this had been the residence of Robbins of unhappy memory.

The glasshouses Bird rebuilt entirely, on the giant scale. They covered two acres at the centre of the garden. They were fabricated on the mainland of iron and cedar, transported by ship from Portsmouth, erected and glazed, all in the space of three months. A collier brought coals for the stoves once a month to the South Quay, and their stoking and maintenance gave work to three men and a boy. A further dozen propagators and weeders and potters were employed in the glass.

If the island welcomed Bird, it seemed Miss Harriet welcomed him too. Before, she had run in harness with her father and the Misses Mentmore. She had taken her responsibilities to the garden very seriously. It seemed to be a relief to be able to delegate them to Bird. Certainly she became less grim, her tongue less sharp, and was even on occasion seen to smile.

It really was going awfully well, as James said to Alice during one of his visits. Alice had smiled, and nodded, and said she was glad of it. She liked to find him happy. He was not always so, since the poor child had gone down the garden stairs. Alice knew what it was to be close to the death of a child.

Meanwhile, James' pleasure was in Miss Harriet, and in being an improving landlord, and in shooting and fishing. Fishing meant trammelling up red mullet in the bay, or trolling for pollack among the Southern rocks.

Or spearing eels in the Pool.

The Pool itself was more than a little magical. Mythically, it was the body of water in which the arm clothed in white Samite, mystic, wonderful, had brought the sword Excalibur to the attention of Uther Pendragon. Actually, it was home to a population of gigantic sow eels. When most eels spent their energies on spawning migrations to the Sargasso, the Pool sows for unknown reasons stayed behind year after year, thriving on a queasy diet of fish, and carrion, and young ducks and moorhen. At the dark of the moon, night-walking islanders from time to time arrived home shaking, having stumbled over leg-thick krakens gorging half-grown rabbits alongside the island cricket pitch.

One hot day in June, James was walking along the top terrace, sweating. It was twenty years since he and Emily had first come to Trelisc. How things had grown. How things had changed. The greenhouses, panes whitewashed against the fierce sun, were a dazzle of reflected light in the garden's centre. They were making their money. The farm was making its money. Money was all right.

James's pulse was loud in his skull as he stood at the top of the Poseidon Stairs. His collar was tight, his waistband constricting. The garden was not the only thing that had grown. He mopped his face with a red handkerchief.

'Nice day for the water,' said a voice at his elbow.

'Hello, Alice,' he said. 'Hot, what? D'you want some strawberries?'

'Strawberries are always nice,' she said.

'I'll send someone up with some.'

'Thank you. How's Harriet?'

'Splendid, thank you.'

'She hasn't been up to see me lately.' Pause. 'Probably got better things to do.'

'Doubt it,' said James. She was getting at something. What?

'What with the new gardener and all.'

'Marvellous chap,' said James.

'What does he look like?' she said.

'Peculiar,' said James, and described him.

'I thought I knew his voice,' said Alice. 'Wrong again. Getting old, I suppose.'

'Both of us,' said James.

Silence, except the sounds of the hot afternoon.

'The gulls are making a racket,' she said at last.

There was indeed a pile of gulls shrieking over the eastern end of the Pool. Like a bunch of ruddy cousins, thought James, squawking, eating, making a confounded nuisance of themselves. 'Lunchin' off eels,' he said.

''Spect so,' she said.

'That's right.'

'If you get a few, bring us one over with the strawberries.' She tapped herself away.

She was right, of course. It was a jolly good day for a bit of eeling.

The water of the Pool was like glass. James stood in the punt in his shirt-sleeves, waistcoat unbuttoned, drifting. In his right hand was an eel-pike, an ash-shafted spear with a four-pronged head the size of a man's hand, the fingers almost connected by barbs. Below him, the level brown mud slid by. A hole; then another. He took a deep breath, to control his thundering heart. Then he drove the spear into the mud midway between the holes.

A heavy, kicking writhe thrummed up the shaft. He hauled in the spear hand over hand. On the end, a three-foot eel was knotting and reknotting itself. James shoved it into the sack on the punt's bottom, and prised it off the tines with his foot. His movements were economical, practised. He pushed at the mud with his spear. The punt glided on towards the Garden House.

Gulls lifted in a screaming cloud. He drifted towards the hedge, waiting for the ripples to die.

The reflections rippled. The bottom cleared. He saw an eel.

It was a vast eel, terrible. Its girth seemed the girth of a small barrel, its length the span of his two arms outstretched. It was the eel of a lifetime, trailing a plume of mud as it serpentined across the oozy plain. His heart was a thunderstorm in his chest. He took the spear in sweat-slippery hands, and jabbed; a short, sharp stroke, the stroke of an over-excited boy, not an experienced eel-hunter sixty-five years old next birthday. One of the tines nicked the eel's tail. The creature accelerated, churning mud, and slid like a piston into a dark hole under a rock, inaccessible.

James swore. The blood was thumping in his temples. He looked around, wheezing.

The punt had drifted across the Pool, so that the lawn of the Garden House was now visible, a green slope heading up from the water in three terraces. Remarkable good garden Bird had made himself in a year. Jolly good *Rosa xanthina* up there over the sort of Indonesian platform thing, *bale* he called it, at the top of the terrace—

The eel vanished from his mind like smoke on a breeze.

There were two people on the *bale*.

One of them was Bird. The other was Harriet. They gleamed a brownish cream, the colour of the skins of two people who spent a lot of time in the sun. Brownish all over, because neither of them were wearing any clothes. At least not as far as James could see; because they were very close together; leaning back, it was true, rocking, apparently, but joined at the . . .

Great good galloping God almighty. His daughter. And that man Bird. And they were . . .

No!

In the chaos of his head, two faces floated. There was the face of the gardener Robbins, broad of forehead, steady of eye, clean-shaven, with a damned impertinent twist to the mouth. And there was the face of this Bird, wrinkled, heavy and black of beard; broad of forehead, steady of eye, the eyes blue without the glasses, the mouth hidden under the beard . . .

The faces settled one on top of the other. The beard undyed itself and vanished. The shaved hair grew back.

They were the same face.

The gulls had stopped crying. Harriet looked past Bird's shoulder. She saw the punt, empty, rocking. Something rolled in the water, making concentric rings of ripples.

And was still.

Harriet screamed. Bird grunted in her ear, his hands digging into the soft flesh of her hips, pulling her onto him. She beat at his face. 'Arthur!' she screamed. 'Papa!'

Bird ran down the lawn, a brown ape, waded into the pool, pulled the body ashore. He crouched by her father, goose-pimpled, penis dangling.

'Put some clothes on!' she said, wrapped in a tablecloth, infuriated by his disrespect.

'Stroke,' said Bird. He reached for his head to take off his hat, but a hat was one of the many things he was not wearing. 'He's dead.'

'Dead.' She looked at the gulls. 'Oh, dear. Oh, dear, dear, dear, dear.' She crouched by the corpse. Its face was black. She stroked its hair. 'Poor, dear papa.' She was talking to herself. 'You. As for you, you will go away again.'

'Away? But—'

'This is your fault. Get out. Now. Go!'

At the funeral Harriet sat in the family pew, George on her left, Babs on her right, holding her hands. Her mother was in Godalming, too prostrate to come. Mr Davies was praying for them.

Oh, Papa!

Chapter Sixteen

Six weeks later, she wrote a letter to Bird in Truro. He came by the next train. They sat in her office.

She said, 'We will get married.'

'Why?' His hair was growing, and he had shaved off the beard. He looked like the old Robbins, but without the self-confidence.

'Because I wish it.'

He said, 'Dearest Harriet,' and tried to take her hand.

'That's enough of that,' she said, pulling her hand away. 'We will go and see Mr Dally.'

Mr Dally was in the rectory, a pink, cringing man much vexed by an unruly flock. 'My congratulations,' he said. 'I shall publish the banns on Sunday.'

'Sooner the better,' said Harriet.

George and Babs also congratulated her, with some reserve. She thought they seemed nervous. 'Well?' said Harriet. 'What is it?'

'Look here,' said George. 'I don't want to teach you to suck eggs or anything.'

'Spit it out,' said Harriet, and smiled; that smile of intense purity that she reserved for George and Babs, and for Papa, when he had been alive to see it.

'When you marry Mr Bird,' said George, 'it all becomes his.'

'I trust him.'

'But . . .'

'Really. You must believe me.'

George nodded. 'Well,' she said. 'If it's good enough for you, it's good enough for us. Eh, Babs?'

'Quite.'

All of which made the shock, when it came, far, far worse.

One evening, ten days before the wedding, Alice Jenkins finished what she was doing, and sealed up the envelope, and walked down her scented path until the road changed under her feet, and pushed her letter under the door of Revel's cottage. Then as was her custom she took the Truro Road north, starting her rounds. The only bird-sound was a curlew on the Downs. By this, and the distant sound of the church clock striking eleven, she deduced that it must be dark.

The grit under her feet changed to granite slabs. She was at the root of the quay. All was quiet, but for the gurgling roar of the Mixer, and closer at hand the sound of someone breathing. A man.

'Good evening,' she said.

The man said nothing.

'What was it you wanted to talk about, my dear?' said Alice. She could smell a sort of sharpness coming off him; also drink. It made her uncomfortable.

'I am to be married,' said the voice of Bird.

'So they say.'

'I am very happy.'

'So you say.'

'What do you mean by that?'

It came to Alice that this voice was not simply vexed, but also, possibly, dangerous. 'Marriage is a happy event, I hear.'

'That is all you meant?'

'What else would there be?' Alice could feel her own anger rising. She was going to say too much, she knew. 'Something about your father, was it?'

'What about my father?'

'Mr James never told his daughter who you are, or why you came here in the first place. Out of consideration for her poor heart, so she would feel valued, not used. I have good ears, you know, and you sound very like Robbins, and he sounded very like Macleod.'

'I love her.'

'So you say.'

'It's why I came back to her.'

'You tried to spoil her once, for revenge. What has changed?'

'I told you,' said Bird. 'I love her.'

'But why should I believe you?'

'All the time I was away, I was thinking about her. People change. Love lasts. Revenge . . . it passes.'

Alice said in a quiet voice, 'Do you think so, Mr Macleod? Well, it was your father put out my eyes. And I find that I don't much like Macleods even now. And as for Miss Harriet not knowing that you're a Macleod, well, I think she should know the facts, and then she can judge for herself if it's love or vengeance you are after. Eh?' Silence. Then she said, 'Put me down!'

She summoned her breath to shriek. But something slapped hard over her face, something cold and wet and earthy, and filled her mouth so she could make no sound. She tried to draw breath. But the clay was in her nose as well as her mouth. She knew that the silence he planned for her was not the silence of an evening, but eternal.

And that his plans had failed already.

Then she was passing through air, and into icy water, and she was being drawn down by her clothes, spun, and none of that mattered any more. The Mixer was swallowing her up, dragging her through the agony of no-breath into the long golden tunnel. At the end of the tunnel there was Trelise: a Trelise she could see, the same old Trelise, but made new, bathed in brilliant sunlight that flooded her eyes with joy. And in the middle of the flower-blazing rockery, waiting for her, good as new, her Joshua.

It was Revel who spotted the thing in the Glory Hole, and dragged it out with his wrecking hook. It was Revel who stumped up to the house, and pushed aside the butler, and marched into the drawing room.

Harriet was sitting with her cousins Miss Barbara and Miss Georgina. They had a tea tray on the bench. The sisters were embroidering. Miss Harriet was looking out of the window, chewing her lips.

'Alice Jenkins is dead,' said Revel. He handed her a letter, which she read. She turned from silver to grey, and fell into the tea tray.

When her eyes opened she was looking into the frowning, sunburned faces of George and Babs. She took a piece of paper from her jersey, beneath which (George could not help noticing) her bosoms seemed bigger and rounder than before. 'Read this,' she said. 'Take it into a room and copy it out, and keep a copy each.'

The letter was appallingly written, too much ink, not enough; but an excellent effort for a blind woman.

Dear Miss Harriet,

I know you are to marry the man who calls himself Bird. I know that you think his name is truly Robbins, and that he is the father of your child.

But his name is not Robbins. It is Macleod. He is the son of the man who blinded me, and killed Joshua Jones. Your Papa knew, but he did not tell you, because he thought you were hurt enough when he chased your lover off of the island.

Whatever he feels now, he began in hate, and is stained with it always. If you marry him, it may be for love, or it may be his trap. All I know is that he thinks he has killed me before I can tell you the above. You may make your judgement accordingly.

If you read this, I shall be dead. I am giving it to Revel, who loves this place and can be trusted in matters affecting its welfare.

Your Friend
Alice Jenkins

'Damn Papa,' said Harriet. 'Damn him. May he roast and stink.'

'Your Papa?'

'A woman is no worse than a man,' said Harriet. 'Why can I not make up my own mind, while being in possession of the facts?'

'What on earth are you talking about?'

Harriet said, 'You are a virgin. You always will be.'

'*Harriet!* How *could* you?'

'My life belongs to me. Not Alice. Not Papa. Not Trelise. Not anybody else. Nobody!' She was shouting. She started to cry.

George moved over and put an arm round her shoulders. Harriet tried to pull away, but George held on tight, and Harriet relaxed, laying her ruddy outdoor cheek against the blue oiled-wool shoulder. 'I don't understand

232

some things,' said Georgina. 'I mean, virgins, yes, I suppose so.' She frowned. 'We are rather poor. Rather managing, I suppose. It is hard to see who would want to marry us. But dearest Harriet, what matters is that we are your friends.'

'Your great friends,' said Babs. 'Until death.'

Harriet looked up. She held both their hands. 'Thank you, my dears,' she said. 'Until death.' Being friends was so lovely. Oh, how she wished it could have been enough.

'Here,' said George, and gave Harriet her handkerchief, beautifully embroidered with needlepoint turks' heads. Harriet dried her eyes. 'Better now.'

'All better.'

'Just us,' said George. 'That's the ticket.'

'No,' said Harriet. 'I am awfully afraid there must still be a wedding.'

Dear Papa,

I forgive you. What you did you thought you did for the best. If it were not for me, you would be alive still, dear Papa, and so would poor Alice. The grief is terrible, but not so terrible as the guilt.

There are two of us guilty. Me. And the man. I should have told you, Papa, the moment I recognised him on the quay. The first time we talked, he told me he was sorry about the child. He cried. Cried like a crocodile. And I believed him, and kept my secret from you, Papa.

And now I am being punished, and the punishment will last for ever.

Dearest Papa, I promise you this.

There will be no more men.

Mr Bishop, the lawyer, had been shocked: shocked at the short notice at which he had been rousted out of his office; shocked at the whirlwind speed of the trap's progress out of Truro and across the causeway; and shocked at the nature of the agreement he was requested to draft. 'But Miss Harriet,' he cried, wild-haired. 'It may do for London. But in Cornwall . . . the irregularity!'

'Do it,' said Miss Harriet. (*So* like Joshua and James, thought Bishop, quailing). 'Here and now.'

'It will not be neatly done, you understand?'

'Will it have the force of law?'

'Under the Married Women's Property Act ... yes, that part of it. Undoubtedly.'

There was the sound of feet in the hall, the butler's murmur, a voice raised, expostulating at a delay.

'Mr Bishop, perhaps you would do our draft in the library.'

Mr Bishop needed no encouragement.

'Bring him in,' said Harriet, in a voice of ice.

When Bird came in, he found the three women equidistant from each other round the room. He went towards his usual chair on the right of the fire.

'There will be no need to sit down,' said Harriet. 'Alice Jenkins wrote me a letter last night. This is a copy. My lawyer has the original.' She watched him read it. 'Well?'

He said, 'Your father wished to spare you pain.'

'My pain is my own business. Where is Alice?'

'Drowned, they say. She fell off the quay.'

'All your corpses,' said Harriet. Her lip trembled, firmed again. 'This will not do, if we are to be married.'

'If?'

'I have had enough of men,' said Harriet. 'It seems that you are treacherous, mendacious, self-seeking. What you offer in mitigation is pleasure and companionship. I have decided that there are other pleasures and better companions. Bishop!' Bishop came in and handed her a paper. 'But there are times when a woman needs a husband, and you will do as well as anyone. Sign this.'

Bird read the paper. It seemed that he hereby renounced all claim on the Estate of Harriet Blakeney-Jones, hereinafter referred to as 'the wife'. He hereinafter guaranteed that all contact between them should be governed by her wish and her wish only. Further, the heirs of his body should be known not as Bird, Robbins or Macleod, but as Blakeney-Jones; and he was to have no say in their upbringing or education.

He said, 'This is servitude.'

'Barbara,' said Harriet. 'Be so good as to send for a policeman.'

'Wait,' said Bird.

There was silence.

He said. 'You loved me, once.'

Her face was made of pale wood. 'I loved the person who deceived me. Now I am undeceived, and I find the person who deceived me no longer exists, so I no longer love anyone. Sign.'

Bird signed with a hand just recognisable as his own.

Bishop took up a pen to witness. His face showed conflict and unhappiness. He ran his fingers through his aesthetic locks. 'Well?' said Harriet.

'If I might venture an observation?' Silence. 'Trelise is not as other places,' he said. 'It is an island, as such a thing unto itself. But it is only an island. Not a kingdom. On it all are subject to the law. It is good practice to avoid what is . . . eccentric. Unnatural. I ask you, is this arrangement natural?'

Harriet said, 'This is a garden, Mr Bishop. In a garden, the owner decides what is nature and what is not.'

'Man proposes,' murmured Bishop. 'God disposes.'

'Woman proposes,' said Harriet. 'As to God, who can tell? Now if you would be so good as to sign?'

Bishop bowed, and signed. 'You understand I felt it my duty,' he said. 'As an old friend of the family . . .'

'I understand,' said Harriet, ruddy face, yellow hair scraped back, china-blue eyes hard as glass. 'Mr Bishop, if you value our association, never have the impertinence to speak of such matters again.'

Bishop's mouth fell open. He seemed on the point of mentioning duty. But Harriet had left the room.

Harriet advanced the date of the wedding. Two days later, she and Bird were married in the church on the island. The pleasure of the guests was sensibly diminished by the necessity of retreating over the causeway even before the drinking of healths, the tide being unfavourable. Some said that the wedding day had been chosen by the bride with this in view. But John Bird and Harriet Blakeney-Jones were at last married, and that was the main thing.

Five months later, Harriet gave birth to twin boys, and ordered that the older be christened Guy, the younger Harry.

*   *   *

Hull Bay was a dry sheet of sand and mud laced with creeks of sky. Victoria followed the dog, Patton, out from the quay, skirting the pool at the end, where *Fly* and the other boats lay and where later on the tide the Mixer would form. She saw herself alone: a tiny stick-figure dwarfed by the heaven and the earth, and the disasters that lay before and behind. She was purposely not thinking of Morgan. But to keep her mind off him, she thought of the skeleton in the Sea Garden. She had almost convinced herself that it had been Robbins, shot by James after the seduction of his daughter. Now it was not. What she had found was more dreadful than bones: the letter in Alice's blind handwriting, that terrible letter, face to face in the folder with Bird's simultaneous binding to exclusion from Harriet's life. Harriet had loved Bird, that much was clear from the diaries. Then she had made her decision to live without men. Nothing lesbian about it, of that she was sure. It was more as if she had retreated into her luxurious certainties, the way she had when she and the Torodes had turned *Fly* for home halfway to the wreck of the *Voltaire*.

As if she had decided to reject the real world, and spend her life in a garden.

One thing was certain, Bird had not taken well to servitude. From the beginning of the summer of the twins' birth, a tide of whisky began to flow through the Garden House accounts. Bird was anaesthetising himself. Victoria found it hard to blame him.

Patton was lolloping foolishly on the sand. She picked up a stone, threw it for him. Married for four months to a man she had been in love with, head over heels, passionately. Now she was having an affair. And she did not know whether it was Guy she had stopped loving, or what Trelise had done to him. It was not even the sort of thing you could talk to anyone about. It was just terrible. Inescapable.

Oh, Christ.

The stone fell. It lay for a moment on the flat brown sand. Patton's merry bark changed. He was whining, now. 'Go on,' she said. But he stood still, panting at the stone, whimpering. The stone was shrinking. No. Sinking.

Victoria stood completely still. There were quicksands out here.

She called the dog. Then she turned and walked a dead straight line back to the shore. She passed the Pool, went up the quay steps.

She stood on granite, but she was still sinking.

Not that Guy noticed.

He was by the tea tray, giving garden history to the English feature writer: a woman called Fiona, a bobbed blonde with a short black skirt and distressing legs and gooey blue eyes. Victoria paused to watch them from behind a Dawkins explosion of *Echium* and *Fuchsia*. She walked across the state room to the library and dropped into her desk chair.

Guy put his head round the door. 'I forgot,' he said. 'Someone called Emma rang. Sounded Australian.' He fished in the pocket of his jeans. 'Here.' He handed her a number scrawled on a plant label.

Victoria dialled the number. A woman answered. The right Emma. 'Alleluia,' said Victoria.

'Hey!' said the voice – New Zealand, not Australian. 'Victoria?'

Emma had shown up at the Museum of America, to film something about waggons. She and Dave were freelance film-makers and journalists, travelling here and there by the seats of their pants. Since they really did not know anything and really wanted to find out, they had no shame about asking the kind of questions that no Northern European would dare ask.

'Someone called Victoria lives at Trelise,' said Emma. 'I saw in *Hello!* magazine. Is that you?'

'That's us.'

'And there's a garden there, that your husband is restoring and filming.'

'That's the one.'

'Dave found it in a book. Looks fantastic. We'd love to take a look, maybe do a little film about the filming?'

'Guy would be deeply moved. So would I. When can you come? Emma, it's so great to hear you.'

'And you, honey. About a fortnight?'

'Just call.'

Oh, real life, I love you. Friends of my own. I dance on quicksands . . .

What am I doing?

She had taken the bottle of Chanel from her desk drawer, was puffing it onto her wrists and throat. In the shed with Morgan's books, the tea would be in the pot, Morgan waiting in the chair.

So off she strode, down the garden path, and the sand rose sucking towards her knees.

Later, Morgan said, 'Would you leave him?'

She was startled. 'Leave who?'

'Guy.'

'Don't be stupid.' She saw his face blank for a moment. Saw through the blankness, into his mind; below all those calm and clever thoughts, into something mean.

Why?

She stood passive as he came towards her, both of them naked, and gripped her by the nape of the neck and kissed her hard. She did not believe what she had seen; not at first. He pushed her back onto the sofa. As he fucked her, she floated up to the ceiling. She saw two bodies, good bodies, the man hard-muscled and slim, the woman long-legged, high-breasted. The man thrust into the woman, and the woman wrapped her legs round him. Her head went back, and she moaned and gasped and made the noises as it spread and connected. But this time, the feelings did not blank out her mind. What she saw from the high corner of the room was an angry man fucking his boss's wife in a garden shed. And a thought came into her head, cold and unnerving. All the kindnesses: the demonstration of the garden, the explanations, the initiation into the debris of Valhalla, the discovery of skull and painting. Not kindnesses. Each one a little wedge to drive between Guy and me. And now this affair. He is doing this to fuck Guy. Not me.

That's why.

When it was over, she dressed quickly.

'Tomorrow?' said Morgan, lounging on the sofa like a small nude pasha.

'I don't think so.'

'Day after, then?'

'We'll see.'

He raised an eyebrow. The heat had left his eyes. What remained looked like calculation.

'Yes,' he said. 'I expect we will.'

She shut the door. She had left herself open to . . . anything he wanted to do to her.

238

She went back to Harriet and Bird.

At first, it was terrible. She was edgy and distracted, unable to settle. She missed Morgan; hated him, but missed him. And feared him, because of the calculation in his eye. What if Guy found out? But if he told Guy, Mary would find out. Did Morgan care? She had to hope so. Her whole life, resting on a Mexican standoff.

Hurt too much to think about.

Work.

For ten days she did not come out of the library except to go sailing, and to be extremely nice to Guy, who was at first stunned, and then visibly delighted. One teatime, he said, 'Morgan was asking after you.'

'Oh?' Face smiling, frozen.

'Wondering if you were ill, or something.'

She yawned, delicately; what an actress. 'Do I look ill to you?'

'You look bloody marvellous,' said Guy, and put his hand on hers. It was Guy's hand again, warm and dry, comforting as a goose-down duvet. She felt she was being rescued. Morgan had been desperation. Guy was the real thing. Always had been, ever since the parking lot at Pinewood Studios. That was how it felt, anyway, as Guy peeled the foil off a bottle of Puligny Montrachet. That was how it felt as they drank the wine. They ended up in bed, to their mutual pleasure and benefit. Lying with her head on Guy's chest, Victoria really thought that it might be over with Morgan. Screw you, Morgan.

Well, she had.

A shadow fell over her thoughts; perhaps the love she had just made to Guy she had made out of spite for Morgan. That was how Morgan would see it, anyway.

Nothing would ever be simple again.

With these and other unnerving thoughts, she drifted into a shallow, unsatisfactory sleep.

Bird could feel the sun on his back like a burning haversack as he trod the Endless Walk. Lady Scudamore asked him a question. He could not make himself listen to her. She was another female friend of Harriet's to be taken on a garden tour, a beanpole of a thing with a face like a horse and a voice to match. There was a bottle of whisky in his potting shed, calling him with a dark, insistent voice. 'Wha?' he said.

Lady Scudamore gazed upon him with disgust. The man needed to be washed. His face was purple and bloated with drink. He smelt as she imagined a four-ale bar might smell. 'I observed that the myrtles are beautifully cool at this time of year.'

Bird experienced a sudden spasm of rage, at this horse, Harriet, what his life had become. 'Cool as your arse,' he said. He shoved his hands in his pockets and walked away. If Harriet wanted horses shown round the garden, she could do it herself, instead of palming them off on him and lurking up there in the house with her man-women and those poor little twins.

The greenhouses drew him like a magnet. Great gleaming beauties, they were. Built to his specifications. No silly show-off tapestry-of-plants womany garden bloody what-goes-next-to-what codswallop here. This was serious stuff, new species and hybrids, reproduction sexual and asexual, division of cells into money. Ali Baba's damned Glasshouse, or was it Aladdin?

The smell of the propagating house was cool and rooty. A shaft of sun slanted in from a high window. His tools hung on nails on the wall, the more delicate scalpels and brushes in japanned-tin cases on the shelf. He sat down at the potting bench. Potting bench. Twice round the bloody world. Two species, hundred and thirty-eight varieties named for him. Married to the owner of Trelise. Back at a potting bench.

He plunged a hand into the bench's dark, moist mound of compost. His practised fingers found the neck of the bottle he kept there. He pulled the cork out and drank. Got to get off the island, get abroad. Get away. Couldn't be done, though. There was his duty, out there on the Mare. And Revel had something on him. Harriet had something on him. Sex and death. What made gardens work. Plus the duty of nurture. A prison. Devil's Island, with Harriet the devil . . .

The thoughts buzzed in his head like trapped bees. His hands worked automatically, fuchsia cuttings five to a pot, tamping down the soil, putting them in the barrow for later deployment in the glass. He noticed that someone else had come in, was sitting on the next stool. A woman;

young woman. Garden student. One of six, come to study what he had to teach. Good strong upper arms, big, firm body. Joan Jarvis. 'Hey,' he said, groping for the bottle. 'Drink.'

Joan Jarvis had a broad face, high cheek-boned, with thick black lashes and narrow eyes, short, broad, straight nose. She took the bottle, and drank. 'Thank you, Mr Bird,' she said, wiping her lips on her coarse linen sleeve.

'George.'

She smiled at him. Down here on an RHS scholarship. Clever girl; the only one. Always at the front of the crowd, asking good questions, listening to the answers, eyes shining, lips parted; all that. She wanted to do man's work in a garden, but she was still a woman with it. Unlike some. She smoked cigarettes and drank whisky. And by the look of her, she liked Bird.

They sat working in the dark shed with its bright shaft of sun. Whisky made Bird bold. He dived his left hand into the pile of potting mixture, let it stray to one side. His fingers found Joan's, firm and strong and smooth. Her hand became completely still. Her face was impassive, touched with light like the face of a temple carving he had seen in Bali. The fingers suddenly took on a life of their own. Quickly, they clasped Bird's—

'George!' said a voice from the doorway.

The hands leaped apart, causing only the smallest tremor in the surface of the dark compost-pile.

'Lady Scudamore says you were rude.'

'Pish,' said Bird.

'You will be civil to my friends.'

'Not necessarily,' said Bird. 'Not when I am running the stove and the cool houses and the orchid house and the cut flowers and the bulbs and the kitchen garden and twelve gardeners and twenty on the farm and old Uncle Ali Baba and All.'

'Reflect,' said Harriet. 'What would you be without Trelise?'

'What,' said Bird, 'would Trelise be without me?' The figure in the doorway lifted its chin and turned away. He picked up the whisky to drown it, drank, offered the bottle to Joan Jarvis, expecting to see in her eye scorn and dislike.

But seeing instead, in the beam falling through darkness onto her face, something like sympathy. Even compassion. 'It's terrible,' she said. 'Those poor children. I'm sure you could do something.'

Bird gripped her hand manfully.

She knew who it all hung on

Extract from the diary of Guido Blakeney-Jones, 2 October 1907

This begins the story of the life of Miss Guido Blakeney-Jones of the Nursery Trelise Cornwall England Europe Western Hemisphere The World The Universe. I write it in the lovely book I have been given by Aunt Babs for my VIIth Birthday. It has got creamy coloured paper. A lovely binding of blue suede leather. A lock. And a special key that I can wear on a special string inside my blouse.

My Life. I live in the Nursery Rooms at Trelise Priory with my mouse Daphne and my brother Harry. Daphne is pink, because Aunt Babs painted her so and she looks so pretty. Harry is bigger than me, though younger. He thinks Daphne looks sissy. He is ushually cross. When other little girls come in to play he sits and sulks and whops things except my camel Dulcie because when he whopped Dulcie I pinched and pinched him and Grant (who is our guvvy and ever so nice) boxed his ears! Harry wants a gun. I have got my own garden, a small one. I want a lute with ribbons, like the Lady of Shallot. It is teatime so now dear Diary I must go to have some scones. Then I will see if Harry will play House but he won't the rotter so I will do my garden insted.

Harriet at fifty was little different from Harriet at forty, except that her hair had faded to a severe mouse, worn in a tight bun. Perhaps it was this tightness that gave her face its look of astonishment with everything that she saw of the world. She was indeed astonished – not because of any lack of familiarity with the world's workings, but because of the world's perpetual failure to operate along lines that she considered reasonable.

Take the reproductive process.

One of the reasons she admired the plant kingdom was its capacity for asexual reproduction, by cutting, layer, division and graft. The business of sex had caused her brief moments of pleasure, but years of misery. The natural law that decreed that fathers be part of the process was also loathsome to her. Male evil roared down the generations like a series of avalanches: Fairey, Joshua, Josia Macleod, Arthur Robbins in all his guises . . . Males should be like the male Barnacles found by Darwin, minuscule, perpetually resident in the female, significant only as inseminators, causing no trouble. She said as much to George as they played Chinese whist in the drawing room.

'How vile,' said George. 'What's trumps?'

'Hearts,' said Harriet. 'Here's tea.'

They abandoned the cards. Harriet watched the household collect: George and Babs (permanent residents, since the death of their poor mother), Mercy, red-bearded Anastasia, Joe, Frau Gertler, and of course the Twins, on parade between schoolroom and nursery. Harriet felt herself wrapped in security and pleasure. After all the dreadful things that had happened, she was safe. They were all safe in this room. She looked after them, and they looked after her.

A movement on the terrace caught her eye. It was Bird, fleshy nose pressed against the window pane. She waved him away. For a moment he vanished. Then the terrace door burst open, and he was in the room. 'Harriet,' he moaned. Drink rolled off him in waves.

'The study,' said Harriet. She stumped into the room at the end and sat down. 'Well?'

'It's not right,' said Bird. 'I was watching you all through the bloody window. Nest of dried-up old—'

'What is not right?'

'The boys,' he said. 'You've got to let them be boys.'

'I am not aware that I have *got* to do anything.'

'Don' you be slippery with me. They've got to get out of skirts.'

'Many children wear skirts.'

'The reason children wear skirts,' said Bird, 'is so when they shit it falls to the ground without messing their breeks. Harry and Guy—'

'Guido. He calls himself Guido, as you would know if you ever talked to him.'

He said, 'They're seven years old now.'

'I think you have forfeited your right to dictate to me the way I bring up my children.'

Bird's head dropped. 'You think I deceived you all along. Never mind how we started, I came to love you, Hatty. And you loved me.'

'So you are always saying.'

'I am a good father, when allowed,' he said. 'You know that too.' Harriet folded her lips, and glanced out of the window at the blink of the Mare. 'But you won't allow me. I can't leave this island, and I can't see my little boys, and I can't do nothing without you say so first, and you never say so. You've got me gutted, Hatty. Gutted and filleted.'

'You have made your bed,' said Harriet. 'Now you must lie in it.'

'Says she with a mouth like a chicken's arse,' said Bird. 'Well you wait, Hatty. You'll get the consequences.'

'What consequences?'

'Wait and see.'

Harriet stood up, smiling infuriatingly. She said, 'I understand that it is not pleasant to be defeated. But you should have thought about that when you wished me to be the one defeated. You have had your turn. Now you will do as I please.'

He trudged past the averted eyes of the spinster army, and onto the terrace. Back among the seed trays and empty bottles of the Garden House drawing room, he thought deeply. What did women hate?

Rivals. Jealous devils, all of them. Get 'em fighting among themselves. That was the one.

He would see what he could do.

The moon rolled up. It was a calm night. As always on windless nights, a punt lay tied up alongside South Quay. He climbed aboard. Puffing and grunting, he began to pull across the silky remnants of the flood, heading for the Mare.

In the heat of the Argand lamp, inside the concentric crystal wheels of the lens, the white world at the root of the Mare's beam. Sweeping the horizon, flash, ten seconds, flash; speaking to the Lizard and the Eddystone, beacon unto beacon, and to ships passing, sparkling like towns in the black night, red for London, green for America. And over towards the land, the lamp-yellow windows of Trelise, shattered by ripples. It was a good flat night, so the boat had come.

Even on a calm night, the tower was alive with sounds: with the majestic rumble of the five-ton lens, driven by its clockwork, spinning on its trough of mercury. With the bubble of stew from the cylindrical kitchen two floors below, where the table was laid for four. With Bird's voice, telling the story of Little Red Riding Hood.

And with the ragged sound of a pair of childish hands, delighted, clapping.

The twins had enquired about their father, of course. Harriet had showed them Bird. They had not been impressed. He looked awful, and smelt worse. It was known that he had done something terrible, the kind of thing that men always did. They had no friends their own age. They assumed that mummies and daddies always behaved to each other like Harriet and Bird, unless they were islanders, in which case they had to work awfully hard.

Harriet made sure the nurserymaids dressed the twins sensibly, of course: calf-length skirts of blue serge, with white blouses on top, and oiled-wool jerseys of navy blue

Harry, the younger, was square of chin and build. When the nursery-maids refused to cut his hair (Miss Harriet's orders) he did it himself with dead-heading shears from the toolshed. The humiliating skirt he wore hitched up like the kilts in the pictures in *Rob Roy*, scratched brown legs sticking out below, feet unshod. He was a dead shot with a catapult, a dab hand with a trap (his room was uninhabitable, perfumed with innumerable moleskins rubbed with saltpetre, pinned out on boards under his bed). His mother he cordially disliked, preferring the company of Farlow the keeper or, failing Farlow, his red-bearded, pipe-smoking aunt, Anastasia. (Actually, Anastasia was not an aunt at all, but a great friend of Aunt Joe, herself only a cousin. Aunt Joe had brought her back from Cowes, where Anastasia was a distinguished figure in Big Boat racing circles. Anastasia was of aristocratic Russian extraction, and Tough as Old Boots. Harry respected her greatly.) On rainy days, he and Anastasia would lock themselves into the dining room and engage in target practice with a .22 rifle, greatly to the detriment of various clay pipes and (as excitement mounted) the Famille Rose porcelain on the great dresser, considered by Trelise frilly and vulgar.

Harry's elder brother, Guy, was different.

From earliest years, he took against his name. At first, he bitterly envied Harry his extra syllable. Then Frau Gertler, an aesthetic Austrian Babs had accumulated on a Danube voyage, had taken a fancy to him, and petted him, and Italianised his name in a way that appeared to his infant mind mysterious and important. Guido, as he was now universally known, was entirely compliant with his mother's wishes. What was on Harry a kilt was on Guido beyond doubt a skirt. His jersey, rough garment that it was, he wore with a subtle Viennese flair. His blouse, which on his brother Harry was an assembly of rags bathed in mole-blood and pollack-slime, was a crisp thing worthy of Bond Street. He wore at all times short socks of dazzling whiteness and black patent-leather pumps. His hair, honey-coloured and shining, descended in orderly ringlets, framing his huge, liquid blue eyes, his bee-stung red lips, and his delicately pointed chin. He had from the earliest age been passionately interested in the great doll's house James had given Harriet, helping with the flowers – Frau Gertler and Babs were great flower arrangers. The sound of Anastasia and Harry making hay with the china would reduce him to tears of grief and rage. But one thing he had learned from an early age was to stay out of Harry's way. And one of his favourite places for doing this was in the greenhouses.

He varied the house of preference according to his mood and the weather. In winter, he would stretch himself on a vacant bit of staging in the Orchid House, revelling in the heat and the humidity and the sumptuous inflorescences of the *Cattleyas* Bird had brought from South America.

But now it was spring; April, to be precise. Harry had been being a beast. First he had sunk Amelia and Dorinda, the two best dolls, in an eel trap in the Pool. Then he had made Guido pluck eighteen sparrows for a sparrow pie. Guido had slid out of the house and down into the greenhouses, but not this time the Orchid House, sweltering with the piped heat from its boilers. The end of a spring day was time for the Cool House.

He sat on an iron bench in the stored heat of the afternoon, and watched the ferns coiled like butterfly's tongues against the pinkening sky. Around him, the greenhouses darkened.

He daydreamed he was a butterfly. A gorgeous butterfly, a peacock, probably, with eyes on his wings; a peacock living in a glasshouse, safe from rain and wind and cold, and Harry drowning her poor dolls—

The daydream came to an abrupt end.

Out in the night, a lantern was moving. Above it was a face, lit from below. Bird's face.

The yellow light wobbled next door, into the Orchid House, and stopped moving.

Two ghostly shapes came into being, illuminated by the lamp, hazed and bent by many layers of glass. One of them was short, the other tall. A man and a woman. They put their arms out. They took hold of each other, and hugged.

Guido's heart banged in his chest. Something awful was going to happen. The man would get the woman into trouble, and leave her. Mama said it always happened so.

Silently, Guido ran through the dark garden to the Priory.

The Aunts were at dinner in the dining room, digging into a cartwheel-sized shrimp and conger pie in their usual silence. Guido whispered into Harriet's ear. Harriet stood up so fast her chair fell over. She said to Guido, 'Stay here!' and ran from the room.

'Guido!' cooed Frau Gertler. He went to stand by her chair. She straightened his collar and fed him prawns and smoothed his ringlets. If *only* he had been a girl!

There was no more lamp in the Orchid House. There was only the half-moon filtering a hard grey light over flower and pseudobulb. There was steam on the inside of the glass, so from the outside it was like a vast prism of pearl. In the places where the condensed water had become too heavy to remain droplets, it had run in drips from top to bottom of the pane. On one pane, near the middle, the drips had united into a sheet of clear glass.

Through that clear glass an attentive eye might have seen two naked bodies, moving together like one body, the sweat on them gleaming in the diffuse, silvery light of the moon.

And the sounds. A man, out of condition, grunting *Joan, Joan*. A young woman's voice, breathing hard. The breathing becoming a gasping, then small cries, pleasure, pain—

Then a new noise. From the door end of the shed, where the boilers are, a muttering. *Not again*, says a woman's voice. *Never again*. The discreet scrape of a shovel on coals. A slosh of liquid, a heavy, oily smell. In the grey night there rolls a flock of orange sparks, scattering across the slatted staging, breaking and glowing. Round the orange there comes a ghostly blue that spreads and licks at the timber. The woman's gasps become screams. The naked bodies separate. The flames are everywhere now.

And from above, with a huge jangling smash, the daggers of glass come raining down.

Chapter Seventeen

Victoria said, 'She killed him.'

Guy put the paper down. 'What?'

'Harriet killed Bird.'

Guy was staring at her. 'Harriet killed the father of her children?'

'Why not?' Fire. Victoria could see it. Fire, heat, noise. Screams. Revenge. No remorse. Remorse came later. 'She found Bird and Joan Jarvis making love in the Orchid House. She thought she was in control of Bird. She couldn't stand it when she found she wasn't. She snapped, blew it, set fire to the greenhouses – they kept paraffin in the Orchid House boiler house for starting the furnaces, it's in the ledger.'

'Maybe she blew it. But *killed* him?'

'I think the way she saw it, she had him in prison. He was killed while attempting to escape.'

'Lord.' Pause. 'So where's he buried? He's not in the churchyard.'

'He's not in the register either. They hushed it up. He left, apparently. Disappeared. Not seen after the fire, not found in the ashes. There's a letter from Joan Jarvis's parents, saying how marvellous it was that their daughter had worked at Trelise, and what a ghastly accident. She was sent home in a box, apparently.'

'Christ,' Guy said. 'Poor girl.' He was not reading the paper any more. 'Mind you, if Bird didn't get away he would have had fillings in his teeth and everything. Maybe he's your skeleton.'

He had a point. Low-speed drill, Helen Torode had said. If Bird had had fillings, it would have been in the low-speed drill era. Worth checking, if she could find a way to check; on its own, hardly definitive – wait a minute. 'How did you know about the fillings?'

The tide of blood spread up Guy's face. 'The report,' he said. He took her hand. 'I told you . . . Victoria, don't give me a hard time.'

'It's just fascinating to hear you're interested, that's all.'

'This is my great-grandmother killing my great-grandfather and burying him under a bush,' said Guy. 'Of course I'm bloody interested.'

'Only possibly.'

'Well, I like it.' There was a stubborn look behind his eyes. Victoria had the strong impression this was something he wanted to believe.

One thing was odd, though.

Guy's hands: warm, dry, strong, one of the things Victoria had first loved about him. But just now, when he had taken her hand, the palm on her fingers had been chill and clammy.

Why?

Fly, sliding along the rocks of the West on a day of green sea and yellow sun. Wake a small crease, Victoria with an arm along the sun-warm tiller, Emma on her back on the deck, small, broad, vigorous, in a lime-green bikini. Below *Fly*'s keel, swimming among the kelp-trunks and the black rocks, the red-rubber pollack baits.

It was a full day since Emma and Dave had turned up. Emma and Victoria had been playing. They had kept out of the garden, so far. The garden meant Morgan—

The line in Emma's hand jerked violently. She sat up and hauled, hand-over-hand, feet planted, the light sliding over the little muscles at the base of her neck. The pollack came to the side of the boat. Emma ran her hand down the trace, wrapped it once round and swung it inboard and into the basket, no fuss, economical, confident. The way she was in life.

'Enough fish?' said Victoria.

'Sure.'

'Lunch.'

'And then the garden.'

The thought of bumping into Morgan gave her a big weakness between the ears. There was guilt. There was desire. There was fear.

Face up to it.

So after lunch, away they went, marching down the stairs, Emma did her inquisition, starting in Davy Jones, history and emotional background of each figurehead, then the bamboo walk, the Antipodes, talking. Victoria had done it all scores of times, but today she found herself as enthused as if it had been the first. That was Emma for you.

They sat on the ruins of the dolmen at the base of what had once been Araby. Victoria was telling Emma about Robbins' seduction of Harriet in the Paradiso. 'Wait'll I tell Dave,' said Emma. 'Notes on technique. Half a bottle of wine and a cheese sandwich, and what about it, right?' They walked up the steps; the original steps, the plantings innocent now, mossy, ferny, the smell moist and bracing. The stern cabin of the *Voltaire* still stood mortared into the rocks. Instead of the day bed there was a wormy ping-pong table, a crumbling model yacht, two or three thousand dead flies. Emma swept flies off the window-sill and sat down, one sturdy brown knee under her chin. 'Lovely,' she said, looking back down the steps.

'Harriet made Bird redo it.'

'Not the garden,' said Emma. 'Nice though it is. Hey, he's coming back.'

She was watching a ten-yard gap between a *Griselina* and a *Camellia* that revealed a stretch of the Endless Walk. Past the gap walked Morgan; Morgan strolling, hands in pockets, ramrod-straight in his jeans and seaboots; face firm and distant, contemplative. He could have been a Greek philosopher out for an evening stroll in Arcadia. Victoria found she had stopped breathing. Don't look up, she begged him. Or I will have to introduce you, and I'll, oh, shit, why did I ever get mixed up with you in the first place? She could feel the blood hot in her face. But at the same time, she was interested to note in a detached, forensic manner, the problem now did not seem to be so much passion as embarrassment, and even dislike.

'Who *is* that?' said Emma, nose against the window pane.

'The head gardener.' Safely the other side of the glass. Walk away, Morgan—

Emma bashed the window open with the heel of her hand. 'Oi!' she yelled. 'Morgan! C'mere!' And she was out of the door.

Numb-faced, Victoria trailed after her.

They were standing in the walk, talking. Or rather, Morgan was talking,

251

because Emma had asked the question. She was giving him tits, eyes, legs and mind, adding up to the kilowattage of a herd of buffalo. Emma laughed, her completely natural laugh that everyone always wanted to hear more of. They were blocking the exit. There was no way round. Victoria said, 'Afternoon, Owen.'

He smiled and said, 'Victoria,' with that focused warmth.

She said, 'I'll see you at the house, Emma.'

As Victoria walked away, she felt terrific. No more quicksand. They would become friends again. Things would get back into balance—

Bullshit. You do not get to be friends with an employee that you fuck on your island. Particularly employees whose motives you suspect.

From the library she heard Dawkins jitter into the State Room with the teacups.

'Hey!' said Emma, bursting in. 'Where did you go? What a guy. What a *garden!*'

Victoria nodded. There was nothing to be relieved about. It was still a quicksand. Emma was talking. Something about a TV series. 'What?' said Victoria.

'We've been looking for someone,' said Emma. 'For bloody months. It's this idea Dave's got – old world, new world, European gardens, new world plants? Stupid boring idea, I told him, unless you get a really seriously good presenter, nice guy, down to earth, sexy, knows his onions from his *Notopanax*, know what I mean?'

'Yes,' said Victoria. 'D'you want some tea?'

'No,' said Emma. 'I've found him. Great face, nice boots, huge mind. I talked to him. He wants you to lend him to us.'

'Lend who?'

'We'll only need him for six weeks. You'll get great coverage. And if you don't let him do it, he'll probably leave anyway.'

'What are you talking about?'

'We are going filming,' said Emma. 'With our new presenter. The man's name is Morgan.'

Victoria stared at her.

Emma made a face back. 'Well?'

It would have been great. But there was no way, not with Guy's film to make.

But when Emma asked him, Guy thought for five seconds, then grinned two-thirds of the way round his head and said, 'Morgan? Sure.'

Victoria could not believe her ears. 'What about the film?'

'We're ahead. Give him a holiday, raise his profile. What about some champagne?'

So at the beginning of July, Morgan left the island, to return in August. For Victoria, it was as if someone had put oxygen back in the air. There were children in the house, cousins staying for the summer holidays. Victoria liked children, even other people's. Everyone seemed to be having a good time. Even Dawkins.

Even Guy.

Victoria's Daddy liked his girls to sail. His girls liked sailing, too, mainly because it was a way of getting away from Daddy. They were taught by Doc Schmelk, who had a large yellow moustache and was a retired fisherman, not a doctor. They came to like different kinds of boat. Martha liked big yachts with walk-in freezers and scrubbed-white teak decks. Sarah liked six-metres and other crisp racing boats. Victoria liked anything, really, as long as she could sail it herself. In earliest years, they had done it from a cottage in North Haven in Penobscot Bay, sailing little catboats. Daddy liked Penobscot, because it was full of the kind of Bostonians who counted God among their ancestors.

It was in Penobscot that Victoria and Sarah were sent out to sail their first race.

There was some kind of regatta on. They had come up to a start line with a lot of other boats. They had been carefully briefed. Windward end of the line, start on the starboard tack. But everyone else seemed to have the same idea, so there was a terrible crowd. Sarah was arguing with the stopwatch in a Donald Duck voice, and waving to Jamie Cabot, so they were a bit confused about the time, particularly because Jamie unsportingly flipped her the finger, and she did not know whether it was because her hair looked terrible or because this was a race. She got pissed at him anyway. 'Asshole,' she said. 'Can we start, and beat him? Victoria?'

Because Victoria had sailed all the way past the marker boat, out of the race and onto the dark ruffle of the bay.

'Victoria,' said Sarah. 'What are you *doing?*'

Victoria pointed to a chunky granite hump, crowned with trees. 'I'm sure there's a quarry on there,' she said.

'So what?' said Sarah. 'We're *racing.*'

'Screw it,' said Victoria. 'There's no record of a quarry. I want to look at it. Now. It could be a discovery. This is important.'

'No it's not.'

'Well, it's very interesting.'

'Jesus.' Sarah stuck her bottom lip out. 'Why can't you ever do what other people do?'

'Because Daddy would be so delighted.'

Sarah thought about that. 'Point,' she said.

And they both laughed like hell, because they thought they were getting away from him.

How wrong could you be?

1915. A sunny evening on the Mare. The lantern full of rainbows, the windows open, for a miracle, the squeak of chamois leather polishing salt off the glass. Few ships in the Channel now, because under the diamond blue of the sea the U-boats were sliding. The plumes of half a dozen merchantmen cut the edge of the world, straggling westward, hearts (according to the experts) high because they were not shepherded humiliatingly in convoys. Closer inshore flocked the tan sails of luggers, hauling mackerel out of the tide under the Lewis gun of a launch with a smoky paraffin engine.

To the north of the tower, Trelise lay calm under the sky. The bulb fields, normally brown ridges at this time of the year, were green with potato haulm and yellowish with corn. Where once the greenhouse ashes had scarred the garden, carrots and cabbages were growing. The island was self-sufficient in food, and sent potatoes and vegetables ashore to Truro, whence they headed east to feed the land at war.

Behind the beaches by Old Hull quay, men had for weeks scurried like wasps on a nest. Now an apron of white concrete covered the foreshore, with a slipway down the beach to the low-water mark. Beyond low water, half a dozen big white buoys floated in line. Long sheds with asbestos roofs stood at the inshore end of the apron, raw and new in the evening light.

There came into the air a buzz, no louder than the hum of a heat-drugged bee in the lantern. The men on the apron stopped what they were doing and looked east. Six dots materialised over the dark whisker of the Eddystone. The dots grew, and became lumbering biplanes. By the lantern of the Mare they stood on one wing, turned, a view of rivets on silver boat-bellies, one, two, three, four, five, six. Then they were settling into white foam-arrows on the mottled blue, and taxiing to the buoys.

The squadron had arrived to fight its war.

The sun was touching the horizon. Squadrons might come, and squadrons might go. Some things must never change.

Lots of pumps on the pressure cylinder, until the valve said hiss. The weight of the clockwork was already up, because you did that at noon, winding the handle by the big winch under the iron stairs. Which is where you went now, to take the pawl off the ratchet.

Once the pawl was off, the lens began to turn, slow at first, then faster, until there she went, smooth in the mercury trough, one spin per ten seconds. Pull the fuel-cock. Smell the paraffin vapour misting out of the mantle. Flick the trigger of the igniter. *Whoomp*, a small, safe sound. On the horizon to the west, the sun was a great half-orange. The shadows rushed across the land, blackening valleys, hiding towns.

'Well done, Arthur,' says Keeper Souter.

Overhead, the lamp swells, and the crystal wheels of the lens blaze.

As every night, the Mare opened its great white eye and began to spin.

Supine on Plum Orchard beach, Lieutenant Charteris floated in pure light. This water, palest turquoise, this sand, silver ground not from dull stone but from purest crystal . . .

He closed his eyes, and let the golden eye of the sun glare upon his naked body. The chesty roar of the wavelets soothed his ears, still ringing from the hammer of the Curtiss' engines. He felt his stomach settling; the castor-oil in the exhausts gave a chap awful collywobbles and Jepson, the observer, was enough to make you cat. Girls, music-halls, beer and more girls, Jepson. Great lumbering land girls that smelt like horses, rough and tumbled with all their ghastly breasts and haunches in dirty haylofts or sordid boarding-houses that smelt of bugs . . .

Charteris breathed ozone. He lay on hot sand, clean and male. *What* a place!

Somewhere behind the beach, a flute started to play.

Charteris did not open his eyes. The flute carried the beach out of the war and into Arcadia, beside a wine-dark sea up which Homeric heroes climbed to monster-haunted horizons. Under a holm-oak in the shade of a rock, a slim-limbed shepherd boy played on a simple pipe a melody clean as his rustic soul . . .

Charteris had left Radley eighteen months previously, and a youth spent in Dorking meant that disillusioning contact with genuine shepherd-boys had been negligible. He turned his head languidly in the direction of the flute-player, and opened his eyes.

There was no holm-oak. But there was bright-green bracken, and mauve sea-pinks, and a granite menhir grey and yellow with lichen. And in the shade of the menhir, sitting on a stone and playing a silver flute, the absolutely quintessential shepherd boy, Dorking edition.

He would have been fifteen. His skin was the colour of honey, the lips pursed over the flute's hole red as cherries. The curls that framed his delicate features were of purest gold. The parts of the limbs visible outside the knee-length shorts and short-sleeved shirt were brown, hazed with golden down. Altogether (thought Charteris, whose classical education had been shallow) he looked a ripping good sort, and it would be awfully jolly to get to know him better.

So he rolled onto his side, and said, 'Awfully jolly tune.'

The boy stopped playing. A blush mantled the delicate features. 'Erik Satie,' he said. 'I'm awfully sorry. I come here to practise. Harry, my brother, he hates it. So I have to get out of the way.'

'Very, er . . . ripping,' said Charteris. He was blushing himself. 'Jolly good tune. Sort of wild. Look here, I'm Charteris.' He put out his hand.

The boy gripped it, firm but delicate. 'Guido,' he said. 'Blakeney-Jones. I say, are you from the flying boats?'

'Spot on.'

'So beautiful,' said Guido. 'Like barges in the sky.'

'Not bad old crates,' said Charteris. He was watching the way the boy's – Guido's – mouth moved. He had never seen anything so ripping in his life.

Guido did not know what you said to tawny hulks who lay on the beach and did not seem to notice that they were naked. He wanted to be embarrassed. But he could not be. He wanted to know more about this chap who could fly, with his narrow hips and square shoulders, who was ... well, beautiful. And who seemed interested in him. Most men were interested in Harry, not him. He said, 'Would you ... that is, could you come to tea?' He hesitated. Today everyone was here, and tomorrow the Aunts were going sailing. But he simply simply could not wait. 'Today?'

'Awfully kind,' said Charteris. 'They're re-rigging the crate, as it turns out. So I'd absolutely love to.'

'Good. Er ... ripping,' said Guido, breathless with joy. 'Half past four. I'll come and find you.'

'Ripping.'

It was only as Guido turned to go that they realised that since their handshake, neither of them had let go the other's hand. Something startled and intense jumped into their eyes. Then Guido turned and ran away down a path in the bracken with (thought Charteris) the grace of a deer.

Guido ran across the island cricket pitch and into the gate by the Sea Garden. By the entrance to Davy Jones he stopped, panting. His mind was turning like a kaleidoscope. Something had happened, and he did not know what. In the foreground, there floated the face of ... Charteris: dark-haired, grey-eyed, sunburned, with lines round the eyes, tiredness, strain, responsibility. The face could have been a boy's, but the eyes were the eyes of a man.

Guido sat down on a stone and looked up the empty Poseidon Stairs. He had been to his cousin Sophia's wedding three years ago, at St George's, Hanover Square. In his mind he saw two figures on the stairs, as Sophia and Horace had stood on the steps of St George's. Except that the face over the tight-belted tunic and gleaming brown boots was not Horace, but Charteris. The other face was hidden behind the white bridal veil.

Charteris paused, and gently lifted the veil. The face underneath it was Guido's. Charteris took off his cap, and bent his head . . .

Crimson-faced, Guido ran helter-skelter back to the house for luncheon.

Harry was there, fingernails black with dried blood, reeking of dead fish. 'What you been up to, Queenie?' he said to Guido.

Guido hated being called Queenie, but it did not do to let Harry know, or he would tease you to bits. 'Practising my flute,' he said, then realised too late that that was no good either.

'Tootle, tweedle, tootle,' said Harry, with scorn. 'Terrific lot of lobsters off the Little Foal's Tail. Which I suppose you will guzzle up even though you don't do anything to bring 'em in.'

Guido hunched miserably over his plate. The table was crowded with Aunts in blue serge. There was little conversation. Lunch was talk of war accompanied by mackerel and potatoes, the mackerel fresh, the potatoes overboiled. The women ignored the boys, as was their wont.

'I saw the flyin' boats,' said Harry, with his mouth full. 'Curtiss C-12 Large Americas. Rippin' great flight of them. Comin' back from patrol. Great work goin' on out there. Bashing the Hun. And all you can do is play the flute.'

'No,' said Guido.

'Well, true,' said Harry. 'I mean you can't even play the flute, not really.'

'I mean, no I spent the morning talking to one of the pilots,' said Guido.

Harry's small, square face seized up with disbelief. 'Pish,' he said.

'And I've asked him to tea.'

The square jaw dropped for a moment. The mouth hung open. Then it closed with a click.

'Today.'

'I'll be there,' said Harry.

Guido realised he had been outmanoeuvred. Harry would talk to Charteris about . . . oh, guns, and fish, and boats, and all the rest of the stuff Guido did not know how to talk about because he was not interested. And Charteris would pay attention to him, and forget Guido, and poor Guido would be adrift in the garden again, playing his flute and thinking of weddings and dances in places where there were only bulbs and potatoes . . .

'I say,' said Harry. 'Ain't you going to finish those spuds?' He did not wait. He scraped them off Guido's plate onto his own. That was the thing about Guido, silly beggar. You could ignore him, really. It would be jolly interesting to talk to this airman chap about guns and the Boche and so on.

Charteris arrived in the courtyard at four-thirty sharp, trussed up to the chin in tunic, breeches and boots. The day had become steadily hotter. His collar itched. He sweated from the feet and armpits. He was horribly uncomfortable. He walked over a courtyard of carefully brushed grit, in which an elderly carriage gleamed from the shadows of a coachhouse, past a wall of blood-red geraniums trained to climb, and up to a front door over-arched with an ogee of carved granite. No such barbaric splendour existed in Dorking. He began to feel not only uncomfortable, but unworthy.

And also slightly furtive.

The RNAS men in the huts behind the slipways tended to be mechanics, not aesthetes. They viewed the Priory with extreme suspicion. There seemed to be a large number of women there, dressed in navy blue. These were known as the witches, and avoided, out of fear of boredom. The witches did not issue the invitations usual from feudal establishments close by military installations. So the airmen directed their attention to the fuggy joys of the Castle taproom, and the succession of clattering lorries that left nightly for the fleshpots of Truro and Falmouth.

A spherical butler opened the front door. Charteris found himself passing through a gloomy chamber lined with ship models, and into a drawing room lined with shapeless figures in navy-blue sailor suits. One of them (it was hard to tell, in the shadows) seemed to be sporting a short but definite red beard along the lines of Sir Francis Drake. But if the human furniture was dour, the flower arrangements were magnificent. Apparently from the middle of one of them, stepped a tall woman with a long nose and mouse-coloured hair hoicked into a bun. There was a golden blur of movement at her side, and Guido was there. 'Charteris,' he said. 'I mean, Lieutenant Charteris. Lieutenant Charteris, Mrs Blakeney-Jones. Mummy.'

Lieutenant Charteris smiled. Harriet did not smile back. She was not impressed by handsome young men. The war had meant that she could get rid of most of the men on the farm and get some gels in, but now the gels were under siege from the men of the RNAS. Harriet was preparing a lecture for later this evening, How to Stay Out of Trouble, none a greater authority than she . . .

'Have a cup of tea,' someone was saying. Frau Gertler. Harriet went to her office and started to rough out the heads of the Land Girl lecture.

After a while, the dim tinkle of music began to filter into the study, mingled with the sound of the flute, beautiful and precise. Not that Harriet could be bothered with beauty or precision. She was on Paragraph Six – Knees and Elbows – Showing him What's What when things get Hot. Paragraphs like Six were delicate things, requiring concentration.

In the State Room, Charteris had forgotten how hot he was. A square-faced brat in knickerbockers had come up to him and introduced himself as Harry and started rabbiting on about guns and U-boats. Charteris had had enough guns and U-boats. He had been watching Guido, whose face had fallen at his brother's arrival and who had slunk miserably away. Charteris had made some sort of excuse, and followed Guido into the next room, where he found himself transfixed by a radiant smile. Now he was sitting in a chair by the piano, on which Frau Gertler was accompanying Guido's flute. He had forgotten that there was a bone-china cup of rather odd tea in his hand ('Camellia leaves – grows in the garden,' Frau Gertler had said as she poured. 'U-boats, you know.') He was no longer aware of the evening sun streaming onto the panels of Chinese wallpaper, the golden gleam of book spines in the tall shelves, the hefty navy-blue Aunts stacked against the panelling. Charteris was transported on wings of music.

He had absolutely no idea what he was listening to, of course. He just knew that once again he was suspended in light. Frau Gertler charted a steady track on the black-and-white steps of the keyboard, and Guido's silver flute danced around that track like a faun in a thicket. The music swelled. The piano clambered to a height that seemed impossible. The flute danced beyond it, forsaking terra firma, treading the very air itself. Charteris forgot to breathe, here in the shimmering altitudes—

From outside the window came two huge explosions and a long, dying scream.

Charteris was standing up, heart hammering. The music had stopped. Guido was ashy grey, staring out of the window.

Outside which, on the terrace, stood Harry. A Harry grim-faced, square jaw set. In his hands was a shotgun, which he was reloading. At his feet lay the bloody corpse of a peahen.

'Got one,' said Anastasia, next to Charteris. She did have a beard. 'Beastly birds. Get much sailin'?'

Frau Gertler came rushing to the window and started beating her fists on the panes and shrieking Mitteleuropean abuse. Charteris saw that Guido was crying. Charteris turned away from red-bearded Anastasia and said, 'Jolly well played, that man.'

Guido shook his head. He could not speak.

'Tell you what,' said Charteris. 'Ever flown in an aeroplane?'

Guido shook his head again.

'Dawn patrol tomorrow,' said Charteris. 'How about it?'

Guido rubbed his eyes with the back of his hand. 'You don't have to,' he said.

'I want to,' said Charteris. He clapped his hand on the boy's shoulder: the bones so fine, the muscles so slender. He found his hand lingering. He took it away. 'Look here,' he said. 'Come to my hut. Second door along, third from the sea. I've got some spare togs there. I'll tell my observer you're a chum of mine from before the war. CO's away, nobody'll ever know. You'll love flying. It's ripping!'

'Rather!' breathed Guido. He watched Charteris go, straight and solid in his beautiful uniform, between the aunts and out of the door. And felt that his departure had left a hole in his life that nothing could fill, ever. Well, not until dawn.

'Sorry,' said Harry, arriving with an arrogant grin. 'Did I interrupt the tootling?'

'Vicked boy,' said Frau Gertler.

'Oh, go back to Berlin,' said Harry, with a curl of the lip.

'Vienna,' said Frau Gertler.

'So you say.'

'Be quiet, Herry, you vicked, evil child.'

'At least I'm not a Boche,' said Harry. 'Or a girl.' He attacked Frau Gertler because he knew it caused Guido pain, and Frau Gertler knew it too, and did her best to defend Guido, who was so sensitive.

But this evening, Guido was not even listening. He was standing staring towards the hall, into which Charteris had disappeared.

He could not wait till dawn.

That night he lay in his tidy bed and thought untidy thoughts. When he shut his eyes he could see Charteris. Nude, tawny. On the beach.

Frau Gertler was all right. Harry was all right, too, except when he was cross or jealous or when the other aunts played up to him, and Mummy was so busy all the time that she just glanced at Guido occasionally, as you might glance at a blown egg in cotton wool, then shut the cabinet drawer. Be a man, people said. Nobody had ever shown him how. Unlike Harry, he did not know automatically. Mostly he seemed to like the things girls liked, not the things men liked.

Guido betted that girls liked Lieutenant Charteris.

There was a banging on his door. 'Queenie!' said Harry's voice. 'You asleep!'

Guido moved his hands quickly outside the covers. 'Go away!' he said.

'Hear you're goin' flyin',' said Harry.

'Who told you?' As soon as it was out, he knew he had walked into a trap.

'So it's true,' said Harry.

'No!'

'Yes it is. Well,' said Harry, 'I think you'll be frightened by all the nasty noise and all that. So it would be wrong to let my big bruvvy go. So I'm going to make sure that everyone gets up early so you can't sneak off with that chap, because they won't let you, you know. Not Mummy.'

'You never will.' But he would. The beast. The *beast*. Desperate tears stung Guido's eyes.

'Mummy's gone to bed,' said Harry. 'And what she don't know is that I've put a cock in a cage behind her curtains, but won't she get a shock at four o'clock! She'll be in a rare wax, and you'll never get past her!'

Guido said, 'You'll get into trouble.'

'Listen to him blub!' said Harry.

'I wasn't going anyway,' said Guido.

'Just as well,' said Harry. 'Because I'm going to come in and give you *such* a lickin', Queenie. Fee, fi, fo, fum – hey!'

For Guido had leaped out of bed, run across the threadbare carpet, and shot the bolt on his room door.

'Well, you can't go now,' said Harry. 'Because I'll be listening and Mummy'll be watching. So there.'

Guido sat and felt desperate. The chintz flowers on the curtains shifted in the breeze from the open window . . .

The window.

Guido tiptoed across the room, and stuck his head out. His room was two floors up in the Tower. Thirty feet below, the East Rockery was a dark tangle of boulders and succulents. If you jumped, you would probably die.

But Guido knew that if he did not see Charteris, he would definitely die.

He put on a blue shirt and knee-length khaki shorts, and pulled the sheets from his bed. He stretched them corner to corner, and tied them together – he had read about knotted sheets in *A Fourth Form Friendship*, but he had no idea really how it was done. Then he tied one end to the mullion of the window and dropped the other outside, shaking it until it lay tidy down the wall. He had stopped crying. He was cross now, dry-mouthed, frightened by what he was going to do, but more frightened of what would happen if he did not do it.

Before he could think, he had his legs out of the window, and he was going down the sheets hand over hand, mewling as he barked his knees on the rough granite. From the yellow-lit billiard room came the grunt and bark of Aunts playing billiard fives. It was hard to hold the sheets, and his arms hurt. But he did not have the strength to climb back to his window, even if he had wanted to.

He went on down. The end of the sheet passed his knees. It still looked an awfully long way to the ground. Too far to drop. What if he broke his leg?

His foot hit something. The outlet pipe from the nursemaid's lavatory.

He swallowed hard. His hands hurt dreadfully. He gave a sort of sob and let go of the sheet and grabbed at the sewage pipe, but of course there was nothing to grab and he was falling back-first and opened his mouth to shout but before he could utter he had landed *crunch* in something terribly painful.

He had landed in the briars that nowadays choked Joshua Jones' secret staircase. He was scratched and prickled. But as he untangled himself from the thorny wands, he found that he was not hurt at all.

A great bubble of joy swelled in his breast. He scrambled down the rockery, onto the Truro Road, and set off along the shore.

There was a chain-link fence round the huts on the Farm. It incorporated the blank walls of a couple of farm buildings, used now for storage. Guido walked past them on the road, pulled up a trapdoor once used for the loading of coal, and let himself down into a dark cellar, where he had once played house with Amelia, the daughter of the parson before the parson before last. Following a gleam of light, he walked the width of the building, climbed a short flight of steps, and emerged onto the margins of the concrete.

There was no moon. But the night was clear, and in the pale gleam of starlight he saw on the sea the awkward shapes of the flying-boats, in echelon at their buoys, awaiting the dawn patrol. This side of the aeroplanes were the huts, four of them, parallel to the sea.

Now the fear came back. But it was too late for dithering. He had to find out. Casually as he could, he strolled across to the huts.

The last twenty yards was like walking in treacle. Eventually, he was outside the door. He turned the handle and pushed. It was unlocked. Heart pounding, he stepped inside, and closed the door behind him.

Creak of springs. Hot, manly smell. A voice. 'Corporal?' Charteris' voice.

'No,' said Guido, with an unsteady throat. 'It's me.'

Silence. Then, 'Is it dawn?'

'One o'clock.'

More silence. Then Charteris. 'You'd better come here, old chap.'

Guido was already moving towards the bed, unbuttoning his shorts as he went.

Chapter Eighteen

The noise was stunning. Guido lay back in it, resting against the leather padding of the observer's seat.

In the grey pre-dawn he and Charteris had walked out of the hut, bundled in scarves, helmets, leather flying coats, fur-lined boots a size too big. Charteris had squeezed his hand and given him a look from his kind, narrow eyes. Then he had pulled Guido's goggles down for him. An erk had rowed them out to Charteris' machine. Now Guido was in the observer's seat, with its Lewis gun, and Charteris was in the cockpit, doing goodness knew what among the switches and dials. The air filled with the sharp smell of petrol. Charteris raised a hand. The erk swung the starboard propeller. The engine caught with a broken clatter. The erk rowed across to the port side. More clatter. The erk clambered into the boat, untied the mooring warp.

Charteris' hand went to the throttles. The clatter became a buzzing roar. The smell of petrol was replaced by the exciting whiff of burned castor oil.

The light was growing now. The flying boat moved towards the fiery orange east along a series of yellow buoys anchored on the bay. At the easternmost it turned, the ribbon telltales on the rigging wires streaming due aft as it came head to wind. Charteris' hand eased up the throttles, a definite, powerful thrust that sent a thrill into the pit of Guido's stomach. The flying boat lumbered forward; trot, canter, gallop, white spray hissing off the floats, the wavelets hardening into a regular tattoo of slap and slam, the tattoo becoming thinner, then ceasing altogether as the flying boat swooped into the sky. Air poured past Guido's face in a steady torrent. There went the beach, the kennels, the Tower – still a pale line of knotted sheets hanging from his bedroom window. Plum Orchard beach glided below, turquoise shallows, deep green sea. Dead ahead the Mare was a great black pillar. The flying boat roared straight at it. The lens spun, drowning them in its huge white wink. Then Charteris put the machine on its side and the lantern was passing forty feet away, a pale, vacant-faced man on the gallery in a blue uniform cap, hand half-raised in a wave. The sun stuck a fiery limb over the horizon. And the flying boat flattened out and crawled south over quiet, glittering leagues of sea.

So there was Guido, leaning against the padding, in all the noise. He had the observer's glasses in his hand. Charteris had said to look through them. So he was looking. But the vibration of the fuselage made the eyepieces rattle against the goggles, and the sea was no better than a blur. So he gave up, really, and let the minutes slide by, happy to be close to Charteris, suspended in the bright air.

After two hours, Charteris altered course, and grinned under his goggles, his lips framing the word, 'Home.' The horizon tilted alarmingly. There was a sharp whipping sound. At first Guido thought the whipping was part of the turn. Then he saw a line of holes come into being across the port wing, and Charteris' face, no longer smiling, looking round at him, his hand pointing downwards, at his feet. When Guido looked down he saw a lever with BOMB RELEASE on a little plaque next to it. The engines were making a new noise now, a screaming. The wind was howling in the rigging, bagging out the fabric where the bullets had holed it. And beyond the nose, lying across the sea, was something low and black with a squat tower in the middle of it. A submarine.

Guido's heart rolled horribly in his chest. If Charteris was like this, it could mean only one thing. It was a Boche submarine. A U-boat.

The U-boat grew on the nose. They were diving straight for it. Charteris had one hand up. Guido understood that when the hand went down, he should pull the bomb lever. He understood that the Boche were shooting, but he knew Charteris would make sure everything was all right.

The U-boat's hull disappeared under the flying boat's nose. Charteris' glove chopped down. Guido's hand fumbled with the lever. He could not make it pull. He bent, found a safety catch, flicked it off, hauled upwards. There was more whipping, a crack, a bang. Something stung his face. The flying boat lurched. A hole had appeared by the bomb lever. Through the hole Guido could see wrinkled blue sea, very close. He sat up and looked round. He saw the U-boat, and the tail of the flying boat, ragged now, full of holes like Gruyère cheese. Between the tailplane and the submarine were four towers of water, drifting away in the breeze. Guido's stomach curdled with guilt and castor oil. His fumbling with the lever had made them miss. Miss by a mile. The submarine seemed to be sliding underwater. Perhaps they had got it.

But Guido knew perfectly well that it was not sinking, but diving.

He turned to look forward again.

Charteris had shrunk.

Before, he had sat up in the cockpit, square-shouldered and strong. Now, only his head showed, slumped sideways, resting on the padded rim.

'Charteris!' shouted Guido. The noise of the engines took his voice. They sounded rough, out of rhythm. The starboard one started to blow white smoke, clattered and stopped. They were flying north, now, a hundred feet above the sea. The aeroplane seemed to be making its way through the air like a crab, as if Charteris was fighting some sort of battle with it, and losing. The sun was well up in the sky. The sea was blue as a sapphire, with a low southwesterly swell.

The port engine started to pop. More white smoke.

Then silence.

The nose dropped. Air wailed in the rigging. Charteris' shoulders underwent a strange convulsion. He was hauling the stick. Surely it cannot be that heavy, thought Guido. Then with a crash and a roar and a cloud of spray the aeroplane belly-flopped into the sea. It rocked, steadied, and became still, rising and falling with the swell.

'Charteris,' said Guido, in a high, shocked voice. 'I say, Charteris!'

Charteris did not speak or move.

Guido stood up and leaned forward. 'Charteris,' he said.

Charteris' face was bluish-pale. His eyes rolled at Guido. 'Tell Mummy I love her,' he said. Blood welled out of his mouth and down his chin. He died.

Guido started to scream. He was still screaming, though faintly, because of the rawness of his throat, when the patrol found him two hours later.

*   *   *

'Guido,' said Harry, shaking his head. 'Who'd have thought it, eh?'

'Stupid boy,' said Harriet. '*Stupid* boy. If it hadn't been flat calm—'

'But it was,' said Harry, cheerfully. 'No use crying over spilt milk, eh?'

'He could have been killed. The pilot was killed. Did you know that?'

'Odd chap,' said Harry. 'Didn't take to him.'

But Harriet had stumped off in her great black boots to the kitchen, where cook had made a milk pudding that could not fail to soothe poor Guido's nerves.

Harry visited his brother the night after the funeral, taking with him a weasel he had caught in a gin-trap in the Duckery. Guido was a very bad colour, and the bones showed under his face. 'Look,' said Harry, holding up the weasel.

Guido turned his face to the wall. The beast kicked its three remaining paws and bit Harry's thumb, drawing much blood. 'Ow,' said Harry, shaking it off and stuffing it into his shirt. He had come out of decency. Like most bullies, he was acutely aware of the difference between right and wrong, and was rather shocked to find himself on the wrong side of the fence. Now, he was embarrassed and somewhat sulky at the rejection of his peace initiative. 'Awful rot about Lieutenant Charteris,' he said.

Guido's eyes filled with tears. Complete nervous prostration, the doctor had said.

'Look here,' said Harry. 'It's pretty mouldy but it happens in wars. And at least he died having a biff at the Boche.'

'I dropped the bombs late, so they missed,' said Guido. 'Or he'd still be alive.'

'Mustn't blame yourself,' said Harry, quoting Harriet talking to a mother who had nagged her son off to the Somme two weeks ago, and received the fatal letter within three days.

'I don't,' said Guido. 'I loved him.'

'Must be awful,' said Harry, out of his depth in this emotional quagmire.

'You don't understand,' said Guido. 'I really loved him. I wanted to be his wife.'

'Be his *what*?'

'I went to bed with him,' said Guido. 'I lay with him. We were man and wife. In the eyes of God. And he asked me to look after his mother.'

'Good *Lord*,' said Harry. There was a stunned silence. Then the weasel bit Harry sharply on the stomach. Incoherent with pain, he reversed out of the room, detached the beast and put it in a shoebox. He had never been more grateful to a weasel in his life. Guido and that . . . apparently perfectly nice . . . Lieutenant Charteris . . .

A strange restlessness overtook Harry. He went out and shot forty-three sparrows. The next day, he was woken by shouting, and the thunder of black boots on stairs.

Note found on the pillow of Guido Blakeney-Jones, 4 Sept 1916.

> *Dear Mummy and Harry,*
>
> *By the time you find this I will have gone. There is nothing but unhappiness for all in me being at Trelise. I have thought of a way I can bring happiness into the world, and do my Duty, in ways I never could have at home. So do not think badly of me, Mummy, I beg.*
>
> *Your child, whom you will never see again.*
>
> *Guido*

'Blow me down,' said Harry, scratching his short curls. 'Perisher's joined up. Who'd a thought it? Ow!'

For Harriet had smacked him on the ear, and rushed to her room, and locked herself in, sobbing.

While the Aunts shouted consolations through her door, Harry walked over the causeway, hopped a cart to Truro, took the train to Plymouth, and joined up himself.

Drizzle was falling as Guido walked down Alsager Road. He had never seen a place with so many houses so close together. When he said good morning to the people in the gardens, they either ignored him or responded curtly, then returned to whatever it was they were doing. The curiosity of Trelise had been like needles in his brain. Guido found Alsager Road wonderfully soothing.

According to the address stamped into the head of the letter he had found in Charteris' hut, 'Marazion' was number one hundred and thirty-six. There was a green gate, some straggling lilacs, and a concrete path winding between beds of *Veronica* and herbaceous geranium infested (Guido could not help noticing) with couch and bindweed. The house looked clean but dreary. He put an unaccustomed thumb on the button, and pushed.

A maid took him into a drawing room with pictures of Highland cattle on the walls. A woman was sitting by the cold fireplace. She was wearing black. On the piano, Charteris looked out from a framed photograph, debonair in uniform. Guido looked away: too late. His vision was blurring with tears.

The woman looked up, now. Guido had been in bed for the funeral, but he knew she had been on the island, because he had heard the aunts talking afterwards.

'See that woman?' George had said.

'The poor boy's mother,' Frau Gertler had said. 'He was her only—'

'Utterly wet,' said George.

'Pippin' like mad,' said Harry.

'Shut up, Harry,' said George, approvingly.

Frau Gertler had kept her mouth shut.

Close up, the face of the woman on the sofa was blindingly, amazingly Charteris'. Guido went down on his knees, and took her hand. It was pale and fine and cold, the fingernails bitten. He said, 'It's awful,' and started to cry.

She started to cry too, without even asking who he was. After a while, he stood up again. 'I just wanted to see you,' he said.

'That was kind,' said Mrs Charteris. She seemed a little frantic. 'I lost my husband at Spion Kop, you know. So now I am all alone.' He looked like a ghost, a thin little ghost in front of the fire, where the dear boy used to stand. 'You were a friend of Alan's?'

'Yes.'

'Please,' she said. 'Would you stay to luncheon?'

At luncheon, Mrs Charteris had a glass of sherry, but not another, which was unusual since the dreadful news had arrived. She could not think where Alan had found Guido – he was more like a little sister than one of the great galumphing friends Alan used to bring home. There was so much you did not know about them, as they got older . . .

As for Guido, he found Mrs Charteris a kind and loving soul, whose lapses of taste in the matter of pictures and garden plants were reminiscent of the manly gawkinesses of Charteris.

To their mutual surprise, the two of them got on like a house on fire.

'Well,' said Mrs Charteris after luncheon, with a sigh. 'I suppose now you will have to go back.'

'Back?' said Guido.

'To Trelise.'

Guido's gaze was vague. 'No.'

'I beg your pardon?'

'I won't go back.'

'But my dear child,' said Mrs Charteris. 'Your *mother*. What will she *think*?'

'She's very busy,' said Guido. Mrs Charteris seemed nice and ordinary. Her house was nice and ordinary too, in a splendid way, solid, part of real life, like Charteris. In his mind Trelise hung from its causeway like an over-ripe fig, ready to fall and burst.

After lunch, they had coffee, intensely rare, in his honour. 'Where are you stopping?' said Mrs Charteris.

'Stopping?'

'An hotel? With friends?'

'Oh,' said Guido, and blushed. Mrs Charteris realised suddenly that he had not thought that far ahead. How extraordinary. How other-worldly! How . . . *charming*! She heard herself say, 'You could always stay here.'

'Could I really?' said Guido. 'How ripping!'

When she dressed for dinner that night, she wore dove-grey, and pearls. Showing, they said in the kitchen, as how she was getting over it; though who the little sissy chap was as had come it was very hard to say, the only undeniable thing being that he would not have done for poor Captain Charteris.

In which, of course, they were right off the beam.

*   *   *

It soon became apparent to Mrs Charteris that she was entertaining an angel unawares.

Guido was the perfect companion. He loved the commuters walking their dogs, and the cycling delivery boys, the bridge, tennis, tea – even in wartime, the tribal rites of Dorking were so much kinder than the dark observances of Trelise.

He had at Mrs Charteris' insistence let his mother know he was alive, a fact that seemed of only marginal interest to her. This settled, he deepened his acquaintance with Dorking. The only thing about it that seemed less than perfect were the gardens.

The policies of 'Marazion', for instance, consisted of patches of lawn front and back, bordered by strips of black mould in which coarse plants competed lackadaisically with soot and cat filth. Guido undertook several railway trips to Kew and the Chelsea Physic Garden. He bought squared paper, consulted deeply with Mrs Charteris, and went to work. When Mrs Charteris' aunt, a leader of thought in Tilehurst, came six weeks later for her annual visit, she walked past the house twice before she realised it belonged to her niece.

A path of stones wound to the front door through an embryonic bamboo grove. A pair of *Yuccas* framed the old familiar porch. Behind the house, a small pagoda ogled a fountain in a pile of boulders across a lawn of sea-washed turf. Beyond the border furthest from the house was the kitchen garden, reformed and enlarged, with a final crop of lettuces and winter greens already showing under cloches. Mrs Charteris' aunt was deeply impressed.

'Marazion' was a delight to its owner and the envy of her neighbours. Guido's relationship with Mrs Charteris swiftly developed rails. He looked after the garden he had created for her. He also designed gardens for people he met at her Thursday afternoons. Word spread in the Home Counties, and even beyond. Reporters arrived. In a year, Guido had a career. In two, he was famous, and started a studio of his own in a rented house in Alsager Road just down the road from Mrs Charteris. He hardly thought about Trelise at all.

Night, stink, the flicker of shellfire. Eighteen-year-old Captain Harry

Blakeney-Jones screwed up his eyes, plunged his face into mud the consistency of porridge, and came up spluttering. It was picnic night. Every night was picnic night.

'All set?' said Harry. 'Off we go.' He nipped up the ladder. *Whit, whit*, said stray rifle bullets round his ears. No whistles heralded this attack, no Staff speeches, no rum rations, except that it was taken for granted that Harry's boys would drink anything they could, whenever they could find it, on the understanding that if they were too screwed to obey orders, Captain Harry would spare them a court martial by administering a Browning round in the soft part of the head.

So up they came, the picnickers, a dozen of them, faces darkened with mud – squelch, pant, creak, and a jingle. 'Racket!' hissed Harry. The jingle stopped as someone padded it with bandage. Thirteen Golems set off into flickering no-man's-land, heading for a gap in the wire. Harry had been in close-order advances. He had watched lines of men blasted to red froth by shell and machine gun. He did not approve, the way he disapproved of all inefficiency. He had designed his picnic nights with ferrets in mind, sharks, skuas. Efficient.

They were through the wire now, slithering through the shell-ploughed filth of no-man's-land like eels hunting in the Trelise bulb-ridges. A German picket sighed and died. A hundred yards ahead, the German trench was a faint dark line in the shell-flicker. Harry put his hand on something soft that burst, emitting a foul gas—

Ahead, the horizon flashed blue and white and orange. Above, the sky moaned and shrieked and rumbled. Behind, the earth stood on end. Harry put his face in the mud and waited. You had to be good at waiting, and to be able to think things out while you did it. He thought it out now, as the air-hammers beat at his eardrums. He did not much like the conclusion he reached. But then there was not much to like in Arras in 1918.

The world over the British trench was going out, the flames dull orange, cowshit green. Smoke. Gas.

Everybody knew what came next.

The barrage ceased. There was a deathly silence, in which Harry could hear coughing, a revolting, vomiting cough, half a mile behind him in the British lines, as some bloody fool got himself gassed. Then ahead came a sound infinitely more dreadful than silence – a grunt and a long, metallic rustle as a sheet of Germans flowed over the parapet and started to squelch towards the fumes masking the British trenches. Harry screwed his face into the mud. Shock-troops, probing. Looking for weakness. Then would come the infantry attacks, concentrated where they would have most effect.

Jolly interesting.

Jackboots stamped in front of his nose. He kept his head down, confident that everyone else was doing likewise. His bowels were loose with fear and the remnants of dysentery. His mind was his own, under control, making a plan and looking forward to carrying it out.

Harry Blakeney-Jones loved a picnic.

The shock-troops ran right over the picnic party without seeing them. To left and right, machine guns opened up. From the British trenches came a steady clatter of rifle fire, with the chug of Vickerses and the clang of trench mortars. A starshell went up. Fumes swirled thickly in the corpse-light, and among the fumes plodded men.

Harry got up and ran, earth-colour against earth-colour, towards the German lines. A pillbox stood squat to the right, the flame of the machine gun dancing in front of its slit, covering the advance.

The thirteen earth-coloured men hopped over the parapet and into the German forward trench. They had done it before. They knew what you did.

You kept close into the parapet, so you rolled inside the bayonets. You kept low, so the men jammed waiting in the trench had to bend to get at you, and in bending collided with each other, and could not find you, and could not bring their bayonets to bear. You had your bayonet, of course, without the rifle, and your revolver, some Mills bombs, and various other weapons made at home and abroad. Once you were into the trench and down among the legs, you got busy.

The mass of boots and greatcoats started to heave and scream. Harry worked hard but economically. He stabbed with his bayonet, twisted, felt a spout of warm blood, moved on to the next stab, twist, scream, spout. The Germans were falling back along the trench, into the arms of the next picnicker. So he took out a Mills bomb, pulled the pin, stood on tiptoe and stuffed it down the back of a greatcoat collar, turned and ran in the opposite direction, hacking and stabbing, pulled out his Browning and shoved it a couple of inches away from a torso (Brownings must breathe) and pulled the trigger. After the flash and the bang came the heavy *blap* of the Mills bomb, then screams (a Mills bomb down the neck turned a human skull into a cannonball, human ribs to shrapnel). A voice started roaring in German. Harry was damned if he was going to learn to talk Hun, but it sounded like orders to him, so even as he stabbed and walloped and biffed he got the Acme Thunderer between his teeth and blew it, two blows. The Boche were pretty restless now. They could not wait to get out of this hideous trench, full of steel and explosions. They went leaping up the ladders, well before start-time of course, and the NCOs were bellowing at them to form up, and Harry and his chaps were up and out too, wearing German helmets now, going up for the pill-box on the left, indistinguishable in the smoke and flash and bang from the milling Boche.

They edged closer to the trenches round the pill-box. Here they began to lurch and weave, as if shocked. The men behind the parapet watched them and shook their heads, and on about the third shake Harry ups and outs with the Browning and bang, bang, bang, quicker than it takes to shout it, three holes in three helmets and Boche brains up the back wall of the trench. Then round the back of the pill-box, and the sergeant pulled out a Mills bomb, but Harry shook his head, and checked the clip in the Browning and bounced through the baffles by the door. There was a big noise of shooting, amplified by the raw concrete interior.

When the sergeant went in Harry was rolling a German corpse off the machine gun. Beyond the gun-slit, dark waves of men were rolling through the gap in the wire towards the gas-clouds over the British trenches. 'Open fire,' said Harry. The gun chugged. Men started to fall down. More starshell. More fire from ahead and on the flank. Hundreds of men started to fall down. The attack faltered and ceased to exist.

When the Germans got back to the pill-box, it was empty. The gas-clouds had dispersed. Far away in the black of no-man's-land, two red Very lights went up: Harry's signal for coming home. Five of the picnic party were still alive. The offensive had been interrupted rather than halted. But it was generally acknowledged to have been a goodish picnic, well up to Harry's usual standard.

In fact they made him a major, and gave him the VC, and shipped him back to Blighty to encourage the civilian population. In the first week he got into six fights, all of which he won. Then he got a fortnight's leave and went to Trelise, and arranged to use the Steward's House as his country establishment. And by that time, people were dancing in the streets because the war was over.

One evening, his mother showed him an article from the *Horticultural Magazine*. There was a sketch of his brother Guido posing next to a herm, expounding his theory of the Whimsy Jungle.

Harry stared at it for perhaps a minute, stroking his blond moustache with his trigger-finger. 'Ugh,' he said. Then he went out to shoot rabbits.

It was agreed by the Aunts that Harry had turned into quite a chap. It was a pity he found so little time to be on the island. But at least he came more than his brother (who was also quite a chap, in his way, though Harriet would not talk about him). It would really be so much better all round if Trelise passed to him, not Guido. But Guido was the elder, and on his twenty-first birthday it would all be his.

Harriet talked to Harry about this. 'All right,' said Harry. 'I'll go and see him.' And off he went, over the top, to Dorking.

The sun was shining as Harry walked down Alsager Road on his way to Get Things Straight. The train had been beastly crowded, and he thought Alsager Road was a latrine: sticky asphalt, hot paving-stones, ghastly little hutches crammed hugger-mugger alongside it. What Alsager Road needed to make it habitable was a damn good walking barrage.

He turned sharply into 'Fernleigh', the house Guido used as his studio. The garden was not bad, in a miniature sort of way. The door was opened by a young man with hair dropping into his eye and unless Harry was much mistaken some sort of black stuff on his eyelids. Guido was in what they probably called the Front Room, working on a drawing at a table covered in plant lists. He was wearing a lilac silk shirt and huge cream trousers. He got up and opened his arms and would probably have kissed Harry on the cheek if Harry had not stepped sharply backwards, crushing a small bag of bulbs.

Guido asked the invert with the eyelids to make tea. 'How are you?' he said. He seemed nervous.

'Never better,' said Harry.

'And Trelise?'

'Farm's a shambles, but can you try to put it straight?' He snorted derisively.

'And the garden?'

'Very pretty,' said Harry.

'The echiums?'

'Fine.' Harry realised something else was expected of him. 'Red. Blue. You should come and have a look.' There was a dogged expression on his face. He had arrived in this bed of pansies to carve himself a slice of Trelise. It was time to *mak' shikar*. 'It'll be yours in a minute.'

'No,' said Guido.

'What?'

'I don't want it.'

'What do you mean?'

'I want to make new gardens, in a new way. Trelise is already there. It's all mixed up with us and Mummy and Grandpa and Great-Uncle Joshua.' He made flopping movements with his hands, as if trying to shake off a lump of well-rotted manure. 'I just don't think I can face it.'

'But when you're twenty-one it comes down to you. I suppose duty doesn't mean anything?'

'What duty?'

'You don't own a thing like Trelise. You look after it and pass it on.'

'To your children.'

'And their children. And their children's children.'

'I haven't got any children. I won't have any.'

Harry stared at him. This was a state of affairs that had never occurred to him. Incomprehension curdled into sarcasm. 'Ah,' he said. 'Too busy sticking his prick into chaps' arses to do his duty and get some.'

'Actually,' said Guido, blushing, 'they stick theirs into mine.' Harry went pale. 'Now I think this is a bit upsetting for you. Shall we change the subject?'

But Harry was standing up, in a panic.

Guido followed him to the door. 'Look here,' he said to his brother's chunky shoulders. 'I'd like us to be friends. I know how you feel. We're the same age. We were brought up together. In the same room, for God's sake. You think what I do's disgusting, well, there it is. But I love you, Harry. Like a brother. I'm doing what suits me. I want you to do what suits you.'

Harry said, 'Not possible. I'm twenty minutes too young.'

'I want to help. Really.'

Amazingly, Harry found himself touched.

'Give my love to Mummy,' said Guido.

'Give it to her yourself.'

'It's so difficult. I don't see her, nowadays. Only Frau Gertler, when she comes to London. She gives me the news, you know.'

So that's that, thought Harry. Guido had done the usual Guido thing. Been meek and gentle and put him on the wrong damn foot again.

Though . . .

Not a bad chap for a bugger, Guido.

Harry still wanted to kill something. But there was nothing to kill in Dorking except people, and you were not allowed to do that any more.

The Rolls-Royce was waiting at the end of Alsager Road; Harry had not wanted the chauffeur to see the queers. 'White's,' said Harry.

As the Rolls glided through Kingston-upon-Thames, desperation settled over him in a stultifying cloud. Major Harold Blakeney-Jones VC was perfectly confident that he could impose his will on anyone.

Except his family.

Letter to Harriet Blakeney-Jones from her son Guido Blakeney-Jones, La Mortola, Menton, 1922.

Dear Mother,

I am sorry not to be able to be with you today. Thank you for asking; it is lovely to be 21, and on the Riviera! I hope you have a jolly Ball, and that everyone is happy and gay. I am in the middle of redoing Lady Hanbury's Roman Terrace, and must not take my eye off these men for an instant.

Mummy, there is something I must tell you. This has been in my mind for an awfully long time but it is only now I am of age that I can tell you. A lawyer chap who is here tells me that I am a fool – but since I insist, he will help me do it properly (!). So, dearest Mummy, I hereby and by this instrument yield to my brother Harry on your decease my interest in the lease of the island of Trelise, the buildings thereon and the monies thereunto pertaining. I don't want anything to do with it, Mummy; something I expect you will never understand. My shoulders are too narrow for such a burden, and it will not go with my dress!! So let Harry have it, with my gracious blessing.

   Your loving son
   Guido

[In a different hand, scrawled with many blots – possibly Harriet, under emotional stress:] *Ain't he gracious, nasty little queer.*

Chapter Nineteen

August came. Morgan had left in a BMW rented for him by Emma's film company. Trelise filled with tourists, lured by the stories Guy had planted in glossy magazines. Hull Bay was full of dinghy sails, cruising yachts lay at anchor off the Mixer, and the Estate Office dealt politely with nose-to-tail complaints about the holiday cottages. At night the Castle's drinkers spilled out under the Arch and onto the causeway.

In the midst of this profitable frenzy, Victoria moved in a zone of calm. The cousins infesting the house were admirably self-contained. She monitored herself for signs of missing Morgan. Then she scrutinised the meter for signs of guilt. Not a flicker of the needle on either count.

The final test was Mary.

It was a morning when you could have fried an egg on the Poseidon Stairs. The propagating shed was cool as always. 'Hello,' said Mary, looking up as she went in.

Victoria found she could smile naturally, no worries, serene even. They took the sour Nescafé outside, chatted about this and that. Morgan was a phantom, vanished, over and done with. Oh, the relief. Then Victoria said, 'Did you ever know Harry?'

'Harry Blakeney-Jones? Hard to say, really.'

'But you were here ten years.'

'Maybe you never get to know the boss.' Is she talking about me? thought Victoria. 'He never seemed all that sure of himself, to me.'

Victoria thought of the Regimental history, the fearsome catalogue of mutilation and slaughter. Unsure? 'What about Guido?' she said.

'Read his books. Bit dated.' Mary was looking at her closely. 'What you been up to, Victoria?'

Victoria's heart stopped. She felt her face heating up. 'Up to?' The needle was jumping. Calm down, calm down—

'You're different,' said Mary. 'Something's changed.'

She should never have tried to pull the wool with someone as intuitive as Mary. She must be crazy. She was sweating, blushing, on the point of bursting into tears.

'Maybe not,' said Mary. She thinks she's being nosy, thought Victoria. So English. Thank God. 'How's the work going, then?'

Victoria found herself back on firm ground. She fell on her face like the Pope, kissed mental concrete. 'No luck with that skeleton; looks as if it was early, from the Joshua days, unrecorded, covered up. I'm still looking. But I've got everything else in order, up to Harry taking over. I've been wondering about Guido and Harry. Why would Harriet be so cold with them?'

'What do you mean?'

'She tried to bring them up as girls. When that went wrong, she just lost interest. And I was thinking, was it something to do with the child she had after she was seduced by Robbins? Maybe the child dies or gets adopted. There's Emily, going on and on at her, on and on and on: you see what you have brought upon yourself and your child, all that. What would that do to Harriet? And what happened to her diaries?'

Mary shrugged. She did not understand, not really understand, thought Victoria. She was not sure she understood herself. But the tears boiled up behind her eyes anyway. Why was she taking this so much to heart?

'Harry could easily have burned papers, diaries, you name it,' said Mary. 'He liked things plain and straightforward. He wouldn't have liked an illegitimate elder brother. Why not ask Dawkins? He looked after Harry. He'd know if anyone would.'

'He wouldn't tell me.'

'You'd be surprised,' said Mary. She screwed the top back on her thermos and got up. As they moved back into daylight, she said, 'You're looking terrific.' She narrowed her eyes. 'You're not pregnant, are you?'

Victoria said, 'No way.'

Oops.

Dominoes were falling in her mind. She had heard about this; blissed-out, matter-a-damn, me-and-my-body, feel-so-good, handle anything, surges of raw emotion sloshing about. Late, too . . .

Of course she was pregnant.

She walked home through the sizzling garden, without looking at it. It could not be Morgan. She knew that for certain. Thank God. She went into the courtyard and climbed onto her bicycle and whizzed through the heat and the tourists to the garage. No bloody specimens-in-the-post for her. She drove to Truro, parked, went into Boots. She saw nobody she knew. The girl at the counter had an up-country accent. This was private, between her and her body. She drove back, walked straight into the Priory and upstairs, alone in her house.

Positive.

Definitely pregnant. Definitely Guy's baby. The past was done, finished with. The future was in her womb, cells dividing. She had never been so happy in her life. She could not imagine ever being unhappy again.

She sat on the terrace and looked across the dark garden at the wink of the Mare. It was an ideal moment for work. But she did not want to work. She was not an observer any more, a bolt-on addition to Trelise's history. The child made her part of it.

A stooped figure panted by in the dusk. 'Dawkins?' she said.

'Victoria?'

'Did Harry burn a lot of papers from the library?'

'Not as far as I know.'

'Are you sure?'

'Well, I didn't actually watch his every movement, did I?'

So there it was again; the brick wall.

Hiding something she was part of.

She shivered, and went in.

Harry applied to the pursuits of peace the arts he had learned in war. The weeks he spent in the City, conducting raids on petroleum companies, and chemical works, and gold mines. Most weekends he was at Trelise, shooting, and fishing, and terrifying the vicar during sermons with the unswerving blue lance of his eye. At times the eye fell upon the Aunts. The Aunts looked straight back, china-blue, wondering what the future held.

Harry seemed to have all the money in the world. Village roofs were mended, the Watch Tower repointed, repairs made to the Quay, and the dry rot in the Abbey Tower taken care of. It gave George and Babs great pleasure to see old *Fan* restored, and the building at Falmouth of a couple of smart Dragons, *Bee* and *Fly*, whose evolutions in the bay led to great flashings of telescopes on the Priory terrace, accompanied by hoarse commentaries from Anastasia.

Then two things took place that shook the Aunts severely. In 1921 Harry met in London – *London!* – a gel called Letitia, who was all right in a frock-wearing, shingled-hair sort of way. Letitia claimed to be a painter. But Babs, who knew a thing or two about painting, said what she did was splodge, splodge, all very modern no doubt but she did not understand it she was pleased to say and hoped she never would.

After five years, the jury of Aunts agreed that Letitia was here to stay. Two children had arrived, a boy and a girl, noisy little Turks. On the minus side, Letitia had put up some unforgivable curtains in the Steward's House. On the plus side, she could stand up to Harry. All in all, the Aunts agreed (taking their cue from Harriet), he could have done much worse.

The other thing was odder. Everyone knew that Trelise chose and paid the keepers on the Mare light. At one of his Saturday-morning meetings with his mother, Harry suggested turning the maintenance and manning of the light over to Trinity House, the body responsible for all Britain's other navigational aids, thereby saving the estate a large drain on its resources. 'I have been to see the Elder Brethren,' said Harry, his moustache luxuriant now, high-crowned soft hat on his knickerbockered knee. 'They agree that in the year 1927 it is just too damn silly that we should be saddled with the upkeep of one of the principal lights of Western Britain.'

'What do you mean, "we"?' said Harriet.

'The estate, of course.'

'Me,' snapped Harriet. 'Not "we".'

'Chance won't come again,' said Harry. 'It's now or never.'

'Never, then.'

The chubbiness of youth had left Harry in the war. Now it was returning, in a tendency to double chin and convexity of waistcoat. He was used to getting his way. He said, 'If you do not agree I shall go across there in the *Fan* and take the keepers off myself.'

She looked at him, and saw her stubbornness in his eyes. She knew he would do it. 'In that case,' she said, 'I shall need two months, and ten thousand pounds.'

'*How* much?'

'I am sure you heard me.'

'Why?'

'Mind your own business.'

'But—'

'There are things you would not understand.'

'I'll be the judge of that.'

'Stop being awkward,' said Harriet, as if to a schoolboy. 'You've got all those stocks and shares, and the market's sky-high, so you can just pay up.'

Harry said, 'Is this something to do with Guido?'

'No. Now write me a cheque.'

Harry glared at the mirror surface of his right brogue. He said, 'I'll tell my people to send it.'

'Cheque,' said his mother. 'Now.'

Harry took out his pen.

Two days before handover day on the Mare, the wind dropped. By next morning the sea was down to an eight-foot swell, too rough to land on the rock, but all right for the breeches buoy. A boat showed up; a steam drifter lettered FH for Falmouth. The drifter took a line from the iron door on the platform high above the sea, made it fast, and steamed away until the line was taut. Aunt Anastasia, watching from the terrace through the big telescope, called out the packages that came down the rope from the lighthouse. 'Trunk,' she said. 'Boxes.' She lit her pipe. 'Piano, could be harmonium.' Puff, puff, blue smoke cartwheeling away east. 'Chap. Keeper, long one. Chap. Keeper, clumsy oaf's lost his hat. Chap. Keeper, shorter. Relief keepers goin' up, one, two. Dropping the line. Off they go.'

And off they went, shrinking, until the black smoke from the drifter's funnel lost itself in the far blue smudge of the hills beyond the Helford.

From the *Metropolitan Enquirer*, July 12 1928.

Ructions in Bohemia
Guido Blakeney-Jones, Artist in Planting, onlie begetter of the
Whimsy Jungle and now a New Constructivist, has fled his old
haunts. Marchionesses are mortified, duchesses devastated, sailors
stricken, and at least three he-decorators entertaining thoughts of
self-ending. Friends say that ultra-smart garden genius Guido has
'left for the west'. Richmond, perhaps? Hounslow? Surely not! Look
out, America! Your croquet lawns are about to sprout palm trees!

It was to the loss of the Mare that people generally attributed the Great
Change. Aunts muttered that if the Terrace could see the gallery of the
Light, the Trinity House keepers (dipsomaniacs, mostly, when ashore)
could see the Terrace. Previously, the keepers had been Trelise employees,
on side. There was no privacy any more.

And after the Mare, Harriet, who had scarcely stirred from Trelise for
years, began to spend more time off the island. The first series of these
absences culminated in a string of secret visits to Falmouth, and a small
bill paid to George Penhaligon, Cabinetmaker, Monumental Mason and
Tutor in Automobilism. Just before Christmas 1928, at low water springs,
a Model T Ford advanced jerkily across the causeway and came to a halt
under the Watch Tower, filling the air with a smell of burning rubber. The
driver climbed out. When she unwrapped her head from an antiquated veil,
she was seen to be Harriet. 'Put it away,' she said, to nobody in particular,
and began to stump back up the Priory Road.

From then on, whenever the tide served, she took off on unexplained
errands in the interior. The routines of the Priory were disrupted. Deprived
of her constant leadership, factions of aunts formed, did battle, re-formed.
The servants began leaving, taking with them the spoons. Housemaids
failed to clean, and under-gardeners turned to drink. With surprising
speed the Priory became shabby and chaotic, an ant's nest deprived of
its Queen.

Harry and Letitia, meanwhile, had made the Steward's House most
attractive. Colefax and Fowler had replaced painted sailcloth. The small
garden was a jewel under the direct supervision of David Carrott, at that

time Head Gardener. But the children were growing – they were seven and eight now, beefy little entities who made a lot of noise – and the Steward's House, designed for the childless middle-aged, was becoming frankly too small.

January 7th 1928 was a day of black east winds, smoking fires, and the lusty screams of the little ones one thin layer of floorboards from the breakfast room. 'Darling,' said Letitia, screwing up her aristocratic face against the pain of last night's cocktails. 'We really *must* get a bigger house.'

'Hmph,' said Harry, engrossed in calculating how many pheasant poults the island's covers could be forced to sustain next year.

'Really,' said Letitia. She was a slim, dark woman, with a Roman-nosed beauty and a firm set to the jaw. 'It's not fair, that they live in the Priory and we're stuck up here.'

'And in London,' said Harry. 'And at Whitefriars.' Whitefriars was his Hampshire estate, seventeen bedrooms, eleven hundred acres.

'The children like it here,' said Letitia.

'You don't.'

Letitia saw her opening. 'I might, if we lived somewhere we could have some people to stay. Some friends. And Guido.'

'Guido wouldn't come. I've asked him,' said Harry. 'Six times. He writes perfectly civil letters, very amusing, actually. He just thinks he'd rather not.'

'I'd love to meet him.'

'Not here. He doesn't like it. It reminds him of his boyfriend. Me, too, I should think.'

'It might be different if we had a bigger house.'

Harry did not answer. Letitia had been brought up in London and Suffolk, the second daughter of a general with political leanings. Early observation of her mother had taught her that it was on the whole wives who were best able to make use of the power accumulated by their husbands. So she started going to tea at the Priory herself.

The Aunts at first received her with grunts and frowns of suspicion. But she was a handsome woman with excellent manners and a good eye. By the fifth teatime, all the Aunts had noticed these qualities, and come round to the view that she might in time make a perfectly good Aunt herself. Their teatime conversations became long and informative.

Letitia would return to the Steward's House from the Priory, and in the cubby-hole of the drawing room that did duty as her study, write up her visits. Her notes featured not only a detailed catalogue of improvements necessary in the house, and lists of plants for the garden, but also notes about the Aunts themselves. She noted that Harriet nowadays seemed oddly happy, but as if her mind was elsewhere; that George and Babs, though still the best of friends, were frail, particularly Babs, who was diabetic; that Anastasia and Joe lived to all intents and purposes as man and wife; and that Frau Gertler seemed withdrawn and depressed, no longer played the piano, and was nowadays used as a sort of servant by Aunts physically stronger than her. Insensibly, Letitia's visits took on the nature of a campaign.

The culminating teatime was on a soaking day in March 1929. She brought the children – Charles and Daisy, blue-eyed, curly-headed, nine and eight years old respectively. 'Grandma?' said Charles, dressed in blue jersey and long shorts. 'May we, if you please, play billiards?'

Harriet actually smiled. 'They do so love the space,' said Letitia. 'Are you quite well?'

For Harriet looked pale and haggard, with dark circles under her eyes. 'Bit peaky,' she said. 'Cold.'

'Not enough air,' said Anastasia. 'Spend more time on deck.'

'We could walk later,' said Joe, who normally spoke after Anastasia.

'Busy,' said Babs.

'Perhaps early bed,' said Frau Gertler. 'I will make you a leetle cake.'

'It's too jolly cold to go to bed,' said Harriet, with a shudder.

'Harry has put an iron radiator in the bedroom at the Steward's House,' said Letitia. 'It's as warm as toast.'

'Tea?' said Harriet.

'Galley fire's out,' said Anastasia. 'No way of boiling a kettle.'

'Oh.' Harriet's face was blank. She was forgetting things, nowadays. 'Damn Heatly. What's he thinking of?'

Letitia looked pained. Actually, she had (after judging the weather) sent Heatly to Truro, to see his sister in hospital. Heatly, though very old, was much at the centre of things in the Priory nowadays. It was well known that in his absence all the fires went out. 'We've got an Aga at the Steward's House,' she said. 'Awful nuisance. Goes out in three days, if you don't stoke it.'

'Every four hours, that range,' said Anastasia.

'Stoke, stoke, stoke,' said Joe.

There was a silence, in which the happy cries of the children came from the billiard room. Then Anastasia started complaining about a deck leak, emanating, it seemed, from the gutter outside her window.

'Oh, *dear*,' said Letitia. 'Shall I see if Arthur Pender's got time to pop down for a look?'

'No,' said Harriet, and started talking in a confused manner about the School Treat, which was not due for another two months. Eventually her voice trailed away. They sat in silence, dark as crows in the drawing room, the rain swishing down on the terrace, laughter from the billiard room speaking of happy, far-off worlds. Letitia knew that Harriet was thinking of the clammy wastes upstairs, the acres of roof that Arthur Pender would never have the time or skill to mend. It was really going rather well.

Harriet had said something.

'I beg your pardon?' said Letitia, returning from her calculations.

'A radiator would be lovely.'

'They are,' said Letitia. 'Well, I think we should be off.'

Out of the kindness of her heart, Letitia went up and put a fire in Harriet's bedroom, and made her a hot-water bottle. She bicycled back to Old Hull with a stomach full of butterflies. Any day now. She was just about sure.

Later that night, there was a knock on the Steward's House door. The butler said, 'Miss Harriet.'

'I must see to the children,' said Letitia, and vanished.

Harriet found the drawing room blissfully warm, the rugs and curtains unsoured by damp, a faint smell of flowers and woodsmoke, Harry leaning on the mantelpiece smoking a Turkish cigarette. Up at the Priory they were clustered round a fire in mittens, and Anastasia was smoking her pipe. She said, 'Will Guido come back?'

'He assures me not.'

'Very well.' Pause. 'Harry, I think it is time you moved into the Priory.'

Harry raised an eyebrow. 'This is all very sudden.'

Harriet shook her head. Her mind seemed far away. 'Things change,' she said. 'It's the car, I think. You can get about so. And actually it's getting to be such a bother.'

'You're sure?'

Harriet shivered. For the first time, Harry saw her not as the mother of steel and ice, but as an elderly woman with cold hands. 'Quite sure,' she said. 'Now, do you think I could have a go with your radiator?'

The Aunts submitted almost meekly to the diaspora. Harry's reforms of the farm meant three empty cottages in the village. In the end, Harriet, George and Babs occupied the Steward's House, Anastasia and Joe moved into the Lookout, by the village, and Frau Gertler moved to South Kensington, where she gave piano lessons and was visited from time to time by Guido and his young men.

Harry, Letitia and the children moved into the Priory. In the early months of 1929, it looked as if peace and plenty would never end.

Victoria was in bed with Guy. She had not told him about the baby; she was waiting her moment. But it was almost as if he already knew. He was being warm and kind and friendly; as if something had changed. As if it had something to do with Morgan leaving. But that could not be right. There was no way he could have known about her and Morgan, and not said something already.

Never mind Morgan. She was into living memory, now. Into questions whose answers might lie with living people, not words on paper; into the story of which she and her baby were a part.

She said, 'Why did Harriet agree to leave the house?'

'I thought because she was too old.'

'Rising seventy. Not old at all.'

'Fed up, though. Cold, harried. Too many Aunts.'

'Maybe.' Silence. 'It's as if her heart wasn't in it, after the Mare went.

But it's odd, that Mare business. Why did she keep it on so long, even though it cost a fortune to keep up?'

'Tradition.'

'Tradition is for people who don't live here and don't know. You told me that.'

'What, then?'

Victoria hugged her knees. Soon, her belly would be out there where her legs were. It was hard to imagine. 'Where was she going when she was off the island? She hadn't been off for years. And suddenly she's away all the time.'

Guy shimmied towards her and put his arm round her shoulders. 'I neither know nor care,' he said. 'There is absolutely no doubt in my mind that you will find out. But later. Please, later.'

It was always awkward bringing boys home in Little Neck. Mom wanted to know too much about them, asked them questions about their grades, for God's sake. And Daddy engaged them in conversation, despising them for not knowing stuff it had taken him forty years to learn. Between them they had a serious gift for making guys feel not at home. So Victoria spent a lot of time in other people's houses, and in the backs of cars down by the River Road.

College came as such a relief: cool, rational, sun lying on blond wood, the smell of chewing gum on breath, conversations cool too, romance cool; everything cool. When she came home at the end of a semester, the house felt like a snakepit, everyone coiling and hissing and biting, not at all cool.

So she had taken refuge in work, and made herself a project: interesting project, on a certain Captain Clough, a Maine sea captain who in 1789 had set off in a schooner to rescue Marie Antoinette from the Jacobin hordes, having furnished the ship in the highest style and remodelled his house to match. His wife had not held with French people or queens, or indeed her husband's spending of all his money on fancy-ass furniture. Victoria had dug up a cache of their letters, some written when the bold captain was in a French jail after the failure of his mission, and put together an edition. It had all seemed amusing, and harmless.

Then one afternoon Daddy showed up on the porch with a man. 'Victoria,' he said. 'I want you to meet Dr Nevis.'

Victoria made tea and conversation of the kind Daddy expected, scheming flight. Dr Nevis had a regular-featured face with a skinned look, and crewcut yellow hair through which his scalp showed. He was thirtyish, but seemed younger, mostly because he was so eager to please. He was teaching history at Princeton. Daddy had met him at an inter-faculty conference. He drank tea and agreed with everything everybody said. Victoria had hated him on sight.

He said, 'I hear you're working on Captain Clough.'

'That's right.'

The tongue went round the wet red lips. 'I'd like to talk about it sometime.'

'It's a free country,' said Victoria.

He shook her hand. His palm was hot and wet, and he would not let go. After he had finally left, Daddy said, 'Fine young man.'

'Really?'

'Stop reading when I'm talking to you. He'll be a professor any day now. Fine sportsman, too. Excellent family. Excellent.'

Victoria laid her papers in her lap. She said, 'Daddy, why is any of this interesting?'

'This is a man of a calibre you don't find every day. I don't know who you see at college, but it seems to me that it is time you—'

As Victoria stood up, she noticed his eyes were glassy and earnest. His breath smelt of drink. She said, 'I hope you are not thinking what I think you are thinking.'

He said, 'Wait a minute. He's a historian. I told him about your Clough research. That's all.'

Victoria tucked her papers tight under her arm. 'Good,' she said. 'Good.'

But Nevis rang, time and time again. After a while, Victoria got one of her sisters to answer the phone. Daddy made noise about it. So she told him she wanted to keep her research to herself. In time, the phone calls stopped, and Nevis wrote letters instead. Letters you could throw out unopened.

So that was that, she thought.

Wrongly, as it turned out.

Harry thought he was probably the luckiest man alive.

It was six o'clock, a brilliant October evening.

There they all were on the terrace, with the smell of roof tar sharp under the lemon verbena: a white tablecloth covered in glasses, Letitia in a cloche hat, Charles with shorts and (miraculously) clean knees, Daisy (equally miraculously) in a print frock. And there were the Aunts, boots firmly planted, with the resolute expressions of longtime residents determined to see all change as being for the better.

Not that much had actually changed. The rotten barge-boards of the house had been replaced using timber from a deck cargo washed up in Plum Orchard. Parts of the terrace wall had been repointed. The roof, which had suffered from eighty years of gales, had been mended, with many timbers replaced. But what the white tablecloth and glasses affirmed was that Joneses had been in possession for eighty years; and that each generation had remade the place; and that now, Harry Blakeney-Jones, using his great wealth, had assured the future for his son and his son's sons . . .

'Come on,' said Harry, a dynamo of charm and energy. 'Let's have a glass of wine. Then I'm going to make a really long speech. Pender, do your stuff.'

Arthur Pender was standing by, smelling faintly of beer. He trowelled up mortar from a spot board, dropped a stone in, pointed all up, and stood back.

'Topped out, be Jove!' cried Harry, square, ruddy and beaming. 'God bless her and all who sail in her. What?'

'Amen,' said Letitia.

'End of speech,' said Harry.

Strother, the butler, materialised at his elbow. 'There is a telephonic manifestation,' he said.

'Tell 'em to ring back,' said Harry.

'It is Mr Cazenove of Cazenove's,' said Strother. 'He desires your most urgent voicings.'

'Speak English,' said Harry. 'Ruddy broker. Pour out. I'll be straight back.' He stumped into the house. The terrace homed in on the glasses. Conversation started, the heavy commonplaces of island life. Letitia was good at it, but it was a relief that next week they would be out of here, heading for Hampshire, then London, Menton, perhaps Paris afterwards. Trelise was lovely in small doses, but the idea of *living* here—

The terrace door opened. Harry walked down the steps. Letitia stared at him.

His face was grey, with black bags under the eyes. He walked stiffly, like an old man. He went to the table, picked up a glass of wine and drained it, refilled it, drained it again. Letitia went close to him, so he could feel her warmth, and said, 'What's happened?'

He swung his head at her, heavy on the powerful neck. His eyes were dull. 'Crash,' he said. 'Stock market.'

'What?'

'Crash, bang, wallop. My poor old girl,' said Harry. 'The bottom has dropped out. We're bust.'

'Well,' said Letitia, brightly. 'Waste not, want not. Shall we have some dinner?'

That night, in their room, Letitia and Harry had an argument.

'What do you mean, you're selling Whitefriars?'

'We only go there for the fishing. It's a place people will want to buy.'

'And Eaton Square.'

'We'll have a flat. Lots of people do nowadays.'

'Menton?'

'Out of the question.'

'But we've got to go.'

'We've got to stay here and see what we can rescue.'

'We could sell up here,' said Letitia, chin out.

Harry took a deep breath. Eaton Square was five floors of splendour. Whitefriars overlooked its calm valley in the best Hampshire style. But Trelise was his home. Without Trelise, there would be nowhere for his mother, the Aunts, no memories for Guido, no work for the islanders, no eighty years of work and history to keep the imagination alive, the blood coursing. Getting rid of Trelise would be an amputation, not a sale.

Not that Letitia could be expected to see it that way. She was a fighter, Lettie. That was why he had married her.

A week later, when the extent of the damage was clear, she faced him across the dining room table. The servants were in bed; moonlight lay on the terrace outside the window.

'You don't think it'll happen,' said Letitia. 'Actually, I think we all got what we deserved.'

Harry looked shaken. 'What?'

'It's all betting, isn't it? We've got no right to win all the time. They were perfectly decent bets. But all the horses fell.'

'How did you know?' said Harry. 'We never talked about this.'

'I checked,' said Letitia. 'You should know by now. I always check.'

Harry nodded.

'And I'm sorry I was a pig,' she said. 'You should certainly sell Number Nine and Whitefriars. The place to be is here. We'll have to change things, of course.'

'Of course.'

'But if we buckle down, we can keep it all going.'

He said, 'Are you going Bolshy on me?'

'I am the wife of a tenant farmer of the Earl of Kernow,' she said. 'I look after the garden. My husband looks after the rest. I have a wonderful boy and a sweet girl. As long as we all work like hell, the future is assured. And if your brother gets himself into trouble, we'll have him back as well, and he can help.'

'No danger of that,' said Harry.

'It's dogged as does it,' said Letitia. She stood up. 'Now would you please take me to bed?'

For five years, Harry and Letitia worked to restore Trelise's fortunes. Harry got the farm organised and the debts paid, and enough put by to be a cushion in times of hardship. And Letitia, charming as ever, kept up a large correspondence with hundreds of friends and acquaintants, making sure in the process that the wonder of the Trelise garden was never far from the public eye.

Among her favourite correspondents – by letter only; never in the flesh – was Guido Blakeney-Jones.

Apparently he now lived in Cornwall. He had been sighted in the gardens of Tresco and Trebah, and rather more often in the public houses of Penzance and St Ives. But he was never seen on Trelise until the January woodcock shoot of 1935.

Charles Blakeney-Jones, now fifteen, had been given the mainland end of the line. The guns and beaters were walking up a patch of bracken dotted with gorse bushes, above the church and its black Irish yews and the cold grey sheet of Hull Bay. A woodcock got up, stood on a wing, and flipped down the line. The bird was missed in turn by a Colonel of infantry, a Liberal M.P., a society portraitist and a Lieutenant-Commander R.N. Charles raised the Holland and Holland to his shoulder, leaned gently towards the bird, and fired. The woodcock folded up, sailed over the rock and out of sight. The Colonel, the M.P., the painter and the sailor exchanged expressionless glances. To say Charles was a good shot was like saying the Duke of Windsor was a silly beggar.

A spaniel shot over the rock, picked up the corpse, glanced back at the guns and bolted over the horizon. A dim roaring came from up the line. *God damn and blast the bloody dog it's going to devour that bird*, cried the voice. *I may weep I shall weep o blow me down here I am weeping already.* The woodcock shoot always made Harry deeply emotional. Charlie unloaded his gun and pranced on long, knickerbockered legs after the spaniel. A funny boy, Charles, great stork of a chap, huge long nose on him, absolutely mad in boat or car.

The spaniel was sitting on a rock plucking the woodcock. Beyond it, the causeway snaked across the puddled flats to the mainland. Across the causeway a figure was riding on a bicycle. 'Unhand that thing,' said Charles to the spaniel.

The spaniel withdrew, taking the woodcock. Charles was a patient youth, and it was the last drive before lunch. He pranced back up the hill and told the guns to carry on without him. Then he went back after the spaniel.

The cyclist had stopped to watch. He was a thin man, about forty, with high cheekbones and a classically straight nose. Despite the icy February rain, he was wearing white flannels and a striped blazer, as if on his way to cricket. He said, 'Is your father about?' His voice was light and high. 'By the way, I'm your uncle.'

'Good Lord,' said Charles. 'Guido?'

'Oh,' said the man. 'They told you about me.'

'Of course. How absolutely topping to meet you.' Charles was a boy of great personal warmth. 'At last, what?'

Guido smiled at him, a smile of exceptional sweetness, and shook his hand. The handshake was a surprise, hard, roughskinned. A gardener, of course. The breath was a surprise, too. It was volatile with spirits – gin, by the smell of it. Close to, the face was mapped with burst blood-vessels. The eyes were unnaturally clear, heavily bagged, rimmed with black.

'Come to luncheon,' said Charles.

'I'm having lunch,' said Guido, looking shifty. 'I'll pop up at teatime.'

'Splendid.' The spaniel had come to bark at the stranger. Charles wrested the woodcock from its maw and loped off to lunch.

In the village, the striped coat on the bicycle wobbled its way not (as Charles had supposed it would) to the Steward's House to see his mother, but to the pub. That afternoon, the rattle trap bicycle was sighted by the garden entrance, leaning against the rock bearing the plinth that said WELCOME, STRANGER. Guido himself was not to be found.

There was a creeper, *Muehlenbeckia complexa*, known as the Muley Bush, that crawled in thick swags and hammocks through the limbs of a *Metrosideros* tree. The Muley Bush had grown, these twenty-four years, but the footholds were still there if you remembered where to look for them. From the platform of woven stems in the upper branches the garden spread out below like a map, the walks, the great ramparts that the Monterey pines now made round its margins, and out to the south the grey sea and the fog-moan of the Mare.

Guido lay in the rain-soaked hammock of the Muley Bush and contemplated through a lot of gin and a touch of flu the development of Trelise.

Everything was extremely neat; the military mind at work. The place where the greenhouses had burned, where in the war there had been vegetables, was now a year of apples and pears, planted in order of edibility. There were no new plants from China. Harry and Letitia had been to South Africa, though. There were Cape marigolds by the score, *Gazania* and *Dimorpotheca*, in the summer bright as a punch in the nose; and less brash and (to Guido) more delightful, the *Proteas*.

In the southern hemisphere, the *Proteas* flowered in mid-summer. They did not seem to be able to rid themselves of the habit. They were still flowering, laurels for Poseidon's head, misty with gin and drizzle at the top of the Stairs. Used to the top of Table Mountain, of course. Funny what you could get used to. Last time Guido had lain up here, he had been fifteen, and life had been warm, and bright, and hellish.

Letitia had looked after things well; a thorough woman. Neat, everything; but not poetic. Guy's gardens were discreet triumphs of form and habit and vista, natural but contrived, free verse. With Letitia, everything had to rhyme. Doggerel, thought Guido. But eccentric, magnificent doggerel. He sighed, conscious of an irksome soreness of the throat. Oh, the magic of Trelise. The gin of breakfast and luncheon filled him with a comfortable nostalgia. It would have been lovely to take possession. But that would have been most unfair. His fate was not to possess, but to be possessed. By Charteris: by Mummy: by his gardens, when the fit was on him: by gin, and sailors, and love . . . He sighed. He laid his poor hot forehead on his cold, drizzle-wet hands. He slept.

It was dark when he woke. He was stiff, and his head ached, and the soreness in his throat had become a rawness, with an agonising cough. The gin, he thought, through the buzz of his head. He climbed down the Muley Bush and walked up to the house.

There was a smell of China tea and toast and Turkish cigarette smoke. Eyes settled light as snowflakes on the thin figure in the drenched cricket whites. Eyebrows rose the significant millimetre. Letitia had been warned by Charlie. She got up and swept across and embraced Guido. His face was dreadfully hot, his skin the colour of lead. She offered him dry clothes, tea, a bed. He refused it all, and asked, teeth chattering for gin. He said, 'I'm awfully sorry to trouble you. The garden's looking marvellous.'

'Bad day to look at it,' said Letitia. 'Would you come back? I'd love to pick your brains.'

He gave her a sort of ghost of the old sweet smile. 'Why not?' he said. 'God willing, and all that. Harry here?'

'He's down at the kennels. He'll be up in a moment.'

'Give him my love.'

'Stay. He'd love to see you.'

'Don't be silly. I just want to nip into the library.' He ran in. She heard him moving around. When he came out, his blazer was buttoned, and she thought she could see a couple of books stuffed down the front of his trousers. Well, she did not begrudge him a couple of books, God knew. He finished his gin, lit a Gold Flake, and coughed volcanically. 'Tide,' he said. 'Causeway.' He lurched out of the room. Letitia went after him, but he moved surprisingly fast. By the time she was out of the front door he was a pale ghost, fading into the black rain – harder now, and cold – of the evening.

She was glad he had liked the garden.

Guido's thoughts were sluggish as he pedalled. He meant to stop for gin and a possible sailor at the Castle, but the wind blew him past its yellow window before he could react. Next thing he was on the causeway and the acetylene light on the bicycle had shrunk to an orange glim. Waves were breaking against the western coping. He rode through torrents of spray, grinning to keep the salt out of his eyes, freezing in his stupid blazer and whites. He thought he would probably be sick.

After days and days and days, he hit the mainland. There he did go into the pub and get some gin, but the man behind the bar had to take the money out of his palm because his hand was frozen stiff. The man got cross when Guido made a grab for his thick red fingers. So off Guido went into the night, shivering horribly. It seemed possible that he had had nothing to eat today. The hills were very tiring. The oaks hissed annoyingly. Left, right, right. Up to the cottage where he rented his room from Mary. Lean the bike against the stone tits on the gatepost, carved by clever old Mary. Granite sculptor. Woman of stone. Stand up; legs shaky. Fall sideways. Too far gone to save himself. Hope for soft landing, books uppermost.

Very soft. Too soft. Ditch, water, mud. Cold. Cold. Freezing.

Go to sleep anyway.

★   ★   ★

Hot, hot, hot, can't breathe.

1) A bedroom, dry sheets, snow-blue sun through striped curtains. Mary's curtains.

2) Can't breathe.

3) Jolt, jolt, down the stairs, into a van. Ambulance? Cornish voices, did you see 'er, the hair the shoes the corduroys? Million to one she's a lezzie. And of course they were right my dear . . .

4, 5, 6) Can't breathe.

7) Great dazzle of white. Doctor's coat. 'Pneumonia.'

8) Mummy, crying.

9) Harry, cold hand.

10, 11, 12) Can't breathe.

13) . . .

And Guido fell upwards, open-eyed, into the still, bright air above Treliske hospital, drifting through the gulls, into the blue calm where once the flying boats had soared.

Chapter Twenty

'How absolutely *disgusting*,' said Letitia.

Mary Brewer, a square woman with a pudding-bowl haircut and blunt stonecarver's hands, said defensively, 'His business. Not mine.'

Harriet was incapacitated with grief. So it had fallen to Letitia to come, bright and early, with Heatly and one of the farm vans, to clear out Guido's rooms. There was a bedroom and a study. Both were squalid beyond anything she had experienced, deep in paper, cigarette ash, empty bottles, small fossils, cuttings in old bean cans, items of jewellery, feminine underwear in Guido's size, dried-up cosmetics, drawings stained and crumpled. Letitia raked the debris with her efficient eye, swept the table clean, and plonked down her cardboard boxes. These she filled with the recognisably useful stuff – books, diaries, ornaments – and had carried to the car by Heatly. 'Well,' she said, dusting her hands. 'That's *that*!'

Mary Brewer was standing in the doorway. 'What about the rest?' she said.

'You can do what you like with it.'

Nobody told Mary what to do. Her granitic jowls reddened. 'Not my pidgin,' she said.

Letitia had thought Guido awfully dear, what little she had known of him, and to think of him wallowing in this filth had upset her badly. She was shocked that she had been too selfish to realise that Mary was probably upset too.

She sighed. 'All right,' she said. 'I'll send someone.'

So in due course Heatly came back, and shovelled the filth and foulness and letters and drawings into tea-chests, and hauled it all back to Trelise. He got as far as the concrete apron that, with a couple of huts, was all that remained of the flying-boat base. Here, Revel told him he needed the

301

van to get a load of flowers on the London train. So they hauled out the tea-chests. Heatly painted on them *Mr Guido*, and numbered them, and stacked them any old how in the first place he found, which was (oddly enough) the hut that had been Captain Charteris' quarters.

And there they lay, forgotten.

At the funeral, Harriet appeared most severely affected. She kept her veil down, and seemed an old, old woman, bowed and shrunken. She was hustled away afterwards by George and Babs.

Two days after the service, Harry looked through the crates Letitia had brought back from the cottage above the Fal. The books he put to one side. The diaries he took out and skimmed – briskly at first, then more slowly. Letitia watched him with growing anxiety. His face was changing. Its ruddiness was departing. It was turning black and grey, the colours it had taken on receiving the news of the Crash.

'What is it?' she said.

'Nothing.' His lips had a bloodless look.

'Bugger's stories?'

He smiled, a haunted grimace so unlike his usual full-blooded grin that it frightened the life out of her. 'Worse than that,' he said.

He picked up the pile of diaries, placed them on the rug in front of the fire, and sat down on the low stool where the newspapers usually lay. He started tearing pages out of the diaries, one at a time, waiting until each was utterly consumed before he put in the next. After an hour, Strother came in. 'Dining,' he announced, 'is commenced.'

'Go away,' said Harry. He did not get up until every page was black ash. He never even mentioned the diaries to Letitia; she knew there was no point in asking. But she would have liked to ask. Particularly, she would have liked to ask why among Guido's diaries there were two volumes in a different hand, bearing the stamp of Trelise; presumably, in fact, the books Guido had made off with on his final visit.

But all the books were burned, now, so it made no difference.

It was terrible. Terrible, terrible, terrible. Sometimes he remembered the Lantern, ages ago, ages and ages. There was no Lantern any more; no rainbows, no feeling you were floating between sea and sky. There was just a square room, a bed with a brass end, a window, square too, hung on the wall like a picture; and beyond the window a flat river with boats on, not sea ships, just rivery sort of boats, no good. He was lonely.

After a bit you could go and look at the window in the brass knob of the bed. Then you could see the room and the window all bent and gold-coloured and that was better, but not the Lantern.

The room was not nearly as good as the Lantern.

The Lantern was the big change. There were other changes, a lot of them. Daddy was gone and Uncle Gee was gone and She was gone and the only person left except staff was the Old Woman, which is what staff called her. The Old Woman was sad and tired and had a cold nose when she gave you a kiss. You could tell she did not like you much. There was something wrong, too. Harder and harder to get out of bed, pain in front, bang, bang in chest. There had always been that, but if things got bad you could go to the Lantern.

Now, all you could do was sit on your chair and look at the brass bed-knob, with the sails in it, moving, but like fish in a bowl, not gulls in air.

Terrible.

Perhaps you could do something.

The brass knob tasted bitter and metally.

Do something.

How did you do that?

On the morning of September 3rd 1939, Harry marched out of the house with his son, Charlie, to supervise the construction of slit-trenches on the downs behind Trelise Church. The war was as good as on, and it was considered that Trelise would be a suitable place to site anti-aircraft guns against German aeroplanes starting bomb-runs on Plymouth or Falmouth.

They were working above the village, among heather and gold-crusted rocks. The tide was in. The *Lyonesse* was heading for the quay, jammed with trippers; war clouds or no war clouds, it was a brilliantly sunny day in the summer holidays. Later, Charles could never work out what it was that made him watch that boatload of trippers while he took a breather. Anyway, he sat on a rock, hearing his father shovelling away with the men, out of sight, and rested his eyes upon the village and the bay.

All the people swarmed off the boat; all except two. There was Danny Pembarra, and another figure; an odd figure, long and thin (it was hard to tell, with distance) sitting in the boat, tense, strung-up looking. And on the quay now, running along the strip of granite paving, another figure, all in navy blue, jersey and long skirt; Charlie's grandmother. Harriet.

Charlie was suddenly possessed by a chill certainty that things were going wrong. He got off his rock, hurdled the churchyard wall, and ran down through the village and onto the quay. His grandmother was standing at the top of the steps, boots planted, fists on hips. 'Go away!' she was shouting. 'You've no business here!'

Another voice answered her, a curious mumble, inaudible over the bag-of-nails clatter of Danny's diesel. Then Danny. 'Couldn't stop 'im, Missis Jones,' he said. 'He just came aboard.'

'Take him away!' said Harriet. 'Show him the Marc, Danny! For goodness sake, get him away!'

Charlie arrived at the edge of the quay. His grandmother's face was a dark, meaty colour. But it was the figure in the boat that caught his real attention.

It was a man; an old man by Charlie's standards, probably about fifty or seventy or something. He was wearing a dark blue jersey and trousers, and on his head was a cap with a shiny peak and a cover that might once have been white. The effect was of a uniform, without badges.

The body and face did not go with the uniform. The man sat with his feet together, his hands pressed palm to palm between his knees. His head looked too heavy for the pale, scrawny neck above the jersey. The face was white and smooth, an invalid's smoothness, with great blue-black shadows in the orbits of the eyes. The lips were liver-coloured. The jaw hung open, and a dribble of spit hung from the bottom lip to the jersey, where dried-up stains showed that this was not an unusual event. The eyes were blue, and clear, and hurt.

'Go *away*,' said Harriet, nearly screaming.

Danny Pembarra looked flustered. 'Yes, Mrs Jones,' he said. 'Ullo, Charlie.'

'Morning, Danny.' Charlie looked at the passenger, who seemed to be trying to attract his attention. 'Morning,' he said.

'Morning,' said the passenger, in a sort of uncontrolled mumble. 'Who you?'

'Charlie Blakeney-Jones,' said Charlie.

The idiot face was suddenly illuminated by a smile of piercing sweetness. 'I seen him!' he cried. 'Mummy, I seen him!' He stood up, wobbling.

Harriet's face had turned suddenly bluish white. She said, 'Go away, I tell you!'

Danny flicked the spring off its hook, whacked the gear lever ahead, and stuck his hip against the *Lyonesse*'s tiller. The pale-green boat slid away from the quay.

It was half-tide now. The Mixer was running, turning a long, slow wheel of water along the shore. The *Lyonesse* moved into the out-flowing side of the whirlpool; the standard method of leaving the quay. Except that today, as the *Lyonesse* slid past the Mixer, the strange old man stumbled aft in the boat, arms up, as if wanting to embrace the people on the quay, mouth open, emitting a cry of pain and loss that clutched at Charlie's heart.

'Stupid boy,' said Harriet, through lips like bone.

Charlie got the idea that the old man would have loved to land, but that Granny would not let him. He said, 'Can't he come?'

Harriet did not even look at him. He was about to ask her again, but the words froze.

The old man had stumbled all the way to the stern of the boat, which was moving away from the quay. He stood for a moment still, arms outstretched, moaning. Then with shocking abruptness he grabbed at his sternum, folded up, and fell into the sea. As he went, his head hit the rudder with a bang audible on the quay, fifty yards away. Danny cut the engine. The current spun *Lyonesse* sideways, away from the Mixer. A limp hand rose. Charlie caught one nightmare glimpse of a white face, wide blue eyes, a black O of mouth sharp in the crystal water. Then the white became pale green, darker green, and faded into the deep.

Harriet's legs crumpled. She sat down. Charlie was shouting, and the quay was full of people, and Danny had backed *Lyonesse* up and was peering over the side, and Revel had found a punt and was heading out into the Mixer. For five minutes, the world turned desperate. But to no effect. There was just Revel in the punt, scratching his beard, spinning: and the man in the sea, God knew where, tumbling towards the Glory Hole.

Charlie helped his grandmother to her feet. Her hand was cold, and she was crying bitterly. 'Who was he?' he said. She could not answer. He felt he should not have asked the question. He took her back to the Dower House, where Babs came to the door. When she heard what had happened she turned white and grim, and helped her inside. 'Bed,' said Harriet in a thin voice. She shuffled into her room. There was the sound of the bolt sliding across, the creak of springs: then more sobbing.

Charlie said to Babs, 'He called her "mummy".'

Babs was white-faced, clench-jawed. She said, 'The man was mad.'

'Ah.' He had looked a bit . . . well, loony. But Charlie felt that did not explain it.

Later that day, war was declared on Germany. The body had disappeared. After things fell in the Mixer, they almost always washed round into the Glory Hole; but occasionally they just vanished out to sea, to be recovered or not, as chance dictated.

Chance, or some other agency.

The rawness of his grandmother's emotions had made a deep impression on Charlie. So had the look on the man's face. Idiotic, perhaps; but there had been that one bright-blue flash of recognition, the stretching out of arms towards Charlie: 'I seen him!' he had shouted. And Granny had sent him away. Why?

It was almost as if in the idiot's mind they were old friends, sundered, re-meeting. And as if Harriet had tried to keep them apart. And now the poor chap was dead.

Charlie was a bright, good-natured boy, and he was really very interested in finding an explanation. But war had been declared that day, and he was eighteen, his father's son. So of course he went straight up to Dartmouth the next morning, and joined the Navy.

*   *   *

A photograph taken on the terrace at Trelise. Harry, feet apart, jaw out; Charlie in navy-blue, with braid on his cuffs and a white-topped cap under his arm. He is smiling, wide, confident, slightly goofy; a young man who has just discovered what he was born to do.

Oddly for a family that prides itself on its punctilious manners, the women are on the outsides of the group. Daisy stands next to her father, lumpish in WAC uniform. On her face is an expression of sullen anger. You can almost feel her straining away from her father, hear him insisting that is where she must stand.

At the extreme opposite end of the group is Letitia. In only a year she has grown thinner. She is smiling, but it is the brave smile of the country at war, a conventional grimace. There are circles under her eyes, and the shadows under the cheekbones are crow-black. The eyes themselves are imploring and terrified, aimed at the camera.

It is reasonable to assume that the photographer had attracted her attention, and that previously she had been looking at Charlie.

'Thank God that's over,' said Harry, when the photographer had gone.

'I thought he was rather a nice chap,' said Daisy, heavy-chinned.

'Hairdresser.'

'There was no need to ask him to come if you don't like him.'

'Since when do I have to get your permission to like or dislike anyone?'

'You do exactly what you jolly want all the—'

'Goodness,' said Charlie. 'There's the yardarm, there's the sun. Gin, mummy?'

Letitia shook her head, smiling at him, thank you. Harry said, 'Yes.'

'And if you've got a moment, could you do me one?' said Daisy, sticking in the knife to Harry, for barging in first, and Charlie, for not managing to offer first, and Letitia, for being there.

'Coming up, dear relations,' said Charlie, bestowing upon them the goofy grin.

That was how it worked, at Trelise.

12th April, 1941

Dear Major Blakeney-Jones,

I have been asked to write to you by George Babington-Drake, because he knows that you and I have been friends for many years. I am afraid the news is as bad as can be. Your son Charles was on patrol on Tuesday night, in command of MTB-471. The boat on his starboard quarter reports that, at 0231, an explosion was heard from 471's position, a large flash, followed by a considerable amount of orange flame and smoke. A search of the area revealed a quantity of wreckage and oil, and some bodies later identified as members of 471's crew. I am afraid that while poor Charlie was not among them, there is no doubt that 471 was sunk with all hands, and that there is no hope. Charlie was a marvellous boy and a very gallant officer, and will be missed by all of us here. I am terribly, terribly sorry.

Yours ever

James Bartholomew, Captain, R.N.

Nobody spoke. Nobody spoke for days, and days, and days. They had a service in the church, White Ensign in front of the altar. All right, there was a war on. But nobody believed in God, not if this was allowed to happen. They had believed in Charlie. Charlie had kept the peace, and been the future.

Now Charlie was dead.

As far as Daisy was concerned, it confirmed her suspicions. Trelise might look beautiful, but it was horrible. There was no one you could talk to about anything interesting (the sonnets of Petrarch, the paintings of Duccio). People shouted at you (Daddy; Christ, Daddy!) or drooped over you and hoped you would get married to some utter wet without a grey cell. The only thing that had made it endurable was Charlie. In a place absolutely completely without a giggle in it Charlie had made you giggle. He never shouted, brought you brooches from London, and nodded affably during lectures you gave him on the symbolic content of Masaccio.

Without Charlie, Trelise was hell.

The day after the funeral she went into the library, awful dark room. She took down Vasari's *Lives of the Artists*. She should put it in the loans book, she knew . . . God damn it all. She stubbed out her Du Maurier in the loans book, slammed it and shoved it back onto its shelf. She put the Vasari in her bag and left the island.

There was no news of a fire, worse luck.

Letitia did not believe what had happened. She knew it was awful, but she was pretty sure, deep down inside, with a mother's certainty, that since they had never found a body there was always a possibility – vanishingly small, diminishing each day, but a *possibility* . . . Meanwhile there was a war on, and other people were far worse off than her and Harry, so the thing to do was get on with it, work like a beaver, expect nothing, but *hope for the best*. She did ARP, had in convalescents, goodness *knows* what she did not get up to. And every night when she laid her head next to Harry's in the Big Bedroom, she dreamed the same dream. Plum Orchard beach. Something in the sea, a nice calm sea sometimes, sometimes rough. She would be looking for shells along the high water mark. She would feel somebody close at hand. She would look up. And there would be Charlie, in uniform, dripping.

'Phew,' he would say. 'Bit of a swim.' And he would come towards her, to hug her. But before those big blue arms would go round her, she would wake up. Then she would walk down to Plum Orchard, so Harry would not curse her for crying. Oddly, she always dreamed right about the weather.

But she never dreamed right about Charlie.

Harry had had enough of bloody women. His daughter had vanished. Letitia had gone quiet. Harriet never went outdoors any more. So Harry talked to a couple of men he knew in the War Office, and outlined a scheme for delivering agents to Brittany by fishing boat from Trelise. This worked quite well. So he and a couple of like-minded neighbours began to hitch lifts across the Channel, stage little picnics at radar installations, that sort of thing, which were quite fun. But there came a time when Harry found himself sitting on top of a wet, dark cliff, having climbed a hundred feet after three days at sea in a bad boat in worse weather. And actually he was feeling somewhat tired.

'You all right, Major?' said the twenty-five-year-old lieutenant sent down by his friend Stirling.

'Course,' said Harry, shouldering his pack and Sten. 'Now where's that damned transmitter gone?'

And off they went, into the night. But the lieutenant had to go slow to let Harry keep up. And he made a report to his CO: game old boy, Major Blakeney-Jones, but anno domini, you see what I mean? The CO saw. A week after they got back, Harry got a letter from his friend Stirling with new orders, someone needed to take care of things at Trelise, wise head on broad shoulders. So from then on Harry went on no more picnics, and did his bit from home.

He did not have much time to think about family matters. But it did strike him that Letitia seemed semi-transparent nowadays; still there, but not there, sort of. He watched her like a specimen, getting thinner. She said things to him, but he was not really concentrating. So it was a surprise to him when she went into Treliske to be operated on, and the same level of surprise when she died. He was sad; very, very sad. He missed her horribly; differently from the way he missed Charlie, but horribly all the same.

It was just that he was concentrating. Charlie had been the heir to Trelise. Daisy was . . . female, not right, never would be.

So what Harry was concentrating on, without a successor, was to live at Trelise himself.

For ever, if necessary.

Victoria was starting to show, but only if you knew where to look. She put her hands over the faint bulge below her navel. Poor Letitia. Poor Charlie; funny Charlie, young, enthusiastic; blown to bits. Poor Guy's mother, so kind, so helpless . . .

She was going to cry.

She was not going to cry. Why should she cry? It was facts from the past, nothing to do with her. She got up, climbed aboard her bicycle, and pedalled down to the village.

The RNAS's concrete apron was still there, crumbling now. The sheds had been knocked down, except the hangar, which was used for the sorting and packing of bulbs, and the officer's quarters, nasty cement shoeboxes with asbestos roofs. The Second World War had left them untouched.

Victoria found Revel in the bar at the Castle. He followed her out onto the concrete. They walked down the alley between the sheds, skirting the rusting corpse of an impossibly huge winch. They stood in front of the door

one from the end, where Guido had stood the night he had climbed from
the Tower window to visit Charteris. Revel picked up a rock and smote
the lock once, with the exact degree of force necessary. 'Christ,' he said.

The shed was full of boxes, bird's nests, batshit, all of it rotting down
into a powdery mulch.

'That was the Major for you,' said Revel. 'Never threw nothing away.
Never know when it's going to come in 'andy.' He waded in, and started
hauling out junk. There were two pram dinghies, a cricket-pitch white-line
marker and a festering piano, cardboard boxes in great profusion. 'Order,'
said Revel. 'System, 'e liked. Then forget about it. What do you want out
of here?'

'Evidence,' said Victoria.

'Oh, ah,' said Revel, out of the dust. The back wall was coming into view:
paved with brown wood, the wall, each paving slab with a rusted-silver
edging. More tea-chests. And on the tea-chests, neatly stencilled in black
paint, writing: *Mr Guido 7* it said.

Victoria felt the hairs rise on her neck and forearms. Here it was; raw
Trelise, the way it had been scraped off Guido's floor; uncatalogued,
unedited, unburned.

They made an alleyway through the other debris. Victoria found a
sack trolley in the packing shed, and trundled the chests outside onto
the concrete, squat and fusty in the sun, numbered one to nine.

There were only eight of them. Number five was missing.

She made Revel go back into the shed to look for it. Clouds of dust
rolled forth. 'Not there,' he said, at last. 'Probably Mr Heatly painted 'em
on wrong.'

They put the boxes on a trailer and dragged them round to the big
shed. There, on an oily work bench lit by a frosted-glass window, Victoria
started to sort through.

Guido had been an enthusiastic user of Max Factor, Chanel, and Gordon's
gin. He had smoked Gold Flake, eaten quantities of caviare and sardines, and
medicated himself with Dr J. Collis Browne's Chlorodyne, Carter's Little
Liver Pills, and Vaseline. There were sketches for gardens he was designing.
There were letters from men, containing news of other men, scandalous
gossip, and (usually) requests for trifling loans. These letters showed signs of

having been crumpled up and flung away, then smoothed flat and answered. And there was a cardboard frame, containing four photographs, filthy, as if it had been face down on the floor, mistaken among the debris for a bit of packing. One photograph was of Harry, square-faced, curly-haired. Another was of an older man with delicate features marred by huge bags under the eyes; Guido. Another, at the top of the mount, was of a pale fellow with a tall white forehead, eyes vague, mouth slack: the face Victoria had found under the clumsy impasto of the water-colour of (as she now realised) Harriet, the boys, and the Aunts on the Top Terrace.

The fourth picture, at the centre, was of an older man, bald, with whiskers, a thick nose, a square jaw and hot eyes over pince-nez. He was dressed in an earlier style; the coat wrinkled, slope-shouldered, flat-collared: late Victorian. Victoria recognised him as Robbins.

Victoria set the frame up in the light, and gazed upon it. A father, and two of his sons, and . . . a stranger.

Why was the idiot in the frame?

A father and three of his sons.

Try this. The face was the eldest son of Robbins and Harriet. Conceived in the Paradiso. Let roll down the Poseidon Stairs by an inattentive nursemaid. Flung from the pram; hit on the head. Not killed; hence the absence of a grave, a register entry. Turned silly by the knock on the head, poor child. Brain damaged. Kept out of the way by Harriet. Cared for by his father. And later by his kind brother Guido. Both of them loved him, as a member of his family.

And were loved in return. The whole family was loved in return. They bloody well did not deserve it.

The accounts of the drowning came into her mind. All witnesses had mentioned the expression of joy on the face: the reaching out of hands to Charlie as the *Lyonesse* drew away from the quay. The expression of an exile from Trelise, who belonged to Trelise but kept away, because he was a reminder to Harriet of weak flesh and divine punishment . . .

Victoria could feel the heat of tears. She told herself to take it easy. They were all dead.

But not gone.

She sat down on a crate. It was the baby, sending all this gooey stuff at her. She was Victoria Kline, who drew conclusions according to the evidence. Not touchy-feely-whispery rumour, myth, speculation . . .

She went through the boxes again.

Besides the photograph, there was nothing of any interest. No book, diary, cheque stub; nothing.

Wearily, she packed up. The letters she had filed, the artefacts she had boxed, the rubbish she had slung. She stacked the last box, stepped back. Her throat was full of the taste of dust.

There was a piece of blue paper on the floor; an ancient scrap, filthy, crumpled. Probably an old bulb-packer's ticket, dropped. She could not even be bothered to pick it up.

Of course she could be bothered.

She bent, stiff-kneed, and smoothed it on the oily timber of the bench.

The blue paper was not a bulb-ticket. It was a sheet of writing paper. Across the light, the letterhead said Shore House, Roseland: on the east bank of the Fal.

It said *Mr Blakeney-Jones. 1 month wages — Usual Nursing Care – Florence Penharrow – £10-0s-0d. Paid with thanks.* In the top right hand corner of the carbon was printed the number 35, in red.

Victoria smoothed the paper on the bench. Guido had lived in Quoit Cottage, not Shore House. So why was he paying for someone to be nursed? Not just once, either. A lot of times, by the look of it. And if there had been other occasions, why were there no other receipts? Perhaps they had been filed, and burned by Harry when he had burned the shocking diaries.

Or perhaps Harry had not been destroying sodomitical filth. Perhaps the book-burning had had other motives altogether.

Victoria found her hair wanting to stand on end. Sorry, baby; adrenalin, not nice for you, honey. Maybe we should forget it. You're the project now, not history—

But she was already out of the shed.

It was evening; she had been at the bench since eleven that morning. The sun was laying a syrupy light across the island, painting the shadows of rocks and houses as long, inky stripes on the ground. She boarded her bicycle and rattled up the Truro Road, through the courtyard and into the garden. She clumped up the stairs to Revel's verandah. He was sitting in an old deck chair, eating a large fish with his fingers. 'Those boxes,' she said. 'You said Heatly painted the numbers on wrong. Left one out.'

'That's right,' said Revel.

'Do you know that for a fact?'

Revel seemed to be weighing something in his mind. He examined the fish bone, then slung it far into the bamboos. He did not speak.

'You're not sure?' said Victoria.

'Difficult, living on an island,' said Revel.

'I'm sorry?'

'The main thing is to keep your head above water, so to speak. So, imagine you've got two stones to stand on, to keep you breathing. What one do you choose?'

'The high one.'

'No,' said Revel. 'You keep one foot on each, until you feel one of 'em start to roll.'

'What exactly are you trying to say?'

'I think you'll last,' said Revel. 'You and Guy. You'll keep him out of trouble.' His eyes had gone deep and dark. 'There's another box,' he said.

'Where?' She was being told something.

'It was took away.'

'Who by?'

Revel said, 'He went through 'em all, put the good bits I suppose into one box, and I put it on the hydraulics and drug it up to his house. About ten years ago.'

'Who did?'

'Morgan.'

'He's your rolling rock?'

'Put it this way,' said Revel. 'Would I be telling you this if I hadn't felt it move?'

Back in the library it was all sitting there, piled, tagged, boxed.

Until today, this had been the history of Trelise, from the arrival of Joshua to the death of Harry, complete as the library could make it. Robbins' bones in the Sea Garden, the succession of personalities and owners established. Until today the past had been complete, the future had started here.

But today was turning into history. The present was moving on. And the past was changing, too.

Guy put his head round the door. 'Good God,' he said. 'Not finished, are you?'

She opened her mouth to say, no, there is more, in a box that Morgan has got. Then she saw in his face the slackening of a tension so deep-seated she had not known it was there.

She gave him a smile that felt as if she had cut it out and pasted it on. 'Just about,' she said. 'The odd loose end.' Well, it was not really a lie. She would have liked to tell him about Morgan and the tea chest. But there came back to her that look in Morgan's eye, threat, calculation . . .

'Great,' he said. 'Look, I think I'm winning, too. Let's go away. In October. Bit of a holiday.' He looked at his watch. 'We're on *Fuchsias* and *Crocosmias*. Then I've got to talk to Morgan. Bottlebrushes in the Antipodes tomorrow.'

'Morgan?'

'He's coming back tonight.' She thought she saw the tension in his face again. Perhaps it was the baby. You saw things differently, when you were thinking for two.

Guy left. It was now or never. Victoria walked past the Pool, out to Morgan's house, and knocked on the door.

There was nobody in.

She thumbed the latch. The front door was open, like all front doors on Trelise.

The Garden House was white-walled and neat. There was no place for old boxes. There was a living room, blond-oak coffee table, Crown of Thorns in the bay window, tray of cuttings on the sill. A study, neat, desk empty. The filing cabinet was locked. There was a kitchen with blue-and-white striped crockery and a big table, bird-table outside. Upstairs there were four bedrooms, two done out for lodgers, one that smelt of Morgan, the other of Mary. There was a big-eyed kitten on Mary's wall. No boxes, no papers.

She went back downstairs. In Morgan's study there was a neat board of keys above the desk. One of them bore a label that said SHED. She took it down and slipped out of the back door. The shed was at the far end of the garden, built of slate and granite, a small barn, really, with a bright-blue boat paint door. She turned the key and went in.

There was a moped, a fishing rod, tottering piles of back numbers of horticultural magazines, many boxes: debris of other lives. She picked her way among the boxes. Her eye fell on a glint of tin. It was the binding of a tea chest. She lifted away a box of encyclopaedias. On its side, in stencilled paint, it bore the legend *Mr Guido 5*. It was half full of papers.

Her heart should have been driving warm, enthusiastic historian's blood round her body. The heart was going, all right. But the blood felt cold and frightened.

It was worse when she saw what was in the box.

She found three old Safeways bags and stuffed them with papers. Then she half-filled the tea chest with gardening magazines, and spread the remaining papers over the top, and put everything back as it had been before. Beyond the shed window the garden stood empty in the sun. She let herself out, went in at the back door, and returned the shed key to the board in the study, and headed for the front door.

As she came round the corner into the hall, the latch snicked, and someone pushed the front door open.

Victoria was only halfway into the hall. She found herself back in the kitchen. She went for the back door, opened it quietly, shut it, could not get the latch to engage, left it open, and scuttled across the lawn and into the bamboo thicket that separated the back garden from the road. She stood between the straw-coloured stools, panting. Morgan came out of the back door and stood in the garden, small, alert, as if sniffing the air. Now she saw that Morgan moved in a world of secrets the way dogs move in a world of scent.

Why am I doing this? thought Victoria. Why am I sneaking around in this way, rather than going up to Owen and saying, look, about those papers Revel says you have, can I have them back, please?

Because Morgan had not wanted Revel to say anything about them, and Revel had betrayed him to her.

She was out of the bamboos now, strolling down the road to the Priory.

Mary came round the corner on a bicycle. Victoria felt the blood rising to her face. Mary smiled and said hello. Victoria smiled back, swinging the shopping bags.

She walked round the pond and up the rockery. Bees hummed, and the warmth of the rocks was powerful with thyme and heath. Dawkins was in the hall, finger on cheek, watching her. She took the bags into her office and started pulling out papers.

They were bills, and letters, and cheque stubs. The bills were letterheaded 'Shore House'. They had been paid month by month until 1939. They started suddenly in 1927. Before then, there were other records, detailing payments to Assistant Keeper Souter. Assistant keeper of what? Or of whom? There were other papers. She could not see where they fitted, or what they were. That would be more research, cool thought.

This was no time for cool thought.

Beyond the window, the sun was setting. It was well beyond the middle of August: the nights were drawing in. The sky was deepening from pink to navy blue. Out in its nest of rocks, the Mare opened its great white eye and blinked at her.

Winked at her.

Gave her a wink of complicity.

The Mare had stood there and been part of the garden, and watched Trelise. The Mare knew.

All of a sudden Victoria knew what Souter had been assistant keeper of.

She saw Robbins on calm nights rowing out past Tobaccoman's Head, across the track of the moon, and into the shadow of the Mare. She could feel the past changing, shifting under her feet, the way the bones in the Sea Garden had changed identities while they lay in the dark ground.

She went to see Revel.

Chapter Twenty-one

Revel had got himself a new boat, used for passengers until the certificate lapsed, the lack of certificate being the reason Kenny had sold it to him.

He took Victoria out next day it was fit, being the third of September. The sea was calm, but still there was a heave out here beyond Tobaccoman's, rumbling creamy in the Foals. As they came to the cylindrical granite base of the Mare the world lifted and sank, six feet at a time. The tower of the lighthouse stretched dizzily into the sky.

'Jump at the top of the swell,' said Revel. The boat came alongside. 'Now.'

Victoria stepped onto the wet, rusty rung set in the granite. She heard the suck and roar as the swell dropped away below her. Knees shaking, she began to climb.

When she looked down, Revel was a doll in a toy boat. She clambered on, hauled herself onto the plinth and stood for a moment pressed against the sun-warm stone of the tower. Then she took from her pocket the key Revel had given her and slid it into the keyhole in the massive iron door.

From the *Independent*, May 28, 1989.

The Mare, one of the last manned lighthouses in Britain, was automated this weekend. Built in 1862 by the Scottish engineer Robert Stevenson, the Mare is credited with preventing hundreds of shipwrecks.

'This is the end of an era,' says Kenny Jenkins, who for thirty years took mail, supplies and relief keepers to the island in his boat Old Joshua. *'Now there's machines up there not keepers what happens when someone gets in trouble out here? Who's going to see him? You tell me.'* A Trinity House spokesman blamed the closure on *'technical advances. You don't need lights any more in these days of GPS. I'm afraid the rock lights are as obsolete as the steamships they were built to serve.'*

There was a chilly stone hallway, a staircase, the ghost of a smell of paraffin. The staircase became a spiral. It passed through a workshop-cum-store with grey-painted tanks, neat, empty, whitewashed, then a galley with a black iron range and a dinette curved to match the wall. Above the kitchen was a room with three curved bunks, each still with a blue-and-white gingham curtain; and above that, a chamber with a stove and a window surrounded with bookshelves painted pea-green. The library, presumably. Here Victoria paused to catch her breath, gazing out of the window, an oblong two-thirds sky and one-third sea.

She forgot to breathe.

The westering sun threw the grain of the softwood end of the bookcase into sharp relief. There was writing under the pea-green paint: writing in pencil, a hard pencil on soft wood, written perhaps when the shelves had been bare, then painted over.

She tore a page out of her notebook. Her hands seemed to be shaking. She laid the paper against the wood and shaded with her pencil.

From the black graphite the writing emerged, clarified; flowing copper-plate, but with Greek E's, and an italic angularity to the pothooks. *Dear Arthur, August 9, 1891*, and then a line. Below it, another line. *Dear Arthur, July 12, 1890*.

It was a year-by-year height chart, of the kind drawn on walls by a proud parent.

She went up through the light room, a place of pipes and valves and new machinery; and up again, up a new kind of staircase, with a brass handrail and arts-and-crafts oak leaves on the balusters.

At the top of the staircase, the lantern was a sea of light. The concentric prisms of the Fresnel lens gleamed silver and rainbow, splitting sea and sky and Trelise into a Cubist cathedral. There were ships on the sea, tractors in the fields, the terrace at Trelise, jumbled and magnified and superimposed. Gingerly, Victoria walked round the gallery. A balcony ran round the outside; on the inside was a parallel walkway. Halfway round the walkway, facing Trelise, was an iron seat. From here, the island lay spread like a map. The bench had a much-sat-in look.

Victoria sat.

Poor child. Rejected by its mother, brought up in this tower by Assistant Keeper Souter. Watching from this glass prison the children of Trelise playing on the terrace. Growing damaged, poor child, and further damaged by life. But Harriet had thought only of Harriet. The child was her punishment, and she hated him for it. Or perhaps it was not that (thought Victoria, hand on her belly; after all, how could you hate your child?). Perhaps she was so frightened of being hurt that she had sent away the people who had the power to hurt her. Never you mind what you're like, Victoria said to her own baby. Mommy loves you. And Daddy will love you too.

Like Arthur's daddy.

Arthur's Daddy, whose writing she knew from the letters. Who had rowed himself out here on calm nights, to visit his son, give him something like a normal life, measure him as he grew, read him books from the library.

Robbins.

Slowly, Victoria clambered to her feet, and started down the spiral stairs.

That evening, she told Guy about the baby.

There was nobody to dinner. Guy had champagne open on the terrace when Victoria came down. He was glowing, shiny. Victoria thought of Robbins, rowing to the Mare on calm nights under the moon. She took her glass away from the bottle half-filled.

'To motherhood!' he cried.

She loved him when he was feeling good. And when he was feeling bad, of course; but tonight, she needed him feeling good.

After a while, she said, 'What do you know about someone called Arthur?'

He was looking away, into the shadows. When he turned back to her his smile seemed hollow. 'Who?'

'Arthur Macleod, I guess.'

'Never heard of him.' The smile vanished altogether. 'For a moment there I thought we could have a real life about us and the baby and never mind the history.' His face was heavy, lit in high chiaroscuro by the patio lamp, the spectacles reflecting the flame.

'Something came up,' she said.

'Oh?'

'More papers.'

'I thought you'd been all through the library.'

'These weren't in the library.'

'Where, then?'

She told him.

His face became stiff and grey. '*Morgan?*' he said.

'Our papers,' she said. 'Our records.'

'Keep your voice down,' he said.

'What?'

'You can't just go round stealing things out of people's sheds,' said Guy. 'What's so bloody important about your bloody research that means you get to ransack other people's private property—'

'It's ours,' said Victoria. 'He stole it. I took it back.'

'Fuck,' said Guy. '*Fuck.*'

Victoria could see all this from the outside: the terrace, the moon, herself. Her husband owned a beautiful island. He was married to a woman who was having his child.

So why was his face in his hands?

Suddenly she was back in herself, on the offensive.

She said, 'What is it about you and Morgan?' That was his cue. I gave you all this, he would say, and the first thing you did was screw the gardener. How do I know that the baby is mine? But he had looked so happy, opened champagne. That was not it.

She waited. He raised his head, and took off his spectacles, and rubbed his eyes. He said, looking down, 'Victoria, don't make an enemy of Morgan.'

'Don't you want to know what's in your papers?'

'Not really.'

Victoria said, 'Not even if I've found you a new great-uncle?'

His face became quite still. 'What?'

'Arthur, he was called. The Dead Child. Not dead after all.'

'What about him?'

'He lived on the Mare.'

The guarded look again. 'What's this got to do with Morgan?'

'He'd hidden the evidence in his garage.'

'Not hidden, surely? Stored.'

'Doesn't matter. I've got it now.'

He opened his mouth to say something. Then he seemed to change his mind. He took her hand. It was as if strength was flowing from her to him. Suddenly he was warm and strong again. He said, 'You and me.'

'You and me and it.'

'Screw 'em all,' said Guy, and leaned across and kissed her.

'Dinner's ready,' said Dawkins' voice from the dark doorway.

Next morning after breakfast, she got out the car – the Golf, not the Bentley – and drove to Falmouth.

Shore House would have been within sight of the sea; no Blakeney-Jones would deprive another Blakeney-Jones of a sea view.

Victoria tried to walk along the water, but came up against garden walls and dead ends. She had not been thinking straight. The name could have changed since the 1930s. And the house itself would be no help at all, of course. She walked up the hill. It was high water. Yachts were coming alongside at the Pandora Inn, their crews swaggering along the jetty, shallow, prosperous, unworried.

At the top of the lane was the church, high and grey. When she tried the door, it was locked. She turned. A woman was coming down the churchyard path. She had grey curly hair and a dog collar. 'Hello there,' she said, jolly hockey-sticks. 'I'm Hilary. You all right?'

Victoria said, 'I'm trying to find out about some people who lived here in the 1930s.'

'Ancestors,' said the Reverend Hilary, nodding understandingly. 'American, are you?'

Victoria smiled sweetly.

Hilary unlocked the church. From the black-iron safe in the vestry she hauled a mighty register. Wetting a professional thumb, she began to turn the pages. 'What name?'

Victoria had a sudden, powerful sense that this was her business and nobody else's. She said, 'Could I look?'

Hilary stepped back, visibly miffed. She said, 'Will you be long?'

'I guess not.'

Hilary made a fuss of putting a chair up to the vestry table and arranging the light. Victoria took out her notebook. 'Not fountain pens, please,' said Hilary, with a bossy smile. 'Wouldn't want to get ink on the registers, would we?'

Nowadays, Restronguet was a suburb of Falmouth. Thirty years ago the place had been more of a village. There were births, and marriages.

And deaths. In particular, the death of one Arthur Macleod, in 1939.

Victoria felt cool and still. The Dead Child was truly dead. Now she knew; cradle to grave.

She started at the beginning: 1854, the register began. There were births, marriages, deaths, the intervals between birth and death often pitifully short, poor babies, the span extending as the years went by.

Hilary's footsteps sounded in the nave. A clock was ticking, gulls crying over the gravestones and the Fal.

But Victoria's world had stopped turning. She read the entry again.

She made a note.

She read on. More notes: keep your hand steady, Victoria, because if you let it shake as much as it wants to shake, you will not be able to read your writing, and what you are writing down is important.

Horribly important.

In 1880, Arthur Robbins had by special licence married Harriet Jones, spinster, of the Parish of Trelise.

In 1928, Arthur Bird had died of delirium tremens.

In 1931, Arthur Robbins, son of Arthur and Harriet Robbins, had taken in matrimony a certain Pansy Jenkins.

In 1938, Pansy Jenkins had borne to her husband, Arthur Robbins, a son, Clark.

Victoria looked at her notebook and let the story form in her mind. Harriet had been secretly married to Robbins, probably at her father's insistence, when she had given birth to Arthur. On Robbins' return from exile as Bird, she had married him under his new name; she was after all pregnant with the twins, Guido and Harry, and needed a husband, but could not admit that Robbins and Bird were the same person.

And Arthur, poor Arthur, had not submitted to being the Dead Child. He had been moved from the lighthouse and Assistant Keeper Souter to Shore House, where he was nursed by Robbins, then Guido and hired staff; a man of fifty-five, by then, deprived by Harriet of companionship, therapy. He had not been a human being. He had been a sin.

But poor Arthur had been human, whatever Harriet thought. He had fallen in love with Pansy Jenkins, who had presumably been his nurse and had presumably encouraged him. This might have been because she loved him for himself, mentally handicapped, fifty-five years old, with a heart condition.

Or there might have been other reasons. The consequences were the same, either way.

Victoria was not seeing the page any more. She was seeing the skeleton in the trench by the new terrace. The skeleton that was not Mendez. And was now not Bird, or Arthur. That could not have been a monk or an islander, because of the filled tooth. Back to the drawing board, with the skeleton. With all her neat ideas.

She said, 'Shit!'

The vestry door opened. Hilary came in, with a mouth that looked as if she had been sucking lemons in the chancel. 'Could you control your language?' she said.

'Shut up,' said Victoria, absently, scribbling.

Hilary began to hiss faintly, like a warm kettle.

Victoria finished writing, closed her notebook and stood up. 'Thank you *so* much,' she said. She thought she might faint. The face above the dog collar was quacking reproachfully. She turned her back on it and went out to the car. She had no idea how she got to the Falmouth registry office, but she did. Later that day she was at Trelise, writing.

At seven, Guy came back and flopped into a chair.

She said, 'What do you want to drink?'

He looked at her sharply. 'Whisky,' he said. She gave him the glass. 'Is something wrong?'

'I've been doing some research into Arthur.' He opened his mouth to say he was not interested. 'Wait.'

He waited.

'Arthur was brought up as a supernumerary keeper in the lighthouse. When Trinity House took over, he was moved to the mainland. Harriet got ten thousand pounds out of Harry. With it she bought Shore House at Restronguet and set him up there. Him and his father. Who loved him and wanted to look after him.'

'His father? Robbins?'

'Bird, Robbins, Macleod, whatever you want to call him. He survived the fire in the greenhouse.'

Guy swallowed his whisky and gave himself some more. He said, 'You're not still on about those damn bones, are you?'

'He's buried at Restronguet. Next to his son, as it happens.'

'So the bones are a monk, all along.'

'Forget the bones for the moment.'

Guy looked pale, and there was a gloss of sweat on his upper lip.

'There was something else in the register. Two things, actually. Arthur got married.'

Guy gaped at her.

'She was called Pansy Jenkins, his nurse.'

'But he was a loony.'

'Pansy didn't mind. His father loved him. Maybe she did too. Sweeping him under the rug was Harriet's idea, nobody else's. But listen. He and Pansy had a son. He's in the register. Clark Arthur Jenkins, they called him; mother's name, father not acknowledged. But they were married all right.'

'Year of birth?'

'1938.'

'And no death.' Guy's face was waxy. 'So he was the son of Guido and Harry's older brother.' He finished his whisky. 'And if he's alive, Trelise belongs to him.' He grinned, a dreadful, skull-like grin. 'Happy now, darling?'

Victoria stared at him. She said, 'You knew.'

He said, 'Actually, I think you will find that everything is all right.'

'What do you mean? How can you know?'

Guy got up, knocking his glass onto the carpet. He said, 'Victoria, you have dug yourself a hole and I am in it with you and I suggest you stop bloody digging before it caves in on both of us.' The whisky had thickened his voice. 'Now I am going to have a bath.'

Victoria saw herself alone in the State Room, in the little pool of yellow light the lamp threw. From the shadows the ghosts of Trelise grinned at her: a woman with a baby on the way, in a country she hardly knew, on an island she understood too well, at the apex of a hundred and fifty years of unhappiness. And a husband who had not wanted her to examine that hundred and fifty years. Who had re-buried the bones of an unknown stranger.

How much of a stranger? How unknown?

She could not bear to admit to herself what she thought her husband had done.

The telephone rang, shockingly loud. It kept ringing. Finally, she picked it up.

'Victoria?' The voice was Morgan's. She had not said anything. Was he out there, watching the lit windows of the Priory?

'Yes.'

'Got a minute in the morning? In the hut?'

'I don't know what—'

'There are things we should talk about.' Still the light, intelligent voice. But there was a hardness to it. It carried a threat. It had plenty to threaten with.

'Eleven o'clock,' said Victoria.

'Kettle's on,' said Morgan. The phone went down.

Jeremy Norris was in his office at nine. The sun was turning the Thames sea-green, and he was fresh from the pool at the RAC. His secretary said, 'There's a Victoria Kline on the line.'

'Very poetic,' said Jeremy, and cast himself into his Girsberger chair. 'Victoria?'

He had known her . . . well, until six months ago. Nice girl, pretty, odd she had got mixed up with that weird Blakeney-Jones crowd. She sounded different. He remembered her as wide-eyed, callow. Now, as she did the pleasantries, she sounded different. Older, wiser. Nervous. Attractive woman. Jeremy wished she could see his new suit. She was saying she did not have a solicitor. She needed to ask a question. Well, Jeremy was delighted to oblige: a Blakeney-Jones divorce would be wonderfully expensive. 'The first one's free,' he said. 'What is it?'

'I'm writing a novel,' she said. 'There's this kind of weird inheritance set-up.'

'Tell me.'

'A woman dies. Her estate passes to the elder of two sons, who has already ceded all rights in it to his younger brother, so the younger brother takes possession, lives there for seventy years. It later turns out that there had been an older brother all along, who has had issue. Who gets the estate?'

Jeremy sucked a Biro. 'Wow,' he said. 'Can you still get away with plots like that? Well. The elder of the two brothers passed it straight to his younger brother, you say. So he was never in adverse possession, right? So it may be that the younger brother was never in adverse possession either. So the oldest brother and his heirs would have a case. Not cut and dried, of course; but a case. If I was doing the work, I mean.'

'So it works?' said Victoria. Her voice had gone dead.

'It works.'

'That's what I needed to know,' said Victoria.

'Any time you want help,' said Jeremy.

'I'll remember that,' said Victoria, and put the phone down.

Victoria wanted her baby to grow up at Trelise; to sleep in its buggy in the smell of pelargoniums and the rustle of palms, splash on the white margins of a turquoise sea. She was ready to fight for that. Which was what Guy had been doing all along, and she had been too dumb to notice.

She looked out of the window, across Great Rocks, at the Mare. Christ, she had been a fool. So arrogant. Chasing after an identity for those bones, when she could have been just getting on with stuff, helping. *Weeding*, for Christ's sake. Instead of undermining the process by which Guy had come into possession, because of a whimsical notion about bones.

Guy had resisted her digging, but he had always gone along with her attempts to put a name to them. A monk; Mendez; Robbins. As if he was anxious for her to accept any solution to the problem—

Too anxious.

Victoria, what are you trying to say?

Nothing. Not that. Please.

She looked at the ormolu clock above the fire. It was five to eleven. Morgan was in the hut. Six weeks ago, she would have put on lipstick, hosed herself down with perfume.

Six weeks ago.

Now, she pulled down her sweater, moistened her lips with an apprehensive tongue, and walked heavy-footed down the terrace and into the garden.

The garden did not change; at least, it changed only in the ways it had been planned to change. There were berries on the myrtle that had earlier been all flower and perfume. Apples, plums. Deadly nightshade, cuckoo-pint, hellebore.

This was her place, now: the Poseidon Stairs, the swoop of the Endless Walk, the wind of the path under the tree-ferns to the bamboos. And through the gap in the bamboos, the shed.

The shed had shrunk. The door handle was cheap plastic, the boards of the door itself badly planed, in need of creosote. When she opened it, it smelt stuffy, with a hint of mould.

Morgan was there already, feet on the table, glancing up from a book, marking his place, smiling. 'You look well,' he said.

'So do you.' It was not true. He looked small, and drawn, and grey, the brightness of his eye not so much intelligent as calculating. 'How was TV?'

'Glamorous,' he said. 'East, west, home's best.' He put down his book and stood up with that grace and fluidity of his. That had been one of the attractions.

Snakes were fluid and graceful, too.

He came towards her. 'I've missed you,' he said, and put out his arms.

She held back. He stopped smiling. He looked for a moment as if she had hit him. His arms dropped. He said, 'It's like that, is it?'

'Like what?' She was dizzy with apprehension.

'Things get awkward,' he said. 'You get tired of me. You send me away.'

'Not tired.'

Morgan smiled, not the old smile, but something new, hard, smug; altogether revolting. 'But I have noticed,' he said, 'that this is what you do.'

She should leave. She said, 'What on earth are you talking about?'

'You left America,' he said. 'In a hurry. Right?'

'No,' she said.

'Yes,' he said. 'Because of a fire.'

'No,' she said, but it was more a way of breathing than a denial.

'Doctor Nevis,' he said. 'What was he doing in your room?'

A terrible night; hot, sweat-slippery, the air thick with thunder. Daddy had walked out two weeks before. Mommy was at the kitchen table, as always, wondering where she had gone wrong, and the real answer was when she had married Daddy, but none of the girls could say that because if there had been no marriage there would have been none of them. So they took it in turns to talk to Mommy, fruitlessly. That night it was Sarah's turn.

So Victoria had been lying in her room in a thin cotton nightdress, sweating, thinking. Daddy had left because his daughters were not sons, and life refused to measure up to his 1956-style high standards, and Mom refused to support him. Because, as she pointed out, this was 1996, and things had changed.

Lightning flashed. The lights went out. Victoria lit the oil lamp she kept in her room for romance and emergencies. Thunder rattled.

So did the door handle.

She said, 'Who's there?'

The door opened. Doctor Nevis was standing there, sweaty and peeled-looking. He said, 'I wanted to talk to you. You said it was a free country.'

'Not now,' she said, sheet under chin. 'How did you get in?'

'Nothing was locked.'

'Well, if you could kindly go right out again?'

But he lumbered in, and shut the door behind him. Last time she had not noticed how big he was. He said, 'There is something I have been trying to tell you.'

'Not now.'

'It can't wait.'

'It'll have to.' She was getting frightened. There was something dogged and infantile about him. 'Please. Go.'

'But I love you.'

'No.'

'Women often say yes when they mean no. I know that.'

Unbelievable. A moron. 'Who told you that?'

'Your father.'

'Get out. Please.' She was really scared. Out of bed now, backing away towards the bookshelf, where the lamp stood, burning slow and steady and yellow. He started towards her. She could see his erection through his trousers.

She threw the lamp.

The fire had run from the top of his head to his Bass Weejuns. He had fallen back into the curtains.

Then she had been on the lawn with Mom and Sarah and Martha, and behind her the house had been burning down, the white wooden house of her infancy. And inside it had been Doctor Nevis. And, as it turned out, Daddy, who had sneaked in the back way to collect some books he had left behind.

She had run from that fire, and kept running, and here she was.

In the shed with Morgan.

Morgan put his arms around her.

They were as hard as she remembered them. Harder. He took her face in his hands and kissed her, closed mouth hard, bruising her lips with his teeth. She pulled her head away. She felt herself turned, the edge of the table on the tops of her thighs, Morgan pushing her so she fell backwards and her feet came off the floor. Morgan was suddenly between her thighs, and his hands were at the collar of her shirt, tearing outwards. Cool air

331

was on her baby-swollen breasts, then his hands, hard, remorseless; and behind the hands his face, dark with blood, not smiling any more, hard, violent. The face of a man who was going to take something he wanted, by force, in a dirty shed full of greasy books and tannin-stained mugs.

She lay rigid with fear. She said, 'Don't do it.'

The fingers hardened in her breasts. 'Try to stop me,' he said.

'That hurts.'

His hands moved from her breasts to her waist. He started undoing the buttons of her jeans. 'If you make a noise, someone will come, and I will explain that this is no problem, just a reunion.'

'Stop,' she said. She was going to cry. It would only encourage him. 'You can't.'

'I bloody can,' said Morgan.

'I don't want to. I can't. Not any more.'

Morgan said, 'So tell Guy.'

'I'm pregnant. I'm going to have Guy's baby. He'll—'

'He won't do a thing. You can tell him I fucked you now, and you can ask him to kill me, sack me, whatever you like. But I promise you he won't.'

She heard a zip unzip. She tried to roll away, but he leaned forward and gripped her breasts again, one-handed, and squeezed so hard she nearly fainted. His free hand was doing things below waist level. Victoria thought she was going mad. Morgan was doing this to Guy. *To the baby* . . .

The panic went, and the tears. What was left was clear white rage. She wanted to claw him to little bits. But scratching was too feeble.

Instead, she jammed her right forefinger into his left eye.

She felt something wet, probably eyeball. Then he was swearing and the hand on her breasts was gone, and the weight between her legs had slackened, and she gave a heave of her hips and heard a crash. She was up from the table, grabbing at her jeans. Morgan was leaning against the bookshelf with his hand to his face, his dick hanging out. Books were falling on him. She swung the kettle spout-first into the side of his head. He fell over. She stumbled out of the shed and slammed the door. She tried to button her jeans and bring her shirt together over her breasts. But her fingers were shaking too hard. Holding herself together with her hands, she ran through the calm, beautiful garden. On the Poseidon Stairs she could run no more. She sat down and hugged her knees and started to cry. She wanted Guy. But Guy would be in the Estate Office, miles away . . .

Feet shuffled past her; trippers, not liking to stop. She was alone, clothes torn, in a strange country, on a strange island, married to a strange man, in a strange life . . .

Someone sat down beside her. An arm went round her shoulders. A woman's arm, light and sensitive. 'You all right?' said a voice. The voice of Revel's Daisy. 'Stupid question.'

Victoria lifted her head. 'Nice to be asked,' she said through lips numb and rubbery.

Daisy said, 'I'll take you back to the Priory.'

'No way,' said Victoria. She could not be seen like this. Guy might be back from the Estate Office. He would ask questions, which she would have to answer.

Daisy said, 'What's happened to you?'

She shook her head. Tears went left, right. She was furious. She was starting to shiver. Shock?

'Come on,' said Daisy.

'Not home.'

'You come with me,' said Daisy. She took off her jersey, and pulled it over Victoria's head, and buttoned her jeans up straight, and led her off down the island, nattering away, dear Daisy, what the gig crew had got up to across in St Ives Friday afternoon, a fight in the Castle, the price of potatoes. At her house she sat Victoria in the kitchen and made clattering noises with the kettle. 'Tea,' she said.

The tea was good. Victoria felt the shaking ease. She started to cry again, a different sort of crying; not desperate and angry any more, just sad, that after everything she had tried, what it came down to in the end was loneliness and confusion.

'What happened?' said Daisy.

Victoria shook her head.

'Someone had a go at you,' said Daisy.

'Fell over,' said Victoria.

'Course you did,' said Daisy. 'That enough sugar?'

'Fine.' Victoria drank, and clattered the cup against her teeth and burned her mouth. She wanted to be anywhere but where she was. She got up and went to the door.

'Where are you going?' said Daisy.

If she went home, there would be Guy, asking questions. If he asked questions, she would ask questions too. And Christ knew where it would all end. But she needed to ask questions of someone.

Daisy, for instance.

She sat down again. She said, 'How long have you lived on the island?'

Daisy looked at her, kind oval face, freckled like a gull's egg. 'Twelve years,' she said.

'And,' said Victoria. 'And . . .' Her voice seemed paralysed. She drank more tea. 'Did you ever come across anyone called Clark Jenkins?'

Daisy looked at her from her opalescent grey eyes. 'There's two Jenkins boys in the village now,' she said. 'Emmy Jenkins's Henry, and Alice—'

Victoria shook her head. 'He would have been a visitor.'

Daisy frowned. 'Not for a long time,' she said. 'There was a chap . . . hang on. There was this Australian feller. Terrible drunk. His name was Jenkins, maybe Clark.' She frowned. 'Are you all right?'

'Fine,' said Victoria.

'But we all called him Max, because he was mad. He worked here for a couple of months.' Her face cleared. 'Quite a gang of them there was. Mr Guy was here, too.'

'Guy was here? How long ago was this?'

'Ten years.'

But Guy had not been to Trelise since he had been twelve. He had told her so.

He had lied.

'They were all together, this time of year, a bit later maybe. There was a fuss of some kind, and Max went back to Australia, I think.'

'Fuss?'

'I dunno. They were always in the Castle, Owen and Mr Guy and this Max. I heard a rumour there was some sort of fight, not amazing really, the quantity they were drinking. Mr Guy was what, eighteen? Owen was twenty-five or so. Max was much older. But they were all tearaways, in those days. People settle down. The work stopped, and everyone left in

334

a hurry. Buggered off in the middle of the night. The Major thought the whole thing was hilarious.'

'What work were they doing?'

'Great big upheavals, there were. It was about the last time anyone did anything big in the garden, till now.'

'Oh, Jesus,' said Victoria. 'Oh, Jesus, no.'

'What's up?' said Daisy. 'More tea?'

Victoria said, 'They were in the Sea Garden. Trenching.'

'Well, bloody hell,' said Daisy. 'How on earth did you know that?'

Chapter Twenty-two

Victoria started home with a headful of dark, brittle truths.

The man who was putatively the rightful heir to Trelise had been present during the last trenching of the Sea Garden, with or in the presence of Guy, the next in line of succession. Owen Morgan knew about it. (Thinking of Morgan made her feel sick and dizzy. But by concentrating on the case, she could turn him into a factor in the equation, without emotional content. For the moment.) One possible construction of the facts was that Guy had killed Clark Jenkins and buried him in the Sea Garden, hoping that if the bones were discovered, they would be thought to be a monk. Morgan knew what had happened, of course.

That would explain Morgan's confidence that he would keep his job even if Victoria told Guy tales of fornication, theft and rape. It would explain Guy's dislike of her research, his eagerness to accept any attribution for the Sea Garden bones.

She turned up Joshua's secret staircase through the rockery; clear now, the staircase, bright with little tufts of *Erigeron* and *Convolvulus mauretanicus*, shoved in there by Guy. She was walking slowly, pressed down by the anvil weight of the arguments. Her legs ached with weariness. She sat down on a stone step by the small green well, out of sight of everyone but the goldfish that was its only inhabitant.

Guy was her husband, the man she loved, the father of her child. She thought of him as many things: kind, awkward, short-tempered, *distrait*, clever, evasive, affectionate. The evidence was against him. As a historian her duty was to the evidence. But his baby was in her belly, and their lives were locked together. Never in a million years could she think of him as a murderer.

And there was another thing. Morgan had Guy in a corner, with no means of escape. Morgan was a clever man. It was not clever to reduce a known murderer to a state of desperation.

So chances were that Morgan did not believe Guy was a murderer either.

The strength returned to her legs. She walked up the steps to the terrace, aware of the spicy smells of myrtle and honeysuckle. Beyond the wall, the garden fell away to the dark sea of trees, and the real sea, and beyond it the Mare.

As it always had.

Trelise belonged to her, and her husband, and her child. Anyone who disputed that fact with a bunch of half-truths had something to lose if those truths were made whole.

The signposts all pointed at Guy.

But the signposts had been put up by Morgan.

She had a bath, smeared arnica on the bruises Morgan's fingers had left, and put on some untorn clothes. Then she took a walking stick from the rack and started back into the garden.

She carried the stick like a club, in case she saw Morgan. But the walks and stairs were empty except for shadows. She walked under the blank eyes in Davy Jones and tapped with the stick on the railing of Revel's verandah. He was inside, hunched over a low table, gouging delicate spirals of limewood from a bas-relief of a mermaid in a field of bladder wrack. Victoria said, 'Have you got a moment?'

'Well,' he said, 'Owen wants me to weed the sodding Union Jack. But Owen's on the mainland.' He fetched two cans from the fridge. 'Guinness?' Victoria watched him pour, took a glass, wet her lips. Strength for you, honey, she said to the baby.

'There was something I wanted to ask you,' she said.

Revel emptied his glass with the air of a man fortifying himself for a long-awaited ordeal. 'Ask,' he said.

'Ten years ago,' said Victoria, 'Guy came down to visit the Major. There was a Clark Jenkins here. What happened?'

Revel fetched himself another can. He said, 'You're not asking because you don't know already, are you?'

'Not entirely.'

'Oh, well,' said Revel. He hesitated; the first time she had ever seen him hesitate. Victoria saw he was weighing it up. Telling her Morgan had the tea chest had been a tentative move. This was the point of no return.

'Yes,' he said. She relaxed. 'Ten years ago, like you said. The Major decided he wanted a bit of work done in the garden, which was a notion something foreign to him I can tell you, bloody jungle was the style of thing he liked after Mrs Blakeney-Jones died. Anyway, this Clark Jenkins chap arrives on the island. He would have been fifty, perhaps. But he had all his hair cut off and a ring in his nose and red bits of veins on his face. He said he'd been a surfer. We called him Mad Max, and he liked it, silly bugger. He turned up in February, just him and a rucksack. Over the causeway he piles and goes straight to the Castle. I remember Johnny, he was the landlord then, he said they had a room for him, ready booked by the Estate Office, bill to be sent to the Major. So he comes into the bar, dripping wet from the rain, nasty look on his face, drinks ten pints of lager hand running and falls off his stool, and we carry him upstairs. Not a word did he say all that time, just looking about him as if he did not like what he saw. Next day he came to work in the garden and first out Darren asked him where he came from and he tries to wallop Darren with a shovel, which by the way was the only work he done with it all the time I knew him. We took it away from him quite peaceful and asked him not to wave it about. He got discouraged and went and lay down in a flowerbed. Funny chap, actually. When he was pissed or hung over he always seemed to want to fight, but he was bloody useless at it. Death wish, he had, really.

'And after a bit, Mr Guy turned up. I saw them one day, Mr Guy and this big lout Max, in the garden. Mr Guy was digging away, not too skilful, but quite enthusiastic. This Jenkins was standing alongside him, black under the eyes, two days' beard on him. The Major came down, limping like he did, Dawkins with his camp chair, and sort of sat in front of them and looked at them, very close. Mr Guy had long hair then, which the Major never did like, but you could see he didn't like the nose ring on Jenkins neither. I remember thinking at the time that he was judging them, somehow. It was a funny old time all right. Very funny time indeed.' He stopped, looking into his glass.

339

'But Jenkins went away.'

'That's right.'

She filled her lungs with oxygen. 'Did you see him go?'

'Not exactly.'

'What do you mean?'

'It was the afternoon, going on evening,' he said. 'A Saturday. They'd been in the pub all dinner time. Max he said he was leaving over the causeway. But by closing time it was gone half tide, so the Castle stayed open, causeway covered, no police, you know. So anyway they were pretty far gone through afternoon closing. Then it came six o'clock, getting dark, and the tide was going out. They started to argue then. Max was trying to wind Mr Guy up about something, don't know what. Then Max said he was going, had to catch a boat to the mainland. He went out onto the quay. Dirty night it was; storm of wind, rain, big tide, the Mixer snoring away out there. When I started off home they were on the quay, still arguing, nose to nose, really. I would have said goodnight except they did not look as if they wanted to talk to anybody. Then it came on a squall of rain so I bolted back into the Castle, and Mary Morgan came in looking for Mr Guy, and I said he was on the quay, thinking matters would improve if she went out, because Mr Guy was a gentleman and drunk or sober he wouldn't start nothing if there was ladies present. So she went out, and I had another pint. And that was that, really.'

'So Mary Morgan went and stopped them fighting?'

'I dunno,' said Revel. 'But I know that I drank my pint and I heard the rain slack off on the panes and I started off out again. And I bumped into Mr Guy, in the road, staggering drunk, blood on his face, and there was no sign of Max. So I thought Max had taken the boat to the mainland.'

Victoria felt cold.

'Only, I heard later on, that Kenny decided that night it was such a bloody awful night he cancelled his last trip. So if Jenkins left that night, he didn't leave by boat, and there was seven foot of water over the causeway. So what I have wondered ever since is, how the hell did he go?'

Bones on red clay. The flick of gull-shadows in the blue roof of the trench.

The shadows were lengthening in the garden as Victoria went back to the house. In the kitchen, Dawkins was reading the *Daily Mail*. 'Where's Guy?'

'Exeter, dear,' said Dawkins. 'He's staying the night. Some sort of dinner, he said. Do you want some now?'

'I'll do it,' she said. 'You'll miss EastEnders.' She wanted the kitchen to herself. Dawkins sighed and said, 'Night, then,' and swished towards the stairs. She waited for his footsteps to creak into silence, the distant yarr of his cats and the murmur of his TV. Then she picked up the telephone and dialled Morgan's number. Mary's voice said, 'Hello,' warm and bright as always.

'It's me,' said Victoria.

'Who?' said Mary, cooler.

'Victoria.'

'Oh.' Cool had gone frigid. Victoria's stomach turned over. 'What is it?'

'I've got to talk to you.'

'Can't it wait?'

'No.'

'You'd better come down.'

'Where's Owen?'

'Out.'

Victoria climbed onto her bicycle and wheeled it into the drive.

A thin rain had started to fall. The windows of the Garden House were warm and yellow, its Victorian gables angular against the thick black of the sky. When Mary opened the door she was not wearing make-up, and her hair was scraped back into an elastic band. Her face looked thin-skinned and old, the jawline beginning to descend into a slope of double chin. She did not offer Victoria a drink. They sat at the kitchen table. 'What can I do for you?' said Mary.

Victoria said, 'I'm still doing history.'

'Ah.'

'I've got to Clark Jenkins. Max, you called him.'

Mary swayed a centimetre left, then upright again, as if something small but potent had struck her on the ear. 'Really?' she said.

The next question could destroy her life, or mend it. 'You saw Guy and Max on the quay, the night Jenkins left the island.'

Mary frowned. 'Did I?'

'So you don't remember?'

There was a pause that patently had nothing to do with memory. Mary was trying to work out how much to tell her. At last she said, 'That's right. It was raining. They were on the quay, pissed. They were arguing. I told them to go home before they caught cold. Guy said okay. But Max said he was waiting for a boat.'

'So Guy left.'

'No.'

'Why not?'

Mary looked Victoria straight in the eye. She said, 'Because Owen turned up on the quay.'

'What difference did that make?'

'The way I'd got Guy to agree to come off the quay was that I was going to take him home and make love to him.' Victoria blinked. 'We were having an affair,' she said. 'Owen is a jealous sort of man. If I'd taken Guy off the quay, he would have got ideas. He had ideas already. So I went. And they stayed. The three of them.'

Victoria looked at Mary and tried to imagine Guy in bed with her. A younger, slimmer Guy, with long hair. A Mary with only one chin, a gypsy bloom on her skin. Ten years ago. Why was it upsetting?

It was fine. She had to think it was fine.

It was not fine. Guy was hers.

She got up and left without saying goodbye. She had learned two things. One, the last person to see Guy and Jenkins on the quay had been Morgan. And two, everyone was frightened of Morgan.

Including her.

The house felt dark and huge. She went upstairs, climbed into bed, and took a copy of the *Economist* from Guy's bedside table. She rested her eyes on an article about something or other. The words did not get through, stupid, shallow male words. She kept seeing Guy and Mary Morgan, naked on a bed in the Garden House; and other pictures, of herself and Owen Morgan moaning in the shed; and Guy on the quay fighting this Mad Max Jenkins . . . oh, Christ, what was going on?

She buried her face in the pillows. She could smell Guy there: the steady, sensible smell of Guy. Her Guy. Not some wild-eyed longhair.

The present is only the past, developed.

The telephone rang. This late, it must be Guy. The shadows blew away. She was suddenly warm and happy. She picked up the receiver and said, 'Hello?'

'You sound well,' said the voice of Owen Morgan.

Her heart wanted to stop. She said, knowing it was stupid, 'Do you know what the time is?'

'Just gone midnight,' said Morgan, cold and level. 'I heard you were down here talking to Mary. I rang to say, you keep away from Mary. If you want to talk to anyone, you can talk to me.'

'All right,' she said, out of a great silence. 'Talk.'

He said, 'I'm coming up to the Priory now. I've got some things you need to know.'

'No.'

'Try to stop me.'

'Dawkins is here.'

Morgan laughed. 'That's all right, then. Don't worry, dear, I'm not going to touch you.'

Victoria's mind whirred; flight, fight; ask questions. 'In the study,' she said. 'In half an hour. Come up the secret staircase.'

The telephone went down.

She got out of bed and clambered into jeans, a jersey, engineer's boots. She ran downstairs and made her preparations. Half an hour later she was behind the desk in the study. Guy's photograph was on the wall beside her, watercolours of the garden and the Mare, a portrait of Joshua, three-quarter face, cool-eyed, watching her. She realised the affection she had come to feel for all these things; how she resented the idea of someone violating their sanctity—

The latch of the French door leading to the secret stairs clicked. The door opened. Morgan stepped in.

From somewhere up by the ceiling she saw him shut the door, neat, precise, economical. His right eye was heavily bloodshot; good. She saw him look for a chair, not find one; she had dragged the chairs into the next room. She saw herself in the desk chair, the desk itself, a heavy partner's desk, pulled across the corner of the room with the door through into the drawing room, so it made a little barricaded triangle with a door for escape. In front of her on the desk was a double-barrelled twelve bore. The safety was off, and her finger was beside the trigger guard. It would have been inside the trigger guard, but now she saw Morgan she could feel the cruel dig of his fingers in her body, and her hands wanted to shake too much to be safe near shotgun triggers.

When she shot him, she wanted it to be on purpose.

He said, 'Can I have a chair?'

She said, 'No.'

For a moment he looked awkward; a short moment, but enough to restore her courage. She said, 'This is loaded.' He nodded. 'What do you want?'

Morgan said, 'Like I said, I hear you've been creeping round Mary. Stop it.'

He was trying to seize the initiative. She said, 'I think you should tell me what you're trying to achieve.'

He smiled. He said, 'You'd better talk to your husband.'

'I'm talking to you.'

He turned round and reached for the door handle.

She said, 'Stop.'

He grasped the door handle.

Her finger found the front trigger of the shotgun. There was an explosion that seemed to bulge the walls of the room. The gun jumped back across the desk. She thought she heard a yell, but it was impossible to be sure, the way her ears were ringing. Smoke eddied in a new wind that came from a hole in the window. She could not see Morgan. Christ, she thought, with a sense of nightmare. I've killed him.

Behind the terror, she found something even more frightening. If Morgan was dead, Trelise was safe. And she was happy—

He was on the floor, face down, wriggling towards the far corner, as far away as he could get. She said, 'Sit up.' He kept wriggling. 'There's another barrel,' she said. 'Sit up. Go on.'

He sat up and propped his back against the wall. His face was a sick beige. A wet patch was spreading on the crotch of his jeans. He looked pretty gross.

She said, in a quiet, reasonable historian's voice, 'You said you wanted to talk. So tell me the true story of your life at Trelise.'

He said in a small, thin voice, 'You don't want to know.'

'One more barrel. A leg, say.'

'You're crazy.'

'I don't like rapists. I thought you knew all about that.'

Morgan got himself under control. 'What is it about you?' he said. He was giving her the eyes, the treatment, for Christ's sake.

She said, 'It is hard to take a guy seriously who has pissed himself. Start when you came to Trelise.'

'Don't say you weren't warned,' said Morgan. 'Good garden, run by a silly old bastard, your grandfather-in-law. He hired me to do what he wanted, which was nothing much, but what there was I did properly. In my spare time I looked around a bit. In papers, registers and so on. I found out about Clark Jenkins. I found out where his mother had gone. Which ship, where to. Then I rang up international directory enquiries. Not many Pansy Jenkinses in Australia. But I was lucky. Sure, I was lucky.' He grinned, pleased with himself. His trousers might be cooling, but his spirits were improving.

'She was dying. She told me Max was in Melbourne. I wrote to him, found out he was in jail, needed a little brightness in his life. And I was . . . well. Thing is about a place like Trelise, you get to like it here. I'm sure you know what I mean, Eh, Victoria? And if you're just a gardener, you're in charge of the garden, all right, and the old ladies are ever so polite, but do you have the security? No, Victoria. Not really. So I thought, well, the Major could die any minute, so I should take some further measures. And I suggested to the Major that he should have a look at your Guy, because he didn't know him and frankly nor did I, and he looked like being the next boss, from what the Major told me. I used to talk to the Major a lot. I told him about Clark Jenkins too.' He looked solemn. 'It's a responsibility, an island like this. A choice of two was better than a choice of one, the way he saw it. So I got Clark to come over, and the Major got Guy. Wanted to see how they did, really.'

Victoria said, 'Jenkins was a drunk.'

'And Guy was bloody useless.'

345

'That's not what I've heard.'

'Oh?'

'He had an affair with Mary.' Victoria shifted the gun. The wet patch on Morgan's jeans made a good target. She could see by his face that he knew that too. 'And what I was wondering was whether that had anything to do with your terrific attraction for me. Or any of the other things that happened.'

Morgan smiled at her. 'How did you guess?'

Victoria felt drenched in a wave of pure rage. She translated it into a smile. 'You do your research, and you get Jenkins on the island, and Guy, and Mary takes to Guy – tells you so, I expect – and you think Jenkins is a drunken idiot, and you're jealous of Guy, so you don't really see either of them as the ideal boss.'

Morgan kept watching the gun.

'So what happened the night Jenkins left the island?'

Morgan said, 'You don't want to know.'

'I do.'

Morgan shrugged. 'Jenkins tried to hit Guy. But he was a great lump of a bloke, drunk, too. Guy isn't a fighter either. So Guy ducked, and gave him a stupid little tap on the chest, and Jenkins fell over and banged his head on a bollard and went into the sea and sank. The tide was going past the quay like a river. First thing anyone knew, there he is, rolling in the Mixer. And that was about bloody that. Well, Guy sat down on a bollard, big girl's blouse your sodding husband, and he puts his face in his hands and starts to cry. But I went round fast as I could to the Glory Hole and waited there, and a couple of hours later sure enough round comes Clark and washes up on the beach. I flopped him into a barrow and pulled his clothes off him and planted him where we'd been digging by the steps in the Pool Garden. Then I told Guy, just between the two of us; our little secret, like. Yours too now. You're fucked, you bloody Joneses. Double fucked, after tonight. You can just lie back and enjoy it. I know you can. I've watched you, Victoria. You're a good fuck, girl, but noisy.'

Victoria looked at her hands to stop herself from crying.

'So Guy killed him,' said Morgan. 'Now if you've finished, I'll be off home.'

Victoria said, 'While you're there, pack. Get off the island.'

Morgan smiled. He said, 'I think I'll wait to hear from Guy.'

Then he unlatched the window and left.

Victoria was sick in the waste-paper basket. Then she started to cry, and could not stop. Eventually she opened the desk drawer, and pulled out the tape recorder, and turned it off, and slid the cassette into the pocket of her jeans. Then she headed into the house.

Dawkins was in the hall, face a coppery moon over a black silk dressing-gown. He opened his mouth, saw Victoria's face, shut it again. He had heard the gunshot. He was waiting. She said, 'The French window in the study needs new glass.'

'Oh?'

'I let a gun off,' said Victoria. 'You can clear up in the morning.' Dawkins was looking at her hands. Victoria realised she was still carrying the gun. 'Ah,' she said. 'Yes. I don't want anyone in the house.'

'Anyone?'

'Not anyone. Morgan, Mary, nobody.'

Dawkins' face took on an expression of Buddhic innocence, all except for the eyes. The eyes knew more than the face. Much more. Infinitely more.

Victoria said, 'See to it, please,' and went up the stairs, resisting a panicky urge to run.

Once in her room, she locked and bolted the door. She put the gun on the dressing-table. Beyond the window, the Mare swelled and died. The night felt full of eyes; worse than eyes; hands, minds, voices. She started across the carpet to draw the curtains. Halfway across she dropped to her knees, and crawled. She pulled the string. The curtains closed. She went back to the bed and yanked the duvet over her head.

The tide was over the causeway. The house was locked. Her bedroom was locked. She had a gun. She was safe. Safe because she did not believe what Morgan had told her.

Did she?

She was suddenly exhausted. Baby, you need your sleep after the horrible bath of chemicals mommy has given poor you. How does mommy sleep during all this? Put head on pillow. Try to stop thoughts spinning—

Someone was banging on the door. Light was streaming through chinks in the curtains. Daylight, autumn-gold, making a stripe across the Turkey rug. She had been asleep. Dreaming. It had all been a dream.

The banging came again. Guy's voice. 'Let me in!'

She sat up and put her feet on the floor. Her fingers fumbled at the bolts. The door opened. And there he was, large as life and twice as comforting. She put her arms around his neck and felt his arms around her and there they were, the three of them, now, and everything for that one second was just fine. Then she felt his body stiffen, and his arms come unhitched from her back. He said, 'What's going on?' He picked up the gun from the dressing-table. 'Christ,' he said. 'It's loaded.' He squinted down the barrel. 'What have you been shooting?'

She said, 'Make some coffee, and give Dawkins the day off?'

'What—'

'Do it. I'll be right down.'

She showered, and put on fresh clothes. He was at the kitchen table, the *Independent* open in front of him. Open at the sports pages. He never read the sports pages. She poured herself some coffee and sat down. He said, 'Would you mind telling me what this is all about?'

She said, 'You never told me about Clark Jenkins.'

His face became quite still; the big face, wide, with freckles, the round glasses, kind eyes behind them. He said, 'Who have you been talking to?'

'Owen Morgan. I've sacked him.'

He closed his eyes. He said, 'Is this anything to do with the gun?'

'Yes.'

His head went into his hands.

'I didn't shoot him, though. I didn't shoot anyone.'

'Hooray,' he said. 'So supposing you tell me what happened?'

'Morgan told me about Clark Jenkins. Why didn't you tell me?'

'I didn't see the point.'

'Are you sure that's right?' She wanted a father for her baby, not this liar. She would leave, take her baby elsewhere.

At that moment, he blushed. He actually had the good taste and natural decency to blush. Suddenly she loved him again. With that in her voice, she said, 'Why don't you tell me what happened?'

He seemed to hear her. He said, 'I was just out of film school. Broke, no work, smoking dope. My father was dead. My mother was dying. Not an ideal moment, really.' He grinned, a tense, artificial grin. 'The parents brought me here when I was twelve. Harry behaved like a shit, apparently. So they said, we don't go where we're not wanted. Or my father did. My mother would have gone along with him. And she really hated Harry.' He smiled, a tense smile. 'And me, well, when you're a teenager and at film school and all that, you don't actually want too much to do with feudal survivals. Then Harry wrote and said there was some work to do in the garden. While he knew I would not be inclined to visit Trelise perhaps I would be interested in a little paid employment, and at the same time to get a look at the place my forefathers had made, bla bla, pompous old fool. Well, I didn't have anything better to do. My mother was dead against it, but I was twenty, I knew what I wanted to do. Plus I was curious, I have to say. You could tell my mother sort of loved the place: she always felt an exile, I think. So I thought I'd take a look, and tell her how it was.

'I stayed in the Tower. Dawkins brought me tea in the mornings. Harry was eighty-something, not receiving. So I sat up there and wrote film treatments and dug holes. Trenching, we were, in what is now the Sea Garden. Bloody hard work. Then I ran out of dope and started to go to the pub, there not being anything else to do much. I met a few islanders.'

'And Max.'

'Yes.' His voice was carefully casual. 'I mean I wasn't much good at digging holes. But Max didn't even try. He just sat on a stone and stank of drink and smoked cigarettes. Then one day there was a wheeze and a shuffle and Harry and Morgan turned up, plus Dawkins carrying one of those picnic chairs. Dawkins unfolds it and Harry sits down and calls me and this Max over, and grins at us, and says, "Which one shall it be?" Morgan is standing behind him, looking bored, like he did. Then back we go to work.'

There had been no mention of Mary Morgan, yet.

'Max was in the Castle on the Friday night, pissed. He started on me. I sort of laughed at him and landed up on Tobaccoman's counting meteorites.' Victoria had a sudden picture of a rug on the heather, Guy on his back in the dark, Mary Morgan astride him, the gleam of her breasts in the starlight, surf, shooting stars. She was getting angry again. She had no right to be angry. 'It started to rain that night. Front came in, I suppose. So there was damn all to do on Saturday except go to the pub. It was one of those days that are wet and hot at the same time, southerly wind, big one, so you can't breathe properly. I remember everything on the island was kind of fretting and dripping: boats in the harbour, trees in the garden, people in the bar. Max said this was no kind of weather for surfers, and he was leaving. I told him not to be so stupid, because as far as I knew he had no means of getting back to Oz, poor bugger would have starved to death, ended up in jail, God knows. Then Morgan came in, and he got hold of Max and dragged him off to one side and they talked about something, me I think, because I was talking to someone or other' – Mary, thought Victoria – 'and Max, who was pissed as usual, he kept looking at me on the quiet, but every time he moved his head it sort of wobbled, so I thought it would fall off. Eventually he shook Morgan's hand and grinned and lurched on back to the bar and started drinking whisky, big time, as if he had something to celebrate. And it all began to come out.'

'What?' said Victoria.

'You know.'

'The Dead Child.'

'And all that.'

'You believed him?'

'Morgan showed me a lot of papers. They looked all right. If you see what I mean. The place belonged to Max, as far as I could see.'

'You were wrong.'

He stared at her. 'What?'

'I called a lawyer. Max had about the same claim as you. No better. Worse, if anything. With a lawyer, you could have won.'

He looked at his hands. 'Now she tells me.'

'What did Morgan say?'

'He said that Harry had got us down for a . . . well, beauty contest, he said. Morgan was just about running the place, by then. Nothing happened without his say-so. Morgan had said he preferred Max.'

Victoria looked Guy straight in his soft brown eyes. 'Why would he have said that?'

The eyes shifted. 'Harry didn't like my parents. Morgan knew that. I suppose he gave the answer Harry wanted to hear.'

'Bullshit. Morgan hated your guts because you were screwing his wife.'

The eyes moved back. He said, 'All right.'

'So he told Max he was probably the Crown Prince. And then what?'

Guy said, 'Max was drunk. He wanted to fight.'

'To *fight*?'

'He was an animal. He seemed to think we could just fight, and that would settle everything. I was not at all sober myself. Not a tiny bit. I told him not to be so stupid. Might as well have tried to persuade a horse down a staircase. He said he was off, going to catch the last boat to the mainland, buy a gun, come back and shoot me with it. I can't describe how pathetic he was. Naive, stupid, drunk, lazy ... hopeless. So I get all sympathetic, and I try to stop him. Because if he gets to the mainland he will get drunk again, and go into a gun shop, and not have a licence or enough money, but this will not stop him and he will try to steal a gun, for Christ's sake, and they will catch him and he will get ten years. But he won't listen. He marches out onto the quay, and we are standing there in the rain, arguing. When all of a sudden he sort of grabs me round the neck and throws me at a bollard, and I hit my head against it, hard.' Guy screwed up his face. 'Max must have fallen off the quay. He was swimming, drunk, shouting that it was all right, he was a surfer. There is a lot of tide along the quay there. I was sitting with bees in my head. And I just sort of watched him go until he was right off the end. I wanted to throw him a line, but I couldn't find one because they had pulled all the dinghies up the beach what with the weather forecast. The last I saw of him he was heading for the Mixer. Swimming. He was alive, swimming, still shouting. Definitely. I thought, he's a surfer, he knows what he's doing.

'So there I am on the quay with blood coming out of my head, thinking oh, shit, is it lifeboat, coastguard, Tuesday or breakfast? When up comes Morgan, going, what the hell have you done? I start being sick. Morgan says, you're concussed, and he was right. He said he'd look after things. I felt so bloody ill that I let him. Which,' said Guy, 'seems to have been a mistake.'

Victoria knew how horribly easy it was to let Morgan take care of things.

'I must have gone back to the Tower. Next thing I remember, Morgan was in a chair at the kitchen table saying that Max had come ashore at the Glory Hole, dead. He marched me down to the beach and showed me.' Guy put his face in his hands. 'His face was purple. There was a graze on the right-hand side of his head, where he'd hit his head on the bollard, Morgan said. But he was wrong. I promise you, I saw him swimming in the tide. Shouting. He was perfectly okay.'

'So what did you do?' She already knew the answer.

'We put him in a wheelbarrow. I helped Morgan bury him by the Sea Garden steps. We burned his clothes in the garden incinerator. Then I kept quiet. And Morgan said, if you oblige me, I'll oblige you. When you inherit, if you inherit, keep quiet, never sack me, double my wages, do as I say, and nobody will know anything about any of this. Well, I didn't expect to inherit, not even then. I mean, Harry hated my parents, thought I was some sort of hippy, and there were dozens of cousins qualified. And it was a crazy way to do things, the way inheritance taxes are, so I thought he had other plans. So when it . . . happened, well, it was a . . . shock. Then first out, you found Max's bones.' He shook his head, dazed, heavy. 'It's like a nightmare, but you don't wake up.'

'Yes,' said Victoria. 'So who killed Max?'

'Morgan. I don't know. It's a nightmare.'

Morgan was right at home in nightmares. Ten years he had held this over Guy. Just so he could sit safe and in control of his little kingdom. His world, of which he had taken her on a tour, the patronising asshole . . . Something was wrong. Something that did not sit properly in the curatorial department of her mind. What?

Nothing important. Nothing was as important as her rage against Morgan. She said, 'Why don't you go to the police and make a statement?'

'Hi, Plod. Here is a load of filth going back a hundred years . . . It wouldn't be just me. You'd have the tabloids camped out along the causeway. I'm the wicked landlord, Morgan's the honest son of the soil. No way.'

'You'd rather have Morgan running the place?'

Silence.

Victoria lay and shed cold sweat into her pyjamas. There was no case to answer. But that did not mean that lives would not be wrecked. She could see Morgan in court. Chapter and verse about what had happened in his shed: Mrs Chatterley's Matinées, My Potting Shed Love Romps. Even if they dug up the bones, and Morgan was charged instead of Guy, and they managed to convict Morgan on Guy's uncorroborated evidence, would she and Guy and the baby survive?

At last, Victoria fell into a doze.

She dreamed of heads: heads of swimmers, above the water. Heads diving into water that turned to earth, heads that became skulls, lying on red clay subsoil, dented and grinning, a grin that opened and snapped at her hand, catching her fingers—

She woke. The Mare pulsed whitely on the ceiling. Guy was awake beside her. The horror of the dream faded. As it went, it left something else: a certainty that filled her with an emotion like fear, but not fear: awe, perhaps; amazement.

She knew what it was that had been buried under the anger earlier.

She said, 'Guy?'

'Yep.' He sounded dry and weary.

'Max's head. Purple in the face, you say. With a cut on the right-hand side.'

'Yes.'

'That was the only mark.'

'Yes. He had a grade one. You could see.'

'That's not right,' said Victoria.

'Of course it's bloody right,' said Guy. 'I saw it. I helped the bastard bury him, for Christ's sake.'

'No,' said Victoria. She was up and out of bed.

'For Christ's *sake*—'

'Come with me.' A spark had appeared in Victoria's mind. It became a flame, grew and spread until it warmed her heart. She grabbed his hand, pulled. 'Come *on*.'

He got out of bed, grumbling. He put on a dressing-gown. She said, 'Get a hammer and a cold chisel.'

'What?'

'Get them.'

The sky was greying towards dawn as she pulled him down the Poseidon Stairs. Finally they were standing under the Priory Arch. By the peach-coloured glow in the eastern sky, she found the stone she had been looking for. 'Knock that one out,' she said.

'Why—?'

'Do it.'

He began to bang away, half-heartedly at first, then more vigorously as his blood warmed. It took ten minutes. The stone dropped. Light from the sky fell into the alcove, pinkening the yellowish bone of the skull Morgan had walled up inside; the skull from which Victoria had stolen the tooth.

'Jenkins had a bang on the right-hand side of his head,' she said. 'You're sure about that?'

She saw him nod against the peachy sky.

She said, 'Morgan told me this was the skull from the grave by the steps.'

'It can't be,' said Guy. He reached into the alcove and took the skull out, holding it in his hand, running his fingers over the dome of the cranium, the side where the bone was cracked and crazed.

Not the right-hand side.

The left.

Chapter Twenty-three

Victoria went to the library, and took one of the papers she had found in Morgan's shed, and went back to the kitchen and showed it to Guy. The new day glowed in the *crocosmias* in the courtyard outside.

'I love you,' he said, when she had finished explaining it to him. 'Let's go.'

'I'll get the Golf.'

'Nope,' said Guy, with a gleam in his eye. 'This is definitely a case for the Bentley.'

Victoria went back to the library, and replaced the paper tenderly in its file. The Bentley whispered in the courtyard, and was gone.

The library door opened. Dawkins came in, unfolding his reading glasses.

> *A sad day, the saddest of my life. He who has made all things good and beautiful is no more, and we have laid him away according to his wishes. For as he said, he would make a Gesture to teach the silly world to be practical. He would put it about that a garden was a Laboratory, while all the time it was a Poem.*
>
> *So Revel has come, and we have gone to the Arch, and the deed is done. And the Mason is gone to cut on Poseidon's socle the words—*
>
> *'Man Proposes – God Disposes.'**

By half past four they were in London Bridge, on the pavement outside the Merchant Apothecaries' Hall. Guy was carrying something that might have been a briefcase, but looked much more like a toolbox.

---

* anonymous letter, scarcely decipherable, dated 1865

Under the sooty caduceus on the keystone, Victoria said, 'Are you sure about this?'

For the first time for as long as she could remember, Guy gave her a smile completely without dark corners. 'Yes, indeed,' he said. 'Here we go.'

The varnished doors wheezed. They went up the stairs at a fast trot, feet echoing in the oak panelling. Guy went straight through the library door. Victoria followed, nauseous, wanting to flee. But Guy was gone, and she was walking into the library, *sashaying* actually, exhilarated, not timid. Tiers of books rose around her to the skylight. She pushed her hair back, and placed one hand on the desk. Beyond green-leather tables Guy strode on, swinging his toolbox.

The librarian was fortyish, male, in a dark jacket and striped trousers. He looked as if he would be indecently interested in Boy Scouts and Dewey Decimal. He raised a white, bony hand at Guy. He called, 'Excuse me—'

'So sorry,' said Victoria. 'But could you help me? I'm wondering if you have early plant lists for Trelise? Blakeney-Jones is the name.'

The librarian said to Guy's back, 'Excuse me, if you wouldn't mind leaving your briefcase at the desk?' Victoria was standing by the flap in the counter. To get at Guy, the librarian would have had to squeeze past her, and squeezing past women looked like something he would be reluctant to do.

Victoria stuck her nose in the air. 'Did you hear my name?' she said.

'Yes, yes,' said the librarian. 'I really *must*—'

'Blakeney-Jones,' said Victoria. 'That man is my husband. We live at Trelise. And that' – she pointed up the gallery, to the glass case where Joshua sat grinning – 'is – was – my husband's cousin.'

The librarian had got it. A treacly smile spread outwards from his septum. 'Mrs Blakeney-*Jones*!' he said. She could hear Guy's shoes pounding the iron spiral staircase.

'Trelise plant lists,' she said. 'Early ones.'

'In the catalogue,' said the librarian, indicating with a doubtless clammy hand the computer terminal at her elbow.

'Computers!' cried Victoria. 'Oh, I don't under*stand* them. Could you *help* me?'

The librarian squared his narrow shoulders. Perhaps she had been wrong about Boy Scouts. 'Definitely,' he said.

It was about then that the noise started.

Guy had gone up the spiral stairs at a purposeful lope, humming a tune between his teeth.

There was a table and two chairs in front of the glass case. He walked round it, and gazed upon the ghastly wax face behind the pane of glass. The glass was mounted in a box frame of best mahogany. There must be a door. But no knob presented itself, no keyhole. The glass looked thick; too damn thick. The toolbox would be no good, not for this part, anyway. The chairs at the table were occupied, one of them by a rangy woman who might have been a botanist, the other by an osteopathic-looking young man. 'Excuse me,' said Guy.

The osteopath looked up, lips pursed.

'I need your chair,' said Guy.

'It's my chair.'

Guy did not have time to hang about. Gripping the chair's backrest, he tipped the osteopath onto the floor. Then he lifted the chair and swung it at the glass. On the third swing there was a huge, jangling crash as the pane disintegrated. Someone started screaming. The osteopath looked as if he might attack, but when Guy raised the chair at him he seemed to think better of the plan and scuttled off down the stairs to the ground floor, from which was beginning to rise a surly rumour of reaction.

Guy paid it no attention. He grasped Joshua's lapels, and hauled. The corpse was lighter than he had expected. It flew out of the chair. For a moment he held it like a ballroom dancer, his face full of the musty, camphorated atmosphere of the thing. Then it fell apart at the waist.

He dropped the ribcage, shocked, and jumped backwards, away from the dusty, musty mess on the floor. The head rolled free. The wig came off

The orange football rolled into the angle between a set of shelves and the floor. Guy pinned it with his knee, opened the box, hauled out a Black and Decker cordless drill into which he had already screwed a half-inch hand bit, put the bit to the wax brow and pulled the trigger. The drill went in easily. Under the orange surface, the wax was yellowish-white;

best quality beeswax, as used in Pharaohs' tombs, fit to last thousands of years.

There should have been more.

Behind the wax face of Joshua Jones there should have been a skull, demonstrating to the world its owner's absolute contempt for the funerary rite, his conviction that notions of an afterlife were sentimental bunk, and his certainty that the mind was as much a by-product of the organism as a fart, but a fart capable of hallucination, one of which was the existence of the soul.

But inside the wax head of Joshua Jones there was only wax.

Guy looked up. A frieze of heads looked back at him. On the floor, Joshua Jones smiled up, a half-inch drill bit sunk in the centre of his forehead. A security man stepped forward. 'Oi,' he said.

Guy said, 'Someone ought to clear up this glass before someone gets cut.' He saw Victoria. She was smiling at him. He had never seen anything so beautiful in his life. He said, 'We should be getting home.'

Hand in hand, they walked away from the ruins.

Revel – A Day in the Life: Autumn*
Alarm seven o'clock. Warnings of gales in Plymouth, Sole, Fastnet, gale force eight to severe gale force nine, northeasterly, soon. Tea, strong, three sugars. Tool shed; chainsaw oil, mixture, ladders. Dead branch patrol, saw into meter lengths, stack, remove slab of lime for later carving. Too much breeze for tree work after dinner. Repair steps, North Rockery, cover work with tarpaulin and boulders against rain and wind. No bloody visitors. Haul boat out with tractor, chock and cover. Fire lit in Castle bar, first of year. Three pints Guinness, one rum and shrub. Lift home with Darren and Daisy on tractor. Rough out new carving, Victoria Blakeney-Jones as St Bridget. Quiet time.

Same every autumn, more or less.

It started raining at Exeter. The voice on the car radio spoke in light suburban tones of a complex low, the remnants of Hurricane Zevon,

* *Country Times* magazine, feature

possible roof damage west of Watford. The equinox was upon them, vast whorls of air and water vapour howling over the Atlantic. Victoria craved peace and quiet, and an end to this dizziness and confusion. A huge drowsiness was pressing her into the soft leather seat. 'That little bastard Morgan was trying to mess your head around,' said Guy. 'He never even took Max's skull out of the grave. Probably wasn't even fractured. Had Joshua's out of the arch, gloating, shouldn't be surprised. Made up his story to fit the facts.'

'And now he leaves,' she said.

'That's right.'

She must have slept, because next thing she knew they were moving over the causeway. The rain had stopped, and Trelise lay ahead, black and unforthcoming under a skyful of stars.

They drove right into the courtyard, and climbed stiffly out.

The hall lights were on. It was just past midnight. In the kitchen, the answering machine was blinking. Victoria fetched a ham from the larder, tore up a lettuce and shoved a frozen baguette in the oven. As she straightened up, she saw Guy's face. He had turned an inhuman shade of grey.

'What is it?' she said.

'Message on machine,' he said. 'Detective-Sergeant Fawcett, Truro CID. He wishes to visit at six tomorrow evening to interview me in connection with allegations made by Mr Owen Morgan. Jesus,' said Guy. 'What am I going to tell him?'

The baguette was thawed and crisp. Victoria poured the wine. 'Not very much,' she said.

'I thought I was telling them the truth.'

'Just leave out the motive.'

'What?'

'Don't volunteer any evidence about Arthur. No motive, no crime. We'll hide the papers.'

She went out of the kitchen and into the library. The papers were on the desk, in their pile. She went through the pile that held the Morgan papers, and her tape of their gunpoint interview.

They were not there.

She looked through the other pile.

Not there either.

She started at the top.

Things were missing. A whole sheaf of things. The foundation of the Dead Child story. Gone. As if having blinked into existence, the Child had blinked out again.

She went back to the kitchen.

'Bread's cold,' said Guy. 'Where have you been?'

From above there came the shuffle of slippered feet, the thump of a door, the hiss of pipes as someone flushed a lavatory.

'I'll just pop and say goodnight to Dawkins,' she said.

'Are you feeling okay?'

She bent and kissed his cheek. 'You could do with a shave,' she said. 'I'll be right back.'

She went up the stairs, stood in the whiff of used cat litter at the top, and suspended her knuckle over the panel. Then she thought better of it, and went in without knocking.

Cats flowed away from her feet. Dawkins was propped up in bed. There was a ballpoint in his hand, the *Daily Telegraph* on his knees, folded to the crossword. 'Louse, confused and more impolite, bursts in,' he said, raising one Norman-arch eyebrow.

'Intruder,' said Victoria. Calm, Victoria; calm. She said, 'There are some papers missing from the library.'

'Surely not,' said Dawkins.

'Did Morgan come in?'

His eyes glittered with fury. 'Of *course* not.'

'Ah. I was just wondering, after last time . . .'

'Last time?'

'Some got thrown away,' said Victoria.

'The ones you left scattered all over the floor.'

'I was just wondering if any of them found their way up here?'

Dawkins showed signs of returning to his crossword. 'Honestly, this is too much,' he said.

'So are they here?' said Victoria.

'I mean you come barging in here without knocking in the middle of the *night*. I know it's your house, but really I think you should perhaps give a little more consideration to the feelings of those less fortunate than yourself—'

'Does this mean you resign?' said Victoria.

'—who are *extraordinarily loyal* to the Family,' said Dawkins hastily.

'That's exactly what I was telling Guy,' said Victoria. 'But I'm afraid he wouldn't listen.'

'I *beg* your pardon?' said Dawkins, more and more the dowager.

Victoria sat down on the end of his bed. The smell of cats was almost stifling. 'The thing is there's some sort of difficulty with the police, goodness knows what, and there's a detective coming tomorrow and I think he's going to have a warrant to search your flat.' Dawkins' face had turned pasty and porous over the lime-green silk of his pyjamas. 'So if you're sure?' she said. 'That you haven't taken anything? Not even to . . . protect anyone? Guy, for instance?'

Dawkins made a bad attempt at a yawn. The hand he raised in front of his mouth shook so badly it clattered the dentures in his head. 'Of course I'm sure,' he snapped. 'Is that all?'

Victoria went back to the kitchen. Guy was gazing dully into his wine glass, poor Guy. She felt nostalgic for him bright-eyed, crouching over the wax head with his drill. She said, 'He's got the papers. What do you want to do?'

'Leave him alone.'

'If you do that, he's got you.'

'He's on my side.'

'You and I are on your side. Dawkins is on his own side, because he thinks he is the Soul of Trelise or something. We should search Guy's flat.' There was movement above. She traced stealthy feet across the flat's floor. He could not come down the stairs, because they led immediately past the kitchen door. That left him only one destination.

She said, 'Too late.'

She took off her boots, and went up the stairs quickly, treading close to the wall to avoid tell-tale creaks. The electricity stopped at Dawkins' door. The stairs went up another floor. There was a landing at the top, with a door to the left and a door to the right. The door to the left was closed, and spiders' webs linked the handle to the frame. The door to the right was open. Victoria looked into the oblong of darkness.

She was looking into the main attic of Trelise, a warren of junk in a room the shape of a hammer. The handle of the hammer, down which she was looking, was sixty feet long. The head of the hammer was a hundred and twenty feet from side to side. Down on the left-hand side, she saw a pale glow that moved. Dawkins, with a torch. She saw its beam in the dust motes as he turned to leave. Too late, too late. She fled down the stairs and sat in the kitchen, heart pounding. The footsteps moved overhead. The door closed. Silence.

'Ho hum,' said Victoria, extra loud. 'Bedtime.'

Guy followed her up the front stairs and into the bedroom. When the door was shut, Victoria said, 'Into the attic.'

'*What?*'

'He's hidden the stuff up there.' The blood came back into Guy's face. The airing cupboard was next to their bathroom. He hauled himself up the ladder of drying racks. His face loomed down at her in a frame of white towels. She took his hand and clambered through the warm, clean smell into the attic smell, bitter, dusty.

'So where did he put them?' said Guy.

They were standing in a little clear space like a city square. Streets of boxes and tea chests led away, a whole city of junk and paper.

They followed the flashlight beam down an alley. When their path crossed Dawkins', there were faint scuff-marks in the dust underfoot. 'Somewhere down here,' said Victoria.

The flashlight travelled down a rickety Tudor alley of piled boxes, the lower storeys bulged out by the weight of the ones above. All the papers Victoria had gone through in the past six months, then repacked and restacked.

'Where?' said Guy.

'I don't know.'

Investigating a couple of boxes at random, Victoria found a solar topee, two rotting umbrellas and a folder that accelerated her heartbeat but which proved to be full of cut-flower invoices for 1924. There were seven hundred and forty-five more boxes to search. It was hopeless.

Outside, the wind thumped and murmured in the slates. It was late. They climbed down through the airing cupboard, and went to bed.

In the night, the wind rose. Threads of draught crept under the duvet and sent her in search of Guy. She awoke sore-headed at seven. Guy was already up.

Dawkins was in the kitchen. 'The wind's blown the Aga out,' he said. '*Listen* to it!'

Victoria said, 'You took some papers. We need them.'

Dawkins pouted. 'I told you—'

'Now,' said Guy.

'I don't know what you're—'

Guy said, 'Nobody's indispensable.'

Dawkins flushed the colour of a ripe apricot. 'You don't understand, do you?' he said. 'I don't mind. I really couldn't care an itty bit. I love this place, Mr Guy. Whether I'm here or you're here or, er, Victoria's here, it goes on. With beauty. With dignity. *Unchanging.*'

Guy sat down heavily. Victoria said, 'Bullshit.'

'You would not understand,' said Dawkins. 'Being American.'

Victoria drew breath to explain exactly what Americans thought about thieving faggots. Guy gave her a warning look. He said, 'I will look after those papers.'

'They are safe with me.'

'Who do you think you are?'

'I told you. I care.' Dawkins struck the attitude of a tragic hero in copper.

Victoria said, wearily, 'Morgan has copies.'

Dawkins smiled. He said, 'I took the precaution of abstracting them from his, er, filing cabinet.'

There was a silence.

'Where are they?' said Victoria.

'Safe,' said Dawkins.

'And what do you think Morgan is going to do when he finds he's been burgled?'

'I neither know nor care.'

'Dawkins, you are out of order,' said Guy. 'You're sacked.'

Victoria said, 'This is not necessary.' She took a deep breath. 'Dawkins has worked devotedly for Trelise. I think we can leave some matters to his discretion.'

Guy was looking at her as if she had turned bright blue. She started making coffee. Dawkins glided out, looking noble.

'I'm giving the bugger notice,' said Guy.

'Not till we find the papers.'

Beyond the window, an *Escallonia macrantha* bowed to a rattle of rain. Guy's eyes shifted into the yard. He was looking for Morgan, out there. Morgan had had the evidence whipped away from him. He would not sit still and wait for things to happen.

But Morgan did not appear that morning, at any rate they did not see him, up in the attic, dust masks on, Coleman lamps hanging from the rafters, sorting through boxes.

By noon they had done half the south side of the alley of boxes. There was dust in their eyes, their ears, their hair. Outside, the wind moaned in the chimney pots.

From the other end of the attic, Dawkins said, in a weird, strangled voice, 'Telephone.'

'I'll call back.'

'It's the police.'

'Coming,' said Guy. Victoria turned back to the boxes, sorting through the weary mass of loose-leaf folders and box files.

A door opened and closed. Guy, back again for the fray, God willing. Another gust shrieked in the chimneys.

'Guy.' said Victoria. 'What did they want?'

Silence; the sound of someone moving. Someone too light for Guy.

'Guy?' she said again.

'Still on the phone,' said a voice.

Morgan's voice.

Victoria froze. The lantern rocked gently in the draughts. She stood up.

Morgan was standing ten yards away, down the alley, his face deeply shadowed in the lantern light. 'Any luck?' he said.

Victoria's lips were numb. 'What?'

'Dawkins has been hiding stuff,' he said, reasonable, matter-of-fact, precise. 'We both want it.' Silence. 'So what should we do about it?'

A gust. The attic shuddered.

'I'm going to have it,' said Morgan. 'And you're not.'

'Don't be stupid.' The alley of boxes was a cul-de-sac. Morgan was blocking the only exit.

'Listen,' said Morgan, and put a finger in the air. There seemed to be blood on it.

From the far end of the attic came a curious sound: a high, awful wailing, muffled by thin walls.

'Dawkins,' said Morgan.

'What's wrong with him?'

Morgan smiled. 'He was protecting your family interests,' he said. 'With his life, if necessary. He thought.'

'What are you talking about?'

'Catch,' said Morgan, and threw her something.

She caught it. It was a ball, small and furry and wet. It had ears.

'I got one of his cats,' said Morgan. 'I pulled its head off.'

Victoria dropped the head. She heard herself say, 'That was not nice.'

'So when I started on the next one, he told me where he had put all these bits of paper. Box two beyond you, I think; north side, in the middle. Pencil cross. I tell you this for information only. As they say.'

She believed him.

He started down the alley towards her. She scrambled up a tottering rampart of crates. He came after her, smile unwavering. Her heart was hammering. He did not need her any more. She was just someone who knew enough to go on collecting evidence that he was a murderer.

If she was alive.

She stumbled under the dark rafters, slithering on the accumulation of boxes. The wind thundered in the roofs. He came towards her, crouched like a shadowy ape, arms crooked, fingers curled. A stray gleam of lamplight caught his white grin.

She was panicking, now, walking backwards across boxes. She opened her mouth, felt herself scream. But the attic was full of the noise of the wind.

Her head touched the slope of the roof above her head. She was under the eaves, driven into a corner, her and the baby. There was a pounding on the door, with shouting now. Guy, shouting. Too late. She could feel death breathing icy on the back of her neck.

Not death.

She put her arms above her head.

The draught was the wind, coming at her through the flange of a trap-door. An access door to the southern valley of the roof. The wind was blowing up that valley . . .

Her fingers had been running round the edge of the frame. On the bottom, they found a bolt, shot it. She flattened her palms against the trapdoor and pushed.

Chapter Twenty-four

The wind caught the lip of the trapdoor and slammed it upwards. In the sudden flood of daylight Victoria caught a glimpse of Morgan's face, white and grey and black under the eyes, no longer ghostly but sick and exhausted and furious. Around his feet the paper surface of the world stirred and shifted. Then it rose up in a blizzard, and hid him. Over the roar of the wind and the mighty rustle of Trelise's paper she heard him shout, and the crash of a falling body as he missed his footing. Then she had grasped the lip of the trapdoor, and hauled herself onto the roof.

The wind was a torrent of air. She flew up the slope of the roof to the ridge and over the other side. There she lay for a moment in the lee, pressed to the solid slope of Boscastle slate.

The not-so-solid slope.

She could feel the roof swell under her body. A slate left its mooring with a crack, started to slide, caught the wind and bowled off along the slope like a playing card. Another went and another. Whole sections bulged up, pushed from below by pressure of wind. Slates broke free of their sick nails and spun away. Batten-barred holes appeared and grew. And from those holes fluttered and spun papers; papers in groups, gaggles, flocks and swarms, whipping down the wind towards the village and the wet black acres of Hull Bay.

Victoria buried her head in her arms, hiding her face from the flying edges. She smelt burning. She peered sideways. The wind was still tearing papers out of the attic. But now they dragged sinister little tails of smoke and orange dots of spark. The Coleman lamp, she thought.

The tiles under her face had gone. She could see a blowtorch of fire below and to the left. And human figures; two of them. Two men. One of them was Morgan. Morgan was near the fire, flames streaming from his coat, yelling, beating at himself—

Doctor Nevis. Nevis with the burning oil running down him, the skin rising and bubbling like wax, and in the middle of it his mouth, a round black shouting hole, starting to bubble too . . .

The other figure in the attic was not burning. It had something in its hand: something aimed at Morgan, something from which there jetted a stream of white vapour. Guy. With a fire extinguisher.

Victoria screamed, 'No!' She wanted Morgan to burn.

But if Guy saw someone on fire, Guy would put him out.

Guy was not a killer.

The flames went out. Morgan put his head down and ran at Guy, screaming. He knocked Guy over, and ran on through the paper, colliding with boxes. Guy looked up at Victoria. He tore battens with his big hands. They came away easily from the rafters: rotten, rotten, rotten. The hands came through, strong and gentle. They lifted Victoria down into the paper blizzard.

'Quick,' she said.

'Wait.' He went down the alley towards the orange heart of the fire. The carbon dioxide plume shot out of the extinguisher. The glow darkened to black. As he walked through the flaky pile, the embers rekindled. Victoria smelt burning hair. Guy paid no attention. He tore open the box with the pencil cross, groped, pulled out two folders. Then he came back through the fire. 'These?' he said. He had lost the hair on the front of his head.

Victoria looked at the folders. One of them was hers. The other was full of photocopies; Morgan's photocopies. She nodded.

Guy turned back to the fire. He opened the folders, and pulled out the papers, and crumpled them into balls, and threw them at the red heart of the flames. They caught and rose in the hot air. The wind whipped them between the battens into the racing black sky. Not until the last paper was consumed did Guy squeeze the extinguisher's trigger again. By then it was too late.

They kicked in Dawkins' door, and dragged him weeping down the stairs. There were voices all around below, and a clank of buckets, and somewhere the clatter of a diesel. The whole front of the attic was burning, the rafters as well as the contents. In the courtyard, Dawkins turned to look at her. His face was red with the reflection of flames in tears. He knew who had caused the burning of the Priory. Then someone took him away.

The estate fire-engine was in the courtyard. 'Tide's over the causeway,' said someone. 'Truro brigade couldn't get across.'

'We'll manage,' said Guy. His eyes were burrowing in the crowd. 'Where's Morgan?'

'Forget the bastard,' said Victoria. She started organising gangs. Things started coming out of the house; carpets, pictures, sofas, china, even the panels of eighteenth-century Chinese wallpaper. Sheets of smoke tumbled down the wind. The water from the hoses was blowing away before it could reach the attics. The sound of the fire was a blowtorch roar. Sweat ran into her eyes. There were piles of stuff in the yard. The flames were through the attic floor. She had no idea what time it was, but at some point she caught a dirty red smudge to the westward that was probably a sunset. Some time or other, someone grabbed her arm. She turned and saw Daisy's face, round and freckled. 'What is it?' she said.

'Revel. He's hurt.'

'Where's the doctor?' There was a doctor here somewhere, from one of the holiday cottages.

'He's seen the doctor. He wants you.'

Victoria found herself being led through the crowd to the stable. The tack room had been turned into something that looked like a dressing station in a Civil War battle. Revel was in a corner on an upright chair. His face was chalky white, and his forehead between his eyes was peeled back into a great pink smile, as if someone had started to scalp him and thought better of it halfway.

'Revel,' said Victoria. The wound in his head was sickening. 'What happened?'

'Morgan,' he said. 'He was on the JCB.'

'JCB?'

'Digging,' he said. 'In the Sea Garden.'

In the midst of the racket, silence.

'He saw me watching,' said Revel. 'He came at me with the bucket.'

'Digging where exactly?'

'By the steps,' said Revel.

Digging for Max's bones.

A woman's voice, now; Mary Morgan's voice. 'He thinks he'll get DNA. To show those are Blakeney-Jones bones.'

'It won't make any difference.'

'You tell him. I tried.' Mary looked closer to seventy than thirty. She was crying, now, frightened. Victoria felt the twilight thickening over the island and folded her arms against the chill of it. She said, 'Mary, they're going to take him away. What happens to you then?'

'I don't know. I don't know.'

'You've been on Trelise a long time.'

'Yes.'

'You should stay.'

'Yes.' She sounded surprised, as if she had never considered anything else.

'But it you want to stay, you'll have to tell me the truth about Owen.'

'What truth?' The eyes held Victoria's, heavy with tears.

Victoria said, 'Guy couldn't kill anyone.'

Mary stretched her face in something that might have been a smile. 'Owen could,' she said.

'Who killed Max?'

'Max got round to the Glory Hole alive as you or me. I was following Owen. I was frightened what he would do. Owen had reasons not to like Guy. And he knew the Major favoured Guy over Max, so he was going to land up working for Guy and it would be handy to have something over him. Owen found Max pissed on the Glory Hole beach. He strangled him. I saw him do it.'

'There was a mark on his head, Guy said.'

'Bumped it while they were fighting on the beach, I expect. I saw him. He put his fingers round that man's neck and he . . .'

'All right,' said Victoria. The sound of the crowd flowed into the stable, the rattle of diesels, the clank of buckets. She wanted to be far away.

She went out, through the crowd, looking for Guy. Nobody had seen him for an hour; not since they had brought Revel in from the Sea Garden.

The whole island was at the fire. The only people missing were Guy and Morgan.

A gust of wind spun in the trees. Victoria kicked her way through leaves and branches to the Sea Garden. Her flashlight beam flicked over raw earth. There was a hole by the steps. She peered in the hole. Scraped red clay, a flood of water. No bones. There was a ragged hole in the new-built wall. The ground was torn up by tractor tyres.

Where the hell was Guy?

There was a long-handled fork stuck in the ground beside the grave. She plucked it out. Keeping the flashlight on the tyre tracks, she began to walk.

The tracks led along the grit road outside the garden wall. The wind came onto her left ear as the road turned north. The tide was four hours into the flood. There were branches on the road as it passed through the woods. Once she heard a long, creaking crash as a tree came down. Orange sparks slid down the breeze overhead. Sparks from what had been her house, and Guy's, and still would have been, if it had not been for goddam Morgan.

Hull Bay came up on the right, fretted with streaks of ice-white foam. Here in the island's lee, the wind was slacker, flawed with eddies. Except for the roar of the wind in distant trees, the night was oddly quiet.

Into that quiet there came the sound of a tractor engine.

It came from dead ahead, from a pale glow that might have been headlights. Victoria broke into a trot.

As she came round the corner of the last house she saw the whole length of the quay, jutting into the dark bay. Halfway down its length a JCB stood, headlights on, illuminating a lobster boat that lay alongside. The digger's bucket was raised.

Guy was on the lobster boat. Morgan was on the quay. She could hear Morgan shouting, but not the words. Guy shook his head. Morgan wanted to be on the boat. Guy was not going to let him get aboard.

Victoria was all the way down the quay now, behind the headlights of the JCB, invisible. She shoved the flashlight into her pocket, grasped the fork's helve with both hands. Her mouth was dry. She wanted to cry, to run away.

She wanted to kill Morgan.

A gust of wind. Something blew out of the JCB's upturned bucket and clattered onto the quay. Something yellowish-white: a human femur. Morgan stooped and picked it up, holding it like a baseball bat. Guy bent to take the key out of the boat.

'No!' shouted Victoria.

The femur whipped through the air at Guy's head. It should have caught him on the temple. But at the sound of Victoria's voice he turned towards her, so it caught him square on the forehead.

Instead of caving his skull in, it merely knocked him overboard.

Victoria held the fork like a spear and ran at Morgan out of the headlights. He looked startled, drew back the bone to defend himself. The tine of the fork sank into the hollow of the left shoulder and went in. He fell backwards. His skull hit the granite coping.

Guy had gone.

She pawed at the flashlight's ON button. She found it at last, shone it between the boat's side and the quay.

No Guy. Only a river of black water flowing to seaward, where the Mixer was churning. She followed the river with her flashlight. Fifty yards away she glimpsed his face in the water, white, like a full moon in clouds. Then nothing.

She took the key out of the fishing boat and dropped it overboard. There was a punt alongside the quay ahead of the fishing boat. She clambered in and cast off. The current gripped the hull. The headlights on the quay were two suns. Then the boat spun, and she was looking at darkness, thick, inky, the after-image of the lights blood-red in her eyes.

She picked up the flashlight from the bottom of the boat. It was all moving slowly, now, calm in the middle of all this frantic haste. Methodically, she searched the water with the beam. The arm again. Guy's head, swimming. He was big; he floated well.

Swimming away.

He must think she was Morgan.

She called him. He heard her: turned in the water, grinning into the flashlight. She saw the water pile up white under his chin as he started to swim back towards her. But instead of coming closer, he seemed to drift further away and to one side. For a second she could not understand why.

Then the punt tried to spin again, and she saw the masts of the boats on the moorings and the lights on the quay shift in relation to each other, and she knew what it was. They were entering the outer toils of the Mixer.

There was not much time.

She put her hands to her mouth, and called him.

'Here!' he roared, faint, but ahead.

She set the oars and pulled, two strokes.

'Here!' Ahead and to starboard now, closer. She let the punt glide forward under its own momentum. The snoring gurgle of the Mixer was dead ahead now.

'Here!' Dead ahead too, but further away; on the far side of the whirlpool. There was no way of getting the timing right.

'Here!' The voice broad on the port bow. He had been swept in a complete circuit of the centre. She pulled one more stroke across the current. The roar was huge now, the sound of a jet engine at close quarters. She thought she heard another yell, but there was too much noise to be sure. The surface of the sea was sloping, leaning downhill. She had missed him. She had missed everything. Something walloped the side of the boat. She found the flashlight. Its beam flicked over the black surface of a glossy funnel of water. The punt lurched and stood on its gunwale. She jumped for the uphill side. There was a whoosh and splash as water poured over the downhill rail. The punt came level again, spinning, rocking, huge, fatal rockings.

There was something pale on the far side of the boat, a crab perhaps, a spider.

A hand.

Another hand. Two hands in all. The vortex roared. Victoria got as far away from the hands as she could. Her mind seemed to have bust loose from its moorings. She could not work out whose hands they were likely to be. Max, the Dead Child, any of the other people who had been sucked down to die here . . .

A head came over the gunwale.

Guy's head.

His body came after it. He rolled onto the bottom of the punt. Another roll, another shining flood of water. Victoria dropped the flashlight. It went out. Now there was blackness, confusion, and far away on the land, the twin eyes of the JCB, staring out to sea.

'Bail,' said Guy.

She found the bailer. There was a foot of water in the boat, slopping from side to side. She heard the knock of the oars. 'When in doubt,' said Guy, 'row uphill.'

She lay there hauling scoops of water over the side. She felt the wet breath of the Mixer's central funnel. Her ears popped. Here we go, she thought, down the well, the last slide, Guy, and me, and the baby. The family that dies together—

She heard Guy grunt, felt the boat come suddenly onto an even keel. The roar of the Mixer faded. 'Christ,' said Guy, in an odd, high voice . . .

The oars stopped. Guy's hand was on her shoulder. She could feel its warmth through her sodden jersey. He said, 'It's all right. Sit up, now.'

She sat up on the stern thwart.

The wind still roared. The sky had split, so stars showed between rags of flying cloud. But the sea was smooth and level again, the sucking gurgle of the Mixer fading at her back.

'Spat us out,' said Guy, flat and confident.

'Of course it did,' said Victoria. Not that she took it as self-evident that the Mixer would protect her and her family. But she heard this new confidence in Guy, that he was the master of this island, its rocks and its house, its whirlpool.

And its gardener.

He said, 'Did you kill him, do you think?' calm as if he was offering her a glass of wine.

'No.'

'Ah.'

He let the punt travel in a broad loop of current, bringing it alongside the quay on the opposite side from the fishing boat. The headlights of the JCB flickered as someone moved across them. She heard boot-nails on the granite. The diesel roared. The JCB's lights began to move backwards up the quay.

Guy brought the punt alongside. 'Stay here,' he said.

'No.'

The lights reached the top, turned right into the village, heading for the Watch Tower, the causeway. The bucket was high, full of earth and bones.

Guy began to run up the quay. Victoria ran with him.

The village street was dark and wet and empty. She saw the lights flick under the Watch Tower arch, kept running. She was tired. Where was Morgan going? Up into the Downs? Surely not over the causeway.

She came out onto the ramp leading down to the causeway. There was no shelter here. The wind was an express train out of the west. Guy was there, a hulking shape in the dark. A mile away, the yellow lights of the mainland twinkled.

Between them, the Narrows were boiling.

The wind had gone round to the west. It had nudged the swells round with it. To the west of the causeway, the rocks were chewing them to a thin salt cream. As what was left of the swells passed over it the crests rose again and toppled, breaking, spending their energy in the sheltered waters of Hull Bay. The line of the causeway was marked by a line of breakers.

And along that line of breakers, bucket high, up to the hubs in sea water, a JCB was ploughing.

'He's dead,' said Guy. It was a simple statement of fact: no horror, no satisfaction.

They watched.

The JCB ploughed on, Morgan and the bones of Max Macleod, heading out of the orbit of the the forensic laboratory at Truro, witness statements, a police investigation. A wave slapped the side of the cab, boiled up in a wedding-cake of spray. When it went, the JCB was still there, labouring on towards the mainland. Another wave, and another. Victoria felt Guy's warm hand tighten on hers.

The next wave was bigger, and blacker, and it seemed to move faster than the others. She saw it hollow out, form white teeth, pause and fall. Its crest smashed into the JCB like a fist. This time there was no wedding-cake of white water, but an explosion, a shell-burst that shot ice-white into the dark and blew lazily off down the wind.

And when it had gone, the causeway was empty. No JCB. No bones. No Morgan.

Victoria and Guy turned away. Their hands locked, hers small, his big and warm and dry. They walked up the slipway and under the Arch. They did not look back at the causeway, where the crabs and eels and tides were already disposing of the past. They walked down the wet lane towards the shrinking glow of the house, and the future.

Acknowledgements

For background appreciation of gardens like Trelise, I am indebted to all my maternal ancestors, particularly my mother and my legion of great-aunts. For loans of and advice about books on gardening history, I am indebted to David Wheeler of *Hortus* magazine and the librarians of the Royal Horticultural Society's Lindley Library. And finally, for his good-humoured overview of sub-tropical garden routine and management, I am grateful to Mike Nelhams, Curator of Tresco Abbey Gardens, Isles of Scilly.

Sam Llewellyn

WIN A FAMILY HOLIDAY TO THE SCILLY ISLES

The holiday covers travel and accommodation for two adults and up to two children:

- Return travel to and from the Scilly Isles departing from Penzance either by ferry (The Scillonian) or via helicopter
- 7 nights accommodation and breakfast in a hotel on St Mary's
- £200 spending money

To enter the competition:

Write your name, address and your answer to the following question on a postcard:

What was the name of the gardener who came to Trelise having served an apprenticeship at Tresco Abbey?

And send to:

> The Sea Garden Competition,
> Headline Marketing,
> 338 Euston Road,
> London NW1 3BH.

Closing date: 28th April 2000

Terms and Conditions

1. The competition is open to residents of the UK, excluding employees of Hodder Headline, their families, agents and anyone connected with the competition.
2. The holiday for two adults and up to two children must be taken during 2000 (excluding July and August 2000) and must be booked within one month of the winner being announced. Additional people can be taken on the holiday, subject to hotel/travel availability and at the winner's cost.
3. Choice of travel (via The Scillonian or via helicopter) from Penzance and hotel (on St Mary's) providing double accommodation and breakfast is at the discretion of Hodder Headline. Lunch and evening meal may not be included in the cost but will be available at extra cost.
4. Closing date for receipt of entries is 28th April 2000.
5. The first entry drawn on 2nd May 2000 will be declared the winner and notified by post. The decision of the judges is final. No correspondence will be entered into.
6. No purchase necessary. Number of entries restricted to one per household.
7. Hodder Headline reserves the right at any time to amend or terminate any part of this promotion without prior notice.
8. No cash alternative.
9. Travel insurance is not included.
10. Proof of posting will not be deemed proof of delivery. Responsibility cannot be accepted for damaged, illegible, or incomplete entries, or those arriving after the closing date.
11. The winner's name will be available from the above address from 2nd May 2000.

Promoter: Hodder Headline, 338 Euston Road, London NW1 3BH